T0026834

The
SISTER'S
TALE *a novel*

BETH POWNING

VINTAGE CANADA

Published by Vintage Canada, a division of Penguin Random House Canada Limited,
Toronto, in 2022. Originally published in Canada in trade paperback by
Alfred A. Knopf Canada, a division of Penguin Random House Canada Limited,
Toronto, in 2021. Distributed in Canada and the United States of America
by Penguin Random House Canada Limited, Toronto.

Vintage Canada and colophon are registered trademarks.

www.penguinrandomhouse.ca

LIBRARY AND ARCHIVES CANADA CATALOGUING IN PUBLICATION
Title: The sister's tale : a novel / Beth Powning.
Names: Powning, Beth, 1949- author.
Description: Previously published: Toronto: Knopf Canada, 2021.
Identifiers: Canadiana 20200278975 | ISBN 9780735280045 (softcover)
Classification: LCC PS8631.O86 S57 2022 | DDC C813/.6—dc23

Cover, interior, and map designs: Talia Abramson
Cover images: main photography by Talia Abramson; (shed door) Larry Farr / Unsplash

Printed in the United States of America

2 4 6 8 9 7 5 3 1

Penguin
Random House
VINTAGE CANADA

To Peter
sea, wind, gannets
always

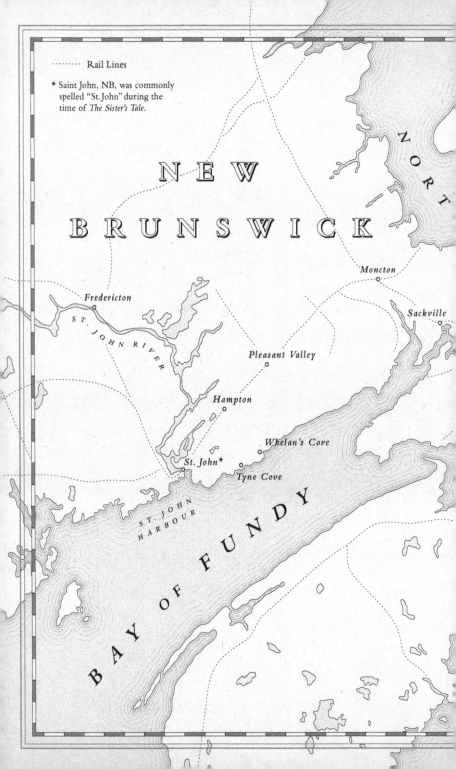

Rail Lines

* Saint John, NB, was commonly
  spelled "St. John" during the
  time of *The Sister's Tale*.

NEW

BRUNSWICK

NORT

Moncton

Fredericton

Sackville

ST. JOHN RIVER

Pleasant Valley

Hampton

Whelan's Cove

St. John *

Tyne Cove

ST. JOHN
HARBOUR

BAY OF FUNDY

The Maritime Provinces of
THE SISTER'S TALE

PRINCE EDWARD ISLAND

MBERLAND STRAIT

Black Creek ○ Pictou

COBEQUID
MOUNTAINS

NOVA SCOTIA

Halifax ○

ATLANTIC OCEAN

N
W   E
S

" . . . each had . . . some remote and distant hope
which, though perhaps starving to nothing,
still lived on, as hopes will."

Tess of the d'Urbervilles
THOMAS HARDY

Contents

PART I

December 1887 – August 1888

Mouse Traps Duly Set

∽

IN JOSEPHINE'S PARLOUR, Mr. Fairweather sat close to the Franklin stove, hands held open to its heat. His eyes were like a dog's, trusting and earnest, and Josephine wondered at his distress. She enjoyed the rare occasions when they were alone together, remembering how, when they were schoolchildren, he had once slipped her a misspelled note, folded to the size of a pansy.

Dear Josephine, will you mary me?

"I apologize for this intrusion, Mrs. Galloway," he said. "It is because of the urgency of the matter, a young girl."

He sat back from the fire, turned to her.

"But first, tell me what you hear from your husband."

"I have only my last letter from him when he was provisioning the ship in New York. Now, of course, he is at sea so I won't hear from him for some time."

She closed her eyes, briefly, rejecting even the possibility of sympathy. Her fingers stroked the nap of her cuffs, like petting a cat.

"It is the way for a sea captain's wife." Her voice was steady, held riches. "I am accustomed to it. But please, tell me. What young girl?"

"As you know, my duties are . . . extensive. We have no almshouse in Pleasant Valley."

A year ago, when Harland Fairweather was appointed Overseer of the Poor by the Justices of the Peace, his wife, Permelia, had whispered the news to Josephine as they were leaving church. *He does not want to do it.* She smelled of the new wintergreen tooth cleaner from McClean's Drug Store. *He will have to pay a substantial fine if he refuses. I told him he must take the position.*

Harland and Permelia lived with four daughters in a mansard-roofed brick house next to Fairweather's Gentlemen's Clothing at the lower end of Josephine's street, where Creek Road met Main Street. Josephine often witnessed Harland in the office at the back of his store, stern and remote, like a display behind glass. All the men in her own family were business owners. Her husband's father owned the town's largest dry goods store; her own father, now in partnership with his two sons, owned a boot and shoe factory.

"I have seen the discussions about the almshouse in the paper," Josephine said. "I concur with the opinion that the poor should have such a place, well-staffed and provisioned by the province."

He paused, surprised, and she surmised that Permelia did not read the brand-new *Weekly Record*. Or perhaps, careful with her grammar, her manners, the people with whom she associated, she perused only the social notes. Growing up, Permelia had been, if not poor, at least disadvantaged; her widowed mother had worked at the steam laundry.

"There is much discussion, indeed," he agreed. Relief, she saw, that he could discuss this with her; and a hint of yearning, quickly hidden by a return of his eyes, and hands, to the stove's heat. "Based upon the exigencies of taxation rather than compassion."

She brushed her hands down her skirts, looking at the tips of her shoes. His care for her held no threat or urgency, only made her feel the poignancy of such a friendship.

At the end of the room was an outflung octagonal turret, where the Christmas tree stood, filling the parlour with the aromas of moss and sap. Last night, Josephine and her daughters had decorated the tree with popcorn chains, gilded walnut shells, and stars made of paper-lace.

"I have read about the auction, Mr. Fairweather. Once a year, paupers are offered for sale." The bidding went downward, rather than up. The lowest bidder won the pauper. "It saves the province money."

"Precisely. There is a girl up for auction. I have visited her. Her name is Flora Salford."

He folded his hands in his lap and watched the fire. She saw his lips tighten, pained.

"Why? Why is she up for auction?"

"Evidently she was brought from England by one of the philanthropic people or organizations. She mentions a lady whose name she may never have known. She . . . Flora . . . has been here in Canada for five years and has somehow fallen through the cracks, as it were. I suspect that Maria Rye is the philanthropist responsible. Have you heard of her?"

"Yes." Josephine had seen pictures of Maria Rye in the newspaper. She was an Englishwoman. The children she brought to Canada were known as "Miss Rye's girls."

"She is a bit slipshod in tracking the children, especially those not taken to her distributing home in Niagara-on-the-Lake but dropped in Halifax or St. John." A log crumbled. He prodded the fire into shape with the poker. "The *short* of Flora's story is that she went to a farmer and his wife, who were both killed in a carriage accident."

"I heard of that accident, on the Mine Hill. Terrible."

"The girl has no one and so has ended up on the pauper rolls. Hence she is to be sold at auction."

"She has no one? No friends of the couple who could take her in?"

"No. I tried . . ."

Harland broke off, leaning forward to peer out a patch of window where the frost ferns were dissolving.

"I *begged* him not to go out this morning. It is *twenty degrees below*, I told him." Harland kept a weather station. Every morning, he raised a flag on the roof of his house so he could see the least twitch of breeze. "It is one and one-half a degree colder on this morning than it has been on any December twenty-third for nine years."

Josephine craned to see out the window, touched by his concern. Snow rose as from the bristles of an invisible broom; drifted, iridescent in the morning sun. Beyond the expanse of snow-covered lawn, she could see Harland's elderly father walking down the street, terrier at his heels, the tassels of a paisley shawl flirting with the tops of his boots. The dog scurried, eyes squinted against the cold—reluctant, obedient.

"There's a reason we call my father The Commodore, you know. He will brook no interruption in his routine. Save for death, as he says." He watched a moment longer. "Ah, well." Harland sat back. "No, as far as I can tell, Flora is utterly alone. I managed to find a family to take the girl through Christmas. They will have her until the auction."

Josephine brought to mind the customary image of a Home Child—"street Arabs," they were called, assumed to be rough, ill-bred, untrustworthy.

"Why have you come to me, Mr. Fairweather?"

"Unfortunately, Mrs. Galloway, I cannot offer her to you as a servant. By dint of poverty, like any pauper, she has been made a ward of the province. I must beg you to come to the auction . . ."

She drew back.

"I have never—"

He raised a hand. "I understand. I beg you, nonetheless, to come to that rabble of hard-faced men and I will hear your bid, no matter how softly you may give it, and I will make sure that my gavel comes down for you. I fear for that child. She is . . ."

He played a few imaginary piano keys with two fingers, looking at the ceiling. A leaf dropped from an aspidistra with a leathery tap.

"You and I have daughters of our own. Flora is fifteen. Despite the evident hardship of her history, despite the lack of . . . all, you know, that we have given our own daughters . . . she is an exceptionally beautiful young person. And what those men will—"

"Ah," Josephine interrupted. She brought the back of one hand to her mouth, closed her eyes and took a long breath. The ticking of the clock, the crackle of the fire—wind-brushed snow spun past the window.

"Yes, Mr. Fairweather. I can find work for her."

"The auction will be held after Christmas," he said. He relaxed back into the chair, crossed his legs. "At the train station. I am in your service, I am indeed. You lighten my heart with your kindness."

"No, no. I have so much. A husband, a family. All of this." She offered him her home on the palm of her hand. "It is the least I can do."

The smell of baking gingerbread rose from the kitchen. A maid, carrying linens, came down the stairs, passed through the hall. The ornaments on the Christmas tree turned, borne on invisible currents of sweet-scented air.

—

She stood in the door watching as Mr. Fairweather walked down the drive between shoulder-high snowbanks thrown up by Mr. Dougan's wooden shovel. Cold thinned her nostrils—like the crisp edges of Ellen's butter cookies.

Lucy, seventeen, and Maud, fifteen, would soon be walking home from the Pleasant Valley Academy, the daughters of a sea captain, well fortified against the cold in their long wool coats, mittens and fur hats. George, attending the University of Mount Allison College in Sackville, was returning tomorrow on the train.

She watched Harland as he swung firmly down the hill in the direction The Commodore and his dog had been heading—towards home, dinner, family; and she was gripped by her husband's absence and the dangers he risked. She tried to dismiss fear, although she could not—it remained, dark, dull, tarnishing happiness.

In the parlour, she resumed her seat before the fire. She took Simeon's last letter from a pile on a marble tabletop and ran her hand over the paper with as much tenderness as if vellum were skin. She unfolded it, read for the fifth time:

My dear Josie,

I write from New York, where I am comfortably installed in The Grand Hotel while "Marianne" is being provisioned. Sailor is curled at my side.

Sailor. His beloved St. John's water dog.

I have agreed to take six women—a mother and two daughters travelling with servants—to South Carolina. Mrs. Holdwell's daughter is to be married in Charleston. I told her we would head southwards in the New Year, passing Cape Hatteras and keeping as far east as possible from the Outer Banks. I struggle to complete my crew. It is getting harder to find seasoned seamen than in Uncle N's day. The first mate is experienced but in poor health. The second mate is only nineteen, although willing and honest. I have not yet found a man as capable of navigation as I am myself.

It was the fault of his Aunt Azuba and Uncle Nathaniel in Whelan's Cove, she thought. All his boyhood, picking apples in his uncle's orchard or sitting on their veranda high over the Bay of Fundy, he'd imbibed seafaring tales: rounding the Horn; sighting a ship stranded on an iceberg; Antwerp's museums; the volcanic islands off Java.

Sea captains' wives are now a rare thing; they are perhaps even pitied. The sea will be my mistress, he'd said, when asking for her hand in marriage. *I will not mind,* she'd murmured. Mount Allison Wesleyan Academy schooled, modern and brazen, she'd been oddly thrilled by the idea of the sea as seductress. And although their parents did not approve, the wedding was sumptuous and Simeon had proved them wrong with his success.

She slipped the letter back in the envelope and held it to her cheek, watching the fire. The sea, as seductress, had become a thing she wished he would renounce.

He would miss another Christmas.

She rose, restless, went into the front hall and lifted a calling card from a silver dish. She studied its scrolled letters, thinking not of the visitor they represented but of the house rising up around her with its routines—polished salvers on the sideboard, the order sent to Mr. Cardwell's butcher shop, mouse traps duly set—and of how she must contrive to cause no ripple, no storm, as if to do so would threaten Simeon's voyage.

—

Josephine heard the harsh jangle of the new telephone. She went to the front hall; lifting the receiver, heard first the operator, then Mr. Fairweather's voice.

"Despite the weather, the auction will go ahead tomorrow at noon. Stand in the front row where I can see you."

She set the receiver in its cradle and stood with her head bowed. She would like to have taken this decision after talking it over with Simeon. He was a man with whom she could discuss things, unlike her father or brothers; or, even, her own mother who had not learned to think for herself, nor approved of Josephine's doing so.

I am at sea.

She said this to him, last time he was home. *Without you, I am at sea.* They were in bed, after making love. He knew how to make her find her pleasure. She lay with her forehead on his shoulder, shy after such intimacy, murmuring into his salty skin. *And? What does that mean?* he said. *You should know,* she answered. *No land beneath one's feet. A wind coming from one way and then another, I suppose, and never sure how to set the sails.*

And he pulled her to his chest and then rolled over on top of her, slowly letting his weight down until, shrieking, she begged for mercy. *There,* he said. *I press you into the ground. No wind will blow you.*

He made the most of his time at home, brightening the future with plans, acting on impulse. *Why don't we build a greenhouse?* Or—*Let's take the children on the train to St. John.* When the children were small, he prowled the house on all fours, roaring and snapping at them like a bear. When they were older, he brought them extravagant gifts from Hong Kong or Paris. He swept away her anxieties with his assurances of boundless good fortune. Master of weather, navigation and command, he exercised the same capabilities as husband, as father. The impulsive side of his nature—announcing, one morning, with great enthusiasm, that he and two friends were going to skate all the way to Fredericton on the St. John River, or, on a summer's day, blithely setting forth into the wilderness with a botanist acquaintance on a quest for a purple fringed orchid—was like a reward, she felt, for his adherences to its opposite.

She walked down the hall, calling.

"Ellen?"

The kitchen was like the cook's own home, with its yellow oilcloth floor, earthenware crocks and copper saucepans, scraps of Irish poetry tacked to the walls like a patina.

Ellen, Margaret, Mary and Mr. Dougan were breaking for tea. Ellen, brisk, stiff-jointed, wearing a cloth cap, poured custard sauce over warm apple cake.

"Will you join us for a piece of cake, then, Mrs. Galloway." Her questions were statements, offhand, as if inured from caring, although Josephine knew how her invariable compliments on dessert or roast brought a glint of pleasure, quelled by tightened lips.

"Thank you, Ellen, but no, I am satiated. That was Mr. Fairweather on the telephone. We're to have a new girl. I'll be bringing her tomorrow. There's been some mistake and she's being sold at the pauper auction."

"Is she from the old country?"

"English. Fifteen years old. Apparently she was sent over as a Home Child."

Looks, exchanged. *Pickpockets, guttersnipes.*

Josephine's heart quailed as she saw the response. They assumed, she saw, that the child would be sullen, bitter, ungrateful.

Her voice firmed.

"Margaret, could you make up a bed for her in the little room at the end of the hall? Make it nicely, with plenty of bedding. She was working at that farm where both husband and wife were killed on the Mine Hill."

Ellen paused, the custard spoon briefly forgotten.

"Ah. I did read of it. Terrible thing." Her tone yielded, allowed the possibility of pity. "Poor wee girl . . ."

—

In the clear morning light, Josephine stood in the hall waiting for Mr. Dougan to come with the horse and sleigh.

She held the newspaper in gloved hands and perused the front page. The words were somewhat obscured by her lace shawl but she did not wish to undo the bow she had tied beneath her chin.

AXE MURDER. The horrible deed of blood which was committed at Tyne Cove yesterday has caused much excitement. A woman, Mrs. Elsa Cavanaugh, was found murdered in the home of Mr. John Tatum, with indications of a violent struggle. Her wrists and hands show marks as if they had been made by the teeth of a human being and her body bears the marks of bruises. The walls of the room in which she was found are finely spattered with stars of blood. The murder weapon, an axe, was in plain sight, leaning against the stove, soaked in blood. Her reason for being at the home of Mr. Tatum, by his accounts, is as a boarder. She was found by him when he returned from St. John. He saw the body lying on the floor, the head red and her clothes tossed up. By his account, Mrs. Cavanaugh, a widow, was of

County Tyrone, Ireland, and has been living in this country for over thirty years. She was fifty years of age, portly, of short stature and ill health. It is not known . . .

The front door opened. She lowered the paper, startled. On the cold air, the smell of horse, the bite of snow.

"Ready, ma'am?" Mr. Dougan gave her his arm as she stepped up into the sleigh. She had asked him not to tip his hat. You are in Canada, now, she'd said.

She settled, pulled up the bearskin rug. A blanket for the girl was folded on the seat beside her. Mr. Dougan handed up a basket prepared by Ellen—gingerbread, a ham sandwich.

"She said the girl will be cold and hungry," he explained.

Dappled coat groomed to a trout-shimmer, the mare snorted, neck arched, as Mr. Dougan climbed into his seat and collected the reins. Josephine, adjusting her collar to cover her nose, felt a wave of pleasure as the sleigh slid down the lane—lindens, snow-covered lawn, the house Simeon had built for them, with its scrolled red trim, turret and verandas.

She leaned forward to enjoy the sight of Hilltop, the town's largest house, built by an English duke for his two childless, widowed sisters. Snow made a conical cap on the roof of its three-storey turret and accentuated its delicious details—veranda railings topping spindled balusters, Gothic windows with stained-glass panes, gingerbread scrollwork.

Everything had become like a painting, Josephine thought—all things made less ordinary by a turn in the weather.

The Auction

∾

A SMALL, QUICK-MOVING WOMAN came up the attic stairs and stooped over the pallet, shaking the sleeping girl, impatiently.

"Dress in your warmest clothes."

She sat up, slumped forward, mindful of the nails poking through the sloped ceiling. Her nightdress was missing a button at the neck, the collar scrubbed to a threadbare finish. She crossed her arms, felt the warmth of her own hair, fallen from its pins. She could not make out the woman's expression.

"Why?"

"Because you . . . And pack up all your belongings."

"Am I leaving?"

"Yes. The Overseer of the Poor will no doubt reimburse you."

The woman's dress rustled as she lifted it to descend the perilous stairs.

The girl dressed in her union suit. She pulled a wool sweater over her dress, worked her feet into long stockings. She knelt to set folded clothing—wool socks, drawers, two merino undershirts, her only other dress—into the wooden box, painted green, that had accompanied her on the ship, the train, the wagon to Ada and Henry's farm, and now here.

She went down the narrow stairs, awkward, one arm barely surrounding the box.

The kitchen was warm, lit by kerosene lamps.

"They've eaten," the cook said, glancing at her. "They let you sleep in. You're to have your breakfast and then go wait in the hall."

She sat at the kitchen table and ate a bowl of oatmeal and a slice of buttered bread with jam made from last summer's raspberries. She went into the hall and slid onto the bench where the children sat to remove their boots. In the cold light, she could see snow falling past narrow windows on either side of the door.

She listened to the ticking of the clock, thinking of Ada, remembering how she'd been glad to see her wearing her red felt hat on the day that she and Henry set out for town to buy the dimity.

The last thing I saw of them. Shooing the barn cats from their feet. Their winter boots.

A knock on the door; she jumped to her feet and opened it. A man stood in the falling snow.

"You Flora Salford?"

"I am."

"Got your things? Hand 'em over . . ."

Bits of hay clung to the man's wool coat. Gobbets of frozen mucus in his moustache. She followed him out the door. He was in a hurry, she thought, and wondered why. An open farm wagon stood in the street, filled with men, women and children. They did not look up at her, but hunkered against the cold and the snow.

The man gave her a hand up onto the wagon's iron step.

"Where are we going?" she asked. Her words hung in the air, an embarrassment, for no one answered. All the people had bags at their feet. All jolted in the same direction as the wagon moved off. A woman lay rolled onto her side, grey hair showing above a blanket. Beside Flora was a boy her own age. He leaned forward, arms like broken branches, hands hanging. A little girl began to cry, a keening mournfulness muffled by an older girl's coat. A little boy huddled on the bigger girl's other side. Flora didn't dare look at all the others—four or five men and women.

"Where are we going?" Flora whispered to the boy her own age. Rheumy eyes lifted only as far as his knees and then returned to settle on his hands. As if, she thought, she had said it to torment him.

The wagon passed through the centre of Pleasant Valley. The street widened, storefronts on either side—dry goods, laundries. Rug-covered horses stood hitched to sleighs. The wagon rattled over the train tracks, turned towards the station.

Men pressed together, jostling, in front of the station house, a two-storey building. People carrying satchels and carpet bags hurried up its front steps, crossed a porch, vanished inside. Across the street stood a long, three-storey hotel. Beyond, beneath the snow-covered branches of elm trees, the town emerged through the snow, a complex pattern of roofs, one higher than the next, planes of white: factories, by their size, and a tannery, by its smell. She thought of the long, dreary days hemming gloves at the workhouse, felt a stab of fear.

The wagon passed the station house and pulled close to the platform along the tracks. She had waited beneath its roof when she arrived, alone, from the Protestant Orphanage in St. John.

In the wagon, people bent to gather their bags. Hands on leather straps, on ropes, on the faded red and blue threads of a carpet bag. A wicker basket, tied with string. The cold air, making noses run. Stepping down, a man's hand, offered.

"Careful, now."

Flora climbed down from the wagon, clutching her box with both arms, fear a blood taste in her mouth. She recognized the Overseer of the Poor; he stood on the platform steps holding a gavel and perusing papers. His cheeks were red and shiny as apples, cold-polished.

She stared at him, terror rising as the situation spread itself around her: the unfeeling clamour—laughter, shouts, jibes; pipe stems clamped in teeth; round hats like a flock of black-headed birds. The people from the wagon filed past, as if they knew where to go.

He glanced beyond her, significantly. She turned to see a woman stepping down from a sleigh driven by a dapple-grey horse. A black lace shawl covered her hat. The woman paused, hesitant in mid-step.

A man approached Flora. He held a pencil and a tiny notebook in purple-gloved hands; she smelled pomade emanating from his froth of white hair, curling, woman-like—white carnation in his buttonhole. His eyes met hers and he raised his eyebrows.

"My name is George Francis Train. Of *The Weekly Record*. I—"

Someone seized her arm. Led her up the steps to a platform beneath the portico.

She saw the sign.

NOTICE OF IMPENDING SALE. ELEVEN PAUPERS . . .

The people who had been with her in the wagon were arrayed on the station platform on two benches. The wagon was parked before the platform so the ill woman could be present. Snow gathered on the blanket covering her.

Flora set down her box and sat beside the little boy. He shuddered, his cheeks puckered with dried mucus and the trails of tears.

She slid sideways. He looked up and she nodded, minutely—*lean on me*—and he did. She felt the contact with a shock, the small breathing body so like her own. The only bodies she ever touched were those of farm animals, solid and hot, their hearts uncaring; they suffered her embrace as they would the feet of a fly. The boy relaxed. His shuddering came in spasms, then stopped. He slipped off one mitten and put his thumb in his mouth. He gazed at his boots.

The station windows were streaked with runnels of condensation; she imagined a pot-bellied stove pulsing heat in the little room, and how there must be tea and gingerbread for those waiting to go wherever they wished. Birds burst from the rafters and out into the snow, their wings making a clatter like a winnowing machine. Flora stared out over the crowd, rage rising at the Overseer's betrayal—putting her on sale like a pig at market.

—

"I beg your pardon," Josephine murmured, making her way to the front as Harland had instructed her, touching serge sleeves; men averted their eyes.

Josephine felt a sense of disorientation. She could not be in her own town. She wished Simeon were here to share her shock. Eleven paupers: an old man leaning forward, hands gripped between his knees, working his mouth over his gums. A boy about thirteen, head back, hostile. Four middle-aged men and women. Three little children. A bedridden person, bundled in a wagon.

A girl, not a child—dark blonde hair caught up haphazardly, coming loose and falling from a knitted cap, bright against a black cloak. High, clear forehead; sad, far-seeing eyes. Hands gripped in her lap.

Surely that is Flora.

Josephine saw her friend Harland Fairweather transformed by his role. On the platform, he sat at a table. He set down a gavel and fussed with his papers, not looking at the crowd below or the paupers beside him. The table wobbled. Someone wedged a pamphlet under one of its legs. At the bottom of the stairs, Josephine saw a man who surveyed the scene and then scribbled in a notebook, white hair curling from beneath a fur hat.

Harland bared one hand, breathed on cupped fingers and worked the hand back into its glove. He would hate being before a crowd, Josephine thought; he was not one to call attention to himself. When she visited Permelia, she might glimpse him in his weather station, a glassed-in porch at the back of their house, where he pored, utterly absorbed, over thermometers and gauges, peered out at flags, entering figures into notebooks. "It's not because of his name," Permelia would murmur, permitting herself an exasperated giggle.

He picked up the gavel and rapped it down. The crowd quieted, shifting. On the air, a hint of the tannery's stench.

His voice, isolated, was as strange as the scene.

"I am ashamed . . ." Harland Fairweather called out, and waited for complete silence, until all that could be heard was the diminution of a sleigh's bells as the driver, seeing the auction, deferential, pulled his horse down into a floating half trot.

"I am ashamed of the task I have to do."

He pointed down at the wagon and its mound of blankets.

"Look," he said. "There lies a woman too sick to rise and sit with the others. Yet not too sick not to be brought here in the cold and snow. I feel I must point out that it has come to my attention as Overseer of the Poor that . . ."

He paused, as if losing his thought. Collected himself and continued.

". . . that during the last year, some of these paupers were kept in onerous conditions. I have seen with my own eyes that they were made to sleep in sheds, given nothing but rags for bedding."

He took a deep breath. He worked a handkerchief from a pocket and wiped his mouth and nose. Josephine saw his hand tremble as he put it back.

"Some have been worked beyond their power of endurance. But as you all know, we have no other way to care for the poor. We have no almshouse. So it is my unfortunate duty to offer these paupers for sale to the lowest bidder. Those who receive them will be paid the amount of their bid by the province, as a monthly sum, for the duration of *one year*. It is my fervent hope that those who receive these paupers will treat them with humanity and decency."

He worked spectacles over his eyes, wrapping the temple tips behind his ears. Josephine watched as the girl sat straight and placed her feet side by side, keeping her eyes fixed on Mr. Fairweather. The girl did not appear to realize that she was a lodestone, every man's eyes sliding, looking away, returning.

"I will begin with these three children so that some one of you will take them home, give them a decent meal, and comfort them in their distress. They are orphans, aged . . ."

He ran his finger down the paper.

". . . aged five, seven, and eight. I offer them as a block."

Josephine covered her mouth. She would bid for them. She tried to think where she would keep them. She could not put them in her daughters' rooms. And George would be outraged should he return to find his room occupied.

"What am I bid for the block of three?"

The little boy sat up and reached for his older sister's hand. Like the mother who should have been there, Josephine thought, and her heart felt thick, shortening her breath.

"What am I bid for the block of three? May I remind you, these are sisters and brother."

No one bid. Josephine felt a recklessness threaten to overtake her.

"I'll take the boy," a man called out. "I bid thirty-five dollars."

No one else bid.

She drew a breath, parted her lips to speak.

The Overseer brought the gavel down. A wail rose from all of the children. Already the purchaser was mounting the steps.

The two little girls went next, bought together.

The blonde girl sat apart from any others, now, as the older boy was sold. Then the old man. Then the bedridden woman, who went for the high price of $101.

"Flora Salford." He pointed at the girl.

He had not named the other paupers.

So I will be absolutely certain.

"Formerly a hand at the Quigley farm. You will know that Henry and Ada Quigley met their deaths earlier this month when their horse slipped on ice on the Mine Hill. By her own account, this young woman is fifteen years of age, able and capable of hard work. She comes with complete outfit except she needs winter boots, which the purchaser must provide. What am I bid?"

Harland's eyes scanned the crowd. Hands shot up. He did not look at Josephine.

He wants me to bide my time? Josephine did not know this game nor how it was best played. I will hear your bid, he had said.

A man's voice called out. "I bid fifty dollars."

"Forty-nine."

The first man, again. Square, fleshy face. He poked up the handle of a cane. "Forty-eight."

Now a third man. "Forty-seven."

Harland glanced at Josephine. She held her hands palm outwards, fingers stretched—*ten dollars less*—hoping he would understand.

"I am bid thirty-seven," Harland said.

"Thirty-six." All three men called out at the same time.

Again, Josephine flashed her hands. Harland brought down his gavel. "Sold . . . for twenty-six dollars."

An uproar ensued. He pounded, pounded, the crack of gavel on maple.

THREE

Polite and Invisible

~

THE DRIVER WHIPPED THE dapple-grey mare into a hard trot. Balled snow flew from her hooves. Flora fell backwards against the quilted padding. The woman who'd won her at auction, jostled, attempted to unfold a plaid wool blanket.

"Pull her down to a walk, please, Mr. Dougan. We can hardly . . ."

Flora turned to look back. Snowy roof of the train station, a white gleam, and men's hats, the size of pebbles.

"There," the woman said, as the horse dropped into a restrained, high-stepping walk. She handed Flora the blanket, which she had shaken from its folds.

"And there's a ham sandwich for you in the basket," she said, lifting up a hinged wooden cover, revealing a paper package. Flora was not hungry, but took it out and unwrapped it. The bread was faintly warm, the ham smelled of cloves. She took a bite, seeing that the woman was watching her.

The woman looked away, pulling the bearskin up over her neck and shoulders. She drew a long breath and pressed the back of her glove to her lips.

She was a woman poised between youth and the beginnings of decline, her cheeks marked with fine, curved lines; a slight downturn at the corners of her lips; a strong nose; full, cold-flushed skin, the skin of shade and expensive soap.

"My name is Josephine Galloway," the woman said, not looking at Flora. "The Overseer of the Poor is my friend. He asked me to bid for you."

Flora parted her lips to speak and did not know what to say. She hardly knew who she had been and did not know who she was to be now. She did not know whether she was going to the woman's home as a servant, or was being sent back to Maria Rye, or was being taken to the Overseer of the Poor.

"It is barbaric. He was afraid for you." The woman glanced at Flora, nervous. Looked away. "I know your name is Flora. You don't need to speak."

The horse leaned into the traces, pulling the sleigh up a steep street, passing large, new-looking houses.

"That sickly woman in the wagon," Josephine exclaimed, a burst. "They were going to put her up for auction! I cannot believe—"

Flora put down the sandwich. She looked out her side of the sleigh, remembering women in the workhouse. Gaunt, motionless. Too sad to eat.

An enormous house loomed from the winter trees, with a tower and gables.

"The MacVey sisters live there," the woman said. She began to lift the bearskin. "Their brother built them that house."

They turned onto a lane almost at the top of the hill, leading to a white house set back from the street by a wide lawn, with a barn and a veranda running around three sides of the house.

"This is my home, Flora," Josephine said. "You will live here now."

—

They stepped into a hallway, surfaces gleaming with cleanliness. The cold, bright day shut away with the closing of the front door.

Flora set her boots on the rack. She followed the woman's rustling skirt over slippery, varnished floorboards, then a soft rug. A babble of Irish accents rose as Josephine pushed open a door and ushered Flora into a kitchen.

Three women, suddenly silent.

Steamy warmth, a spill of flour on the yellow floor, green wainscot. Verses tacked to wallpaper, to the sides of cupboards.

"Flora, this is Ellen, my cook. Ellen, this is Flora Salford."

Ellen was built like a goat, the framework of bones visible. Sagging cheeks, their lines compressed into riverine maps offset by sharp, percipient eyes. She wiped yeasty hands on her apron and took Flora's hand. She did not shake it but made certain that Flora stood and returned her close look and allowed herself to be examined. Flora's heart thickened.

"Flora Salford, is it," she said. "Well, then."

"This is Margaret," Josephine continued.

Margaret was tall and raw-boned, with large front teeth that protruded. She held a bowl in the crook of her arm and braved a glance into Flora's eyes. She nodded and turned away, stirring with a wooden spoon.

"And Mary."

Mary was small and quick. She put her hands on her hips and stared at Flora. Her voice was flat; friendship, Flora knew, was a thing to be earned.

"You got a head of hair on you, girl. Some beautiful. Wants untangling. You can use cider vinegar rinse."

Mr. Dougan came into the kitchen. At Josephine's bidding, he took away the green box. Flora heard his steps, clumping up uncarpeted stairs.

Standing close to her new mistress, Flora glanced at her. She did not know if thanks should be given, or apology. Josephine returned her look, hesitating, as if she, too, did not know what to say. The lines beside her mouth deepened.

"Mary, take her up, show her to her room."

Boiling hot water hissed from the spout of the claw-footed tub, with its palm-sized spigots, like metal daisy heads. Flora stared at the black grime outlining her toenails. Scraps of sock wool rose from between her toes and floated on the limpid water. She leaned forward and grasped her legs. Ribs; flat skin between her pelvic bones. The door opened just enough for a hand to drop fresh clothing onto the seat of a chair. She pushed herself up to look. Black dress with a white apron and a white cap. Black stockings. Leather shoes. Black, white, starched.

Servant's clothes.

She slid under the water and opened her eyes.

They'd made her wash on the night that she arrived at the farm, five years ago. She was ten years old and had disembarked from the ship in St. John and been driven to the Protestant Orphanage, but no family in St. John offered to take her and so the matron hung a placard around her neck reading *Flora Salford* and put her on a train. She arrived at the Pleasant Valley station on a cold spring night and Henry Quigley picked her up. Utter darkness, save for a flicker of light in one window, when the horse came to a stop before the farmhouse. Smell of cows and forest, and the thin throb of peepers. On the scarred linoleum, a washtub in front of a wood stove. Ada sent Henry and their two hired men out of the house and told Flora to take off every stitch of clothing and climb into the hot water. The tired farm woman gave her a fist-sized ball of hard soap.

In the morning, Ada told her to make bread.

I never made bread.

Nor, she told Ada, when questioned, did she know how to make butter, or knit a sock or even use a hoe. At the workhouse, they had lined up and shuffled single-file to long tables, where they were fed like beasts at a trough. They were led up into high rooms—hot in summer, cold in winter—and given baskets of gloves to hem. They were told they were being punished for the sins of their parents, who were poor.

They were lucky, they were instructed, to be fed and clothed, since the outside world was a place of danger and terror. Old women spent their whole lives in the workhouse. Men walked and murmured in their own yard, beyond a wall, making an unrelenting din with their hammers, splitting stones.

Flora sat up suddenly, attempting to lose her memories in a rush of soapy water. She reached forward to adjust the magical spigots.

Ada had not learned the whole of her shame. How workhouse children were made to stand in tubs while women rubbed them down with rough cloths, talking of boyfriends, insults and secret matters. How it made her feel as if her filth were intrinsic, something she had no power to remove.

In this bathtub, where fresh water could be summoned at the turn of a tap, dirt separated from her, her legs were turning pink. She leaned forward, cupping her hands beneath the faucet.

—

On Flora's third day of work, Ellen told her to take tea to the front room, where Mrs. Galloway had a visitor.

"'Tis her husband's first cousin Carrie. Her that went around the world as a child and was almost killed by pirates." Ellen held a silver pitcher between dainty fingers, set it next to a plate of sliced cake. "Set the tray on the table next to Mrs. Galloway's chair."

Carrying the tray down the hall, Flora felt she had no under-pinnings, might stumble and fall, since she did not know what kind of expression to put on her face, whether to smile or show fear; she knew only to be as invisible as Ellen, Mary and Margaret had instructed her, a costume hung on a line.

She set down the tray so carefully that the porcelain barely shivered. She straightened, wanting to hurry back to the warmth of Ellen's kitchen, where she could resume rolling dough thin enough to be pressed with a star-shaped cutter.

Josephine's guest was leaning forward, hands shaping a story.

". . . she had written and passed the matriculation exam. In fact, she placed second. It is a requirement for a student wanting to enter the University of New Brunswick. The law states that any person passing that exam, paying the dues, and agreeing to abide by the rules of the university will be accepted. Well, she—"

"Excuse me, Carrie." Josephine held up her hand, apologetic. "I would like you to meet Flora Salford. Flora, this is my cousin, Mrs. Emmerson."

"Good day, Mrs. Emmerson."

The woman looked up with acute, curious eyes.

"I'm happy you've come to this house, Flora."

Flora dropped a knee, awkward.

"Pleased to meet you, ma'am."

Leaving, she wondered if Josephine would have introduced Mary or Margaret to Mrs. Emmerson, girls whose last names Flora did not know.

—

Wrapped in shawls, Josephine and Carrie watched Flora leave the room. Sunlight shimmered in the frosted windows, stretched across the Persian carpet. New Brunswick was in the midst of a spell of intense cold.

"She was not admitted," Carrie said.

Josephine was momentarily puzzled.

"Oh, the student." She laughed. "Yes. I'm sorry. Would you like milk in your tea?"

Carrie accepted cup and saucer and sat back. "Mary Tibbits. She was not admitted into the university. Do you know why? Because even after interceding with a lawyer, even after going directly to President Harrison, she was *denied entrance*. They said, in effect, that a woman was not a person."

Carrie herself had been sent to a boarding school in Boston and then attended the Wellesley Female Seminary. She was married to a lawyer, lived in St. John, gave private lessons in French, German and Italian.

"A woman has graduated from the University of Mount Allison College, you know," Josephine said. Proud, because she herself had attended the female branch of Mount Allison Wesleyan Academy. "The first woman to receive a bachelor of arts degree in the British Empire."

"Yes. I'm sure Mary Tibbits called that to the attention of her member of the legislative assembly. He took up her cause, you know. He threatened to withdraw provincial funding unless she were admitted. The university reconsidered its position. She is there now. The non-person became a person." Carrie drew a long breath and Josephine thought, inconsequentially, of a battered doll she had once glimpsed lying on the pillow of Carrie and her husband's bed. They had no children.

"It makes me angry." Carrie stirred the milk into her tea. "*Very* angry."

Carrie's visits always left Josephine feeling half-formed, tattered, and infused with a determination to join the Women's Christian Temperance Union, as had Carrie, or visit the poor, as Carrie did, or start an organization of her own, as Carrie had done, several times— resolutions that faded as she discussed the week's menus with Ellen, or sorted through calling cards in the silver dish, or wrote to Simeon telling him of lectures at White's Hall, skating parties, the cornet band concert. Only this morning, she had been asked to join the town beautification committee, and had accepted, and did not tell Carrie.

"The position of women is not that different from that of the paupers," Carrie said, after a silence broken by the icy spit of snow against windowpanes. "Despite some progressive laws giving women like ourselves, *married* women, more rights to our own property, judges continue to adhere to narrow and patriarchal interpretations. By the way, did you see today's paper?"

"No."

"You know that American who writes for *The Weekly Record?* Mr. Train?"

"Yes, I saw him at the auction."

"He has written a diatribe comparing the pauper auction to the infamous slave sales in the southern states before the war. He's renowned in the United States, you know. Pleasant Valley will come to international attention."

"It was terrible, Carrie. There were three little children, a brother and two sisters, separated. My friend begged me to rescue Flora. Men were bidding for her."

Carrie set down her tea. She had not touched her cake.

"There is so much wrong with the way things are now."

Her face hardened. Her voice acquired an elevated, strident tone.

"Perhaps you don't see it, Josephine, living here in this quiet little town. In the city, you can hardly hear yourself think, you can hardly breathe the air, there are so many manufacturers. There are women working in those mills. Children working ten hours a day. In dreadful conditions. And we women, who understand their needs better than any man, have no say in either drafting legislation or voting. Because, like your Flora, we are non-persons. We have been pauperized."

She is not *my* Flora, Josephine thought, resenting the implication, intimidated by the word *legislation*.

Carrie sat forward on the edge of her chair. Josephine fancied that the years at sea had formed the freckles mapping her cheeks, and the remote, musing expression with a hint of remembered hardship that reminded her of sea captains—Simeon, Uncle Nathaniel.

Carrie frowned, tapped her knuckles on the arm of her chair.

"I am starting an organization to fight for women's suffrage."

Suffrage. The word was appearing in the newspaper with increasing frequency, and Josephine sensed its peculiar complexity—*suffering, muffins, rage*—and could not help understanding why its adherents were mocked. The organization would be based in St. John, too far away for her to feel the obligation of joining. A relief.

Carrie glanced at the clock on the mantelpiece.

"I must go, Josephine. I told Mr. Dougan I would be ready by four."

In the hallway, Carrie fastened the clasp of her cloak, worked her fingers into wool-lined gloves.

"I will be back to attend Mr. Train's next lecture. Did you know he intends to dress a pauper in the finest Savile Row suit and put him on the stage? He intends to show how we judge by appearance and circumstance. Will you come with me?"

"Yes. Well. Unless Simeon has returned."

Carrie's face gentled. She patted Josephine's shoulder.

"My mother told me this was why she wanted to go to sea. She was tired of *waiting*. Always waiting."

—

"Go on to bed with you," the cook said. Flora had dried the last pot and was hanging the cloth on the wood stove's handle.

Ellen sought her chair as if it were the day's single consolation, a sigh carrying her down, feet rising to a footstool. She had snapped at Flora, today; harried her, hurried her. She had been exasperated over all the things the girl did not know how to do.

"I have to sweep," Flora said.

"Only me to look at it." Ellen flicked her hand at the floor.

Flora stood with her feet set neatly side by side and looked at the floor.

"I know about loneliness," Ellen said. The cook was gazing at her as if seeing someone else. "You go on up to your bed."

As Flora climbed the stairs, the conversation she had overheard this afternoon ran in her mind, a quiet murmur spiked by occasional audible words—*education, angry, conditions*—and wondered at these tea-drinking, educated Canadians. *What they have. Houses and husbands.* In her room, the kerosene lamp guttered; she turned the knob and the flame leapt up behind the smudged glass. Snow sifted under the window, made a line along the sill. She put on wool socks, a flannel nightgown and a woollen cap. She blew out the flame and slid between the sheets.

In the unfamiliar darkness, death was close. She could still hear Ada Quigley's voice over the clicking of knitting needles and the crackling fire in the wood stove.

I'm going to make a baby dress.

Can I help sew it?

If you get yer chores done.

She wished she had seen the dimity that Ada had gone to town to buy. Ada didn't usually go to town with Henry, especially not in winter, but she had not yet seen her daughter's baby and wished to have a tiny dress ready for the child when she did.

Did you get them caulked shoes on the mare?

A sharp question to Henry. The last thing Flora heard her say.

She rolled onto her side, arms around her knees. The story unfolded, over and over in her head.

At the church, a woman pulled the cover over the keys of the pump organ. All the black-coated people filed out and into buggies and carriages, bound for Ada and Henry's house. The kitchen was packed with people smelling of horses and wool. Women poured boiling water over tea leaves in pitchers, passed plates of pie, just as if the kitchen were their own. People ate dutifully, without pleasure. The hired men packed up their belongings; they paused, looking at Flora—before leaving, they filled the wood box with maple chunks, split fine. She watched Ada and Henry's daughter bundle up the baby whose gown had caused her parents' deaths. And then, once everyone had left, she stayed in the house all alone, because no one knew what to do with her. Beads of sap froze in the joists and swelled against the sinews of their encasement, waking her with cracks as loud as gunshots. She'd clutched the quilt to her mouth. *Ma? Ma?* Longing for a ghost to breathe on her cheek, even cause her death if it might take her home to a meadow in the Cotswolds, lacy with the umbels of wild carrots, shining with hovering damselflies. The next morning, neighbours arrived in their wagons to do the chores. They came stomping into the kitchen and fired up the wood stove. They started at the sight of her.

The Overseer of the Poor arrived. He set his cane against the scarred wainscot, sat in a straight-backed chair. He folded his gloved hands.

"You're a Home Child, of course, but we've lost track of your papers. In such a case, the province will assume your care. You'll spend Christmas with children your age. After that, we'll see what can be done with you."

"I want to go back to England. *Please*. Send me on the boat. Send me home."

"We'll see."

He'd patted the back of her hand. She got in his carriage and they drove out of the valley, passing the cemetery where Ada and Henry would be buried in the spring when their bodies were taken from the icehouse.

Children your age.

Had the Overseer truly thought she would spend a happy Christmas with the Pleasant Valley family?

Once she had been placed on Henry and Ada's farm, she'd tried to change the way she talked, copying the cadences of the hired men. In the one-room schoolhouse where she had gotten a bit of learning on days when she was ahead with her chores, the children had teased her. They had mocked her strange dress and stockings, as if the workhouse were an odour emanating from them, even though the clothes were fresh from Ada's soap. The children in Pleasant Valley were no different. They imitated her accent, dropped dead flies in her porridge.

She was made to sleep in the attic on a pallet whose buckwheat hulls, leaking from its seams, crunched and slithered, leaving little but cloth beneath her. The ceiling slanted close, stippled with nails whose points bristled with frost. On Christmas morning, she had peered out the attic window and seen smoke drifting from the chimney, separating into white strands, like angels on the point of dissolution. Downstairs, a fir tree stood in the parlour, hung with painted baubles, but she had been told to remain in the kitchen, helping the cook.

One day she would tell the Overseer of the Poor. How she had thought she would have turkey and mince pie, as she always did on Ada and Henry's farm. And instead, at the cook's sharp call, had steeled herself to leave her warm cocoon and put on the clothes that hung motionless as frozen rabbits, and had gone down the back stairs to the kitchen on the day she was supposed to spend *with children her own age*.

She yawned, closed her eyes. Today's images pressed close: wax on wood, her rag, circling: custard, crinkled with nutmeg—*you're going to let it burn*; icicles holding a rainbow shimmer, vinegar on windowpane; Josephine, hand on forehead, an urgency in her pen's scratch. Maud and Lucy, home from school with frosted eyelashes.

Thoughts tipped, slid, ran together, glossy and warm, sweet smelling.

—

By bedtime, Josephine had not had time to peruse *The Weekly Record*, so she took it upstairs. Heat radiated from a stovepipe, which rose through the hall floor and separated into three pipes. She always warned her daughters about the hot metal. *Careful. Hold your skirts tight*.

She twisted, unbuttoning the back of her dress; worked at the hooks of her coralline corset. Her skin relaxed, like a jelly tipped from a mould. She rubbed at the red creases in her flesh. This was the time when she would read the paper out loud to Simeon, feet in his lap as he eased her arches with his thumbs.

In nightgown and wrapper, she sat in an armchair; paused for a moment before opening the newspaper's virgin pages, smelling of ink. Mr. Dougan always spoke to her before shutting up the house. "Storm coming," he'd said, tonight. "There's a smell of the beautiful on the air." When Simeon was on furlough, he spent his days at his father's store, and in the evening she shared the day's stories. *Your cousin Carrie came. Mr. Dougan called snow "the beautiful" again. Flora served tea for the first time*. She gazed at Simeon's untouched pillowcase and felt herself changing. Her lips, held more tightly. A sadness within her as the stories she wished to tell him bloomed, faded, dissipated.

She looked down at the news.

IS SLAVERY ABOLISHED?
By George Francis Train

A veritable slave scene was enacted on Saturday last in the civilized village of Pleasant Valley by the annual sale of Paupers. Although no slave driver was present with his long whip to drive the poor creatures to the block, the sale recalled in all its degrading colours the scenes that were enacted in the long ago Slave sales in the Southern States . . .

She felt her heart speed as she read, as if the article had been written specifically to her.

. . . inhuman . . . just as unchristian as when the poor black man . . . nefarious business . . . degrading not only to the paupers themselves but to all those who take part herein . . .

Excuse me, Carrie, she'd said. *I would like you to meet Flora Salford.*
She felt her face grow hot. She dropped the paper and walked to the window. She closed her eyes, pressed her forehead against the cold glass, listening for the approaching storm.

—

Ellen, in her bedroom, also read George Francis Train's diatribe on the pauper auction, finger running beneath the words. It did not occur to her that Mrs. Galloway had done anything wrong by purchasing Flora and saving her from the men gathered to bid for her.

Then she read the next installment of the axe murder trial.

The first witness, Mr. John Tatum, is a bachelor. Elsa Cavanaugh has resided with him after her husband's death for about four years. The witness slept on a bed in the kitchen and she slept in the bedroom. On the day of the murder, Mr. Tatum left the house at about seven o'clock. Elsa Cavanaugh was still in bed at the time he left although she was awake. He spoke to her and asked her to be certain to lock the door after he had left. She said yes. He took his dinner and went to his job, taking a new axe and leaving the old one leaning against the stove. He was chopping cordwood for Mr. Cardwell . . .

She snipped the article from the newspaper with quilting scissors, thinking what she would say to Mr. Dougan.

"The old axe," she would point out, shrewd. "He said himself 'twas too soft and the edge turned over. He testified that he bought that new axe the very day before the murder. Now do you think . . ."

They would discuss the details all week, until the next installation came in *The Weekly Record*.

—

Shaking out a cloth on the side porch, Flora squinted in the morning sun, glittering in last night's snow. She could see farm wagons on Creek Road—horses, with icy fetlocks, stepping high; farm couples and half-frozen children looking eagerly at the big houses, reminding her of herself when she lived on Henry and Ada's farm and was familiar with manure, teats and the butter churn. Here, her maid's uniform was made of finer linen and edged with more piping than what she had then worn to church.

She went back inside and down the hall, where she opened the door of the broom closet.

This brush is for cobwebs, Mary had taught her, that first week. *Mind you don't use it for anything else. And this is for the outside of windows. This here's a coat broom. This one's the whitewash brush.* Her finger, moving, ticking each one like a checklist. *Stove brush, shoe brush, common broom, dust brush.*

So much to learn. How to make peaks in egg whites for a dish called *meringue*. How to turn a mattress and put the marked part of the sheet at the top. How to polish silver. How to iron collars without leaving a scorch mark. How to brush a hat. How to walk. *Don't be a lummox. Step softly, like a cat. You come and you do your business and you go.*

"Flora?" Josephine called.

Flora thought of this now, walking quietly by stilling herself from the inside. In the parlour, Josephine was sitting at her writing desk. She put down her pen when Flora entered. Sunlight hazed her loosely pinned bun, its wisps. She wore a scarf wrapped round her neck—blue cotton, with white dots. She smiled, although her eyes held worry.

"Ellen has spoken to me about a little problem."

Flora looked at the carpet.

"It's nothing much, Flora. You have been learning very fast. I have nothing to complain about. It's only the grate."

The grate. Flora frowned, looked up, surprised.

"The kitchen grate," Josephine explained. She capped the pen and leaned forward, tapping it against her mouth. "When you scrape it out, you leave ashes all over the floor. She has told you twice."

Ada's country kitchen. The stove wood was kept in a box, pushed up against the wall. Ada did not mind a drift of ashes. It was the maple-wood table she insisted upon being scrubbed to whiteness.

"I forget," Flora said. "I got so much to do in the mornings. I will remember." She tightened her hands on the whisk broom behind her back. Her heart speeded, she bit her lips. "I'm sorry."

Josephine turned to her desk, pressed blotting paper against the letter she had been writing.

"I always tell my girls," she said. "Both my own daughters, I mean. And you, too, Flora. You and Mary and Margaret. I tell them that they . . . you . . . can always talk to me. If you have any questions. Something you don't understand. Or . . . or problems of your own. I like to have a happy home. My husband and I. We like to have a happy home."

The clock on the mantelpiece ticked more slowly than Flora's heart. She thought of the question. She had held it so carefully, like the egg basket when she walked across ice.

Unasked, she could still hope. She had pondered this. If the answer was no, would she leave this house? Would she somehow find her way back to England?

"I do have a question."

"Yes?"

The oak-cased telephone rang and they both jumped, but it was three rings, not one.

"I never asked," Flora said. She tightened her hands on the whisk broom. "Whether I am to be paid."

Josephine smiled, this time without worry.

"Of course you'll be paid, Flora. I pay the others every two weeks. You'll be paid along with everyone else."

Flora could not bring herself to say that she did not have a single penny saved. In Ada's kitchen she'd been led to think she was a member of the family. *You can go to school if your work's done.* Eating at the table with them. Hearing the rumble of Henry's stomach, seeing Ada's hand over her mouth to cover a belch. She got the same serving of food as Ada; slept in the same cold house; shared the same kerosene-lit parlour on winter's evenings.

"I have a sister." She drew a breath that strained the buttons between her shoulder blades. "Her name is Enid. They told me she would be sent over to be with me. They told me I could save up my money and better myself. For when she came. I wouldn't have left if I'd have known it wasn't true."

She had been waking at night from a recurrent dream. The matron, looming with a giant blacksmith's nipper—*Have you no appreciation!*—Enid's fingers, clasping Flora's arms. The nipper, *snap snap.* Screams.

"I want to save my wages."

Josephine's eyebrows shot upwards, her mouth fell open for a moment. She pushed back her chair. "You have a . . . Flora?"

"And I want to find her. There was a lady came to the workhouse. She's the one who told me about bettering myself. She's the one who brought me over. I gave a paper to the Quigleys but I never seen it again. Think they must have lost it. So I can't remember her name or where she is. I thought the Overseer would help me."

"You have a *sister?*" Maud had stayed home from school with a sore throat. She stood in the doorway holding a cup of tea, wearing housecoat and slippers. Her hair was pillow-flattened, her eyes earnest—shocked, she looked at Flora as if seeing her for the first time. "A *lost sister?* Where do you think she is?"

Flora spoke to the carpet. "I don't know. Think she's still in England."

"They made you come away without her? How *could* they?" Maud said, stepping into the room. "Mother, isn't it terrible?"

Flora glanced up at Maud.

Who am I? Who does she see?

"I will ask Mr. Fairweather. The Overseer of the Poor," Josephine said. Her words chased one another, a cascade of promise. Her eyes, as earnest as Maud's. As shocked. Her hands, clasped tightly and pressed against her breast. "I will ask him to help us. We will try to find your sister, Flora."

—

"She was violated," Ellen said, after the staff had finished their noon meal. She sipped her tea, pointed at the newspaper. "She was a woman of *fifty years of age.* In poor health. And she was violated. Can you imagine, now? Bruises on the insides of her legs. Teeth marks."

The Weekly Record was lying on the kitchen table. Its headline was larger than usual. *Is Slavery Abolished?*

Flora picked it up. She read the article, running her finger under the words.

"Can you read, then, Flora?"

Flora stopped. She was silent for a moment, stung.

"I can. Even though I'm only a pauper."

"Flora. You're not a pauper."

They didn't know, though, Flora thought. She set down the paper as if it were one of Josephine's freshly ironed blouses. No tears, never tears, only hurt that occasionally shook her like a fever, so much of it that she realized how long she had been patient. Trusting. Waiting.

They could scoff at her feelings and hand her a cup of tea and a bowl of raisin pudding. They could teach her to knit, tat, play cards. They could show her how to skate, holding the back of a chair. They had never stood before a crowd of men and known that those men had the power to buy her because of how her body might serve their lust.

"You'll be getting paid like any housemaid," Ellen added. She was watching Flora closely, running a finger around the rim of her teacup. Margaret's back was turned as she washed dishes in the sink. Mary, on her hands and knees, rummaged deep in a cupboard. "Mrs. Galloway told me she spoke to you about the ashes. I'm sorry, Flora, I did tell you twice. I lost me temper, I shouldn't have said anything."

"It's all right. She was . . ."

"She's a fair person, she is. Like her husband. They're good people. We're lucky to be here."

Her gentled tone brought an unaccustomed prickle to the back of Flora's nose, a rush of tears.

No tears. Never tears.

"I told her something," she said.

Mary sat back on her heels. Margaret turned from the sink. Water plinked into the dishpan.

"I have a sister. I have a little sister. Three years younger than me. Her name is . . . her name is Enid. We was orphaned and put in the workhouse. So I guess we were paupers, in England, anyway. A lady told me if I came to Canada I could save my money and bring Enid over, and she made me feel like I had to do it if I loved my . . . if I . . . so I left her behind, I told her she would be coming over soon as could be. And not a word since. Years ago, it was. I asked Mrs. . . . . I wanted to know if I would be paid, like."

Margaret put both hands over her mouth.

"Did she get brought over too?" Mary asked.

Flora shrugged.

"Sent, more like," Ellen muttered. "The likes of that *lady* wouldn't of held you by the hand, would she now."

One tear slid down Flora's cheek as her secret was told, and taken from her, like handing over a baby, watching as it was cradled, passed from person to person, revered.

—

George Francis Train's vitriolic comments dominated *The Record* for the next three weeks.

> She's a pauper. There's a bid! That face he turns to us is stamped as only Satan stamps the faces of men. If he were dumb, and we heard not his rude and filthy jesting, the sensuality of his heart would be revealed in his face. But he is the lowest bidder and the woman pauper is handed over . . .

The diatribes found their way into the international papers. For the first time, the rector of Josephine and Harland's church preached a sermon attacking the pauper auction and advocating the building of an almshouse. The St. John paper printed its own headline: *Terrible Dominion Slavery*. George Train reprinted articles from England and the United States expressing shock and outrage, and condemning the country that could allow such *outrage to human dignity*. Letters to the editor reflected the town's seething divisions: fury at Train—*A shame that the fair name of one the most beautiful spots in Canada . . .*—or appreciation—*May heaven send us more such cranks . . .*

Josephine, learning that Flora was fully literate, knowing that she was reading the paper, sent Margaret to ask Flora into the parlour. She sat at her desk, exasperatedly jiggling the handle of a jammed drawer. She explained to Flora that both she and her friend Mr. Fairweather were joining the voices calling for an almshouse.

"He would rather not be the Overseer of the Poor. It is an appointed position. He and I and my husband went to school together."

Flora stood stiffly, stroking the turkey feathers of her duster. She wondered if Mary, Margaret, Ellen or Mr. Dougan were ever invited into the parlour to talk to their mistress about anything other than the day's orders.

"He and I do not believe in the pauper auction, you see."

Flora didn't know what to say, or what was being asked of her. She wondered if Mrs. Galloway wished her new servant were in an alms-house.

"I am very happy to have you here, Flora. I want you to know that I am *very* sorry about the way I had to . . . acquire you. I know you are not a pauper, not really."

Josephine leaned forward on her chair, almost, it seemed, asking forgiveness. Flora did not know how to respond, how to feel.

In her bedroom, she looked into a mirror on her dresser. She could not remember what she had looked like as a child. There were no mirrors in the workhouse. She and Enid saw only vague reflections in the long windows, before the lights were extinguished. She did not understand why men looked at her and then looked again as if they did not believe what they had seen. She did not care about beauty nor know if it was what she possessed.

—

Josephine answered the phone. She heard the operator's baby making happy sounds.

"Good morning, Mrs. Galloway. How's Maud?"

"Good morning, Mrs. Martin. She's fine, back in school."

Carrie's voice came on the line.

"Good morning, Josephine. I'm not coming today. Did you hear? The show has been cancelled. The pauper's owner will not let Mr. Train exhibit him. Moreover, Mr. Spooner has let him go."

"Let who go?"

"Mr. Train. He's to pack his bags and leave town. My mother phoned to tell me the news. She heard it from her brother."

Josephine pictured George Francis Train holding a leather suitcase in one purple-gloved hand. He would not mind, she thought. He would return to the greater world and continue ferreting out injustice. She would follow his career in the newspaper. She felt an emptiness within herself, however, as if his energy had ignited a spark that would die, unused. She had planned to invite him to dinner. She wanted to ask him about his wife and his children and why he had written that his favourite thing was to sit on park benches feeding squirrels and listening to *the sagacity of children*. She had planned to tell him that she, herself, had once felt the urge to help those in need. How, as a schoolgirl, she had been known as a person with the ability to protect, heal, tame, love. How she had not known in what capacity she might use this skill, and, in any case, realized that there was probably none for a woman outside of mothering, and yet because of her desire could understand his own fierce outrage. She had thought that he would press his lips to her hand, and that she would feel the brush of his pomaded moustache.

"We held our first meeting," Carrie rushed on. "Twelve of us. We read papers written by the English and the American suffragists. We planned to join the national organization. We felt that what we want to do *will occur*. It will! We all felt it."

Phone conversations were unadorned. Clicks indicated the presence of listeners.

"Just as well not to travel, Carrie," Josephine said. "A storm is coming." She set the receiver back in its cradle.

The house was quiet. The girls, at school. George, away at university. Smell of roast chicken and rhubarb sauce. Thud of feet overhead —voices.

She had a meeting of the beautification committee this afternoon to discuss the year ahead. The planting of trees. Street cleaning. A town picnic.

Feathers ruffled by Mr. Train, Pleasant Valley would resume.

FOUR

Ocracoke Island

~

THE LETTERS LAY ON the hall floor. Josephine gathered them and went into the parlour, her mind on the bulging plaster in the upstairs hallway which she must discuss with Mr. Dougan.

She sat at her desk, shuffling the letters. She separated out one with unfamiliar handwriting. She picked up her reading glasses, worked them onto her nose and peered at the frank. Her heart stuttered.

Ocracoke, North Carolina.

The envelope was brown, its edges soft and blunted.

Mrs. Simeon Galloway, Creek Road, Pleasant Valley, New Brunswick, Canada.

She lifted a brass paperknife and sliced open the envelope. Her hands trembled—withdrawing the paper. Unfolding it. Smoothing it.

Elbows on blotting paper.

Fingers to temples.

> *January 15, 1888*
> *Dear Mrs. Galloway,*
>
> *I write to you from Ocracoke Island, where I am the lighthouse keeper. It is my sad duty to inform you that the ship "Marianne"*

went down off our island in a gale. Many were saved but unfortunately your brave husband was not among them. At the time of
writing, his body is washed and decently clothed in our parlor. By
the time you have received this letter, he will be carefully interred in
our own family cemetery rather than in the dunes, as is customary
with the many unfortunates who have washed up upon our beaches.
We await your instructions as to marker, hoping for a visit from
you and your family. My wife and I extend the greatest sympathy,
and invite you to stay in our home for the duration of your visit,
but should you wish privacy, there is a fine hotel.

As for the particulars, it was seen from shore that the ship made her
way northwards in a tremendous gale. It was feared that Ocracoke
Light was mistaken for Hatteras Light, in which case such a course
would have been correct, but unfortunately this drove the ship
directly onto the shoals where she was instantly rolled onto her beam
ends. People gathered on shore as enormous breakers crashed upon
the vessel. It had commenced to snow and hail. No lifeboats could
set out, such was the extent of the surf. In the mist and spray, we
made out several men clinging to shrouds on the bow, and could see
that they flung an item overboard. Through the telescope we made it
out to be a dog, which after a gallant and desperate swim, came upon
the shore with a line attached to its collar. By means of this rope,
we were able to rescue all the women aboard the ship and some of
the men. Most of the men who assisted in the rescue perished in the
attempt. Among them was your husband. From his belongings, and
once the vessel's name was discovered, we ascertained his identity.

My wife has cleaned and set aside all the property he carried on
his person to return to you. We were told by the women who were
aboard the ship that the dog, Sailor, was the beloved companion of
your husband and so we will guard this precious animal and return
him to you, as well.

*It is one of the worst of my duties to send letters such as these,
and I come to a quick finish in order to place it on the ferry as soon
as possible.*

I remain your servant . . .

She was standing, now, the letter clutched to her breast.

Her own voice, swollen.

"Ellen!"

She bent forward, collapsed back on the chair. Her voice came, weaker.

"Ellen! Ellen!"

*Dog. Gallant and desperate. Body is washed. Cemetery. Enormous breakers
crashed. Beam ends. The worst of my . . .*

Ellen, Margaret, Mary, Flora—rushing from the kitchen, trampling
down the stairs. Arms around her waist, breast-tightened cloth, voices,
urgent and meaningless as her knees gave way. Falling. Vomit. Cheek
pressed to the carpet. Mr. Dougan, smell of tobacco, her head rolling to
his tweed vest. "Let her down gently, now. Gently." A pillow beneath
her head. "Holy Mary, Mother of . . ." Struggling to rise. "No! No!
No!" Her own voice again and then blackness sweeping up, pressing
down, within it a glowing core, a single point of light. Ocracoke Light,
not Hatteras. Not Hatteras. Not Hatteras.

—

Mr. Dougan went to the school with the horse and sleigh to collect Lucy
and Maud. He warned them of very bad news, and they went upstairs
into their mother's bedroom and learned that their father was dead.

George was summoned from Sackville via telegram.

Simeon's parents and Josephine's parents came.

Ellen bade the housemaids to strive to their utmost. Roast chicken,
biscuits, apple pie. Flora flew back and forth from kitchen to dining
room, setting out cups and saucers, plates, silverware.

After nightfall, a firm knock sounded on the door.

"Let me see it."

Nathaniel held out his hand. One eye was narrower than the other, as if from years of squinting, with a thickened, drooping lid; his "kind" eye, Azuba called it. The other—held wider, as if in compensation, its expression grim, brooking no nonsense—he levelled at merchants or at workers sent into his orchards. Josephine saw this eye harden, now. She gave him two letters, the most recent one from Simeon, sent from New York, and the lighthouse keeper's.

She watched as he read Simeon's. She saw the moment when he encountered Simeon's words—*I struggle to complete my crew. It is getting harder to find seasoned seamen than in Uncle N's day. The first mate is experienced but in poor health. The second mate is only nineteen, although willing and honest. I have not yet found a man as capable of navigation as I am myself.*

Nathaniel gripped his mouth. His chest expanded with a long breath.

George, seated beside him, looked up, and Josephine noted his resemblance to Simeon as well as the difference. His face was the unmarked template of his father's—square forehead, thin nose—but its expression was habitually worried rather than keen; whereas Simeon had been lanky, athletic, George was stocky. He sat on the edge of his chair gripping his hands, his jaw thrust forward to keep tears from falling. Upon arrival, he had suffered their embraces, unable to speak or look into anyone's eyes. Later, he'd stared at the floor, pressed his face to windows. Had chosen a seat next to his great-uncle. White-faced, he did not look across at his mother or his sisters.

Josephine sat in the middle of the chesterfield sofa. Maud, curled on her side, buried her face in her mother's lap. Lucy sat on the other side, as silent as Josephine, who had become stunned, numb, her eyes turning from George to people picking at the plates of food on their laps, to Mr. Dougan kneeling before the Franklin stove with tears on his cheeks, to Flora setting down a bowl of biscuits—feeling as if she were a stranger, watching people she did not know, wondering at their grief.

Nathaniel opened the travel-worn envelope from Ocracoke Island and withdrew its letter. His eyes flickered down the page. He had followed Simeon's progress as cabin boy, second mate, first mate, captain—avidly, as if encouraging a second son. Nathaniel and Azuba's own son, Bennett—born in Antwerp after a nearly disastrous voyage—had declined a life at sea for a career in law.

He laid down the letter and stared at the pulse of flame behind the stove's window.

"He would not have mistaken Ocracoke Light for Hatteras Light," Nathaniel said. "I daresay he . . ."

Azuba leaned forward, abruptly; caught Nathaniel's eye. Her face, like his, was weathered, darkened both from the sun's brilliance as it beat down upon their clifftop house and the refracted glare of the seas upon which, once, they had travelled together.

He checked himself.

"He was at sea far longer than he had expected to be, Josephine. There is no doubt that he ran into storm after storm. In that latitude, winds would have forced him into the Gulf Stream, which runs northeastwards, contrary to his direction. He may have taken sick. Or one of the women might have needed him and his medicine box. No doctor on board, of course. Just for one fatal watch, he might have had no choice but to allow someone else to navigate."

He came across to the sofa and went down on one knee. He laid a hand on Maud's head, the other on Josephine's hand.

"The seas off the Outer Banks are shoal-ridden, Josephine. And the winter storms are worse than anything you could possibly imagine."

His hand tightened on hers. She looked into his eyes, so close to her own.

"Think of it like this, my dear. I am certain that he had no choice in the matter. He would have died doing his utmost to save his ship and all the lives on board."

With a straitened crew, no choice but to catch some sleep . . . Was what Nathaniel had been about to say, Josephine thought, detecting a beat of censure. Was he thrown from his bed tangled in blankets as the ship slewed violently into sand? Was his first thought fury at himself?

She pictured Simeon lifting Sailor to his chest, standing at the rail. His last words, perhaps.

Go. Good dog.

—

The mare stood with head low, rain making rivulets in her thick coat, percussive against the carriage's leather roof. Mr. Dougan stowed satchels and hat boxes. Three days had passed since the arrival of the letter. Simeon's distraught parents planned to meet her at the station. Together, they would travel by train to North Carolina, where they would fetch Sailor, collect Simeon's possessions, visit the cemetery and give instructions as to the gravestone.

Josephine, tearfully, bid Lucy, Maud and George goodbye.

She watched the house diminish behind her. The mare high-stepped down the lane, broke into a trot on the street.

Earlier, she had gone into the kitchen to speak to her servants. She did not know how long they would be living under her roof, but this, along with many other issues, she could not consider in full. Grief balanced bewilderment at the incomprehensible fact that she could never chastise Simeon for his foolhardy decision. *You could have told that woman you had no crew, she could have found another ship.* And other things, things that she would not have said, even if given the chance. How Simeon's erect, carefree bearing, the smile lines beside his mouth and his teasing eyes would have overridden any misgivings the woman may have had; how she would have ignored her own instincts, trusting the captain.

Just as Josephine had—in all things.

—

The maids and Ellen ransacked the house, looking for a will.

"She remembered him saying something," Mary said, now, in the attic. "*Under* something."

Ellen was on her knees turning over the contents of a trunk.

"Why he'd put it in here, now? In with this lot of stuff."

She pressed her temples with the heels of her hands.

"Floorboard, more likely," Mary said. "My father had a floorboard where he kept his whiskey. Me mam never knew but I did."

"Think how many boards there are in this house," Margaret murmured.

Flora, tugging out drawers of a dusty bureau, could not speak. All the weeping had unlocked her own grief, returned her to the rain of England, pattering on the thatch, trickling down the windowpane, on the day when Ma's screams stopped and the midwife came out of the little bedroom and told Flora and Enid that they had a baby brother, but he was dead and so was Ma. Father and mother, stronger than walls and roof, shielding Flora and Enid—guardians of hope and of life's goodness. Both gone, for Papa had died in an accident at the farm the previous month. She and Enid held each other, too shocked to weep. Women came to the cottage. Through the bedroom door, the sisters glimpsed the women at work: rags dipped in a basin of soapy water, Ma's arm being lifted, her hair being brushed. Moans and whispers. Men, arriving, with two boxes, one long, one tiny. At the funeral service, they could hear rocks rolling in the river, a hollow sound like the clopping of hooves.

Hapless, the rocks. Worn smooth as eggs. You could see them when the river was reduced to a stream in August.

If Enid were here, Flora thought, rummaging in a trunk, I could ask her. Did she remember Papa's funeral and then Ma's? At least Maud and Lucy and Josephine had one another, and George, and grandparents and aunts and uncles, and all the people of the town. *But I want the funeral here,* Josephine had cried, before leaving for Ocracoke. *I want the cornet band. I want the procession. I want Simeon buried in our own churchyard.* Face, swollen, her cheeks chapped from tears. Her eyes, bloodshot. Staring and not seeing. Handkerchief, twisted in her hands.

Eat, now, Ellen had coaxed, the morning after the letter's arrival, setting oatmeal and applesauce on Josephine's lap as she huddled in bed—*eat for your strength, now*; and Flora sensed the cook's tenderness and wondered why she was unmarried and mentioned no children. For days, Ellen insisted on carrying meals to Josephine's bedroom. Holding the door as the cook staggered beneath a laden tray, Flora had glimpsed Josephine sitting in bed with letters clasped to her breast, like trying to hold an armload of autumn leaves. Her hair down, her dressing gown fallen open.

—

On Ocracoke Island, the lighthouse keeper's wife stood in her garden, bonneted and skirt-blown, deadheading roses. Chickens blustered at her feet. Her eyes were deep-set, sad; a thin-lipped mouth warped downwards. Simeon's father bent, gravely, and shook the woman's hand.

"Please give our thanks to your good husband and his crew for saving so many of my son's sailors and passengers."

The woman clutched a handful of crinkled dead roses. "Your son's body was respected and washed. We saved all we could find for the widow."

Josephine could not speak. She stared up at the white-shingled tower with its light that had not saved her husband's life.

"You'll be wanting to have the dog. Sweet thing, it is . . ."

She broke off, looking at Josephine, and released rose petals into the wind.

They followed the woman across the scoured grass. Refusing tea, they waited by the door. She returned with a small wooden box. Sailor pressed past her; seeing Josephine, he began to bark. He ran to her, and she fell to her knees and tried to hold him in her arms but could not. The dog was in a frenzy, whimpering, wagging his tail, licking every piece of exposed flesh he could find.

They walked back along the dirt street, having elected to stay at the inn. The dog trotted, anxious, at their heels. Simeon's father carried the box. He and Josephine went up to her room; he set the box on a table by her bed. She did not touch it, waiting until he left. He stopped in the hall to ease the door shut, making only the smallest click.

She listened to wind in the evergreen oaks, constant as the distant, murderous roar of surf. She heard Sailor, below her window, barking as Simeon's mother threw a stick for him. Slowly, Josephine lifted the lid of the box. Inside, she found five items: a folding knife with an ivory handle, a pocket watch, the garnet ring she had given Simeon, which he wore on a chain around his neck, a lock of her hair wrapped in a square of ironed cloth, and a mass of swollen paper, dried, bearing the faint traces of her own handwriting. She hung the ring around her neck, tucking it out of sight beneath the crepe mourning dress.

Later, they walked to the beach where his body had been found. From behind her black veil, she watched the waves, building and surging and breaking towards her, like breath that could not be stilled.

—

The dog searched for Simeon in the Creek Road house. He raced up the stairs, panting. He sniffed under Simeon's chair, the bedposts, the crack of Simeon's closet door. He came back downstairs and begged to go out. Josephine stood on the back step, weeping. The dog ran to the barn and pawed at the door.

A funeral was held.

The cornet band came to the house.

The family followed it down the hill to the church.

—

On a warm Tuesday in the second week of April, Josephine sat in the office of her lawyer, Mr. Eveleigh.

"We could not find a will," she said.

His skin was as if pumiced; dark eyebrows accentuated a humorous expression. He wore a high, stiff collar and a pocket handkerchief with blood-red edging.

"Did you ever hear him say he had written a will?"

"I think so. But I can't be sure. He was most business-like about his voyages. When he was home, he was so . . . Well, he was happy to be home with me and the children. He did not want to attend to business, just for awhile."

She paused.

People passed the window, heading for the grand opening of the new tin store.

"My maids told me that they opened every drawer, every box, they searched to the back of every cupboard. I sent Mr. Dougan to tap with his hammer for hollow places. We looked in the carriage shed. We found one loose floorboard. Nothing. I fear it slipped his mind, although I know what his intentions were."

"What do you mean, his intentions?"

"That he intended to write a will. And I am certain that he intended for me to be comfortable should anything befall him."

Mr. Eveleigh pressed the side of his hand against his upper lip. He remained in thought, finger passing up and down over the corner of his mouth.

"Mrs. Galloway. I'm afraid I must tell you the law, and it will not be happy news for you. I can give it to you straight away, in point-by-point fashion. Are you agreeable? Or would you rather I told your father? That would probably be best."

He smiled to himself, turning over papers on his desk.

"Then he could guide you through the particulars. I always feel that Mrs. Eveleigh needs a soft chair and a cup of tea by her side when I present her with difficulties."

She thought of how men exchanged looks, in the presence of women, as if some things should not be inflicted upon them. Her father, leading her down the aisle, handing her to her husband. Giving her away. She felt space, now, making silence around her.

Where is your husband?

Single. Just one. Alone.

"Tell me," she said. She straightened her back and stared at the rosy-faced man with his manicured fingernails. At first, force of thought had carried her through one day and then another. Thought rode atop feeling and was still floating, fragile. *Do what they tell you. Try not to cry. Do not eat in bed, get up, get dressed.* So she did, trying to resume. She asked Ellen not to bring food to her bedroom. She made sure to let no tear fall unless she was alone. She began making a scrapbook with Lucy and Maud, gathering every single thing they could find about Simeon: a poem little Maudie had written for him when she was four years old; from his handkerchief drawer, an outsized acorn found on a walk with Lucy.

"Tell me now," she repeated, forcefully, and he looked at her, surprised.

"Very well, Mrs. Galloway. I'm sorry to have to . . ."

He located the papers; worked pince-nez onto his nose. "This is the Intestate Estates Act chapter. I will read: *His real estate . . .*" He broke off. "Meaning land and things fixed to land. Such as a house . . . *shall be divided equally to and amongst his children. If there are no children, then to his next of kin.*"

He looked over his glasses. "A widow is not kin."

A widow is not kin.

"Excuse me? I don't . . ."

"A widow is not kin," he repeated, pausing between each word.

Her hand flew to her breast. She pressed hard, fingers spread.

"However, the Dower Act ensures that you have one-third life interest in the real property. It is a *life* interest, which means you own one-third of the real property as long as you live. In theory you could identify your third and rent it out, but it would be rather . . . awkward. You see, who would buy your house, for example, knowing that you still owned one-third? You could always sign away your dower rights, of course. For a price. Now, as for *personal* property. You knew, of course, when you married, that all personal property you brought to the marriage vested absolutely in your husband."

"Yes."

"So now we are discussing everything that you may feel you and your husband owned. After estate expenses, one-third of this goes to the widow and the residue *in equal portions to his children* . . ."

He paused.

"You do not own the house and property outright, in short. Nor are you the legal guardian of your minor children. Since they are the owners of the house and land, as well as of two-thirds of all personal property, this is what you must do: you must apply to the Supreme Court in Equity to be declared their legal guardian—"

"I am not their legal guardian?"

He shook his head, no. "So that you can deal with their portion of the real property until they decide what is to be done with it. They cannot sell the house, in short, until they are all over twenty-one years of age, and they all agree to sell, and you agree to sign away your dower interest."

Josephine reflected that Mr. Eveleigh would go home to his house after his day's work and remove the collar, which was surely uncomfortable. He would unbutton and remove the starched shirt. Perhaps he would shrug into a looser shirt and a smoking jacket. He would light a pipe and wonder what kind of trees to plant in his yard, elms or lindens.

"Moreover, it will be incumbent upon you to keep very good accounts, as all portions of the estate belonging to the children must be used *only for their benefit*."

A young woman, passing the window. Looking not at them but her own reflection. A new bonnet trimmed with feathers and silk flowers.

Watching the girl's self-satisfaction, Josephine pressed at her cheekbones with her fingertips, forcing her eyes half-shut.

A wife is not kin.

A mother is not her children's legal guardian.

"Simeon would be horrified," she said. Her voice broke. "He would be furious."

"Yes," Mr. Eveleigh agreed. "The law can be cruel. It does not bend."

She stared through the dusty window. Spring sunshine, warm on those heading for Howe's Tinware. Faces, smiling, anticipatory; people thinking of a new teapot or jelly cake pan. She sensed the change in her body—skin, bone and blood adjusting to the meaning of this news.

"You can look again," he suggested. She felt it as mockery—an insult to Simeon, and to the hard work of her maids.

Not my house.

Not my children.

"Make me an appointment, then," she said. Her words were not as commanding as they would have been several weeks ago, when she was still Simeon's wife. She felt a shiver of uncertainty.

His eyebrows raised. "With?"

"The Supreme Court in Equity. I will be their legal guardian, at the very least."

"Very well," he said, pulling papers towards him, reaching for his pen. "And we will see how much money you have when all is done. In the meantime, you may continue to draw on the funds as you have been. But I would advise beginning to . . . modify . . ."

FIVE

Mirror

JOSEPHINE JOINED HER PARENTS for midday dinner and told them what Mr. Eveleigh had said.

"Oh, Josephine," her mother said. Emmeline had short eyebrows, like a terrier, and a patient, worried face. She glanced at her husband, who set knife and fork to pot roast, repressingly, not looking at Josephine. "I'm sorry. I *am* sorry. You are sorry, too, aren't you, dear?"

Josephine watched her father, Gordon, his fork scraping the plate as it pierced a cut of beef.

"The law is the law," he said.

"It's a terrible law!" Emmeline protested. "If women had the right to vote, there would never be a law saying that wives are not kin. That women do not have custody of their own children. That women are men's property."

He paused, knife raised, shocked. He pointed the knife first at his wife and then at Josephine. "And you never will have the right to vote, my dears, because women are not capable of logical thinking. There's a very good reason for that legislation."

He sliced his meat, and chewed another mouthful. He sighed, patting his lips with his napkin.

"Eat, Josephine," Emmeline murmured.

"We looked," Josephine said to her father, leaning forward with her hands flat on the linen tablecloth. "We tore the house to pieces. It must have been thrown away by mistake."

Choleric in any event, spots of red bloomed on his cheeks. "Simeon should have taken more care with the disposition of his will. He should have informed you of its whereabouts. It should have been in a strong box."

"I—" She looked up at him. Formidable grey-streaked eyebrows bristled over blue eyes, whose expression softened. He was angry *for* her, frustrated by the law. She saw that he was torn between caring and propriety, and was forcibly reminded of the number of people in this town he employed.

"I'm sorry, my dear." He folded his napkin slowly and laid it beside his plate. He brushed the starched linen with his fingertips, not looking at her. "I am very sorry."

She picked up her fork, stared at her uneaten dinner. She felt their guarded sympathy as a renunciation of Simeon, the young man who had refused a job in the boot and shoe factory.

"I will pay for the rest of George's education," he said. He drank deeply from his water goblet. "I will offer him a position in the factory as soon as he has graduated."

No mention of the girls, Josephine thought. She felt both anger and the inability to express it. Embarrassment, shame. Her father had offered her a gift without asking her if she would accept it.

Her mother murmured into the maid's ear. A dog barked in the yard.

—

On the day that Josephine met with her lawyer, the household was in a state of limbo. Normally, Mary told Flora, on such a warm day they would begin preparing for summer. Winter curtains would come down and be washed and folded and put away. Summer curtains would be hung. Carpets would be cleaned.

"Every carpet. Usually we take them outside about now and whack the bejesus out of them."

She and Flora were sitting on the lower step of the attic stairs. They had put everything to rights, keeping an eye out the whole time for the missing will.

"Do you ever think of going home to Ireland?" Flora said.

Mary tugged at a string in her apron, broke it. She wrapped it around her little finger until the skin turned white. "No home for me back there. Don't know what became of my father, and me mam's dead. Brothers are . . ." A wounded expression, and Flora wished she had not asked.

They did not hear the front door opening, only the slam of its shutting.

A crash. Tinkle of glass. Sailor.

The girls ran down the hall, down the stairs. The dog stood in the door to the hallway, barking.

Josephine was walking in circles, grinding the shards of a small smashed mirror into powder. Her hat lay halfway into the parlour, on the Persian rug. Its feather still quivered.

She looked at the girls: furious, blind. She turned to the large hall mirror and began to lift it. Mary ran forward. Josephine threw down her hands. She went into the parlour and stood staring down its length towards the sun-filled turret room.

—

"They're calling more witnesses," Ellen said to Mr. Dougan. She was following the axe murder trial as if it were the one sure thing in her life. She was certain that the bachelor had done the deed. Single, sex-crazed. Why else would he have invited the victim to share his tiny house?

Mary and Margaret, eating rice pudding, were subdued. Their mistress was in the process of "asking around"; she assured them she would keep them until such time as good employment could be found. Mr. Dougan sat in the kitchen more often, since Josephine gave him no instructions about the gardens, the paths, the shrubs. She did not order him to purchase pullets to replace the old hens. She hinted that the mare might have to be sold.

He refused pudding, but accepted a third cup of tea.

Ellen filled his cup and then sat in her rocking chair by the window. She resumed her perusal of *The Weekly Record*.

"Mr. Tatum, the bachelor, says he ran to a neighbour. Now. This is what the neighbour has to say."

She adjusted her reading glasses.

> *We went into the house—and got there about twenty minutes past six. It was dark and we lighted the lamp and looked at the body. We did not examine it. She was lying on her back. Her clothes were turned up leaving her person exposed. The cat was in the room and eating at her head. I saw quite a stream of blood flowing down near her left side . . .*

She skimmed ahead, reading silently.

"Oh, Lord. Now here he talks about the murder weapon."

> *We took up the axe and examined it. The axe had been used. It had blood on it about one quarter way up the handle. There was quite a lot of blood on the axe itself. The blood was quite fresh. Cannot say if it was damp, but it was high-coloured and fresh . . .*

"Why would he have left the axe?" Mr. Dougan began, his voice comfortable with the beginnings of the evening's speculation. What *he* would have done, he would begin; and Ellen, then, would tell how *she* would have committed such an atrocity. They both seemed intent on proving their cunning, their devious natures, their contempt for the clumsiness of the murderer.

It was not real to them, Flora thought, only a story. It made her think of the time, crossing the Atlantic, when a storm had made the children cry out for parents who would never know of their terror. It made her wonder where Enid was, whether anyone was watching out for her safety, teaching her to avoid men, lock her door, walk with her face to the ground.

It was raining and the lily of the valley was in bloom. The cloying sweetness came in on the moist air. Maud appeared hesitantly in the doorway and asked if she might have a slice of bread and butter. She had not been hungry at suppertime.

"I'm sorry, Ellen," she mumbled, glancing at Flora. Maud and Flora were the same age. "It was a lovely meal."

Maud was fascinated with Flora but did not dare initiate conversation, nor ask questions, only listened, watched, was quick to respond if Flora spoke first. Where Lucy was built like Josephine, tall and slender, Maud was stocky, with reddish-brown hair and pale skin. She had been her father's pet, Flora guessed, since her eyes filled with tears at the slightest reference to him.

Ellen buttered slices of oatmeal bread and arranged them on a plate.

"Here you are, Miss Maud, come back if you want more."

After Maud left, Flora sat with ankles crossed and hands folded in her lap.

"What is it, Flora?"

I must have sighed.

"I was only thinking about my sister. Wondering if she is in Canada."

Enid, Flora wanted to offer, to dispel the unspoken, the word like a bud; but she remained silent, seeing how Ellen shook folds from the paper, how Margaret rose to find her work basket. Distractions, to cover Flora's pain.

She pulled a shawl around her shoulders.

Picturing.

After Ma died, she and Enid were like rabbits or foxes. Crouched, scurrying, crawling. Fingers scrabbling through dirt, separating baby potatoes from rootlets. Washing in icy river water. Kneeling beneath placid cows and milking into a cup. At night, they crept into the shuttered cottage, where Ma's dress still hung on a hook, Papa's straw hat on a nail.

A man came on the morning after the first frost. He held a felt hat over his nose and then fanned the air with it.

They stared dumbly as he told them to get whatever they wanted, for they would never come back here again—*You are going to the workhouse*; and she'd said—*Ma told us never to go there*; and he said—*Did she, now, Missy, she'd be happy to see you there now.*

Three years later, Matron came to the workhouse schoolroom and led Flora downstairs to a room where a lady waited. The lady was tall, with a long, thin nose and goose-glossy black eyes. Gold dress with lace at the neck; black gloves with lace at the wrist. Hair, a massed coil held by netting, pierced with tortoiseshell pins. Flora noticed the woman's false patience—how her finger tapped as fast as Flora's heart. She knew, too, that she was being tested, for the woman asked questions to which she already knew the answers. What did she do? (*Felting, ma'am.*) Did she have siblings? Were her parents alive?

Do you wish to better yourself? Do you wish to help your sister?

Like a hawk, circling the stubbled fields.

The day the green box arrived at the workhouse. Sent by the lady, filled with clothing for the trip. Flora took out a pair of mittens and slipped them on Enid's hands. Brown wool, they flopped at the tips and Enid covered her face with mittened hands. Her arms, shadowed with grime.

No, Flora. She began to cry. *Don't go.*

Later. In the yard. Enid, a thin little girl, knelt on the packed earth and played with the petals of blossoms that drifted down from an apple tree on the other side of the wall. She nested them, like piles of saucers.

And the day that Flora left.

Flora flung her arms around Enid, the little body more familiar than her own—silky hair, warm curve of neck.

Don't go, Flora, oh, don't go.

Matron's helpers pried up their fingers, one by one.

Flora stood abruptly, flinging away the memories, like the shawl, which slithered to the floor. She bent and picked it up, hung it on the back of the chair. Mr. Dougan, too, stood and set his cup and saucer on the counter. Mary was scraping her pudding bowl with a spoon. Flora lifted it away.

"Wait," Mary cried. "I didn't get—"

"You did," Flora said. "I hardly need to wash it."

—

George came home for a short visit.

On the first morning of his return, he appeared at the breakfast table wearing a freshly washed shirt, with starched collar, and his best jacket.

"Why are you all dressed up?" Lucy asked. She offered him the teapot, which he waved away, asking Margaret for coffee.

"Because I am going to visit Grandfather." Frowning. Lofty.

Josephine, watching the exchange, pondered how George bore his father's death with conscious silence, pained if anyone invoked Simeon's memory. He asked no questions, was uninterested in doings around town—the vandalism that had occurred on Main Street, the neighbour's noisy new rooster. He brooded over his food, applying butter to toast with concentrated energy. Perhaps he felt himself as the man in the house and did not know how to behave under such a burden. Perhaps, she pondered, sipping her tea, he protected himself from grief, more easily quickened at home.

From her desk, later that morning, she watched him depart. The sky lowered, dark with clouds, over the budding trees. George strode down the lane. He carried Simeon's umbrella, furled, touching down the ferrule like a cane.

He was gone all day.

At supper, he sat stiffly, hands folded in his lap and head bowed as he spoke grace. Maud and Lucy exchanged glances, eyebrows raised. They were accustomed to hearing their brother ask the Lord's blessings on the food they were about to receive. Tonight he intoned the words like a priest.

Margaret served leek soup, delicately seasoned with dill, perfectly salted. George tasted it, put down his spoon and turned to Josephine.

"Grandfather told me about your visit to the lawyer, Mother."

"Did he?" He had been a stubborn child, she remembered. Serious, cautious. "I didn't tell you last night because you were late arriving and I thought you would like to go to bed."

"Apparently the house belongs to me, Lucy and Maud once we are all twenty-one. Grandfather explained to me that we are the owners of the house and the land and of two-thirds of all the personal property."

Lucy and Maud lowered their spoons, slowly, at the same time. Lucy's eyes, slitted, furious. Maud's, round, amazed.

"I feel a great sense of responsibility, Mother." His voice was pained, as if she should have been making allowances for this new burden which had been added to the weight of his grief. "My sisters and I . . . we now . . ."

"George. *George.*" Lucy reached forward and grabbed the cuff of his jacket. "You are being *so rude.* Nothing has changed—"

He pushed his chair back. "*Everything* has changed. Grandfather explained it to me. He will pay for my education, and he will give me a job in the family business so I can . . ."

"Oh, the family business," Lucy snapped. "I'm sure I speak for Maud and Mother, too . . . we are so *grateful* that you are going to get an education and go to work in the *family business* so you can take care of us."

"Well, I . . . that *is* my responsibility now. Why are you so angry?"

"Don't you think your sisters might like to go to college? Don't you think we might like to be offered a manager's position in the factory?"

"But that's—"

"Absurd, yes, George. *Absurd.*"

He flicked his eyes over her, pulled his chair back to the table, and lifted a spoonful of soup to his mouth, carefully.

"Lucy," Josephine ventured. "Enough." She glanced at George, picking up her own spoon. *Remember,* she wanted to say, but did not dare. *Remember how you loved hearing your father tell you about commanding his ship?* She pictured George, a small boy, listening, entranced; he had played at being Simeon, standing on the veranda, feet spread as if on a tilting deck, barking imperiously into an imaginary speaking tube.

It crept over her, an added weight to her heavy heart. How, taken under the wing of the men in her family, George would slide away, bit by bit.

Less a brother. Less a son.

—

On the day that George left for Sackville, Maud and Lucy, too, returned to school. They wore black dresses, despite the spring warmth, and black straw hats. Flora stepped out onto the veranda, broom in hand, and watched as they walked side by side down Creek Road. They passed the gingerbread shingled houses, in whose gardens protective spruce boughs had been removed to reveal green shoots. They went slowly, not speaking. Lucy stared straight ahead, Maud's shoulders drooped—like their mother, afflicted with exhaustion of spirit.

—

The next morning, a horse and wagon came up from the depot. The women of the household stood on the lane, squinting in bright sunlight as the depot man lifted Mr. Dougan's things onto the wagon.

Flora was the last to shake his hand, being the one who had known him the least amount of time. Mary ran a few steps behind the wagon, waving, teasing, shouting. Ellen did not watch him leave, but walked away.

Josephine hurried after her. She slid an arm over Ellen's shoulders.

—

Hands in apron pockets, Flora slipped out behind the barn to see the state of the vegetable garden.

Mr. Dougan had pulled up last summer's cornstalks and rotting cabbage stumps. Beneath a bloom of weeds, the ground lay soft and tilthy. He had planted no seeds.

She heard a rattling jingle and the rapid clopping of hooves as a horse and carriage passed southwards on Creek Road, away from town, heading towards the forested hills. A breeze lifted her hem. Her gaze traced the horizon. She picked out a darkness in the folds of the hills, wondering if it was the valley cupping Ada and Henry's farm. Far, far to the east, farther than she cared to recall, was England. She pictured herself in a desolate, echoing building—chill light, cold air—and saw herself enduring, making herself like an empty dress, a deserted body, expressionless, stepping in the right places, Enid, a tiny imitation in her wake, pattering down the corridors of the workhouse, bowed over the bowls of gruel, agreeing with the assessment of their parents' wickedness, *O dear Lord, please do not mind their present evilness and the evil that brought them to this place, I try to correct them,* Matron praying over the dry bread, the rice and suet.

She would find a shovel, dig up this garden, plant peas, spinach, lettuce, carrots, beets. She would take the vegetables into the kitchen and help Ellen make soups and stews. She would become like a burr attached to Josephine, Ellen, Maud and Lucy.

She would not be cast away.

—

By the beginning of June, Margaret and Mary were gone. Their bedrooms were tidied and untouched.

The barn, too, was empty. No hens. The horse and carriage were sold.

Maud and Lucy spent the long-lighted evenings in their rooms, studying for their exams. Occasionally, they argued; Lucy's voice, vituperative, subsuming Maud's hesitant words. Ellen, in the kitchen, grumbled over the lack of parties or dinners for which to plan.

George graduated. He wrote to Josephine, telling her he would board with his uncle's family in order not to burden her. She had expected this; her sister-in-law had revealed her pleasure in "fixing up" the guest room for George, assuming that Josephine would be equally pleased, even grateful. Her mother had asked for George's various dimensions, collar, waist, pant length; she was going to Fairweather's to buy her grandson proper apparel, since he would be working in the factory office. Grandparents, uncles, aunts, cousins. Like a windstorm, sweeping up her son.

Josephine fretted over Sailor, afraid that he would be hit by a carriage or run away seeking Simeon. She put an oval rug beside her bed for him to sleep on. Afternoons, she sat in the parlour, listless, an unopened book on her lap and Sailor curled at her feet.

She had a court date to appeal for custody of her children.

—

Flora had noticed Josephine glance at her with a hint of worry. She knew that as a ward of the province, her keep was paid; Josephine passed on to Flora what she received from the government and gave her more, besides, as wages.

Flora set a teapot and a cup and saucer on a wooden tray. Wind roared in the trees; lilac branches scratched against the kitchen windows. She carried the tea into the parlour, where Josephine slumped at her desk, head in hands, staring at pages densely covered with spiky words. Beside her, Sailor looked up at Flora, showing the whites of his eyes. His tail stirred, hopefully.

"Why," Josephine said, surprised, "that is so thoughtful of you, Flora."

"Mrs. Galloway," Flora said. "You don't need to pay me. I'll work for room and board."

She wanted to say that she was a good gardener. That she had learned, from Ada, how to barter. How to keep hens. How to milk a cow, make butter and cheese, feed a lamb. She wanted to tell her these things. *You* will *keep me,* she was moved to say, but did not. Rather, she sensed a change, as the emptiness of the house allowed what little she did say to have more significance.

"I don't . . ." Josephine gestured at the page of handwriting. "I don't know if I *can* pay you anymore, so I am glad you say so. But I will return the money to you that the government pays me. I insist on that, at least."

Josephine slipped her hands over her face. Her hair was stiff and oily. Flora did not know when the widow had last bathed.

"Mrs. Galloway?"

Josephine looked up.

"I could wash your hair for you."

Such grief and incomprehension came over Josephine's face that Flora wondered if she had heard her correctly.

"Your hair, Mrs. Galloway," she repeated. "Shall I help you wash it?"

Josephine cried out, as if putting into words her utmost despair.

"Oh, Flora. Call me Josephine. Please . . . just . . . call me Josephine."

SIX

A Futile Fussiness

~

LUCY STOOD IN THE doorway of her mother's bedroom. Sailor scrambled to his feet, nosed his face beneath her hand.

"I am going to live in St. John."

Josephine slid shut the drawer of Simeon's dresser. She had been going through his clothing, which she had not yet removed from drawer, cupboard or closet. She sought frayed collars, loose buttons, telling herself she could not give away anything that showed evidence of her own inattention.

She sat on her bed, frightened by the expression in Lucy's eyes. Josephine still wore full mourning. Black dress, black shoes.

"I am going for various reasons, Mother. One, because Uncle Charles has decided to take George as his 'son.' Two, because Grandfather has offered to pay for George's education. Three, because no one has offered to do a single thing for me. You are not even my legal guardian . . ."

"But I—"

"I will go to work."

A clatter. Downstairs. Something falling, ordinary.

"Where, Lucy?"

"The St. John Cotton Mill. I have secured a room for two dollars a week."

Josephine clutched one of Simeon's handkerchiefs. She had embroidered it herself and given it to him as a Christmas present. She had sewn his initials entwined with hers within a chain-stitched red heart.

"Oh, Lucy. Oh, my dear. I *beg* you not to do this."

Lucy's jaw crept outward, her eyes hardening. "Begging is entirely pointless."

"Why are you angry with me?"

Lucy strode to the open window. She, too, wore a black dress. There was no sound but the hiss of rain, the dragging rush of wet leaves.

"Don't you miss your father, Lucy? Don't you . . ."

"Of course I miss my father." She turned and sat at Josephine's dressing table. She tossed her hands into the air. "I'm used to missing my father." Her voice rose to a shout. Sailor slunk to his rug. "He's been gone for half of my life, Mother. He could have been working here, in town. He did have that opportunity. And *you* could have been learning something. *Doing* something. Other than . . . sorting through your calling cards. Deciding what to tell Ellen what to make for your dinner parties. Living in this . . . ridiculous enormous house. *Favouring your son.*"

Her voice was strained, tear-filled.

"I . . ."

"I know what you're going to say. This is what you were *supposed* to do. Well, *I'm* not going to do what is expected of me. I am not going to wait for a man to treat me like a princess, then expect me to behave like one. I will *never marry*. I will make my own money and I'll keep it."

Josephine folded her hands, crumpling the handkerchief so Lucy would not see the embroidered heart.

Sailor whimpered, repressing the wagging of his tail to a suggestion.

Lucy kicked a footstool, sent it skittering. She stalked from the room.

Josephine unfolded the handkerchief, smoothed it on her lap. Last week, George had made a visit. They had sat on the side veranda drinking tea and he had introduced the idea of selling the house. He was investigating how much money they might receive from the property if they sold it, once all three siblings reached their majority, and how much Josephine might expect to receive for her one-third. He argued that she would be better suited to a smaller house, with less to take care of. She imagined Lucy listening to his opinions, silent, hostile, evaluating.

What children do not know, she thought. *What children can never know. How parents suffer their rage and always, always, always forgive their cruelty.*

—

June 12, 1888

Dear Cousin Carrie,

I write to tell you about Lucy in the hopes you will look out for her. She has taken a position at the St. John Cotton Mill. She left this morning on the train. She will be residing at a boarding house. 15 King Street. She tells me the house is at the bottom of the street overlooking the water. I beg you to go look at it and meet the owner and see whether it is a safe place. I could do nothing to stop her. She blames me for my situation.

I cannot think what I should do to support myself.

Love,
Your cousin,
Josephine

—

Carrie stood on her doorstep, pulling on summer gloves. Elms arched over a grass strip dividing the street, where two gardeners knelt, planting geraniums. She set off towards the city centre. As she turned down the hill towards the harbour, brick houses with bay windows and decorative detail gave way to rows of Italianate commercial buildings.

A few square-rigged ships lay at anchor. She viewed them critically, comparing their shabbiness to her father's ship, *Traveller*. Rigging creaked as the ships rocked on the rising tide; and memory came to her of the time *Traveller* had been boarded by pirates in the South China Sea.

It was a horror that had awakened her from nightmares all her childhood and, occasionally, did so even now: her nursemaid's searing wail as she was carried off—*Madame, Captain, Madame*; her mother, Azuba, forcing her to feign death in a pool of her father's blood; her mutism, and an English doctor, in Hong Kong, looming over her with an anxious expression, unsure of the cure. She knew that Azuba blamed herself for these terrors and for Carrie's childlessness, as if the two were related; and yet had never said *I should not have gone to sea*. Carrie had overcome her resentment of this, respecting the risks her mother had insisted upon taking, understanding how a woman might feel trapped by a life into which she did not fit.

One day, she thought, Lucy will understand her own mother, as I now understand mine.

She reached the bottom of King Street. Number fifteen was a shabby, three-storeyed, flat-roofed wooden house. Horses stood in a yard next to it, harnessed to slovens; beyond was a maze of shed-covered wharves where water sucked and slapped, filthy with tobacco leaves, vegetable peelings and dead fish.

A woman let her in. Thin, unsmiling.

"First room on the right."

Carrie climbed the stairs. Knocked. Lucy opened the ill-set door; she stepped back, startled. Carrie swept into the room. Another girl curled on the single bed, sleeping.

"That's Min," Lucy murmured, pulling out a chair for her cousin. "We have to share the bed."

Min, evidently a sound sleeper, did not stir.

Carrie sat, arranged her skirt, surveyed the room.

"Good for you, Lucy. I'm proud of you."

Lucy slipped onto the remaining chair. Her forehead bore a red crease from the elastic of a mill worker's mob cap. Her face had lost flesh; her dress was loose on her frame. Intense eyes bore the narrowed focus of fatigue. The window was set in a crooked frame, or perhaps the house had shifted. Salt air seeped over the sill, bearing the squabble of gulls.

"Tell me about your work," Carrie said. "What do you do?"

"It is loud. *So* loud." Lucy fanned her hands beside her ears. "I can still hear them. The looms."

Carrie, along with other reform-minded, well-to-do women, was working to improve the Factory Act legislation, passed but not yet in effect. She had toured cotton mills, rope manufacturers. She had visited confectioners, shoe factories, biscuit companies, box and match makers, brush and paper factories, potteries—all within the city of St. John. She and the others planned to tour the province and speak on the conditions. Lack of separate toilet facilities for men and women. Underage children. Unequal pay, unsafe conditions. Molestation. Punishment.

"I tend a spinning frame," Lucy said. "Just one frame, till I learn. I have to draw out the carriage and revolve the spinner. I have to actuate the fallers. Check for broken threads; if there are any, call for the doffers. They come racing down between the looms, the little girls."

Carrie nodded. She had seen this, on her tours. Wearing soiled aprons, the gang of doffers scuttled between the looms with their boxes, tearing off the full bobbins, replacing them with empty ones.

"It's hot, too. They keep it hot and moist so the thread won't snap. There are rules posted everywhere."

Lucy glanced at Carrie, who was more like an aunt than a cousin. She looked down at her hands, worried at a welt. Carrie, for her part, gazed at this girl upon whom she had showered gifts. They sat listening to the gulls.

"I came, Lucy, because your mother is worried."

"I'm all right."

"I know you are, Lucy. I'll tell Josephine that you are."

Carrie was certain that Lucy was hungry; that she had not expected to have a strange girl in her bed; that she was appalled to be living in a place that stank of the privy and was liable to flooding by any exceptionally high tide; that she was shocked by the factory conditions. She saw, too, that the girl was fiercely animated by the death of her father, which she had not yet grieved or accepted.

She handed Lucy a slip of paper.

"This is my address. Women meet at my house every Thursday evening at seven p.m. We are trying to change the laws so that what happened to your mother—having no custody over you children, you know, and all the rest of what happens to a woman when her husband doesn't . . . when a will can't be found—can never happen again."

Lucy did not take her eyes from Carrie's face.

"We want to make laws so that no children will work in factories or be without education. So that not only young men will be expected to attend university or to become doctors and lawyers. So that women will *have the vote* to ensure these changes. Even become lawyers and write new legislation. The women in the group are not all privileged, Lucy. There are single and working women, too."

Lucy took the card and angled it, tipping her head. She drew a long breath as if overwhelmed by the challenge she had imposed upon herself and which, Carrie could see, far surpassed her imaginings.

—

Flora stepped onto the porch of Fairweather's Gentlemen's Clothing store. A boy was painting the railings. The paint in the bucket was skimmed with dust and contained a half-drowned butterfly. A bell tinkled as she opened the door. Inside, it was cool and smelled of sizing.

She approached the counter where a girl was absorbed with folding a shirt.

One of Mr. Fairweather's daughters.

"May I speak with Mr. Fairweather?"

The girl's eyes shifted with a sequence of expressions that Flora had become accustomed to: surprise, jealousy, disdain—the paradigm of finding Flora inadequate to her beauty.

They went to the back of the store.

"Visitor for you, Mr. Fairweather."

"Come in."

Over the girl's shoulder Flora glimpsed the Overseer perusing a catalogue with drawings of men's collars. He rose to his feet, flustered.

"I am the one who . . ."

"Yes, yes, yes. Of course. I remember." He scurried away his papers. "Are you happy at . . . of course, such a sad time. Do close the door. Sit, sit, Miss Salford. Please."

She sat, thinking of the butterfly and wishing she had paused to pinch it, for she'd seen its paint-coated wings stirring. Mr. Fairweather, too, resumed his seat, gripping his hands together on his desk.

A nice family, he'd told her. *Where you'll spend Christmas.*

He coloured, a flush that began above his collar and streaked up his neck.

"Is Mrs. Galloway . . . something . . ."

"Please, I wondered if Mrs. Galloway told you about my sister."

"Your—" The colour subsided as his thoughts cleared. "Ah, yes. She did tell me."

His temporary confusion emboldened Flora. She sat forward on the edge of her chair.

"I want you to help me find my sister. Me and her were separated. Like them children at the auction. They told me I was to come to Canada and better myself. I was to make a home so me and Enid wouldn't be in the poorhouse. I promised my sister that."

Fists, white-knuckled. Pressed to her knees.

"I promised her."

He drew a breath, picked up a glass paperweight, watched the play of light in its suspended flowers as he turned it.

"I'm sorry for what happened to you, Miss Salford. After Ada and Henry died, you know, there was simply no time. It would have taken weeks, perhaps months, to determine which of the philanthropic organizations brought you here. Or to search the ships' passenger lists. We had to find a place for you."

"It's all right, Mr. Fairweather. You done a good thing for me. I am happy to be with Mrs. Galloway. But I have to find Enid."

He nodded, held up a hand.

"Yes, yes. Of course. I will make a start to look for your sister." He retrieved a sheet of paper, slid a gold pen from its holder, a tiny ear spoon at its tip. He rubbed the spoon between two fingers. "Let's begin with what you can remember. All right?"

He met her eyes and she saw his shame.

—

At church, the following Sunday, the minister preached on the evils of the pauper auction and the need for an almshouse.

"*For the love of money is the root of all evil,* 1 Timothy 6:10," he said. "We should not begrudge our taxes for this use. It is our duty to our fellow man."

Permelia and Harland sat in their usual pew.

It was mid-July and the heat was oppressive, extending even into the night. Permelia chafed at Harland's presence in the bed, calling him a stove. He began sleeping on the porch where he could smell the sharpness of dew-wet soil, loosened around his perennials. He listened to the town's quiet—no horse hooves, no strike of hammer or cry of child, only the chirr of insects. Up the street, Josephine slept alone like Permelia, only not by choice. He imagined that she curled on her side with arms spread around the phantom shape of Simeon. He'd hardened and relieved himself, guilty, ecstatic.

He flushed, in church, remembering. Handkerchief in his hand. Washing it.

It would never happen again, never. He stared straight ahead, listening to the minister, but could not help glancing sideways. Josephine wore black, a lightweight crepe. Her face was veiled, her Bible bound in black Moroccan leather.

He would help the girl, he thought, and felt a lightening, a relief from the weight of guilt. He sensed the justice of doing so. The expiation. For he had followed the progress of the little boy separated from his sisters and discovered that he was hard used by the man who had purchased him.

He thought of renouncing the job of Overseer of the Poor. Paying the fine. Permelia shifted on her seat, plucking at her skirt, a sheen of perspiration on her face. She fretted over the fit of her clothing and complained of the cook's food.

—

Maud answered the telephone. It was Mr. Fairweather.

"I have purchased bicycles. I wondered if you and Flora would like to try them. Perhaps Mrs. Galloway, too?"

Josephine smiled when told of the request.

"Goodness, no, Maudie. You go. You and Flora. Does he want you now? You go right down. The dishes can wait."

Maud and Flora went to the store. Mr. Fairweather wheeled out two brand-new bicycles.

"My wife, Mrs. Fairweather, you know, she won't try," he said. "Nor any of my daughters."

"You first, Flora," Maud said, nervous.

He held the bicycle steady while Flora clambered onto the seat, hitching up her skirt. He held the back of the seat and ran behind, letting go only long enough for her to feel the thrill of freedom.

—

Fireflies blinked, the darkness lilting with their interrupted wander. Maud and Flora had taken to playing checkers on the front veranda, evenings, by the light of a kerosene lamp. Both would turn sixteen in August.

Josephine stood in front of the linen press, fingers lifting hair from her scalp.

She sighed to enable herself to breathe. Her body was as if drowning in something other than water.

Long ago, before Simeon's death, she had agreed to host a tea meeting. The meetings, Permelia said, were to raise money for the projects planned by the beautification committee: paint for picket fences, new trees for Arbour Day, hiring a lamplighter for the new street lamps. Last Sunday, after church, Permelia had reminded her of this obligation, how it would need to take place soon.

"We usually put little tables in our front parlour," Permelia had said.

"How many?"

"Oh, six or so."

Tablecloths. The white ones with a pattern of embroidered forget-me-nots. Blue napkins to match.

On the veranda, Maud laughed. "Oh, you!" She did not mind being bested by Flora, who would not be smug, like Lucy, or dismissive like George.

Flora's English accent, broadening. "Sorry, Maudie."

Josephine heard the girls putting away the game, the scrape of chairs, their footsteps going through the parlour, their voices, muted behind the kitchen door.

Quiet.

Quiet was like the reaper; she felt his presence in corner or doorway, cold, silent—an essence, expectant. She closed the linen press and stood with her forehead pressed against it.

And there must be freshly polished silverware. Cucumber sandwiches and lemon cake. Bouquets of snapdragons and baby's breath.

She went to her desk and opened a large black book. Every evening, she entered the day's receipts in their narrow columns, writing carefully and with a sense of obligation. Mr. Eveleigh had shown her how to keep accounts. *To prove to the court that you are not squandering the children's inheritance.*

The children, she thought. Not *hers*, as if the court-mandated custody rendered them more their own people, now, than their mother's children. They seemed, all at once, to have become an independent unit, when such change should have happened incrementally, by dint of new loves, new friendships, new occupations.

She put her face in her hands.

Simeon must have left a will. Perhaps a maid, illiterate, tossed it out.

He would be so angry to know this. He would be furious to learn that all he had planned for her—the turret room, the greenhouse and roses, the house with its varnished maple floorboards—was in jeopardy.

The pulse of insects, a murmur of voices in the kitchen—she heard not the quiet of a summer night but the absence of Simeon's voice. She felt the yawning stretch of her life without him, a pain from which she could not run, that she must accept. With which she must live. That could not be ameliorated, save by sleep.

Tea meeting.

If Mr. Dougan were here, he would have brought down the freshly painted chairs. He would have set up the tables. Margaret and Mary would have found and washed and ironed the tablecloths and the napkins. The details which must be correct—gleaming silverware; spotless, starched folds of linen; place markers on flowered cards—seemed an attention to minutia which Josephine, at this moment, saw as a means to fill the moments of a shallow life. A futile fussiness.

She broke into a sweat. She stood and staggered, light-headed, the black dress encasing her in heat.

She made her way down the hall and pushed open the kitchen door. Ellen was reading aloud from the paper.

"*There was blood and plenty of it outside the left leg. I mean by plenty of it a stream as wide as one's three fingers* . . . Oh, Mrs. Galloway. I'm just reading that old axe murder trial. Mr. Dougan got me into the habit. They're going over it now. They expect a verdict tomorr—"

Josephine collapsed.

Flora jumped from her chair, tossing down sock and darning egg.

Maud shrieked.

Sailor scrabbled from his pillow.

A tiny, muscled, sun-bronzed woman started up from the corner. Indigent Ida, well-known in the town and surrounding countryside, had just arrived, coming at nightfall, as was her habit. She carried herbs and ointments, asked for nothing more than a meal and a single night's lodging. Always, she would be gone in the morning, vanishing into the dawn like a stray cat.

She knelt by Josephine.

"Water," she said. Her voice was husky from disuse. "A cloth."

Flora brought a basin and a cloth.

Ida bathed Josephine's face, unbuttoned her cuffs, ran the cloth over her arms and wrists. She held a small leather pouch to Josephine's nose.

"I fell," Josephine murmured.

They helped her into a chair. Maud ran into the parlour and returned unfolding a fan—red, a golden crane spreading its wings. She stood by her mother, frantically stirring the air.

"The tea meeting," Josephine said. Her fingers stroked Sailor's head, automatically. He showed the whites of his eyes, looking up at her. "I can't."

"The *likes of them*," Ellen muttered. "When they know you're shattered." She pulled the kettle to the hot part of the stove, jabbing a stick of wood with unnecessary force into the fire box.

"Tables and . . . Mr. Dougan not here for the little . . ."

"*Them little chairs.*" Ellen imitated a simpering voice. "And you with no Mr. Dougan. No Margaret and Mary." She scooped tea leaves from the canister, an irritable motion at odds with the worried look she sent Josephine.

Flora watched Josephine straightening her sleeves, brushing down her skirts. She had changed from the self-possessed woman who had purchased her at the auction into a person whose movements were uncertain, half-formed. Who wandered the house, staring from windows at the flicker of tree shadow, the late roses; who picked up misplaced objects—an eyeglass case, a book—and put them down again. Who forgot to bathe. Whose hands trembled. Who slept on her chignon and did not notice when her hair slipped from its pins.

Ida settled back noiselessly in the corner. The lamp began to smoke and Maud turned up the wick.

"I'll tell Mrs. Fairweather, Mother," she said, her voice earnest. "I'll call her on the telephone and say you've fallen ill."

Maud was the best telephone operator in the household. She loved to use it.

They sat drinking tea and nibbling gingersnaps. In the circle of caring women, Flora felt a sense of being part, no longer abandoned: the house rising above and around them—closets, hallways, turrets, gables, verandas. The barn, with its empty loft, its vacant stalls. Her garden, growing in the darkness. Baby beets, slender carrots. Rows of potatoes, with purple blossoms. Mr. Fairweather, asking questions that might lead to Enid's discovery. Josephine, always kind. Maud and Ellen, like friends.

"You should keep a boarding house," Indigent Ida remarked, from the half dark. "Got the space. Got the women."

PART II

October 1888 – April 1889

SEVEN

Emissaries of Winter

~

MRS. BEAMAN, A SEAMSTRESS, covered Josephine's bureau with a collection of hats.

Miss Harvey, who worked in the boot factory office, settled gladly for Maud's bedroom. She was gaunt, a minimal presence, and would not mind a smaller chamber.

Flora and Maud decided to put Mr. Sprague in Lucy's room, overlooking the side lawn. Thirty-five and unmarried, he was a typesetter and Pleasant Valley's newly hired lamplighter. From his window, overlooking the roofs of town, he could check the lights' glimmer.

The boarders had use of the parlour and the front door. They were given the large, new bathroom and were provided with breakfast, boxed lunch and dinner.

George's room remained empty until the early evening of October seventeenth.

In the kitchen, Ellen, preparing for tomorrow's lunches, carefully tipped eggs from a spoon into boiling water. Josephine and Flora bent over sewing and knitting, while Maud spread a letter from Lucy on the table and read aloud.

". . . *a spirited meeting, run by Cousin Carrie. We discussed how women constitute a 'sex class' in society, which is deemed inferior. Lydia Mills read a paper written by an American suffragist. We spoke of joining the Canadian Women's Suffrage Association. I was excited and have made new friends. There is a woman who runs a boarding house, there are two artists, and some who have gone to university in the United States. I—*"

A knock came on the front door. Ellen started; an egg slipped from her spoon. Maud, apprehensive, looked up at her mother.

"I'll go," Flora said.

She set down her knitting and slipped quietly along the dim hallway. As she opened the front door, the sharp decay of autumn entered— peony bushes frozen to pulp, decaying leaves.

A man.

Holding a kerosene lantern. Face half-darkened in shifting shadow.

"This a boarding establishment?"

"It is."

"You got a room to let?"

"Wait, please."

She went to the kitchen.

"There's a man, asking if we have rooms."

Josephine sighed. She had not slept the previous night and had been listless, fatigued, all day long. She went into the hall, turned up the gaslight. Flora and Maud stood behind her as she interviewed the man on the doorstep. The man said he was from Gloucester County, gesturing northwards. He was a carpenter. He had secured work here in town. He needed a place to make the miniature houses that he sold. He was not married and had no references other than one of the actual little houses, which he could show Josephine, if she wished. He bowed, slightly, when he told her his name—Jasper Tuck—and reached into his pocket, withdrawing bills ready to pay for one week in advance. He said he would be gone all day during the week and would need a space for his woodworking. He had noticed the barn. Could he pay extra for use of a bit of it? He had noticed that the trellis had come unattached and that there was a rotting step on the veranda, on the kitchen side.

"I can fix those up for you," he said.

Then he stood silent. Josephine asked him to step inside.

—

Once it had been decided to turn the premises into a boarding house, Josephine and Maud had joined Ellen and Flora in the row of small servants' rooms that lined a narrow hallway—beadboard walls painted white, sun-faded quilts, one bureau in each room and a row of hooks. As the nights grew longer, the rooms grew cold, their only heat source the stovepipe that rose through the hall floor from the kitchen below.

Josephine asked Flora to bring her a cup of tea in the mornings, and to sit on the single chair by the door while she drank it so they could discuss the day's doings.

She does not realize, Josephine thought, sitting up against her pillow and taking the cup and saucer from Flora, *how the sadness in her eyes has changed to a quick attentiveness.*

Or how we have all begun to rely on her.

"Thank you, Flora. I find it hard to get out of bed in this cold room." She sipped at the tea. Felt the hot drink warm her from inside. "Did you find a man to supply wood?"

"Yes," Flora said. "He will bring it cut, cured and split."

"How much will it cost?"

"He will take trade. I offered onions, and weekly delivery of gingerbreads, and eggs as long as the hens are laying. Is that all right?"

"It is."

"And I found a rooster. From the same place as is bringing the cow."

"A cow, Flora! And you know how to milk it, of course."

Flora looked at her hands, lying open in her lap. She curled them into fists. A hardness crept into the corners of her mouth, vanished. She nodded.

"The cow is being delivered next week, but we need hay so I thought we might ask Mr. Fairweather if he knew of someone who could bring a few loads, but I don't know how we . . . how . . ."

"To pay for it. Yes."

Josephine cradled the cup in her hands, as if it did not have a handle. "I will sell a bracelet. To pay for the hay. You can tell him that."

"And Mr. Tuck," Flora said. "He could put a stanchel in the horse stall, maybe widen it."

Josephine felt herself yield, incrementally. To Flora's competence. To a sense of comfort, derived from the tea's steam. To small losses and odd gains.

—

Twice a day, Harland went to his weather station in the veranda. He opened a ledger and wrote with his finest nib. *November 7, 1888.* He looked out the glass walls, saw that the flag hung limp. He tapped the barometer, checked the thermometer. He entered the statistics and then added: *Skies overcast.*

He pondered. He would enter: *No wind.* Yet he felt the poetry inherent in his pen, ink easing down the nib's tapering slit. Instead, he wrote: *Air still.*

In the shadow of the fence, frost lay within declivities—cupped leaves, an empty space where he had dug up a day lily—and he saw where a cat had walked. He was tempted to write of this, the meandering black dots of a cat's paws, how this record of an encounter between fur and ice in the autumn stillness was equivalent to his own feelings; and then he thought of the rooms of his house, the glossy furniture and the smell of dinner, his skates hanging by their laces and Permelia's thick woollen coat which she had disinterred from the attic this morning.

Heavy frost, he wrote, bearing down so that the ink welled and made a bubble, which he blotted with the edge of a cloth. He compressed his lips. *Smell of snow but no flakes as yet.*

He slid the pen into its holder. He could not tell Permelia what it had done to him, being featured in Mr. Train's articles, articles that had been read in Toronto, New York, London. *White slave auction. Degrading, inhuman, unchristian. Slave driver with his long whip.* She could not know how it was when he met with town officials, their pens etching for posterity the various reports—amounts gathered from the town for relief of the poor: from the Christmas day collection, from the tax on dogs, from the penalty on horses running at large. Amounts billed by him, Overseer of the Poor, for items purchased by pauper owners and due payable: twill homespun trousers, socks, shoes, burial shrouds, coffins. How, at these meetings, he read aloud his accounts written over the past months, hard voice masking his increasing shame: a chair ruined as a result of being thrown out the window of Joshua Calkin's home by an angry pauper; a doctor's visit occasioned by a knifepoint struggle between Abraham Guntery and Miles Perkins; ditto by two boys turned out on a winter's night, walking twelve miles until they found someone to take them in; coroner's charges for a man found frozen to death in a shed. He passed over his ledger for inspection, expenses neatly itemized, stories dutifully dated.

At the last meeting, after receiving back the inspected book, which he privately thought of as a codification of despair, he softly settled folded hands on its cover. He knew that with this gesture he both protected those shut within the book's darkness and made his decision to resign as Overseer of the Poor, imagining Permelia's fury yet forgiving her in advance, for she could not imagine these meetings: glazed eyes, yawns, arms stretched overhead pulling shirts from waistbands. Jokes and guffaws. Self-important solemnity. His own hidden self-loathing.

Or, perhaps, yes, she could imagine this, and would not find it shocking. Nor be disturbed and moved to protest.

Before leaving for the store, he asked Permelia to join him in the parlour. She sat beside a hanging ivy, absently picking through its leaves for those turned leathery and brown.

"Whyever are we sitting in the parlour, Harland? Do you want me to call for tea? Although I am replete. We only just finished breakfast."

"I need to discuss with you a decision I have taken."

She gave him her full attention, repressing a belch, hand against lips. They had been good friends, once. She had found Harland handsome and pleasant. That, with his promise of financial success, was enough to convince her to bring all her persuasive seductions to play, when she was seventeen and slender.

"My dear, I am going to resign my position as Overseer of the Poor."

She glared at him over her hand.

"You are not allowed. You will be disgraced. You will . . . you will be forced to pay a fine!"

"Yes. And the fine will go towards the upkeep of the poor. Goodness knows they deserve it."

"They do *not* deserve it. They are uneducated, lazy good-for-nothings prone to drink."

He considered her outraged face. She had been, if not poor, then perilously close to being so: her mother's house, in need of paint; her own dresses, painstakingly repaired. The self-righteousness, however, was occasioned by propaganda. Permelia had recently joined the Women's Christian Temperance Union. He pitied those husbands now lectured upon the evils of alcohol in the home. He did not drink, did not like the way it dulled his mind. He observed the loudness of men at gatherings and the way in which they were liable to become expansive, making disastrous personal confessions, revealing alliances best kept hidden.

"Forgive me, Permelia, but you do not know of what you speak. I am familiar with many cases—"

"You always take this tone with me, Harland. *You do not know of what you speak. You* do not know the needs of young women, of how every cent coming into this house counts, and of what your decision may cost us. *Shop at Fairweather's Gentlemen's Clothing? Why, he's the man who . . .*"

He looked out the window as she spoke. He saw the cat whose prints he had seen earlier. It was a calico, white with splotches of butterscotch and black. He watched how fastidiously it negotiated the damp leaves, as though treading upon them only out of necessity.

—

Flora was coming from the barn with a basket of eggs when a farmer drove horse and wagon up the lane. He carefully lowered a burlap bag bulging with chickens.

"Here you go, then, miss."

"But Mr. Franklin, we didn't order . . ."

"No charge, had more than I needed."

Flora set down the eggs and reached up with both hands to accept the neck of the lively bag, which made sudden explosive heaves.

Josephine's parents were visiting; Mrs. Linden had tiptoed upstairs to console her daughter, bearing a tin of toffee, since this morning Josephine had been unable to leave her bed.

Swinging the heavy bag before her with two hands, Flora caught sight of Mr. Linden at one of the front windows, scowling. He would not want it getting around town that his daughter was accepting charity.

"Thank you, Mr. Franklin," Flora said. "Thank you *very* much."

She stalked up the lane past the house, disgusted by this factory-owning father. Ellen, once, had hissed into Flora's ear, furious. She'd overheard a conversation in which Mr. Linden told Josephine she was *paying the piper* for her husband's mistake.

"He sees fit to let her *get by*," Ellen muttered, "since he is giving so much to George . . ."

Remembering this now, heading for the barn, Flora wondered if Ellen's dislike of George had begun only after Simeon's death, when the contrast between son and daughters had been laid bare. Or if it were a part of a disliking of men in general.

Simeon, of course, and Mr. Dougan excepted . . .

"Shush," she commanded the chickens, who had burst into violent squawks.

—

The following Sunday, after church, Josephine and Maud walked home together. Josephine paused in the outer vestibule, gathering herself for the ordeal of passing the boarders, who occupied the parlour. She fussed at her gloves, watching as Maud entered the house and strode down the hallway, pausing to wave at the boarders in their armchairs, reading books, perusing the newspapers, waiting for their dinner to be served.

Young people learn to accept change so easily.

She felt tears pricking her eyes.

I can't keep telling myself that it is not fair. I have to accept, as the minister said. Be grateful for what I have. She had not recovered from the smallest of moments, grown larger in her mind as she walked up the street, when a circle of friends outside the church had taken just an instant too long to admit her, as if without Simeon she were invisible.

She slid quietly into the house, brushing at her skirt. Smell of roast chicken and apple pie. Chinking of porcelain plates being set down. She forced herself to stop in the parlour door. Peered in, made a tiny wave. The boarders looked up. Mr. Sprague placed a finger, ostentatiously, on the passage of the newspaper he was reading, his eyes clouded with some salacious story.

"Did you enjoy your services?" asked Josephine.

Mrs. Beaman went to the Catholic church. Miss Harvey and Mr. Sprague were Baptists. She did not know if Mr. Tuck attended church.

"It was lovely, yes, Mrs. Galloway."

"Very nice, Mrs. Galloway. And you?"

They, too, like the people outside the church, made a community, like a family, and their politeness to her was another exclusion; she was their landlady, and their money gave them the privilege of coming in at the front door, using their own keys. Of spreading their belongings in the parlour. Of going up the front stairs, not bothering to tiptoe if they came in at a late hour. Mrs. Beaman slept in the marital bed. The children's rooms were littered with the possessions of strangers. The women used the large bathroom with its hot and cold running water.

They cannot see it as my house. Mine and Simeon's.

She went down the hall towards the kitchen. The incident at the church had quickened her grief, making her steps waver, her hand seek the wall for support. There was no room in her mind to make decisions, to consider the needs of simple living. She was, like Simeon, suspended in waters that rendered her helpless, floating without volition. She felt a kind of shame, and a rage, that she could not share her grief. It was neither wanted nor comprehensible, and no one could understand its weight, so heavy that she did not wish to rise from bed, knowing that she must take it up.

Nor could anyone understand that all the endeavours of life—polishing brass, mending, peeling apples, sewing hems—seemed now as strands in a web of deceit, netted in as fine and elaborate a mesh as possible, all for the purpose of obscuring death's dominion.

Stop. Breathe. Look at one thing. One small thing.

She leaned against the wall for a moment, watching closely as she turned the ring on her finger. Straightening with a long breath, she opened the door and stepped into the kitchen. The dog scrambled to his feet in one convulsive motion of gladness.

—

Winter crept, seeped, silenced. Skies were grey for a week. Mornings, the grass bore a blanket of frost.

Josephine appeared in the kitchen door.

"I couldn't sleep again last night," she said. "Could I have a cup of tea?"

She wore a long muslin nightgown, her hair loosely braided.

Flora and Ellen were drowsy in the warmth of the wood stove, the steamy, sweet air. Their desire to gather Josephine into their contentment quivered, an arrow held to string. Ellen wiped floury hands, reached for the kettle. Flora lifted cup and saucer from a shelf. Unnecessarily, they made the tea together, Ellen pouring, Flora holding.

"Warm milk didn't help, then?" Ellen said, handing Josephine the cup of tea.

Josephine shook her head.

"I lay awake ever so long."

She lifted the saucer so that the steam caressed her cheek. Flora and Ellen exchanged a knowing look as she left the room and trod heavily up the stairs.

"Oh, they loved each other, they did," Ellen murmured. She returned to the table, where she set hands back on the pillow of dough, pulling it forward, then folding it back into itself. Her face was warped, mouth awry, eyes yearning. "You never saw it, Flora. The way she could be. Laughing, like. Coming in all blowed about by the wind and never a care."

—

Flora tipped the hen gently so that its head lay on the block. She brought the hatchet down on the cord-thin neck, saw the head drop into a bucket, golden eye still fixed on her. It was a Saturday and she could hear the *tap tap* of a hammer. She set the carcass upside down in another bucket and went into the barn. Jasper Tuck had fitted up the tack room as his workshop. He was gripping a ball-peen hammer, tapping tiny nails into a narrow piece of wood. Sheets of glass. A jar of putty. Strips of cedar.

Flora came up close to his bench. She wiped a hand on her skirt and reached out to touch the bright wood, reminding herself that this was not a dollhouse but a work of art—to be displayed in parlours, set in windows, lit at night and admired by passersby.

"One day, I would like to have one of your houses," she said.

"Well. You will, then. Strikes me that you're a girl that makes things happen. Like you do around here." He grinned. His look was sly, containing a hidden, alternate conversation, not with her, she sensed, but with what she looked like. What people called her beauty. He was missing a wolf tooth. He slid his tongue up to cover the gap. His eyes were the colour of silty water.

"When my parents died, I learned how to make do," Flora said.

He set down the hammer. His eyes bored into hers and she looked down, suddenly wishing she had not come here. He reminded her of men she and Enid had encountered in the village, after their parents died. Leaning against cottage walls. Coming up lanes. Their eyes crafty, their hands like spades.

"*My* parents died," he said. "What do you think of that? You and me are alike. How old were you?"

"About seven."

He was silent. She looked up; he was studying her. Her heart skipped a beat and she turned to leave, but his next words arrested her.

"That's how old I was. Seven years old. My mother and father were drowned."

"Oh. That's terrible."

"Ferry. The river ferry. Bashed in by a floating log."

"I'm very sorry," she said.

He returned to the meticulous, almost mincing *tap tap* of the hammer. She felt that he had left an opportunity for her kindness. That she should ask him if he had a brother or a sister and why he had come to this town. She hesitated, not wanting to be the subject of his scrutiny.

He looked down at the side of the little house, held in the vise. He ran his finger along the row of nail heads. His eyebrows raised and vanished under hair that had escaped his cloth cap.

"You could help if you want," he remarked, offhand. "You got them little fingers, you could set glass into the windowpanes."

She waved away the suggestion with a blood-speckled hand.

"I . . . I'll try, but I probably can't. I got too much to do."

He shrugged, resumed hammering. *Tap tap tap*. Gentle. Like tiptoe-ing instead of striding.

She went back outside, relieved, conflicted.

Josephine faithfully gave her the quarterly stipend sent by the government. Other than that, Flora had only free room and board. Nothing had been said about letting her go or about her position in the household. She was pleased to find that Mrs. Beaman and Miss Harvey and Mr. Sprague often came to her for advice or information; they even complained, which she did not mind, for she was in a position to reassure, to make improvements. Mr. Tuck, now, was asking for her help, even though he usually did not need anything. He brought energy into the house. She felt it emanating from his shoulders when she set the teapot on the table. She felt it breathing from the sheets of his bed, when she stripped it.

She buried the chicken's head. The air smelled of soil chilled by morning frosts, dead grass, blood. Lifting the carcass from the bucket, she walked back towards the house carrying it by cold claws. She flung her thoughts forward only as far as was necessary to keep her momentum, as she had when Mr. Fairweather showed her how to ride a bicycle. She saw a rolling succession of chores: *Strip, gut, then drop the chicken in boiling water, add dried rosemary from the bunch; bake the squash; bring up potatoes from the root cellar. Mend Mrs. Beaman's pillow. Put oatmeal and candles on the shopping list.* And hovering, always, was a tiny image of Enid—a river, an elm tree, a farm.

A carriage was coming up the lane. Mr. Fairweather held the reins in one hand, the other lifted to greet her.

"Flora," he called. "Wait, please."

He climbed down and clipped a line to the horse's bridle, looping it around the hitching post. She approached and stood holding the headless chicken, watching, curious, as he pulled an envelope from his pocket.

"I have heard from Miss Rye at last. I was forced, finally, to have my lawyer contact her, threatening consequences if she did not investigate, and so she did."

His fingers trembled, slightly, as if with excitement, and he had some difficulty extricating the letter from the envelope.

"We have, finally, some news about your sister."

The house, suddenly, seemed like a painting—trees flat against a sullen sky, she herself a girl in a book about Canada, standing by a wood-shingled house before a man in a long frock coat and a beaver hat. She clutched her waist with her free hand. Her belly cramped with a swoop of fear.

"Miss Rye confirms the date that an Enid Salford arrived in Halifax. She said only that Enid went to some *trusted friend of hers* who found a situation and sent her off on a train. She did not name the trusted friend, nor tell me anything about the 'situation,' so I will have to ask my Halifax acquaintances if they have any ideas who that friend might have been. Less than I hoped, Flora, but we can surmise that she is in Nova Scotia."

Nova Scotia, Flora thought, stunned. The sky itself seemed to come closer, now that she knew for sure that her sister was alive and living in the next province.

He tapped her on the shoulder with the letter, smiling. "I'll let you know when I hear anything. You'll say hello to Mrs. Galloway for me, won't you?"

She watched his carriage retreat down the lane beneath the leafless branches. The sickness in her belly remained, but changed—both dread and excitement.

Snowflakes fell, wavering down like emissaries of winter.

She heard the *tap tap* of Mr. Tuck's little hammer, persistent, as if nothing had changed.

EIGHT

Tin Reindeer

~

"YOU WANT TO WATCH out for him," Ellen said, kneading dough.

The wind moaned and whistled, carrying the snow in twirling columns and forming drifts on the veranda. Flora opened the firebox to insert a stick of wood, and the dance of flame made a liveliness in the wintery light. Maud sat at a small table in the corner, her pencil scratching, muttering breathily over her algebra.

Flora closed the firebox door and resumed her seat by the window. She was turning a collar for Mr. Sprague.

"I see him looking at you, Flora."

Maud raised her eyes at Ellen's insistent warning, but Flora held the collar closer to her face, tugging at the stitches with a curved ripper.

"Who?" said Maud.

"That Mr. Jasper Tuck. I don't trust that one."

Ellen was kneading dough at the long, central table. Press. Turn. Fold. Emphasizing her words. "You're a rare beauty, Flora. It will get you into trouble."

It, Flora thought. *Not me, but it.*

She knew how Mr. Tuck looked at her. It was nothing more than the way most men looked at her. Women, too.

"Flora?"

"What?"

"Are you listening to me?" Ellen laid the shaped dough into a bread pan and sprinkled it with cornmeal. "Girls like you end up . . . well. Do you *know* what men want from the likes of you?"

Maud turned on her chair. "Don't say 'the likes of you,' Ellen. You make it sound as if Flora was a low woman. We *know*, you know. We are modern girls."

Ellen's mouth hardened. Maud, her pet, seldom offered opinions. "I was only thinking," she said, chastened. "Of that poor woman who was murdered."

"Oh, that. Ellen, what could you expect? She was *living* with him. She had taken a room in a tiny house with an unmarried man. Flora is not like that. She is not stupid."

—

It seemed the world was lost. There were no houses, no people, no horses or trains or towns. Only the whiteness, a muted roar, and flakes that came endlessly from nowhere, from nothing, unbidden, mysterious and persistent, piling on the porch railing, obscuring the trees.

Cold seeped through cracks in the plaster walls; snow found its way under loose windows, lay on sills and did not melt in unheated rooms. No mail arrived, the phone did not ring. Josephine could not track the progression of the sun.

So it must have been for Simeon in storms at sea.

She stayed downstairs only long enough to forbid Maud from going to school. She spoke to Ellen, knowing that her orders lacked conviction, and that if she asked Ellen to make apple pie, the cook might make lemon and no one would care. She sensed Ellen's pity, was made to feel like an invalid as Ellen cajoled her with tea, rusks, puddings.

Josephine continued to worry over Sailor, forgetting that he had survived the perils of shipboard life. She stood in the back door wrapped in a housecoat, arms around her waist, watching as he went into the snow and hunched to relieve himself and trotted back obediently at her call. He followed her upstairs, wet, dripping. She sat in her bedroom, her housecoat dark with melting snow.

She bent forward, moaned into her cupped hands, rocked.

His letters.

My dear Josephine, I sit in the presence of monkeys. They have white faces and shriek with bared teeth.

My dear Josephine, it is late at night on a calm sea and the monotony cannot be described. I miss you, my dearest.

My darling, I miss you. Have you purchased the croquet set and bid Mr. Dougan flatten the yard?

She had been like a child, believing expectations would always be realized. Her imagined future was the engine of her self. Always, upon his return, she had been borne by his enthusiasms. Always, when he was gone, his energy remained, a source never entirely tapped. Enough to see her through.

She crawled into bed with Simeon's letters, his dog at her side.

Pity, sympathy, warmth, caring. She felt it, tepid water lapping at her shores. She stared, wide-eyed, dry-eyed, at what it had been to be loved.

—

By midday, snow skirled faster past the windows and the howl in the branches of the trees grew louder. Ellen, reading the newspaper, clucked her tongue. The boarders had all walked to work this morning, even Mrs. Beaman, vanishing into the thickly falling snow.

"Thank the Lord your mother kept you home," Ellen remarked to Maud, lowering the newspaper at a gust that shook the house.

Maud had seemed relieved when Josephine told her to stay home—*whether or not school is cancelled*—but Flora thought that if she were in Maud's place, she would have protested, determined to hand in her homework, not wanting to miss a single moment of learning.

Learning.

It was the same as freedom, for at the workhouse schooling had been the only time that she and Enid were without fear. Neither Matron nor her henchwomen stood along the walls of the classroom—as they did in the lunchroom, in the welting room, in the yard. Matron must have assumed that the young teacher would discipline them as she did— boxing ears, smashing heads into walls—but he did not. Every girl or woman or child in his classroom was eager to sound out words, listen to stories, hear about kings and queens and the shape of the world that spread beyond the workhouse walls.

Flora noticed that Ellen was fascinated by a newspaper column far removed from cooking, murder, or Ellen's own prospects. It was called *About Women*, reprinted from the American papers. Today Ellen read out loud about a Miss Letta L. Burlingame, of Ann Arbor, Michigan, who had been licensed to practise law; of women granted patents, in New York State; and of women university students.

"*The name of the first woman graduate of Columbia is Miss Mary Parsons Hankey. She is about 20 years of age . . .*"

Flora, her mending complete, sat across the table from Maud. She watched equations—$-2x - 3 = 4x - 15$—emerging from the sharpened tip of her pencil.

"I could get you some books from school," Maud remarked, setting down her pencil and working at the paper with an eraser.

One day, Flora thought, when she and Enid were reunited, she would need to go to a real job, every morning, like the boarders.

"All right."

She tipped her head to read the spines of Maud's books, piled on the table. *History, geography, English*. With Maud's coaching, she could study after her work was done, late into the night. She did not know what this learning would do for her, whether she would ever go to school or become a lawyer like Miss Burlingame. She knew what it was to ferret and scratch and kill and steal to keep a little sister alive; she had seen old women, stunned with loneliness and hunger, waiting for gruel at long tables; had stood on a station platform and looked down on a sea of men willing to purchase her. She ran her palm over the cover of the topmost book—she would become educated.

"*Mrs. Elizabeth Cady Stanton . . .*" Ellen looked up. "Now, who is she?"

"She's a suffragist," Maud said. "She's fighting for women to have the vote. And to have equal rights to men."

Ellen nodded, repressing comment, momentarily at a loss, her opinion uncertain on this topic. "*. . . in a recent visit to Paris, met some of the most distinguished suffragists of France at a reception given at the residence of her son, Theodore Stanton.*"

"Women like Cousin Carrie," Maud murmured, making an equal sign with two short dashes of her pencil. Satisfied, Flora thought, wondering if arithmetic was fun.

Ellen lowered the newspaper onto her lap with a sudden rustle.

"Is Cousin Carrie a suffragist?"

"Haven't you been listening to Lucy's letters, Ellen?"

Flora realized that not a sound had come from Josephine's room since she had gone up to clear away her breakfast dishes. Leaving Ellen and Maud arguing about the difference between suffragists and suffragettes, she went up the stairs, knocked gently on Josephine's door, cracked it open. In the dim light, she saw a mound of bedding strewn with papers. Josephine had fallen asleep propped against her pillows, hand on one of the pages.

—

At six o'clock, when only Mr. Tuck had returned, Ellen covered the serving bowls with tea towels and slid them into the warming oven. Flora ran up the front stairs and knocked on his door.

He was sitting on a straight chair in the room that had once belonged to George, hunched over a wastebasket, carving, his blade gleaming in the light of a kerosene lamp, which illuminated only the knife, his hands, his knees, and a patch of flowered wallpaper.

"We haven't rung the dinner bell because none of the others have come home."

He glanced up at the window. Black, speckled with knots of ice.

She put her hand on the pleated folds of her gingham bodice. He looked at her from beneath his shock of hair. Comfortable in his warm room, with his knife. Waiting. She wondered if he wrote letters, if he had friends.

He set down the knife.

"Suppose you want me to go look for them."

He followed her down the stairs, sock feet making no sound. He lifted down his coat, still wet. He pulled a damp cap and mittens from the pockets.

"Wait," she said. She rummaged in the hall closet for dry mittens and cap.

She watched as he suited himself for the weather. He took his time, tugging the laces of his boots, pulling the cuffs of his coat down over his mittens, wrapping a scarf around his neck and mouth so that only his eyes showed. His movements were contained and she could not tell if he resented being called upon to help or relished the task, tucking it away as a bargaining chip.

She held the door as he trudged away into the darkness, leaning out to watch the rays of his lantern lighting streaks of wind-raked flakes.

Returning to the kitchen, she retrieved her work basket and sat by the stove. Josephine soothed Sailor, stroking the concave silkiness beneath his jaw. Maud fitted a sock over a darning egg. Ellen picked up her knitting.

"They can die within sight of home, you know," she said. "Oh yes, they can. Mr. McFee was lost until two a.m. His wife, poor thing, nearly died herself of the fright. He came staggering in, half-dead. *I've lost the horses,* he said. *I had to leave them.* Well. His men went out and found them. They were almost to the barn."

"Do you think the boarders could be lost right here in town?"

Ellen looked at Maud over her busy fingers. She sniffed, speaking as if reluctant. "Only 'tis good we had a man to send."

'Tis good we had a man.

Flora noticed that Josephine turned from the words, setting her chin on the heel of her hand. The house was silent, save for the sounds of the storm. Even Ellen sighed rather than spoke, all during the hour it took until the front door opened and Jasper Tuck stamped in, having located Mrs. Beaman two houses down the hill, Miss Harvey shuddering in the lee of the skating rink, and Mr. Sprague in the process of knocking on doors, seeking Miss Harvey.

"Got 'em," Jasper Tuck called.

A tremendous stamping in the hallway. Boots, the snapping of coats, exclamations.

Ellen flew up from her chair and Flora knelt to retrieve her knitting, which had fallen beneath the table, five stitches dropped.

Three days later, on a Saturday after the roads had been cleared, the trains were running, and the sky was blue, a knock came in mid-afternoon. Josephine opened the back door to find Cousin Carrie and Lucy on the step.

They stepped in, both talking at once, exuberant, eyes swimming and cheeks red from the frigid air.

"We just came from a Women's Christian Temperance Union meeting," Lucy said, pulling off her mittens.

"We'll catch the four o'clock train back to the city." Carrie's words tumbled over Lucy's and she laughed, unwinding a red paisley scarf. "I know it's awkward, too late for lunch, too early for tea. Never mind. We wanted to see all of you."

Another knock came on the door. Carrie opened it. Her mother, Azuba, stood on the doorstep. Azuba's hair was still dark and glossy, streaked with grey. She bore the brisk competence of a woman who cares for a husband's hidden illness—Nathaniel suffered from dizzy spells, induced by a pirate's bullet. She began speaking and removing her gloves as soon as she stepped over the doorsill.

"Darling." She kissed Carrie, hugged Lucy, turned to take Josephine's hands. "Nathaniel had to see the cooper about ordering apple barrels. I knew Carrie was coming here after her meeting, Josephine. Well, I decided to come up with Nathaniel. I wanted to hear about the meeting." Her voice softened. She looked into Josephine's eyes with an understanding that accepted its own limitations, allowing Josephine the singularity of grief.

"And I needed to see you, my dear."

Maud flew down the stairs, thrilled to see her sister, cousin and aunt. The women trooped through the kitchen.

"Hello, Ellen, how's… Flora, isn't it?… How did you… when… so much snow…"

"Tea. Some cookies," Josephine whispered to Ellen.

Flora stirred the coals, took split maple logs from the wood box and worked them into the stove. Ellen foraged in the cookie jar.

"Should have made . . ." she muttered.

Mothers and daughters—Josephine, Lucy and Maud, Azuba and Carrie—went down the hall and out to the turret room.

"It was a special meeting of the suffrage committee," Carrie said. She spoke in a firm, declamatory voice, accustomed to teaching. She laid out a petition on the round, carpet-covered table, smoothed it with the palm of her hand. "They are going to expand their mandate to include social issues of concern to women, not only the problems of alcohol. They've agreed to endorse our petition demanding universal suffrage. The WCTU has great influence over both men and women. Their endorsement will carry weight."

In the front half of the parlour, Mr. Sprague and Miss Harvey were playing checkers. Mrs. Beaman observed, making wry clucks at moves whose consequences she could foresee.

Josephine listened as the women embarked on a lively discussion, so absorbed by the content of what they had to say that they did not notice her silence, nor bother with etiquette—dashing away statements with the back of a hand, interrupting, correcting or contradicting without apology.

"... federal Franchise Act? Yes, it does, truly. It *explicitly* excludes all women, most status Indians, and all Asians."

"Only white men merit full citizenship?" Maud was hesitant, taking her lead from Lucy's excitement. She glanced at her mother.

Lucy set down her teacup. "Well, of course. If *we* vote, it could lead to a decline in the birthrate. Didn't you know this? No, really, I read this in the paper. The vote would 'unsex' and degrade us, it would ruin 'domestic harmony' and therefore lead to a *decline in the birthrate*. Does it not make your blood boil?"

"The States are ahead of us," Carrie said. "Wyoming and Utah territories granted suffrage to women in sixty-nine and seventy."

"Well, but we have Emily Stowe. Without her, the University of Toronto would never have opened their medical school to women. Now she is working for better factory and health laws."

Azuba looked up from a calm perusal of the petition. "What does Premier Blair think?"

Lucy rushed to answer. "He argued for the enfranchisement of spinsters and widows, didn't he, Cousin Carrie? But his bill was quashed by the legislative council."

A silence fell. Josephine felt a rush of anger towards the unknown men. She knew none of this. She had not attended any of Carrie's meetings.

"They do not reckon on our independence," Carrie said, pointing a finger as if at Premier Blair. "They have *no idea* what is coming. Look at Emily Stowe. A woman doctor. Look what will happen when we have women lawyers. We will make a Married Women's Property Act . . ."

She looked intently at Josephine, raised her voice.

". . . that is not liable to a man's interpretation."

Lucy's cheeks were flushed; she pressed hand to heart as if to slow its beat. "And *then,* once we have a proper property act, perhaps Maudie and I will get married. And provide you with grandchildren, Mother.

Otherwise, there's really no point, is there. In marrying and giving away our freedom."

Azuba glanced up sharply. She flicked her eyes between Lucy and Josephine. Carrie pulled the petition across the table, perused what she knew by heart.

No marriage for my girls? No happy companionship with a man, no babies, no grandchildren? Josephine realized, suddenly, the extent to which the girls had been influenced by Simeon's death. They could see what happened to a woman upon marriage, everything—belongings, beloved home, sense of self—invalidated upon a husband's death.

She gazed at the women's hands variously arranged on the carpeted table—loose, folded—and imagined a future in which Lucy might become a lawyer, Maud, a doctor. No matter if they had husbands or not. She envisioned her daughters, coming home to visit. Vigorous, intense. Telling of their work, their happiness. She felt a shift inside herself, like a room pierced by sunlight after days of cloud.

"Do you want us to sign this petition, Carrie?" she asked.

Carrie looked up at the clock. Squat, on the mantelpiece, with a hand-painted scene of a Dutch windmill. Delicate hands touching three-thirty.

"Yes, of course."

Lucy ran for a pen. Maud slid the chess board beneath the petition.

Josephine angled the paper and signed it in black ink, her signature firm.

Josephine Linden Galloway.

Not Mrs. Simeon Galloway.

Click of a checker piece. *Jump, jump, jump.* Mr. Sprague's exclamation of disgust.

—

Lucy sat at the foot of Maud's bed and looked around the narrow space. Deal floorboards, uncarpeted. Clothes draped on hooks. Faded wallpaper, curling from the plaster above the door. One small window.

The house in which she had grown up was now a boarding establishment.

"Was this Margaret's room?"

"Mary's, I think. Mother is in Margaret's room. Next to Ellen. And Flora is just across the hall."

"At least you have your own bed." Lucy smoothed the coverlet. "I have to sleep with a snoring girl. I use six inches of the mattress and she has the rest."

Maud sat at a small table. Fingerless gloves were draped on a pile of school books.

"Maud, what do you think of George's plan?"

"To sell the house?" Maud picked up the gloves and pulled them onto her hands, slowly, not looking at her sister. "I don't like to think about it. This is home."

"Home? Not the home I knew."

"No," Maud said. She folded her hands and her eyes filled with tears. "Of course not. It's not the same home. Not without Father."

"Oh, Maudie. I meant . . ."

"It's too soon to be talking like this," Maud said, suddenly vehement. "You and George. Talking about selling this house."

Lucy picked at a loose thread in the coverlet, cast a sly look at her plain, earnest sister. "We do need to consider it, you know." Her voice was pleasant.

"Don't take that tone with me. I am so sick of it, Lucy. *I'm* the one who is helping Mother with her grief. *I'm* the one who has to see our home turn into a . . ."

"But you know, Maud, once you turn twenty-one, it becomes *our* house. Yours and mine and George's. Not Mother's."

"We all need to agree, and I will never turn Mother out of her home." Her hands trembled, tearing off the fingerless gloves. She slapped them down.

"A smaller place would be better for her, Maud. All of this, you know. It's just keeping up appearances. When in truth, you're now living like servants. You *are* servants. To those . . . boarders."

"You are a hypocrite, Lucy."

Now Lucy's cheeks flared. She sat up straight and glared at her sister.

"I beg your pardon."

"Yes, you are. You speak of women's rights, yet you treat Mother like a child. You treat honest work as if it were demeaning. You and George. You are thinking *only of yourselves.*"

Lucy was silent. Maud fussed with the gloves, glancing up at Lucy, who did not meet her eyes.

"You know, Maud." Lucy's voice was less sure. "He's so . . . so persuasive. George. You're right to be thinking for yourself. I just realized that he . . ."

"But he could be right, I suppose." Maud, quick. Unaccustomed to being heard. "It *is* hard on Mother. It *is* hard."

"Maud." Lucy paused, glanced uncertainly at her sister. She took a long breath. "No, really, George is only trying to do the right thing. We have to . . ."

"Lucy?" Carrie was calling up the stairs. "We will miss the train."

—

Harland made a more elaborate window display. He added a Christmas tree: loops of popcorn chains, dangling silver-painted walnuts, candles in tin clasps. Beneath it, he set a wooden crèche, with carved figures: Mary, Joseph, baby, wise men, camels, donkeys, and sheep. Overhead, he hung the usual tin reindeer, suspended on wires.

This afternoon, laying silk scarves and shirts in tissue-filled boxes on which the store's name was printed in raised script—*Fairweather's Gentlemen's Clothing*—Harland's hands moved as if independently, making small, fussy tucks. Miss Floyd stood across the aisle at another counter, doing the same with muslin night shirts. Harland's eldest daughter draped white fabric over plinths, creating a necktie display.

He strove to make himself see the store as a stranger might, in order to keep it fresh. His father—who had recently died, leaving the business to Harland—had been his employer, and he remembered doing his father's bidding, every Christmas draping the same white fabric over the same plinths; unpacking shipments of handkerchiefs, gloves, bow ties, French suspenders.

The store's quiet was broken only by the rustling pluck and crimp of tissue paper as he and Miss Floyd made fluted petals around the patterned silks and fancy-front shirts, yet Harland was oblivious of scarves or tissue paper. *Yesterday.* He had asked for a special meeting of the justices of the peace. His cheeks burned as he remembered. His words, prompting a speculative silence, and then delicate questions. As if *there must be something to account for such a decision*: ill health, mental incapacity, domestic turmoil? When he avowed that none of these things had caused his decision, rather that *he could not in good conscience continue to provide his wholehearted support*, he felt their disapproval. And then the shift of status, just as Permelia had predicted. Their eyes, meeting each other's and not his. A peremptory politeness, harbinger of exclusion. He had pushed his resignation letter across the table, as if bidding farewell to a part of himself.

He moved down the counter to begin on the bow ties.

Outside, Josephine Galloway passed the window. She paused to look up at the tin reindeer, so delicately suspended that they turned on the slightest draught, galloping on air. She opened the door.

"The reindeer! It was a treat for me to see them when I was a child."

He fumbled as he set the box aside and came around the counter. He joined her outside. Stepping into the cold was like plunging into the sea.

"I wanted to tell you, Josephine—"

He caught himself, flushed.

"Excuse me."

"No, I am glad. I would like to call you Harland."

She smiled at him through the black veil sewn to her hat.

"I am no longer the Overseer of the Poor. I have resigned."

"Why?"

"The three children. I begged someone to take all three. I should have taken them myself if no one would. I fear for the little boy."

He saw how their reflections in the store window watched them, blind.

Josephine laid her hand on his sleeve; quickly removed it.

"I understand," she said.

Her voice trembled. She seemed as if she was, like him, without layers against the cold.

He shivered, ran his hands up and down his arms. "I am going to help Flora look for her sister. May I stop in from time to time to keep her informed?"

"Please. Please stop in and visit us."

Her words were plain, unadorned, separate from this season of excess; he watched as she continued along the plank sidewalk and then stepped down into the street, pausing to wait for a wagon to pass. He went inside and resumed laying scarves and shirts into tissue. He thought of how he had begun to loathe Christmas and by extension, it seemed, his own wife, and how this terrified him, as if it were a thing beyond his control, a disaster sweeping down upon him.

NINE

Someone Who Talks Back

~

IT WAS PITCH DARK by five o'clock in the afternoon. A hanging paraffin lamp made the dining table shine like a stage in the shadowed room. Flora set down a bowl of stew; steam furled as she lifted the lid.

Hands, reaching for ladle. For salt and pepper shakers.

"I seen your light down on the corner, Mr. Sprague," murmured Miss Harvey, lifting her fork with ink-stained fingers.

"I endeavour to please," he said. He fussed through his stew with the tines of his fork, turning over pieces of potato, carrot, turnip.

Flora left and returned with a covered bowl of buttermilk biscuits. She set down the bowl in front of Jasper Tuck. He glanced her way. Keeps to himself, Flora thought, with a pang of hurt. Even though they had spoken together a few times, he did not acknowledge her as anything other than a servant.

She checked the table. Pitcher of tea. Milk and sugar. Butter on a covered china plate. Water in Josephine's plainest glassware. Dilly beans in a dish. Sweet pickles, sliced cheese.

"That fellow who was here, George Francis Train," Mr. Sprague said. He took a breath, preparing to hold forth. He was fascinated by The Comet, as Train referred to himself, who had exposed the pauper auction. Flora paused on her way out, pretending to inspect the candles. "We thought he was a crank—but you know he truly did go around the world in eighty days. I was reading about it. New York to San Francisco, seven days. Clipper ship to Yokohama, then over to Singapore. Up to France, across to Liverpool, back to New York. Imagine that. And he really did own a town in Omaha. He really did have a mansion in Newport, Rhode Island. I seen a picture of it." He paused to break open a biscuit, reached with a knife for a pat of butter. Lips pursed, he spread his biscuit with tiny dabs. Silver and glassware gleamed in the pool of light. "He's fallen on hard times now. Gone bust."

Flora ate her stew in the kitchen, along with Josephine, Ellen and Maud. Occasionally, she rose to check the boarders' progress. She cleared the table, served tapioca pudding, listened for the scraping of chairs and the thud of footfall—into the parlour, up the stairs.

When the dishes were done, Josephine bid them goodnight, saying she had a headache and was going to bed. Maud and Flora exchanged glances. The quieter Josephine became, the more, it seemed, her grief deepened.

Maud decided to study in the kitchen, where it was warm. Ellen settled in her rocking chair with her knitting.

"Couldn't you sell those, Ellen?" Flora asked.

"Who would want my old mittens, now," Ellen said. Her voice was exasperated, as if her mittens, like herself, were without value, and it had been rude of Flora to point this out.

"I didn't—"

"Anyone can make a mitten." A thumb was growing, stitches shifting from needle to needle on a spiky triangle.

The two girls exchanged another glance. Neither understood the reason for Ellen's unpredictable moods, yet they were complicit in their tolerance. Flora untied her apron and hung it on the back of the door, feeling that she had space within herself to absorb Ellen's prickly retorts. She had a room of her own, a quarterly stipend now, all the food she could eat, and a status in the household that revealed itself like a plant, its growth imperceptible but steady.

"I'm going up to read," Flora said.

Maud ran a hand down the seam of her open book, smoothing. "Come down if you need help."

Flora caught Ellen's sharp observance and felt a sear of frustration. Ellen wanted Flora to remain forever at the back of the house, in the kitchen, a procurer of needs, whereas she expected to see Maud finish her education, marry, and have a house such as this one had been before Simeon's death.

"*You* learned to read," Maud remarked, also noticing Ellen's expression.

"Yes, but I know my place." The rocking chair and the needles went faster.

"What a thing to say, Ellen. If Flora wants to become educated, there's every reason in the world she should. Don't you be like one of those—"

Maud paused, pursuing her thought.

"Look at what they did to Mother when the will couldn't be found. Those *men*. With their laws. Saying she had to go to court to claim her own children as hers."

Flora went up the back stairs into the chill of the hallway. One dim gaslight mounted on the wall illuminated the spruce floorboards. Josephine's door was cracked open for heat; she could see a slice of light. Her own room was freezing. She wrapped herself in a yellow and brown plaid shawl and sat at a small table. She had stood the books that Maud had brought her from the school so that their spines were impeccably aligned. Embossed titles gleamed, golden.

The Practical Speller.

An English Grammar with copious and carefully graduated exercises.

Literary Extracts.

A Practical Introduction to Arithmetic.

Shavings dropped into the wastebasket as she sharpened her pencil with a small knife.

She began writing out tonight's spelling words: *obvious, thorough, simplicity, courageous, impetuous, field, yield, incessant.*

She worked until she could no longer keep her eyes open, writing these words over and over, until both penmanship and spelling were perfect.

—

Every Saturday, Flora had a half day off. She felt guilty.

"I could do the baking," she said. She had put her apron on, pretending to forget that it was Saturday.

"Go," Josephine said. She did not meet Flora's eyes, as if to open herself to sympathy was a thing she could not bear. She waved her hand, the motion unnecessarily emphatic. "Leave everything behind, do something nice."

None of the women in the house had any enthusiasm for the holiday. They were not making cookies or new decorations for the tree. The tree had been set up mainly for the pleasure of the boarders, and the Christmas dinner was prepared only for their sake. George, living at his uncle's house, would have afternoon dinner with his mother, sisters and Josephine's parents; then spend the evening with Simeon's family. Ellen and Flora would eat the boarders' meal, only in the kitchen.

Sunlight slanted through the frosted parlour windows, broken and made lively by crystals. Flora hesitated. *Do something nice. With whom?*

"I could stay here," Flora said. "We could . . ."

Josephine looked up, attempting a smile. "I'm all right, Flora. Take my skates, we have the same size feet. Or you could go to the hill with a sled. They're hanging on the wall in the back shed. You could walk along the river. You could go into the shops."

She put out a hand, as if to be shaken, but slid her fingers around Flora's own and brought them to her cheek.

"There's nothing you can do for me," she whispered.

Flora untied her apron and dressed for the cold.

As she passed the barn with skates hung over her shoulder, she heard a tap on the window of Jasper Tuck's workshop. She saw him, dim behind the frosted pane, beckoning; so she went into the barn, unslung the skates and sat on the edge of a chair. Warmth emanated from a small wood stove set on a slab of stone.

"Saved this for you. Don't think there's anyone else could do it."

"Why not? You could." A bit of cheek, in her words, to cover how he set her akilter.

"My fingers are too big. See."

He had laid out miniscule windowpanes, a jar of paste and a fine brush on a table. She could not resist the little windows with their empty muntins. Like playing with the toys she had never had. Making something that had no plain use. He leaned over her, showing her how to set the panes. She felt his solidity, like a horse—a contained energy. He unscrewed the jar of paste, made sure she understood; then settled back at his own workbench.

Mr. Tuck was making a replica of the house across the street—gables, veranda with matchstick railings, tall downstairs windows. He was attaching its gingerbread trim with tiny tacks. He held his mouth in a tender grimace, almost feminine, as he rapped gently with his ball-peen hammer.

"Is it hard to go back to real carpentry?"

He sat back, adjusted his vision to take her in. "What do you mean?"

"During the week. When you got to use an ordinary hammer and ordinary-sized shingles."

His jaw crept out and he looked out the window at snow unspooling from a high drift. His eyes hardened.

"I guess it would, yes. As you said. But I'm not working right now. At carpentry. I got no work. So I got to sell these, see."

He seemed irritated, whether at her or something else she could not tell. She worked at the windows in silence, waiting for his mood to pass. She could be skating. She pictured the rink, the music, the laughter.

Flora dipped the brush into the paste, drew a bead along the wood. Another bead, and two more. She held her breath, set down the brush, gently picked up a square of glass and eased it down onto the glue. Tapped it with a fingertip, felt it settle into the paste. Done, perfect. She set another pane, and then another, until the grid of sticks, the pieces of glass became a window. A thing to enclose a house, to repel wind and rain, to keep its inhabitants safe. She sat back, astonished. She picked up the brush to begin another.

"You should make little people," she ventured.

He had resumed his careful tapping. "You're a funny one, you are. Little people."

"Why not? Like a doll's house?"

"This ain't a doll's house though, is it. This is a *replica*."

"Sorry."

"Aye, you should be. Sorry."

Was this teasing, she thought, not liking his tone, or testing? Or something else, dangerous? She had never spent time with a man. Perhaps this is what they were like. The windows and dusty walls of the workshop shut away the brisk air she had been enjoying when she had started off down the lane. She wished she had not answered his beckon.

"What was it like, up north?"

"Up north where?"

"Here. In New Brunswick. You told Mrs. Galloway. Where you came from."

He ran his finger over the tacks to make sure they were flush with the wood.

"Cold," he said, after a pause. "It was brutal cold up there. Nothing much to do. So I came south to find work."

A log settled in the stove.

"You're a one with the questions today. What was it like over there? In England?"

"Cold," she said, impulsively, trying to match his teasing tone, never having played such a game. "In the winter. Cold and damp. I was in a workhouse, you know."

"Were you, now." He stroked his cheeks, pulling down his eyelids so his eyes showed their meaty red, like Sailor in a melancholy mood.

She felt his gaze settle on her. Coals shifted in the wood stove. She determined to leave as soon as she had finished this one window.

"Got no people, then," he said. The sentence hung, as Josephine's words had, earlier. *Do something nice . . .*

She wiped the paste from the brush, abrupt. "I have to go."

She gathered up her skates and let herself out of the barn. Ada had told her that men could sense when you had begun your bleeding. That they always knew when you had become a woman.

—

Two days before Christmas, Josephine brought a letter into the kitchen. She paused in the doorway.

Maud stirred a saucepan whose contents slapped and bubbled. Ellen stood at the table with her hands on her waist, observing Flora as she came from the stove carrying a small cast-iron skillet. The room was vaporous, cloud-like: steam rose from the boiling cranberries, rice cooled in a bowl. Flora poked a strand of hair into her bun, carefully poured melted butter over a beaten egg. Rice croquettes, Josephine thought. Cranberry sauce.

"Like this?" Flora asked. Josephine noticed how she glanced at Ellen, nervous. Ellen was a painstaking baker. She had her methods.

"Yes, and then you sprinkle in the sugar and the nutmeg."

The room was at once kitchen, dining room, living room and study. Ellen's chair by the window held a basket with indigo-blue and grey wool. Josephine's armchair, in a corner, was flanked by a pie-crust table loaded with newspapers, books, a wooden writing box. She sank into her chair, working spectacles onto her nose.

"It's from Lucy. Shall I read it aloud?"

"Mother, is she coming home for Christmas?"

"I hope so, Maudie. We shall see, I guess. Here's what she says."

> December 21, 1888
> Dear Mother,
>
> Cousin Carrie invited me for Christmas dinner so I will go there.
> I get only one day off.

Josephine set down the letter. She was silent for a long time before sighing, resuming.

> I'm sorry to miss all of you but at least I will be with family.
> Aunt A. and Uncle N. are coming.
>
> Work is hard. I objected when our lunchtime was cut short. It is not
> a place for someone who talks back. My overseer for work discipline
> and production is nasty. He has already given me two fines which are
> taken from my wages. One was for inferior work which I could not
> see was fair at all. The other was for giving one of the doffers a snack
> from my apron pocket. There is a man who pinches me every morn-
> ing when I go through the door. He waits for me. What should I do?

"Pinch him back," Ellen said, savage. "The brute."

"Tell the overseer?" Maud suggested.

"No." Flora overturned a spoonful of sugar. "That don't . . . that doesn't work. They get worse if you snitch."

> We have to eat our dinner in the same room we work. There are
> chairs in the corner. That is when we can use the convenience which
> the men use as well so it is very sticky and smelly. When I am
> not too tired I go to the Free Public Library reading room in the
> evenings. That is where I am now. It is quiet and my roommate is

not here to stare or chatter at me and drive me to want to slap her face. There is a section about law and I am reading a book called "Blackstone's Commentaries." It is the history of English common law and it is very interesting. Did you know about "the doctrine of marital unity"? It sets out that at marriage the woman becomes absorbed by the man and is nobody aside from him. It makes me see why we women are treated like brainless non-persons and why it is so important that we have the right to vote. Cousin Carrie's meetings are SO exciting. Oh how I wish you could come to them one day with Maud and Flora. We are working on many fronts, as we say. One of us writes to the WCTU . . .

"Women's Christian Temperance Union," Maud murmured to Ellen, who had raised her eyebrows.

. . . who as you know are endorsing our petition calling for full suffrage. We keep each other up to date on our efforts. Also we are going to have a woman come to speak who is an authority on child labour laws and the needs of women factory workers. Ha ha I could do that. There is no fire escape from this building, for one.

How are all your pampered boarders? Is George coming home from school for Christmas? I suppose he will stay with Uncle Charles and Aunt Lavinia, the spoiled thing.

Did you put up a tree in the parlour? I don't know when I will be home again but likely when Carrie starts going around to give talks about suffrage and labour. I miss you, Mother, and I hope you are well.

Love,
Your daughter,
Lucy

No one spoke. Maud concentrated on her stirring. Josephine opened her writing box, slipped the letter inside and closed the lid. She felt a prick of jealousy, picturing Lucy's animated face at Carrie's Christmas table, seeing Carrie take hold of her headstrong daughter, convincing her that to remain unmarried was a political act. She could not bear the thought that Lucy would forego the love she herself had had with Simeon, or that Maud, over whom Lucy had great influence, might do the same.

Flora's spoon batted the side of the bowl, a rhythmic knock as she mixed the butter and egg.

Josephine rose and left the room with apparent purpose; then stood in the hallway, dreading her cold bedroom, the line of mourning clothes hanging as still from their hooks as if they dressed a row of corpses. She remembered her delight in Harland's window display. She could visit again, to see if he had added anything new.

She pulled on her wool coat, wrapped a scarf around her neck and let herself out the back door. She headed down the hill, following a pathway in the snow beneath the branches of naked elms.

They had skated together as children, before Simeon came to town. Hand in hand, the band playing. Recently, in a schoolbook she had gotten out for Flora, she'd found the note he'd written to her when they were children. *Dear Josephine, will you mary me?*

I am drowning, Josephine thought. *Drowning people reach up for something to grasp. Why will I tell him I have come?*

She remembered that he had started a petition for an almshouse. She would ask if she could help. She would go into the store and offer to circulate Harland's petition.

Lucy's letter had made her feel old and relegated to another era, but now her steps quickened. The smell of wood smoke was on the air, and her heart lifted at the thought of Christmas cookies. She would ask Ellen to make some, after all.

—

"He's to be hanged," Ellen said, after Josephine left the house. "Oh, I wish Mr. Dougan was here."

Flora mixed egg, sugar and cinnamon with the rice. She plucked handfuls of the sticky mixture from the bowl with floury hands, making croquettes to store in the ice box for Christmas day.

Maud was stirring the cranberry sauce, watching it thicken. "Who?" she said. "Who is to be hanged?"

"That axe murderer, Mr. Crowley. He's to be hanged tomorrow."

Alongside her Irish poems, Ellen posted with hatpins the most salacious of the newspaper articles about the trial. She unpinned one and waved it at them, then read it aloud; triumphantly, Flora thought.

"*Unless the hand of Providence intervenes between John Crowley and the gallows, he will undergo sentence of death tomorrow, for one of the most heinous crimes on record in New Brunswick. By the judge's request, the hanging will not be made public.* Well, now, we can all sleep safe in our beds."

Maud stared at her. "That's horrible."

"Don't you be feeling sorry for the man," Ellen snapped. "Remember what he did. This is the coroner's testimony: *I lifted the woman's skirts up to examine her. I saw that there were bruises on the inside of both thighs and scratches on the right groin. The bruises appeared to be from a man's hand and the scratches from a man's fingernails.* Then he goes on about the blows of the axe. *The whole forehead was broken in.*"

She pressed the paper back on the wall, pushing the hatpin deeper than necessary, as if she wished a permanent testimony.

"Good riddance to him," Ellen whispered.

TEN

A Wooden Wheelbarrow

~

MAUD AND JOSEPHINE WRAPPED themselves in ankle-length wool-blanket coats with scarlet stripes on sleeves and hems. They pulled caps onto their heads, tied woven sashes around their waists. Maud's skates hung over her shoulder and she held out a pair for her mother.

"I want you to skate too, Mother. Please. There's a boy that's been ogling me."

Josephine took the skates.

Flora, rummaging in the front hall closet, dug out an old toque, a worn canvas coat that had once been George's, and a pair of fleece-lined rubber boots. She sat on the bench, pulling heavy socks over her black stockings.

"It will be lovely in the rink," Flora said. She heard her own accent, how words were changing in her mouth, less fluid, more like solid, sharp-edged blocks. She exchanged looks with Maud. They had talked of how they must contrive to get Josephine out into the cold air, to talk and laugh with other people.

Maud and Josephine stepped into the snow-refracted light. Jasper Tuck, at the door, returned their greeting and came into the house.

He stared at Flora. Boldly, she thought, looking away. She was tugging rubber handles at the top of the boots.

"Wondering what you was doing this morning."

"You need help with the miniature house?"

"I was going to ask you to play a game of checkers with me. In the parlour."

She dropped elbows onto knees, boy-like. "It is Saturday afternoon, Mr. Tuck. I took my half day this morning. I am going out to clean the chicken pen."

"Well, then. I guess I'm goin' to have to help you."

"I don't need no . . . any help. Thank you, though."

Going to the barn, her breath came in clouds, the skin of her face papery.

Checkers!

He could not be sweet on her. He was too old. He must be lonely.

This morning she had awakened from her recurrent dream, tears on her cheeks—*Don't go, Flora, don't go!*—Enid's hands torn from hers, a carriage grown to vast proportions rumbling over cobblestones. She sat up violently, arms around knees, head buried, striving to balance the dream's essence—betrayal, rage—with determination.

She is somewhere in Nova Scotia, Flora thought, pushing a wooden wheelbarrow into the empty stall where the chickens lived in the winter.

My sister, at this very moment, working like me, in the same freezing air.

The hens burst out in a flurry of scaly legs, feathers and dust. She set the tines of a pitchfork into the bedding, releasing hot, ammonia steam. She pried and lifted, cleaning away the manure and dumping it into the wheelbarrow until the floorboards were visible.

Jasper Tuck came into the barn from his workroom. She pulled the toque from her sweating scalp, panting; her hair slid from its pins, unfurled onto her shoulders.

He took the handles of the wheelbarrow, pushed it out the door and down the shovelled path to the manure pile. He tipped the handles as if it were no weight and returned it to the barn.

He reached for the pitchfork but she snatched it close.

"No. I can do it."

He looked down at her. A veil tore between them.

"You come get me for the next load, then. That's too heavy for a girl."

Her heart speeded. She was not accustomed to kindness, could not sort it out from cruelty or expedience. She thought of how the wheelbarrow's iron wheel sank into the snow when she cleaned the cow's stall, loaded with less.

—

Harland went down on one knee, balanced on skate point, tightening Josephine's laces. She saw silvery hairs poking from beneath his astrakhan hat and remembered how, at this same rink, sixteen years old, she had skated arm in arm with a friend, having spurned his advances.

"I never *could* get them tight enough," she said.

She stood, took his arm and made a few trotting steps; then bent her right knee as he bent his. The cornet band, seated on a raised platform, played waltzes and polkas: "Beautiful Dreamer," "My Bonnie Lies Over the Ocean," "Funiculì Funiculà." Beneath the music, scraping blades made a sound like hundreds of miniature saws, while light shafts slanted down from windows set around the high pyramid roof. Smell of wool, of cold. Her heart began a healthy pounding—one of his arms snugged hers close, the other beat time at his side, his legs were transformed, supple and smooth, sweeping them around the rink. Permelia, circling in the crush, skated arm in arm with one of her daughters; her fingers fluttered from the girl's arm as Harland and Josephine swept by. With her privileges, Josephine thought, she could afford to be generous. Her husband merely took pity on a widow.

"I have good news for you," Harland said, on shortened breath. "Concerning Flora."

She felt his commiserating glance, but fixed her eyes on the striated ice, seeing things she would not tell. Simeon's letters in a hatbox beneath her bed. How she now understood Flora's stunned silence after the auction. How she now knew that life was a structure whose frame could collapse, all at once and without warning.

"You know that I received a letter from Miss Rye saying that Enid Salford was delivered to Halifax."

"Yes."

"I wrote to a close acquaintance of mine there. She knows a woman who is one of Miss Rye's 'trusted friends.' These people keep in touch with the girls and convey details of their well-being—or ill use—to Maria Rye. My friend gave me an address, so I have written to this woman, asking if she placed Enid Salford. Or if she knows the person who did."

Josephine looked up at him. Their eyes met and saw more than each intended. She tightened her mitten on his arm—looked away, examining the musicians. They wore black caps with gold badges; matching jackets with stiff, raised collars. Fingerless gloves.

"That's good," she said. "Shall I tell Flora?"

They went halfway around the rink before he answered. "I was going to say no, let us not get her hopes up, but then it came to me that this girl has been kept like a . . . like a tiger in a cage. She has been effectively imprisoned most of her young life. This must end, don't you agree? She has proven herself intelligent, capable and strong."

"Yes, oh yes. She is a wonderful help to me. She should know you are sending the letter, even if it ends in disappointment."

Harland's chest lifted and his stride shortened while maintaining the music's rhythm. She saw that he bore a pleased expression.

"Tell her that I'll be sending a letter by tonight's mail," he said.

Men passing on skates, wives on their arms, nodded to Harland; their eyes dropped to Josephine and sobered, remembering Captain Galloway. Women's sympathy came a beat too late, after a flash of pity, self-satisfaction and a shameful pride, knowing that unlike Josephine they were still married women, fully employed as such, loved and augmented, one-half of a sum greater than its parts. *Permelia's husband is so kind to poor Mrs. Galloway,* women would murmur to one another over the rims of teacups, speaking of the cornet band and the rink and the lovely morning.

"Have you begun circulating your petition?" she asked.

"For the almshouse? Yes. I wondered if you would care to present it at a tea meeting. Not at your own . . . place," he added. "Mrs. Smith has said she would support the cause but has no interest in *presenting* the petition. Someone needs, you see, to explain the situation."

"I . . ."

. . . *sometimes cannot get out of bed in the morning* . . . She sensed that Harland wished to meet her eyes, in query or to exchange a smile, but she stared straight ahead, letting her skates find their way, wondering if Maud and Flora would come with her to the tea meeting. Despite her misgivings about Lucy's fervour, she felt an unusual sense of anticipation, picturing her own signatures—on the almshouse petition, on the suffrage petition—like promises to herself.

—

January 5, 1889

Dear Mrs. Jonah,

I write to you from New Brunswick, where until recently I have been serving the position of Overseer of the Poor. It is in this capacity that an English girl, Flora Salford, came to my attention. She was brought over as one of Miss Maria Rye's orphans. It is thought that her younger sister, Enid, was delivered to Halifax in a similar group of girls.

I take the liberty of contacting you since my dear friend, Alicia Alward, informed me that you are a trusted friend of Miss Rye, and may have placed the younger sister.

*It will be my utmost pleasure to hear that this was indeed the case,
and I remain in eager anticipation of anything you can tell me
about this girl, Enid Salford, for whose welfare her sister, Flora,
is in constant agitation and worry.*

Thanking you in advance for any information you may send,

*I remain,
Yours truly,
Harland Fairweather*

—

At Mrs. Smith's tea meeting in aid of the almshouse petition, Josephine, Flora and Maud were given a little round table next to the piano. Josephine sipped tea, her heart racing. She could not take a single bite of the pound cake filled with strawberry jam and whipped cream. Harland had made the assumption that she would describe her experience, and the organizer had simply sent her a note to confirm the date. Flora, too, was to speak; her cheeks flamed, and she had not picked up her fork. Josephine reached over and patted her hand.

"It's only Pleasant Valley women," she whispered.

Gaslights burned on the walls; in the low, amber light, ornaments glittered—beads, sequins, brooches. A woman stood, tapped a glass with her fork.

"Mrs. Josephine Galloway will now . . ."

"You'll be all right, Mama," Maud whispered. She had worn her best gauze blouse; Ellen had repaired the jet buttons. Maud had insisted on adjusting Flora's hair, easing the tight topknot into a looser pillow.

Josephine rose and stood by the piano. The drawing room was crowded with the round tables; she saw the relaxed, expectant faces of women, some half-turned on their chairs.

"I was asked by Mr. Fairweather, who was then the Overseer of the Poor, to attend the pauper auction and bid for a young girl. She should not have been sold as a pauper, he told me, but he had no choice in the matter."

As she described the crowd of men, and the way she had elbowed her way to a place below the platform, the tinkling of forks and cups and saucers faded to silence.

"They were lined up on the platform in the freezing cold. One woman was so sick that she lay beneath a blanket on a wagon, but not so sick, apparently, that she wasn't brought out to be sold. There were three little children, a brother and two sisters."

Flora's eyes, unblinking, glistened with tears. Maud flipped a butter knife over and over, eyes sending encouragement to her mother.

"I was the only woman there, I believe. Have any of you ever attended our annual pauper auction? I bid against three men for Flora."

Josephine's voice ceased its trembling and she felt, suddenly, like a teacher she remembered at the Sackville academy. *What is the meaning of écrasement? When was the Treaty of Utrecht? How would you compare the Renaissance to the Middle Ages?* She slid into the truth of the remembered moment, her horror at the mechanisms of the sale, her anger at seeing frightened people being treated like animals at market.

"This should never happen again, not in the heart of our quiet town, nor anywhere else. The province should build almshouses and take on the care of people who for any number of circumstances find themselves homeless. It may mean higher taxes. But Mr. Fairweather told me that this is not a certainty, and may in fact prove to be untrue in the long run. It is not the dollar that we must have our minds on, in any case. It is our humanitarian impulse."

She finished to applause. She made her way to the table and lifted a glass of water to her lips with shaking hand. The women had listened with grave concern. No man had risen to interrupt her, nor whispered to another man behind a hand. She felt a new sense of herself, dignified not by a husband but by grief and the knowledge that she must make her way alone.

Mrs. Smith went to the front of the room.

"I would like to introduce Flora Salford, who, to our great sorrow, had to endure standing on our station platform and being bid for at auction."

Flora took her place by the piano and told her story simply, a slight tremor in her voice. The audience leaned in to hear the Queen's English, even if marred by a country accent.

"I was alone after they died and then the Overseer came. He took me to some people just for Christmas. I wanted to be sent back to England. No one told me anything. One day a wagon came. It were filled with . . . paupers. I wasn't no . . . I wasn't a pauper. We were made to sit up on the station platform. Then one by one the names were called out and the people all got sold. I stood up when he called my name and Mrs. Galloway, she put her hand up for me."

When Flora was done, Mrs. Smith asked if she would take questions. Flora's eyes turned to Josephine's, pleading, and Josephine shook her head—no. The meeting was concluded.

Josephine sensed an air of suppressed excitement as the women gathered at the coat rack; it was as if, should someone say one funny thing, delighted laughter would burst from one woman, for sheer pleasure of the evening just passed; and it would be like fire—kindled, catching, flaming.

"It was an excellent talk, thank you, Josephine."

She pulled her collar up, flushed. "Thank you."

"You opened our eyes, you certainly did. You and Flora."

"Thank you."

The door opened to the frozen trees and a moonless night, the Milky Way netting stars and planets. Josephine stepped outside, hearing her own voice in her head—*may prove to be untrue in the long run*—knowing she would not sleep all night long.

Josephine, Maud and Flora turned into the street. They strode fast, bent by the cold.

At the corner, a street lamp glimmered, lighting ice-glazed picket fences.

"Thank you, Mr. Sprague," Maud remarked. "Mr. Fusspot."

Flora spoke through her scarf, muffled. "How that man ruins his collars I don't know."

Josephine laughed. Her heart lifted and she felt Simeon, somewhere in the cloud of stars, relax his hold.

ELEVEN

A Man's Kindness

~

FLORA STOOD BEFORE THE house gazing up at the lindens. The sky was the chill blue of a winter evening, the branches so still they did not seem part of growing trees.

She went to the back of the barn, let herself in. There was not a sound from the workshop, yet Jasper Tuck must be there, since she'd seen him crossing the lawn, breath scarfing the air.

She listened.

The opening of a drawer.

A click.

She tiptoed to the wall that separated the workshop from the rest of the barn. She put her face to a crack, making a frame with mittened hands.

She could see him only from the shoulders down. He knelt at a tool chest with many shallow drawers. The lowest drawer was half-opened. It was filled with handkerchiefs, perfectly folded, laid side by side. His hand passed over the contents, back and forth, as if deciding which one to pluck out.

She could not understand why he would keep clothing in the barn.

Not handkerchiefs. Banknotes! Twenty-five-cent notes. One-dollar, two-dollar, four-dollar notes. Orange, grey, green.

His hand paused, as if he had heard her thought. The fingers, out-stretched.

She held her breath until his hand resumed its soft to and fro.

—

Ellen frowned, a streak of flour on her forehead and her mouth in a knot as she kneaded dough with stiff arms. Flora, chopping carrots, listened as Josephine and Ellen continued an argument, about herself both in its particulars as well as its unspoken underpinnings. Flora felt her position in the house shifting. Much of the food Ellen prepared would not be there unless Flora had grown it, or bargained and bartered, or sold mittens. Ellen was oddly in her due but would neither acknowledge this nor show gratitude, clinging to her authority over Flora, her only remaining "girl." Josephine often came to Flora with questions about the house's running; and Flora responded with caution, thinking that to rise above her station put her in a precarious place whose dangers she could not foresee.

"Why not, Ellen?" Josephine persisted. "Lucy will be at work, but Flora could visit Cousin Carrie. Couldn't you, Flora? You could see the ships, the market. We'll make up a package of food for you to leave at Lucy's boarding house."

She broke off as if struck by an idea.

"You've never had a holiday, have you?"

"Only to pick blackberries," Flora said. "At the workhouse."

Once a year, the children of the workhouse were loaded into two green omnibuses, one for boys and one for girls, and taken to the country to harvest blackberries. With seats inside and on top, the carriages swayed like bloated beetles. Jolted, wide-eyed, the children watched the profligate, dizzying, deafening world. Shop windows with gilt-lettered signs, delivery men, women wearing skirts with street-sweeping hems, shiny horseflesh, whip-wielding coachmen, butter-coloured stone buildings side by side like sheaves of barley . . .

Flora slid a lock of hair behind her ear and resumed cutting carrots on the scarred wooden block, a whole winter's worth of carrots having been acquired in exchange for six pairs of men's mittens. She wanted Josephine to think she had enjoyed her trip to the English countryside, with its hedge-lined fields and air smelling of wildflowers—daisies, lady's pincushion, foxglove, poppies—names that made her think that her mother, who had taught them to her, could not possibly be dead.

Holiday. . .

. . . Matron. Handing out men's shirts to all the children. *Roll up the sleeves. Be careful of thorns.* Arranging the children all along a row of blackberry bushes. *Pick, pick.* She walked up and down behind them, poking with her cane, and Flora saw a place where she and Enid could push through the hedge, dash into an oat field, hide in a stand of willows. Her thought. Like a flung pebble striking the matron's head, who whirled and caught the very instant of Flora's reaching for Enid's hand . . .

Tears sprang to Flora's eyes.

"Oh, dear," Josephine said, watching her. "It wasn't a holiday, was it."

"Nor will be a visit to St. John with the likes of him," Ellen muttered, scooping up the dough and slapping it into a greased bowl.

Mr. Tuck needed to go to St. John to purchase fittings for the little houses—tiny weathervanes and grommets, a miniature boot scraper. He needed a new knife, special varnish, bits of carpeting to cut into playing-card-sized rugs. He was leaving on the morning train and would be back at ten o'clock in the evening. He had asked Flora if she would care to accompany him.

"I think it will be fine, Ellen," Josephine insisted. "Flora, I will phone Cousin Carrie and see if she can meet you at the train. I don't expect you to spend the day with Mr. Tuck. Certainly not, Flora. You let him take you to the train and you see that he watches out for you on the trip down and back."

How he had asked her, Josephine did not know and Flora did not tell.

She remembered the silence before he'd asked. The way he'd considered, his lips tight together like the mouth of a bag. He had been whittling wood, the knife held between finger and thumb, more gentle scrape than carve. She could not reconcile these tender gestures with his lean, intent body, his secretive eyes. He did not love the houses. They were matters of profit. The money-filled drawer made her uneasy and she dropped her eyes a fraction more quickly, now, and he noticed that she did so. I'm going to St. John on Friday, he had said. Wouldn't you like to come with me. It was almost a taunt. You *want* to come with me, don't you, was what he really said, like another voice whispering in her ear, telling her her own desires. He peeled her back, revealed her to herself. He looked up sideways and she thought that once again her thoughts were like a flung pebble, as when Matron had read her intention to flee.

Yet. *To go somewhere!*

"I would like to see St. John," she said. She scooped the pennied carrots in both hands and dropped them into a saucepan. "I'd work Sunday to make up."

"That's all right, Flora. For goodness' sakes."

Flora looked up to see that Josephine was suddenly on the point of tears. Her voice faltered, became breathless. "You work harder than all of us combined."

—

Flora sat with her nose to the window, the parcel of food on her lap.

"You ever been on a train?" he asked.

His hair, combed, bore the grooves and smell of pomade.

"I was on this train five years ago. The orphanage gave me a paper bag with a piece of bread and some cheese and a hardboiled egg. I had to wear a placard around my neck and people stared at me. Like as if I might steal from them. Like I were an urchin."

"Well, you were, weren't you. An urchin."

"I was not. I was an orphan. Like you."

Abruptly, he leaned across her to look out the window at the sight of a burning barn: flames bursting from a roof, running men, a rearing horse. The scene was snatched away, the snow-covered landscape resumed. He did not move back entirely. The side of his leg pressed against her. She inched sideways on the wooden seat, her shoulder cold against the glass, a draught chilling her neck.

You want to watch out for him.

He moved back to his side of the bench. He flipped his checking receipt over and over in his palm, staring straight ahead, mouth closed and tongue exploring his teeth. Flora was lulled by the regular, ratcheting movement, the floral carpet under her feet warmed by water pipes in the floorboards. Amid the close-set walls, the varnished wooden ceiling, the murmuring voices, she felt as if she were in a kind of church, a place where people were subdued by a power they could neither understand nor control. She gazed at a hat perched close before her, so close she could touch it, decorated with lacquered berries, feathers. The woman's neck; a shadow in its groove.

Her eyelids thickened and she felt herself on the point of sleep.

She felt his hand on the back of her head, pulling it down onto his shoulder. She sat up, not acknowledging that this had happened. Perhaps it had not. She pressed her forehead against the cold window to keep herself awake.

—

"Wouldn't you like to go to college, Flora?"

The narrow room smelled of beeswax, its ceiling decorated with scrolled friezes and medallions. Side windows faced the harbour, where blanketed horses lined the wharf, icy rigging drooped against a white sky.

"I'm learning to better my reading," Flora murmured. "So I can help."

Carrie sat straight-backed, alert, hands folded in her lap. On the desk beside her was a stack of books in Italian, German and French. Neat piles of paper, clipped together. She smiled at Flora's answer.

"That's wonderful to hear. You know, you can be anything you want."

Flora wondered whether Carrie remembered that she was speaking to a girl who had foraged in the frozen remnants of gardens and stolen milk from cows' udders.

"Look how many mills and factories there are here in St. John that employ women. Like Lucy. Soon, women are going to realize that they're working as hard as men, if not harder, and being paid far less."

Words came from her mouth in a sleek tumble, like polished stones. Flora held one hand against her cheek, feeling the need to brace herself against the outflow. She strove to understand their meaning—*socialism, political economy, pecuniary.*

"We have such stimulating meetings, Flora. I wish you could come. We talk about all the places women should be serving, and you know, when we imagine such a world, a world of equality between men and women, it is as if it has already happened, and were we to walk out into the city we would find women supervisors in women's prisons, serving as school trustees or on public health boards. In government."

She paused, her face rapt with the vision, and Flora, trying to think of a suitable response, found it hard to imagine Carrie the way Ellen had described her; *her that went around the world as a child and was almost killed by pirates.*

"Last night we agreed that popular government is founded on the principles of representation by population and taxation. Well, you know the women of New Brunswick form at least half of the population. Many of us already have the required property qualification. And the rest contribute to the public revenue in one way or another."

She took a long breath and sat back in her chair.

"We read a satire in the paper, written by a man. *Imagine a stout lady, Honorable Mrs. Jemima this or that, holding the office of the Provincial Secretary . . . Imagine the speaker addressed as 'Mrs. Speakeress'. . . .* Some of us said that we should fight back with our own ridicule of men. Others said we should maintain our dignity."

Flora could hear the quiet, absorbed chirpings of caged budgerigars and a clatter coming from the back of the house; a cook, she thought, in the kitchen—*where I should be*. She thought how childless women bore a slight wariness, as if they were in the midst of something which they had abandoned and expected to be asked about.

Carrie's eyes cleared of the things of which she had been speaking.

"Oh, Flora," she said. "I do apologize. I start on this topic and I am a runaway horse."

She rose, brisk. "Let's walk to the market. I told my cook I would buy some fresh halibut. And we can deliver that parcel to Lucy's boarding house. You can tell me about Josephine and Ellen and your boarders."

They lifted coats from the hall rack, worked buttons into holes.

Carrie opened the door and they stepped down onto the street. Flora heard the searing shriek of gulls, smelled salt on the winter air.

"And who is this man who makes miniature houses?"

—

On the train coming home, Flora struggled to stay awake. She had not slept the night before; the day spent in Carrie's energetic company, meeting women in the market and in the shops and on the streets, hearing their bold words, seeing their intelligent, forthright eyes shining beneath fur hats, had left her exhausted.

Flora is from England. She works with my cousin Josephine, they run a boarding house together. She's studying at home.

Carrie had prompted her to recite the names of her textbooks and to tell about "her" tenants; in response, the women had asked her if she had brothers or sisters, and so she had talked of her search for Enid. Encouragement, advice, kindness. *One of us. Come to the next march.* All day long, she felt as if she were a suffragist, a member of the sisterhood, not a servant but Carrie's friend. Now, in the train, she returned to herself in her brown wool coat and red scarf, a brand-new basket in her lap filled with gifts of cheese, butter, maple-cured bacon, pamphlets.

Mr. Tuck was watching her.

"Slept on the way down, now you're sleeping on the way back."

"Sorry. Did you have a nice day?"

"Nice enough. Got my stuff. Got some bits of carpets for you to cut up."

"*Me* to cut up?"

"You're my helper, aren't you?"

"Sometimes." She yawned. "When I have time. Which isn't much because I am busy taking care of the likes of you. Your sheets. Your dinners."

"You're a sassy one."

A chill in his tone, a warning. She wondered if he knew that she had crouched on the other side of the barn wall, watching him fondle his money. She wondered why he was no longer working at anything other than making the houses.

"That's why I like you," he added. His eyes slipped away from her, rested on a strand of blonde hair lying against the wool coat. His finger touched the hair, stroked it, moved it gently from side to side.

"Take your hand off me," she whispered.

He picked the lock of hair up between finger and thumb, rolled it thoughtfully, set it behind her shoulder.

"I wouldn't hurt you," he murmured. A question. *Would I?*

She snatched up the basket, held it like a shield. "Why would you even say such a thing?"

"It's what you were thinking. *He's dangerous.*"

Her heart began to hammer.

"And you like that about me," he added.

The white flash of teeth.

Behind them, a man snored. Oil lamps flared and guttered, their reflections bent up against the black windows. She stared straight ahead, clutching the basket, thinking of the long walk through the winter's night from the train station to the house, and how Jasper Tuck was meant to protect her from anything untoward—a rabid dog, a drunken man.

—

Josephine was visiting the Fairweathers for the evening, since Permelia's brother and family were visiting from Boston. The son, an accomplished pianist, had brought a book of songs. The parlour was filled with women—Josephine, Permelia and her four daughters, the sister-in-law with her two daughters—and an excess of ornament, the women's dresses with shawls and lace-edged ruffles, the room's fringed table-cloths, peacock feathers, stuffed quail in a glass case. The daughters sang duets and trios; the young man urged his father to join them.

"We need a tenor. Come on, Father."

Permelia's brother waved away the suggestion. He leaned forward and engaged Harland, shifting his eyes only to his son as the story progressed. The girls clustered around the piano, held in check.

"One minute I look out the window and see a moose. Belly deep in snow, staring at the train. Then my eyes fall on a headline—*Captain of German ship Goes Insane at Sea, Jumps Overboard*. He had an obstruction of the bowel, apparently. Made insane by the pain. They gave him laudanum and he seemed to recover but then he decides that various members of the crew desire to shoot him and begins to fire at random. Subsided after assurances to the contrary. Smoke was smelled, it seems he set his cabin afire. Jumped overboard."

His eyes widened, unfocused. He narrowed them, satisfied, lifting a glass of port.

"No, darling. You couldn't possibly have read that." His wife laughed. "Impossible."

"What would you know? Do I ever see you reading a newspaper? No, you only ever study your Godey's Lady's Book." He turned to Harland. "And they talk of wanting the vote."

Josephine felt a headache begin, a slender fracture zig-zagging its way from temple to eye. At the far end of the parlour, tables were set for whist, but after each song the young man swept the page over and the girls remained standing, flushed, and sang again.

Harland spoke into Permelia's ear, then beckoned to Josephine. She followed him down a hallway into his weather station. The long room was cool, smelled of geraniums and leather.

"I told Permelia I had an important message to give you regarding Flora. I mentioned, also, that you seemed to need fresh air."

"I do have a slight headache. I am not accustomed to wine." She felt the fatigue of being a widow in the midst of other women and their families. The effort of repelling regret.

"I never touch it, as you know. Permelia's brother was unaware of her temperance pledge. We said nothing, not to offend. They arrived with lavish gifts."

He struck a match, held it to the wick of a kerosene lamp. She saw a table laid with notebooks, pencils, graph paper.

"My weather notes."

She saw how he marked the passage of his life, in solitude, and had become accustomed to it.

"I received a letter from my acquaintance in Halifax. She knew nothing of Enid, but has discovered the person who delivered her to the train station. A Reverend Snelcroft. I've written to him."

Her eyes went to his fingers spread on the letter. She considered what would happen if she should lay her hand over his. She wanted, only, to be held in a man's arms. To lay her head against a man's chest. To be easily, thoughtlessly, *part*. Not apart.

"You and I both seek forgiveness, Josephine. In my case, it is necessary. But you have no cause for guilt. It is I who asked you to purchase Flora. And you know that you did not truly *buy* her."

"I take money from the government. But I give it to her."

"Well, there. You see."

She had not thought she was seeking forgiveness and saw no way forward in the conversation, since it seemed to be not about Flora but about themselves.

Wet snow adhered to the windows and slid down the glass, dissolving.
Undone, she thought.

I am undone by a man's kindness.

He set a glass paperweight onto the letter. A posy of glass cane
forget-me-knots floated in its interior.

"We are on the hunt, now. We will find this lost child." He looked
at her but she could detect only concern.

"I do hope so," she said, taking a step back from the table, seeing his
anxiety to return to his duties as host.

He extinguished the lamp's flame.

TWELVE

Soft as Flannel

~

March 10, 1889
Halifax, Nova Scotia

Dear Mr. Fairweather,

*I am in receipt of your letter concerning one of Miss Maria Rye's
girls. I did indeed receive three girls into my home and assisted with
their placement with farmers or families that had requested them.
I am happy to report that one of them was Enid Salford. She was
placed with a farmer on the Northumberland Shore, in a place called
Black Creek. I delivered her to the train but did not accompany her
to her final destination. I trust that she was received as arranged
by mail with a Mr. Albert Mallory. I have not heard from Enid
although I have sent several letters, as I promised Miss Rye I would.
It is too great a distance for me to travel in order to make an inspection, and I am not myself a young person nor am I in good health.
I would be grateful if you would undertake this yourself if possible,
although I see that you are in New Brunswick and realize that it*

will be a considerable journey. There is no financial compensation available, of course. We do these things out of the goodness of our hearts to raise these English children from the gutters in which they were found. I am sure you understand and feel the same.

I am,
Yours truly,
Reverend Charles Snelcroft

Harland stood by the window, holding the reverend's letter to the light. Permelia, in the kitchen, was engaged in a shouting match with the cook.

"Let me go, then. I'll go back to me own people."

There had been a burned crust on the apple pie. He was certain that Permelia raised her voice for his benefit, since the stove was, in fact, in need of replacement. She had brought him an advertisement for a nickel-plated range, pointing out the capacity of its water reservoir, the size of its oven, its nickelled towel rod and teapot stand, its *handsome skirting*.

Against the sky, the flag's snap or sag revealed the wind. Just now, it hung limp, as if spent.

Variation within a pattern, he thought, looking at his notebooks, yearning to sit at them for an entire day, comparing temperatures, humidity, pressures and wind speeds for all his recorded Marches. He would comfort himself with the earth's renewal, how its season of torment and persecution faded in fits and starts, how it did not cease its stubborn efforts.

He would take the letter with him to the store; from the quiet of his office, he would write to Josephine. *Please tell Flora* . . . He imagined travelling to Nova Scotia with Josephine and Flora. Dismissed the idea, as if should it linger in his mind Permelia would prise it out like a spider in a cupboard.

—

Sailor lay at Josephine's feet, snuffling for fleas. The piano had been shifted to provide a bulwark, giving her privacy in the turret room, although on this Friday morning the house was empty save for Ellen, in the kitchen, and Flora, who sat facing her. Pots of geraniums—coral pink, red, white—bloomed in the deep windowsills.

"You know, Flora, I can't help but think that it is bad for us to wear these corsets," Josephine said. She sighed and then coughed. Sailor looked up, sharply, and she dropped a hand to stroke his head. "They make *actual dents* in my flesh. And I can't breathe, you know. I really can't. I've read that the organs are displaced and that the muscles of our backs become flaccid."

Flora, sitting on a satin-cushioned chair, felt incomplete without handwork and was unaccountably nervous, not knowing why she had been summoned and sensing, in Josephine, some unwarranted mood. Josephine would never invite Ellen to visit her in the parlour—like a friend, come for a visit.

"Carrie doesn't wear one," Flora murmured, embarrassed by the subject yet emboldened by the currency that intimacy offered. "She told me so. She said it is a thing that men want us to do so that we can be beautiful objects, like a horse or a fancy house."

"She might be right," Josephine said, pulling back her shoulders.

They sat listening to the patter of rain on the window. Flora gazed up at the trees, indistinct against the sky, like charcoal sketches. The smell of smoke from the kitchen stove sharpened the room's book-ish odours.

"This room is so special," Josephine said. Sailor raised an eyebrow.

"Why is it special?" Flora asked. She folded her hands; unclasped them, pressed palm to palm; slid her fingers into a fist.

"Simeon asked me what I wanted in a house. Tell me *one* thing, he said. One thing I had always dreamed of. Would it be a widow's walk, he asked? So I could stand in all weathers and watch for his return? Would it be a gazebo in the garden? Or a library of my own? I said

I would like a place of windows, round, with cushioned seats and stained glass and deep sills for ferns and flowers. So that I could have summer in winter. We sketched it together, drawing after drawing, until we created a room that both of us loved. He added the pointed roof, like a dwarf's cap from a fairy tale. I designed the stained glass. Calla lilies."

She leaned forward to trace one with a fingertip.

"I couldn't sell this house—how . . . how could I?"

Tears welled in her eyes.

"You know, Flora, I thought that when I arrived on Ocracoke Island I would find that there had been a misidentification. That they'd given me some other man's possessions. I have a dream that comes night after night. A man appears at the far end of a beach, so far away that he is but a black speck, and he walks towards me, and suddenly I see that it is Simeon. He begins to run and I, too, run. The sand drags at my feet, and I stumble, panting, calling his name, holding my arms out. For months, I have dreamed this same dream."

"I have a dream just like that," Flora said. "I dream that I see Enid on a road. At first, I can't tell if it's her or not. Then I begin to run. I always wake up too soon."

Josephine lifted her finger from the stained glass, slightly bewildered, and Flora realized that she had awakened to the fact that she spoke not to a friend of her own status, but with a workhouse girl, who, once, might have been called a guttersnipe. She turned to the table and lifted a letter, worked spectacles onto her nose.

"Mr. Fairweather has found someone who knows where Enid was placed."

Flora's hands flew up; she slid to the edge of her chair.

"Enid? *Enid*, my sister Enid?"

Josephine put the letter down, pulled off her spectacles. "Oh, Flora. I'm so sorry. I read it just like an ordinary thing, didn't I? She was placed with . . . let me see . . . a Mr. Mallory. Mr. Albert Mallory, on a farm in Black Creek. On the Northumberland Shore of Nova Scotia."

Sailor opened his mouth in a sudden pant. He looked back and forth between them, his eyes anxious.

Flora flushed with a complexity of feelings she could not control or disentangle, stunned that Josephine could have held this news inside of her while speaking of stained glass and corsets. She could not speak.

Sailor scrambled to a sitting position but did not wag his tail. Josephine looked at Flora, waiting for her to react, and when she continued to stare, silent, reached down and stroked the dog.

"Yes," she said. "It's extraordinary, but it affirms that that is where she is. We can look on a map. You can try sending her a letter, although . . ." She picked up the letter again. ". . . this Reverend Snelcroft says he sent letters and didn't hear back."

"Oh, but Enid would have written." Flora felt a visceral power—in her jaw, in her voice—as she spoke in defence of a sister. A family member. Here, in Canada. She felt taller, her eyes saw more clearly. "She's not well lettered but she would have written back. I know she would've. Maybe she's not . . . maybe there's been a mistake. Maybe it's not her but some other girl."

"No, no. Don't worry. He says right here, see?" She handed Flora the letter, pointing at the sentence.

I am happy to report that one of them was Enid Salford.

Flora went back to the beginning and read to the end . . . *raise these English children from the gutters in which they were found . . .*

She stared at the letter. The words were true, she was now convinced; but she felt a great mistrust of the people who had been put in charge of her little sister and wondered at the reasons for her silence.

"Why hasn't she written? It must be the people she is with won't let her. Or don't mail her letters. Like what happened to me. Or don't want her to be found."

Her voice raised. Hard. Wild.

Josephine took off her reading glasses and set them on the table. She contemplated the stained glass, chin in hand.

"Mr. Fairweather said he would try to send for Enid."

"You can't *send* for someone you don't hear from. This Mr. Mallory doesn't even write back. We can't just . . . just . . . *send letters*."

Josephine turned on her chair. Flora had slid to the edge of her chair, holding the letter with both hands. She stared at Josephine, furious. Accusing.

"Someone needs to *go*," Flora said. "Someone needs to *go to Nova Scotia*. Find her and bring her back."

"We will write . . ."

"No. No!"

"Flora, I—"

"It's not enough. She could be in danger." Her voice trembled, broke.

Sailor scrambled to his feet and nosed Flora's skirt. Josephine, too, laid a hand on Flora's skirt. Patted her knee.

"I will talk to Mr. Fairweather again, Flora. I'll tell him that someone should go over there."

Flora stroked the dog's silky black hair. Through tears, she saw Sailor's eyes soften, relax.

She could not speak.

"Maybe Mr. Fairweather himself will go," Josephine said. "I will ask him, Flora. I promise you. I will ask him to go fetch her back."

—

On the following afternoon, Jasper Tuck took Flora into his confidence.

"I have a plan."

Flora cut a piece of carpet into small squares, leaning forward in a wicker chair, a basket of samples at her side. Her scissors chewed through the carpet with a final effort. March wind rattled the window in its frame, rampaged through the treetops with a sound like surf. Last summer, she and Maud had sat on these same wicker chairs, set around a wicker table on the veranda—drinking lemonade, playing checkers—and heard a frantic peeping. They climbed onto the roof and inched on their bellies to peer into a swallows' nest. The babies clustered like a handful of finely feathered bones, beaks gaping. She would show all these things to Enid. She would show her a clutch of chicks, in the henhouse. They would stand in the summer sunshine. Enid would hold a bucket, scattering corn. Her hair—dark, now, or blonde? Short or long enough to braid?

"You figure in it," he added. He lifted a compass, punched it into a sheet of paper with a crispy *pop*. He swung the pencil, little finger lifted.

He's a strange one.

She set the small square on her knee, smoothed it. Her job, now, was to stitch over the cut edge and attach a knotted border.

"I'm going to make that house down the street. Hilltop, I hear tell it's called."

Of course, Flora thought, with a sudden thrill. Pleasant Valley's most elaborate house. Where the MacVey sisters lived, purportedly holding seances and musical evenings, hosting visiting dignitaries. She always paused to gaze at the terraced lawns and the rose gardens.

"First . . ."

He did not finish the sentence, sliding his pencil along a protractor.

"First, we need to talk about that money."

"What money?"

"Don't be smart with me. You know what money."

"I don't know what you're taking about." A flush started in her neck, creeping upwards in revelatory petals.

He exploded from his chair. He seized her arms, half lifting her from her seat, squeezing, his breath sour in her face.

She dropped the scissors, the little carpet. "Let me g—"

"You shut your mouth. I heard you on the other side there. Watching me. Now you listen to me. I been thinking what to do about you. That's my life savings and it's my business and nobody else's. I don't want one word spoken about my money. Not one word. If you say one word about that money to any of them," he nodded at the house, "I will know." He lowered his voice. "I'll see it in their eyes just like I seen it in yours. People look different at a man with money."

"I won't say anything. Why would I? Let me go."

He released her arms. She fell back in the chair.

"You promise?"

She rubbed her arms. "Promise."

"Say 'I promise I won't say anything about your money.'"

"I promise I won't say anything about your money." She stared at him, suddenly emboldened by curiosity. "Mr. Tuck, it's only money. Why do I care? Most men have money, I suppose. I don't know why you don't put it in the bank, though. What if there was a fire?"

He kicked his chair back to its place in front of the table. He sat, staring coldly at the drawing he had just made. He placed his palm on the paper, gathered it by slow increments with the tips of his fingers, knuckles whitening as he worked it into a ball. He slid a fresh sheet of paper towards himself. She felt the prickling of sweat beneath her arms.

"I got to go," she said, winding the excess thread back onto the spool. "I got to clean the upstairs."

"My plan," he said, beginning again with the compass, "is for you to go to Hilltop. Talk to them ladies. In your posh accent."

"It's not posh."

"They will not look at the likes of me coming up their path, but if we dress you up in some fancy clothes, they'll open the door to you."

"And then what?"

"Then you tell them all about the houses I make and why they should buy my miniature of Hilltop. You'll have samples of them little carpets, curtains, a bed, say, complete with quilt and pillows. All the fixings. Everything but the people. I suppose I could make people if they wanted. Like you suggested."

"I don't have time. I got too much spring cleaning. I'm fixing on getting another cow. There's the garden. And could be I go to Nova Scotia."

"Yuh. Your sister. You and Enid going to want to set up housekeeping."

He moved his chair back, reached down and pulled open the drawer. She averted her eyes. It seemed an intimacy, his savings. The flush had not entirely subsided from her face.

"Look up, Missy Flora."

He was holding a handful of bills. He leaned forward and laid them on her table.

"Count them. That's a start. Once we start selling houses there will be lots more. I'll be employing other girls. To sew all them little things. Your sister, I'll wager she's a hand with the needle. Once we get things going, I'll set up a big workshop. Not here. Down in the town. There's your job for life. You'll go to them fancy houses and show off the merchandise. You'll manage the girls; I'll manage my men."

She touched the money with one finger.

"Count it," he said. "It's yours if you say 'Yes, Mr. Tuck, I'll go up to them ladies at Hilltop.'"

The bills were soft as flannel, as if they had been held, caressed, smoothed, passed from hand to hand. Their creases were like the wrinkles in weathered skin.

"I'll have to tell Mrs. Galloway that I'm getting paid for my work on your houses. Otherwise she won't like me spending so much time out here."

"You can tell her. Just don't say how much."

She should ask him what he would pay her beyond the bribe, but did not, stunned by more money than she had ever seen before, a wild prelude to her changing fortune. She murmured, yes, yes, she would do it, and looked up, glimpsing how his small, square teeth had been revealed but quickly covered, his face assuming its usual cold watchfulness.

—

Maud sat on a chair in the hall, reading a letter. Flora, smelling of wood shavings, hair blown and cheeks reddened, sat beside her, unlacing her boots. The ticking of the parlour clock was like a shore against which the moan and whistle of the wind dashed, was rebuffed.

"George," Maud said, violently clutching the letter to her breast and closing her eyes. "Oh!"

"What?" Flora said. Maud amused her sometimes. She was so often outraged on behalf of someone else, often disproportionately.

Maud's voice dropped to a loud whisper. "He thinks he's looking out for Mother. Truly, Flora. It makes me wonder if he can *see* himself. He is treating Mother like a child."

Flora wrenched off the boot. It was too small and she massaged her toes. "How?"

"He is still trying to get Lucy and me to see that as soon as we turn twenty-one we should sell the house."

"Well. That's a long way away."

"Yes, but you see, he wants me to start *dropping hints*. Make Mother see that she would be better off in a smaller house. Even get her to consider remarrying. He says to me in this letter that he is strictly . . . wait, I will read it to you. *Believe me, Maud, when I say that I look at this in a strictly utilitarian fashion. We would incur a fair amount of money from the sale of the house. If Mother relinquished her dower interest, she would be given her share. We would all be able to get ahead with our lives.* Then he even describes the little house Mother could buy. Apparently, he has spotted just the place. On Queen Street."

Flora noticed the banging of pot lids in the kitchen. She was late, and Ellen was annoyed. Still, she sat with her foot in her lap, her skirt hitched. Indecorous, but it was only two girls, in the cold hall, on a March afternoon.

"We have the power to force the sale, George says. You know, Flora, I truly believe he is thinking only of himself, even though he pretends to be thinking of Lucy and me and of Mother. I believe he's begun to think of this house as his. I believe he's begun to think of himself as head of the family."

Flora said nothing. Josephine, living in a small house. With no need of servants. Pictured herself and Enid, standing on a railroad platform, heading for a destination she could not imagine.

"*I* think of this house as Mother and Father's house," Maud continued, not noticing Flora's sudden stillness. "The house they built with dreams of a long, happy life. Even after we children were grown and gone, they saw themselves living here together."

Flora pictured her own parents. The wretched straw-thatched cottage. Yet they had made dolls for their little girls. They may have bolstered one another's courage with the same kind of dream.

She put her hand on Maud's, knew not to speak.

"I *won't* do it," Maud whispered. She stuffed the letter back into the envelope without properly folding it. "I will resist his idiotic plan. Lucy and I will stand up to him."

—

The Intercolonial Hotel rose, three storeys high, against the blue sky. Flora, gazing up, wondered who might be inhabiting its rooms. She stood in a crowd of women, next to Josephine and Carrie.

Carrie had given a speech to the WCTU in Permelia's parlour, on the subject of the suffrage petition. Afterwards, the women had felt the need to mount a protest. Impulsively, they had swept down Main Street, their heels clicking on the wooden sidewalk—twenty women carrying parasols, white ribbons pinned to white dresses, bright under the early spring sky; their reflections flickered in the window of McAllister's Dry Goods, crossed its display of chinaware—berry sets, dessert bowls. They flickered, too, across the grocery store window, making a watery, layered painting: hatted, veiled women overlying rounds of cheese, a display of raisins and nuts, strings of sausages, brooms with green and blue handles.

As they had crossed the railway tracks, nearing the hotel, Flora had been pricked by memory of her arrival in Pleasant Valley. The track ran due west, merging to a single, silver glint; picking up her feet to step over the steel rails, she felt the culpability of not having told Josephine that Mr. Tuck had offered to pay her for her work, nor that he wished her to visit the sisters at Hilltop. She polished the intention to tell, like something fragile that must be perfect when eventually offered. She prepared her words, trying to see the situation from all angles.

She needed to save money, especially now that Enid had been found. She would need real work once she and Enid set up housekeeping. Jasper Tuck's little houses were exquisite and she was not ashamed to endorse them. Yet she sensed that she was taking a backwards step, one which was dangerous and predicated on fear; and like so much else in her life, a thing about which she had no choice.

The talk increased as they gathered in front of the Sample Room, a small pub attached to the hotel with one large window whitened by drawn curtains, like a blind eye. Around Flora, excited voices gained strength.

". . . things that Premier Blair says about us, I become angrier . . ."

"They think we don't want to vote."

". . . said no privilege has ever been denied us."

"It shouldn't be a privilege. It's our right."

Flora noticed that Josephine was listening, intently, turning to gaze at whichever woman was shouting the loudest.

Two men wearing suspenders, coats slung over their arms, approached the pub, intending to go in. They stopped, staring at the women, muttered to one another. They continued on down the street, glancing back.

Mrs. Humbolt, the president of the Women's Christian Temperance Union local branch, made her way to the front of the crowd.

"Christ's kingdom is based on the principles of human equality and brotherhood," she called out to the women. "*Human* equality means the equality of men and women. Since men appoint us as the repositories of religious and moral virtue, we must use our influence to perfect society. Now, we know that it is women and children who suffer from the evils of drink. We seek a *modest and pure world*. As the Greek writer Xenophon said, *moderation in all . . .* "

The upstairs window opened. A man thrust his head out.

"Ladies, I am going to ask you to leave my premises. You are keeping the gentlemen from my door."

A chorus of responses rose.

". . . send them home to us drunk . . ."

". . . our sidewalk as much as . . ."

". . . *things healthful; total abstinence from all things* . . ."

Mrs. Humbolt finished her speech and the women bent their heads in silent prayer. Some held prayer books. Pages rippled in the breeze. Approaching men veered, crossed the street, gathered to stare.

"Now," Carrie remarked, once the bowed heads raised, "we will take the suffrage petition from door to door."

A bucket, out the window over their heads. Icy water unfurled, a fringed wave, billowing, widening, the spume separating into silver bullets. Outraged screams. Another bucket followed, another deluge.

"And don't come back!"

Flora received the full contents on top of her head, water running down her neck, soaking her cape as she ran forward to salvage a prayer book, lying upside down on the wooden walk.

THIRTEEN

Green Rabbits

~

FLORA SHUFFLED SPRING DIRT from her boots on a pattern of green rabbits. She waited on the mat, just inside the door. The Hilltop house smelled of beeswax, oranges and roast beef. A piano went abruptly silent.

A tall, frail woman drifted down the stairs. Another, older and full-bodied, came along the hallway. Both carried the air of having left more absorbing tasks, yet their faces opened on seeing Flora and she realized that her hair, loosened and wisped around her exertion-flushed face, would be holding the sunlight; and saw an expression of delight and wonder creep over the women's faces.

"My name is Flora Salford. I work for Mrs. Galloway. She has a boarder who makes little houses. He asked . . ."

Her voice trailed off. She gestured behind her towards a miniature house in a child's wagon, parked on the stone path.

"Oh, *my*, Rosamund," the thin sister exclaimed, looking past Flora. "Isn't that something!"

They followed her down the steps to the walkway. The morning was warm, an earthy scent rising from soil soaked by night rain. The thin sister gripped her hands and pressed them to her breastbone. Flora knelt.

"See how he carves the shingles." She pointed at the pieces of cedar, shaped like fish scales or arrowheads.

The sisters walked around the house, tapping at the glass windows, stroking the frail railings. Flora summoned a tone of proprietary pride.

"These are *spindled* porch railings. And see how the trim is painted a different colour."

Flora tipped back the hinged roof.

"Oh, how *clever!*"

One by one, she extracted a four-poster bed covered with a quilt, a cast-iron stove and a tiny Persian rug. She set them in a row on the path. "He could provide doll's house people, if you want."

She paused.

"I could tell you the price."

Rosamund, the heavier and evidently elder sister, made a hasty, dismissive motion with the tips of her fingers.

"What do you think, Grace?"

Grace stood wide-eyed. "Oh, my, Rosamund. Oh, yes. Yes, we must have one."

—

Through a daze of fatigue, Flora chewed toast. The kitchen window was propped open and she could hear the liquid burble of what she had learned were the first birds to return to the north country, red-winged blackbirds. Sun loomed behind a thin veil of clouds, although snowflakes fell like remnants of plenty.

Ellen was avidly following another murder trial in the *Daily Telegraph*, reading bits out loud, ruminating about the details as she stirred puddings or kneaded bread; but it was not as satisfying as the axe murder. A man had sent poisoned chocolates to prominent St. John businessmen, including a clergyman whose wife had opened the package, eaten the candy, and died.

"Serves her right," Ellen said. She sat at the table, leaning on her elbows, the newspaper stained with blueberry preserves. "Greedy thing."

"*Chocolate*, Ellen."

Ellen half closed her eyes, shrugging, absorbed in the paper. She cut no slack for women she considered pampered or spoiled.

Still no letter arrived from Nova Scotia. With difficulty, Flora had located Black Creek on a map. Halifax, Pictou and New Glasgow were large dots along the road's twisting thread, their names printed in bold, black ink, but *Black Creek* was printed in pale, spidery font, like flakes of pepper. Mr. Fairweather would need to take several trains, spend a night, or even two nights, then hire a carriage. No date had been set for his journey since Permelia forestalled it, listing the state of the roads—*pure gumbo at this time of year*—and when that danger had passed, making fresh excuses: their daughters' dances, plays, recitals, her own health, Harland's obligations.

At the root of it, Flora thought, buttering another piece of toast, was Permelia's sense that the journey was another one of Harland's ridiculous notions, the way he had quit his position of Overseer *for the sake of some pauper children*. Increasingly, an idea nudged Flora like a cold snout—she must undertake the search on her own. She pondered, spreading blueberry jam on her toast: she could slip away without telling anyone, leaving a note; better yet, confide in Josephine, seek advice and help—but there was so much work on these lengthening spring days that she was exhausted by nighttime and had to force herself to sit down with her books and had neither time nor energy to plan such an overwhelming project.

"Listen to them blackbirds," Flora murmured, sending her toast down with a swallow of tea. "*Those* blackbirds, I mean."

"Now the axe murder," Ellen continued, as if she had not heard. "That was a thing to read, now. Did the accused leave the gate open or shut. Oh, first he said one thing and then another. First he says when he left the house his clothes were hanging on a hook. Then someone else says they saw the clothes on the floor. Every single thing on her dresser, I can see it all. A reel of white cotton thread, a fine comb . . . Even the print over the bed, St. Patrick in the robes of a bishop. Oh, I can see it all. And the blood. *Nearly a large pailful,* do you remember? Mr. Dougan loved that part the reporter wrote, something about Shakespeare, oh, you know, like how he must have seen some such tragedy to have had Lady Macbeth say her piece: *Who would have thought the old man to have had so much blood in him?*"

Flora watched her, both hands on her teacup. Ellen missed not only the daily drama of the axe murder, but Mr. Dougan. The story had bonded them in anticipation, like one of Charles Dickens's serials.

Ellen sat back and swept closed the newspaper. She ran her hand along the fold, creasing it; smoothed the pages, like a pillow, with a brisk stroke. Straightening, hand to back, she set the newspaper on the table beside Josephine's chair.

"And what are you about today?" she asked Flora. Sharp, with a worrisome cognizance.

Everyone, Josephine, Maud, the boarders, knew that Mr. Tuck was building a replication of Hilltop. No one could quite believe that he would be up to the task and yet, intrigued, they had clamoured to see his drawings, which he spread out on the parlour floor. He held a new status in the household, as if, consorting with the sisters, he was dusted like a bee with the pollen of superiority. Flora kept the money Mr. Tuck paid her in a sock, beneath a loose floorboard in her bedroom. He had forbidden her to deposit it in the bank. After every payment, she lifted the board, slid coins or notes into the sock, hefted it in her hand, pushed it back into the dusty darkness.

Flora sipped her tea. She was determined that one day she and Enid would no longer work in someone else's house but would have one of their own, with white-painted shingles, a yard with raspberry canes and a vegetable garden. A chicken house would be concealed by red rambling roses, like the ones hiding Hilltop's laundry yard. Enid would work in the office of the boot and shoe factory; she herself would be in charge of the women working at Mr. Tuck's miniature house factory. She pictured a summer's afternoon, Enid coming up the path to their house, chin raised, shoulders back, accustomed to the need for courage.

"Josephine was blessed the day the likes of you walked in her door."
Startled, Flora looked up. Ellen was looking at her, fondly.

"It was me was blessed. What if that man at the auction had got me? He was enormous. He had a big, nasty fat face. Mr. Fairweather slammed down his gavel before the bidding had ended."

"Disgusting, now. That you should even have such things in your brain. That our Flora should have sat there in front of all them men." Ellen dug in the flour crock with a scoop. It made a dry scrape. "You working on that little house today?"

"Yes, but I will do all my other things, too, Ellen. You know I will."

Flora carried the cup and saucer to the sink, rinsed them in a trickle of cold water. Neither spoke of what was most on their minds, that Josephine had come down early this morning, gotten her cup of tea and explained that she was going back to bed, since she had lain awake most of the night. Such occurrences happened less frequently, although pain was visible in the shape of her mouth and the uncertainty of her steps as she drifted about the house adorned in black. She had only one dress in spring weight, which grew dirty, grease-spattered, speckled by an unfortunate spray of ink. The first thing that seem to have brightened her, it seemed to Ellen, Maud and Flora, who discussed her in whispers, was the suffrage petition. For this, her suffering quickened, was of use, its darkness like a timber beneath a bridge. Mr. Fairweather's efforts to find Flora's sister, too, brought her back to her old self—capable, steady. But yesterday, she had expected a visit from George. She had invited him to tea, and Ellen had made a sponge cake, and George had phoned, just as they were setting out the tray, to say he could not come. He was *too busy at the office*. She had hung up the telephone and sat by the instrument for a long time, while Ellen and Flora, in the kitchen, paused. Hands hovering, the cake uncut, a napkin half-folded. Josephine had been disproportionately devastated. She had gone upstairs for a nap, instead.

"There was a letter from Carrie this morning," Ellen remarked, measuring cinnamon.

"Thank goodness. I'll see that she gets it as soon as she's up. Well, I'm off to do the rooms," Flora said, tucking pins more firmly into her hair. "Oh, I *will* be glad when Maud is done school for the summer. Four hands are so much better than two."

Ellen tipped the cinnamon into a bowl of flour, her expression wry.

"Maud will be married as soon as can be. Then, Flora, you'll be thanking the Lord for your sister."

—

After dusting the boarder's bedrooms, smoothing their coverlets, sweeping their floors, Flora ran downstairs, tearing off her apron, stopping in the kitchen to pick up a bag of dried peas.

My garden!

The new cow stood in the pasture, sides heaving as she stretched her neck in shuddering moos. Flora ducked under the fence, put her arms around the cow's neck, stroked the sleek hide.

"Shush, shush, it's all right. You'll have another calf."

She left the cow and went to the garden. Sun broke through the clouds; snowmelt sharpened the soil's scent. *People actually do kind things, right out of the blue.* Last week, a farmer arrived with horse and plough and turned the soil. He returned the following day with a harrow and chopped the rolled slabs into friable earth. Then he brought a wagonload of seasoned manure. Ellen baked him two rhubarb pies. Flora gave him a dozen eggs and a pair of socks. He turned red, protested. Said he took them only for his wife. *Save her some knitting*—tucking the socks into his coat.

Flora set sticks at either end of the plot, a string stretched between them. She raked a furrow, knelt and worked her way along the row on her knees, dropping last summer's pale, wrinkled peas.

Wind lifted a new bang from her forehead, cut by Maud. The bang curled.

Beautiful, beautiful, beautiful.

The Hilltop sisters used the word often, referring to her. She had become a go-between, hurrying back and forth to Hilltop with

Mr. Tuck's drawings, upon which they pencilled changes. They insisted she have a cup of tea, gazed at her as she drank it. *Oh, my dear, but do you know your own beauty?* They murmured about it to one another, discussing the fashions she could wear. Once, they placed a feathered hat on her head and bid her look into the mirror. It was play to them, Flora saw. They assumed an equivalency between beauty and happiness. In her bedroom was a mirror on a stand, two little drawers for hairpins. Arms up, sweeping her hair into a chignon, she saw not a beautiful face but the expression in her eyes—a dark, puzzled yearning.

—

"I had a lot to do today," she apologized, slipping into Mr. Tuck's workshop. Dusty windows hazed the light, muted the blackbirds' joyful burble.

"I seen you running back and forth, in and out," he remarked. He dipped a brush into a can of glue.

"You want me to work on these shingles?"

He pursed his lips, nodded very slightly, drawing the bead of glue.

He had made a cardboard template. Diamonds, today. She laid the pattern over paper-thin cedar and picked up a knife. She set her feet on the chair's rungs, leaned forward, concentrating. It did not, in fact, seem like work. There were parts of the house that she longed to be allowed to assemble. Setting the completed glass windows into their frames. Gluing batting onto the bed frames to make the quilts appear mounded.

"They're nice," she remarked. "The sisters. I was so scared to go there but I don't mind, now."

"Give you biscuits, do they?"

She flushed.

"I'm not a dog, Mr. Tuck."

"Just teasing. Never say the right thing, do I. Why I never married." He spoke without expression, as if he were reading lines in a play. He pinched his brush between finger and thumb, dipping it daintily into the glue can: he was surrounded by all things miniature—fine-tipped paint brushes, arranged by size; a small mitre box with a sharp-bladed saw; a rack of chisels; boxes filled with copper brads.

The sisters had paid a substantial advance.

"How long will it take, do you think?" she asked.

"Four months, maybe. Five."

Enid would be here for its completion. Enid could help sew the quilts. She could go with Flora and Mr. Tuck to present the finished house to the sisters.

Mr. Tuck put down his brush, wiped his hands on a rag and walked to the window. He made a clearing in the dust and stood looking out, his forehead pressed to the glass.

"Racket," he remarked. "Them birds."

Those birds, she thought, but said nothing. Mr. Tuck was not a person with whom you became more familiar the longer you knew him, but rather less so. She could not reconcile all the parts of his personality; fussy, tough. Crooning teases, then hands grinding her shoulders. He was like a dog into whose eyes you could not gaze for fear of a sudden bite. And yet, he'd rescued the other boarders, lost in the storm. He kept his room immaculate. He paid his bills. Perhaps it was because he was alone in a place where every person had parents, grandparents, aunts, uncles, and cousins. A place where people's minds were dense and rich with memories whose recounting formed a language of its own—sentences that need not be completed; names, words or remarks that evoked laughter or the shadow of remembered grief. A place where, as a single man, he should be a member of something—church, civic group, club, skating team, cornet band—and was not. Perhaps, she reassured herself, it was only his solitude, like her own, that she pitied. And feared.

PART III

June 1889 – August 1889

FOURTEEN

Turrets and Gables

~

JASPER TUCK WORKED LONG into the evenings, a lingering twilight reflected in the workshop window until almost ten. It was June, and the miniature house was framed, sided and roofed. He was making the intricate turrets and gables.

Flora sat at the kitchen table. She was polishing silverware that she'd soaked in a solution of salt and baking soda, then washed in warm, soapy water. In the half-dark, a sugar bowl shone as she rubbed it with a piece of cotton. She was working late to make up for the time she'd given Mr. Tuck during the afternoon. She felt a gathering frustration, a longing to be preparing for Enid.

The next day, as she worked for Mr. Tuck, he noticed a slip of her knife.

"You got to take your time," he said. "I ain't got wood to spare."

She hunched over her table, folding her lips between her teeth, slicing cedar into fine strips.

"Sorry."

Sighing, stretching, she looked out the window. Fat raindrops were battering the lush summer leaves. She watched with a flicker of envy as Maud let herself out the back door, raised an umbrella, and set off down the lane with a basket over her arm.

Making windows, cutting strips of wood, laying down glue with a toothpick, teasing the squares of glass into place. Her fingers, though much smaller than Mr. Tuck's, were less dextrous. She could not draw the glue in as fine a stripe. Her knife, held less firmly, was too easily misdirected by twisted grain.

He ran a metal file along a board's edge with short, practised strokes.

"You hear anything about your sister?"

"Nothing more. We know where she is but no one answers our letters. Mr. Fairweather must find a time to go get her. Or maybe search for her."

He hung the file, cleared the dust from his work table with a piece of flannel. She noticed that he eradicated every trace of creation, just as he made the miniature house to be so perfect as to bear no mark of its maker.

"I got something for you," he said. "Not *for* you, exactly." He rose from his workbench.

She only half heard what Mr. Tuck said. She sat back, sighing, hunching her head into her shoulders, drawing her shoulder blades together. Nubs for sprouting wings, her mother had said. *One day you will have angel wings*. After their mother died, Flora had told Enid that their mother had grown wings. *White, like our chickens, but much bigger.*

"Did you have a little brother or sister?"

She could not contain the question. She would have asked it of whoever was in her presence at that moment.

He paused and studied her, tongue thrust over his upper teeth, a snakelike plumping. He returned to his chair and sat back, one leg crossed over the other. Blue trousers, sawdust-speckled. Shirt open at the neck, the sleeves rolled. His hair was oily, slicked back over his forehead.

"I did. He was . . ."

He drew a finger along the edge of the workbench.

"What? He was what?"

"I told you my mum and da died on the ferry. Drowned, eh?" He tipped his head back until his mouth slacked open. "I had a little brother. I didn't tell you about him, did I?"

"No."

He sighed. He closed his eyes and pressed fingers to forehead, his lips moving against the palm of his hand.

"He was just a baby. I remember him. I was big enough to pick him up. There was a little boy used to come to our house. He was the child of my ma's best friend. On this one day, when I wasn't home, the women were gabbing or drinking tea or some such in the front room. The baby's carriage was in the kitchen, by the stove. It was winter. The baby was fast asleep and that little boy lifted our baby out of its carriage so carefully the baby didn't make a peep. He went out the back door and carried him down the road and threw him over the railroad bridge into the river."

"Oh." She cried out, horrified. "Oh, Mr. Tuck."

"Shouldn't have told you. You'll have fits like me mum."

Pattering rain. Smell of drenched lilacs.

"I'm sorry," she whispered. "Your poor mother."

He came over and touched her shoulder, lightly. She did not flinch, consumed by the thought of him bearing this monstrous story all his life.

"I have something for you, like I said."

He squatted by a chest, lifted the lid. She heard a rustle of paper. He stood, a dress laid over his arms like a limp girl.

"I want you to try this on."

"Whatever for?"

"For you to wear when you go to them fancy places."

She rose, slowly, and took the dress from him.

"I'll go stand under that tree." He pointed. "You can see me from the window. I'll keep my back to you."

"You'll get wet."

He went out and shut the door behind him, jiggling the latch to ensure that the door was secured.

He crossed the lawn and stood under the tree, facing the street. She retreated to the far corner. Rows of buttons to be slid from their holes; silk lining, the frou-frou of a petticoat. She stepped into an underdress of blue velvet, reaching behind to snag hooks into eyes. Then an overskirt of soft white wool, draped from pleats at the waist to expose the blue dress. A short jacket of the same soft white, reaching only to the edge of her breasts, connected across the blue velvet underdress with wide tabs. Like a fruit, half-peeled, she thought, working at the buttons. At the jacket's neck was a stiff lacy frill. She tugged at the skirts, patted them in place, and looked up to see a girl precisely her age, staring at her. Shock conveyed an instantaneous impression, the girl like the heart's longing made visible, barely flesh, a blue mist of loveliness in the dim, dusty light. Mr. Tuck had stood a floor-length mirror at the back of the workshop.

She lifted the dress to keep it from the floor, went to the door and opened it.

He turned. She could not see his expression as he stood with his arms folded, looking across the sodden grass.

—

June 10, 1889
Niagara-on-the-Lake, Ontario

Dear Mr. Fairweather,

I rec'd yours of the first concerning Enid Salford. I am happy that she has been located and I trust in your good intentions to unite her with her sister, Flora. It is difficult when running an enterprise as complex as my own to keep track of every child after they have been placed, especially if their people do not take the time to write or they fall into circumstances beyond my control, as with these girls.

It is good people like yourself that I trust and expect to come forward in this fine country. Please know that Enid was sent with a kit worth £8. If you take her yourself I will send you all that I have concerning her parentage. If you decide upon adoption perhaps you would be so good as to remunerate me this amount. Excuse the brevity of this letter, I am in much haste due to a shipment of children arriving this morning.

Yours truly,
Maria Rye

—

On the brilliant, windy day of June 20, the regatta began at nine a.m. sharp in St. John harbour.

Harland and Permelia stood on the deck of the paddle wheel steamboat *David Weston*, off her thrice-weekly St. John–Fredericton run. Luncheon would be served in the dining room on the saloon deck, windows flung wide so diners could watch the races. Harland lifted his binoculars to observe the sculling teams in their red, blue, yellow, or white jerseys, their striped caps. Oars flashed as the rowers pulled out into the harbour, circled, jockeying for position near the start off Reed's Point at the foot of Prince William Street. The falls, reversed by high tide, made no roar. Three canoes emerged from the shadow of the cliffs, passed close by the steamer. He had noted, in his program, a one-mile canoe race—*Indians only*.

Scanning the city, he could see that the streets were rivers of heads, hats, parasols. Flags snapped over the brick buildings.

"The judge's boat," he remarked, shifting the binoculars back to the harbour. He pointed with one hand, following the enlarged scene: a man stood in the bow of an open boat. The judge, Harland presumed, miniaturized by distance, pressed binoculars to his eyes, staggered and put one hand to the gunwale; his binoculars, briefly, crossed Harland's. He thought to mention this to Permelia, the oddity, but said nothing, assailed with a familiar weariness—how he would need to endure her perplexity at his comment, her lack of interest.

She had not wanted to attend the regatta, but changed her mind when she learned that they would not be standing in the crowds but dining on the steamer, where she might show off her new lavender dress and straw hat with purple grosgrain ribbons.

She tugged at his sleeve. "I need to sit, Harland. Let's go to the Grand Saloon. We can see perfectly well from there."

They found a small marble-topped table next to a window. Harland ordered tea, followed the three canoes with his binoculars until they arrived at Reed's Point. Permelia leaned back, took a breath through her nose. She was suffering the constriction of her lungs. Her corset had become difficult to hook.

He opened the program, read aloud.

"The race should start any minute for the centreboard sloops. After that is the fishermen's race, *no less than sixteen-foot keel, one mile.* Then the sculls. There are . . ."

"For goodness' sakes, Harland." She pulled a fan from her tapestry handbag. "I can read it myself."

He set the program on the table and spread his hands on either side of it. White marble, cool beneath his palms. He turned to face the window.

"I *am* interested," she said. She opened the fan, rotated the program. "Let me see. You have a friend competing in the single scull?"

"Professional four oars."

"You see," she whispered, fanning herself, watching women descending the circular stairway. "I was right, Harland. There should be less trim on the hat. Puffs and plumes are *out.* Just look at that one. And that one." She pointed behind her fan at a woman seated on a plush covered chair, another on a leather chesterfield. "Awful."

At the bang of the starter's pistol, the white sails aligned, then began to spread across the harbour, bent upon Partridge Island.

He pressed the binoculars to his eyes, keeping a particular sail within the eyepiece, as if he himself were the man at the helm. "I have chosen a date to go to Nova Scotia," he said. "I cannot keep putting off poor Miss Salford."

"You can't choose a date without consulting me."

The sail tipped dangerously close to the water. The captain stayed his course, his crew leaning far over the opposing gunwale.

"I have consulted you for two months, Permelia. I have come to the conclusion that you will *indefinitely postpone* my expedition."

"Oh, for heaven's sake, Harland. There have been—"

"Don't bother. Please. I know what there *has* been. I am going to inform Mrs. Galloway and Miss Salford that I intend to go after my mid-summer sale."

The wind strengthened as the boats passed the headland; a sloop was gaining on the leader. Partridge Island loomed over the boats, the quarantine buildings black, blocky shapes against the sky. The bell buoy clanged, dim and intermittent across the harbour.

"It will be so hot in July."

"Yes, it would have been better to go sooner, but you expressed concern about the state of the spring roads."

"Really, Harland. You have no reason to care about that girl, Flora. Even if she is outrageously beautiful."

He kept his hands steady, sweeping the binoculars over the flotilla.

"Perhaps if she were a fat little thing with spots you wouldn't care."

She might be right, he thought, picturing Flora. Her firm, desperate expression. The fierce set of her shoulders. The competence of her hands.

He set down the binoculars. The boats were about to round the island.

"Miss Salford is the age of our own daughters. I would be shocked indeed if you were to accuse me of an attraction to such a child."

"No, I . . . no. Of course not."

"I put young Flora up for . . . I tire of this conversation, Permelia. Mrs. Galloway feels herself both responsible and indeed indebted to

Flora. The girl has helped her a great deal. You know that Simeon's death..."

The waiter arrived at their table, carrying a silver-plated salver. Permelia and Harland sat back as he served tea with sugar cookies and cherry bread.

"Josephine has had a dreadful time," Permelia murmured. Prim, her face closing as she sipped. "She should not have chosen a sea captain for a husband."

Harland watched steam spiralling from the teapot. He smelled the saloon's sun-warmed plush. Clink of china, spoons on saucers. Permelia's skirts filled the space beneath the table. He remembered the moment when Simeon, a new boy, had come into their classroom. Insouciant, composed, Simeon had slid behind his desk and Josephine had lowered her face to glance from beneath a fringe of hair. And he himself had felt helpless, like the regatta's early leader, now fallen back into the flotilla.

"That comment exhibits a remarkable lack of feeling," he said. He felt an ugliness in his nostrils, the set of his mouth.

"Oh, goodness, Harland. I feel very sorry for her. And I can see that you are too prone to exhibiting sympathy for her."

She stroked her linen napkin, folded next to her plate. A garnet ring, too tight, compressed the wrinkles of her knuckle.

"Indeed, I have changed my opinion, just now. I have been so foolish. It is because of Josephine that you are so keen to undertake this journey, isn't it. You have a desire to impress her. You wish her to admire you. It is shocking. It is *hurtful*. I do believe you are in love with her."

They met each other's eyes.

He remembered how, during the first year of marriage, she had strewn ill-considered opinions, and he realized that she was someone other than the small, full-fleshed, cheerful girl he had thought her. In the second year, he left her to her interests: baby, servants, dressmaker, the orchestration of status; and learned to hide his own enthusiasms—the sight of dawn's flush on the lilies, his inordinate pleasure in the decorated shop window. He found refuge in his weather station. In his civic duties, now abandoned. And, lately, he admitted to himself, in Josephine's need.

"I consider that comment beneath my dignity to answer," he said.

He resumed watching the race, breath shortened by anger. The boats had disappeared behind the island. He realized a strange relief in this, the disappearance of the boats, the momentary absence of their crews' striving, the ocean leading his eyes to the horizon.

"There is such a thing as compassion, or civility, Permelia." He spoke to the window. "In the eyes of most people, what you call being *do-gooders* is, in fact, doing the right thing."

"But you are *not* doing the right thing, Harland. You are using false civility to hide the truth of your attraction to a widow. If you go on this journey to seek that girl's sister, you will prove this to me. And I will *not* be quiescent. I will take it as *your answer to me*, since you refuse to admit what is obvious."

It occurred to Harland that they could not continue like this. He watched the coruscating light, a passionless occurrence signifying that nothing was of consequence save cause and effect.

—

The morning air was cool, although already the promise of heat warmed the veranda. Josephine noticed dew on the rocking chair and saw last year's leaves drifted in the corner, making a musty smell beneath the sweetness of honeysuckle blossoms.

She sensed a change in herself, ever since Harland told her that Permelia refused to allow him to make the trip, and that he had acquiesced to her demand. *Permelia does not want me to go,* he said, *she feels the store cannot afford my absence*—and she realized her dread of Permelia's smothering anger, which she had sensed ever since the trip had been proposed.

She wondered if she, herself, alone, should go to Nova Scotia. I am an independent woman, she thought, I need ask no one's permission.

It was a new perspective on widowhood, this sense of freedom; and yet she did not dare.

She stood and leaned against the veranda railings.

"Simeon?" she whispered. She realized, suddenly, with fearful honesty, that she was the only one listening.

Someone must go.

She could not imagine who it should be. She could not bear the thought of Flora's disappointment. It was a problem she would have to solve, like so many others.

—

After breakfast was served, the dishes washed and put away, and the tea towel hung on its rack, Flora stood beside the cupboard, hands clasped in front of her.

"I have decided to go to Nova Scotia."

Josephine started, pricked herself. She was repairing a sleeve's cuff.

"No!" She sucked her thumb. "Certainly not, Flora."

Ellen put a finger on the line of the recipe she was studying. She looked up, considered first Flora and then Josephine. Sailor, on his rag rug, abandoned his snuffling. He watched, poised.

"She'll be capable, Mrs. Galloway. She's got a good head on her."

"I'm afraid for you," Josephine said, ignoring Ellen's comment. "You don't know what you might find. You don't know where to look."

"I crossed an ocean," Flora said. The words were dark, the weight of cast iron.

Sailor barked, once.

"Now, my girl." Ellen abandoned the recipe, put a hand on Flora's shoulder. She patted it, gently. "We all know what you've seen."

Flora's hands flew up, fingers outstretched. "I know what to look out for. I can take care of myself. I'm afraid for my sister."

"I suppose." Josephine's words wavered between fear and fact. She set down her sewing. "I suppose. There's no one else."

"That Mr. Fairweather," Ellen flicked a crumb from Flora's shoulder. She stomped to the stove and lifted the lid. The coals lay red, winking. "He could pave the way, so to speak."

—

Later that morning, a letter came from Lucy. The rocking chair was now dry. Sailor made a bed for himself on the drifted honeysuckle leaves. He dozed, but peeked every once in a while, checking on Josephine.

June 28, 1889

Dear Mother,

I do wish you could come to our meetings. They are the focus of my life. They make me able to endure the living conditions I am suffering, and, of course, the work, which is dreadful, especially as the days get hotter. But I am only in the position of thousands of others, and have no complaint to make—personally. Of course, I'm glad that it makes me able to speak from a real perspective.

What we are challenging is the idea that in the home there should be harmony between a dependent wife and a protective husband. In the home, as well as in every other place, women are seen to be in a dependent and secondary position. But we are not Lesser Beings! We are not by nature weaker, less smart, less able, or in need of protection. Oh, it makes me so angry, Mother, and so determined, and so proud to be part of this movement! We seek nothing less than full recognition as human beings.

Josephine caught Lucy's excitement, found herself nodding in agreement. She felt purpose steeling her backbone, firming her jaw. Pride, warming her heart. Her girls would have opportunities she could never have foreseen.

Cousin Carrie is particularly interested in Married Women's Property Rights. She has presented papers concerning the topic, showing us that even the new and improved legislation is subject to interpretation by judges. It seems, Mother, that we are still treated as helpless, only worthy of protection, no matter what the law says. I am quite certain I shall never marry.

Presently, we are putting all our efforts into this petition for full suffrage, which is gaining momentum. We are writing letters to our Members of the Legislative Assembly, seeking their opinion on the bill. We are writing letters asking support from the trades union, and to many other public bodies. We are asking the newspapers to support our position. I do hope, Mother, you will put pen to paper. How is everything at home? Are you going to find Flora's sister? I hope . . .

Josephine put down the letter.

She drew a long breath.

Yes.

She would contact Harland, as Ellen had suggested. If Flora were to go to Nova Scotia, she would ask him to pave the way.

—

To: The Proprietor
The Pictou Inn, Pictou, Nova Scotia

July 10, 1889

To Whom It May Concern,

I write on behalf of Miss Flora Salford, who will be arriving at your hotel sometime in the week after your receipt of this letter. She is travelling on my behalf, seeking a young girl, her sister, who may be

*in the vicinity of Pictou. My wife and I would have accompanied
her, but I find that I cannot leave my business at this time. Please
assign her a good chamber. She is visiting on a mission of possible
unpleasantness, since we do not know in what circumstances she
may find her sister. I beg your kindness in attending to her needs,
which I cannot at this time anticipate, as well as satisfying with
your fabled hospitality her general well-being. Please send me the
bill for any and all expenses.*

With kindest best wishes,
Harland Fairweather

—

Two weeks later, Flora boarded the Intercolonial early in the morning,
changed trains in Moncton, and then changed trains again, boarding
the Short Line in Oxford Junction. Sweat trickled down her back as the
train laboured through the Cobequid Mountains, steam billowing past
her window. A small folding table separated her from a sleeping boy,
sprawled in the adjacent seat. She lifted a cedar writing box from her
carpet bag, given to her by the Hilltop sisters. She opened the lid. The
box was lined with black velvet and contained pen, ink and lavender-
coloured paper.

"Write to us," they had said, as if Flora were embarked on the
Grand Tour of Europe.

I might well be having a holiday, she thought. *Who would know?* She
closed the box. Boarding the train, no one had stared at her. She was
not wearing a placard around her neck, nor shabby boots, nor carrying
a paper bag smelling of hardboiled eggs. She was seventeen years old,
now, not ten. Folded in her purse were paper notes, money Josephine had
given her; Reverend Snelcroft's letter; and the address of the Pictou Inn.

The boy next to her rolled over, tucking up his knees. His cheek
was sheened with perspiration. He placed his hands as if in prayer,
worked them beneath his face.

The whistle sounded. The train was crossing a road.

Drowsiness unmoored her thoughts, thickened her eyelids. The iron wheels clacked over the ties, the car rocked.

—

As she carried her carpet bag from the train station to the hotel, Flora felt she hadn't left Pleasant Valley, only stepped into the train while the town's elements were rearranged—picket fences, shop doors open to cool interiors, awnings casting shade across wooden sidewalks. Different, in Pictou, though, was the mewing of gulls and the sound of the docks—clangings, the shouts of stevedores.

She let herself into her room but did not unpack, only sat on the edge of a chair, one hand clutching her bag. The window offered a view to the harbour; on the far side of the water, like a dash of paint, were light-burnished hayfields. She glimpsed her reflection in an ornate mirror. Her hair, slipped from the brown velvet hat, her eyes, startled, half-frightened, oddly surrounded by things not her own: a tall dresser with lace runner, a red Turkish rug. She saw, in the reflection, the net curtains billowing up, settling down, in air that touched her face, smelling of wood shingles and the sea.

She imagined mown hayfields on the farm where Enid lived. A tiger cat, perhaps. A puppy. *You can bring them.* She saw Enid's face, puzzled, gazing at her as if she were a stranger come to take her away from a place she might not wish to leave.

FIFTEEN

Enid

≈

THE FAINT ROAR OF the sea came from beyond a small woodlot on the far side of the road. There was no breeze. She squatted, prising a handful of weeds from around onions planted in the back garden; blackflies settled on her temples and the back of her neck. She ducked her face into her arm, raked the itchy bites with her fingernails. She could see the dog, panting on the dirt in front of the unpainted house where chickens had made hollows. Aprons and tea towels hung from the clothesline. Heat shimmered from the rust of buckets half-lost in grass, from the nails of pigpens built with scrap lumber.

She heard hoof beats and the rattle of wheels; a wagon emerged from the trees and came down the hill, a small bald man driving with a woman on the seat beside him. He stopped in front of the house. The sound of his voice was strange in this place, where she heard only the voices of Mr. and Mrs. Mallory.

"Whoa."

She dropped the weeds, slipped through the grass and worked herself into an alder bush that had grown against the kitchen window. From there, she could peep around the corner and see the yard and the front of the house.

The woman climbed down from the wagon. Her dress was clean and without patches. White, with tiny pink flowers.

A girl, really. Maybe only a few years older than me.

The dog scrambled to its feet and began to bark. Mr. Mallory appeared at the front door.

"Shut that."

The girl walked towards the house. She wore a straw hat with a blue ribbon around the brim. Curls on her forehead. Hair caught up in a soft roll, wisping over her collar. She put down a hand but did not look the dog in the eye. Careful. She continued straight to Mr. Mallory, not knowing that she should be afraid.

Mr. Mallory braced himself in the door, arm over his head, elbow against the frame, hand dangling loose. A shovel leaned against the house.

"What do youse want?"

"Are you Mr. Albert Mallory?"

She's British.

"Yuh."

"I am looking for Enid Salford. I heard from Reverend Charles Snelcroft that he sent Enid to you. You applied for a child from Miss Maria Rye."

"We got no Enid Salford."

"Why did he give me your name, then?"

"You telling me I'm a liar?"

The girl looked straight into Mr. Mallory's eyes, as neither the dog nor Doreen ever did.

Nor had Fred.

"Excuse me. I am trying to understand. Perhaps someone made a mistake."

"Must have."

"But how could Reverend . . . how did he come by your name?"

A spider crouched beneath the window's rotting frame, only inches from her face. *Enid Salford.* She had almost forgotten her own last name.

She was *the girl*. She had been called nothing else since she had stepped off the train and been snatched by the collar; looked up, struggling, at a tall, misshapen man. Beard. Angry eyes. *I asked for a boy.* Arriving at the house, he had flung her to Doreen like a scrap of meat. *Got you a girl.*

Mr. Mallory widened his stance, filling the door.

"You got any more business with me? You and Perley Hayes?"

The driver stiffened at the mention of his name.

"Hey, now, Perley."

Perley Hayes lifted his whip, minutely. He hunched forward, studying the ground behind his horse.

The girl returned to the wagon. She climbed up. The man circled the wagon, flicked his whip; the horse broke into a trot. The wagon disappeared into the trees.

Enid clutched the stem of the alder bush. Longing for the horse to stop. Longing for the girl to change her mind.

—

Who was it came in that wagon.

He muttered it at the supper table.

She wanted to hear him say that someone had come looking for her. Someone who knew her name.

Doreen placed a plate of flapjacks on the table. Flies landed on them. The flies had tiny feet, like socks. The flies had been in the pig-pen. Enid wanted to nudge Fred's foot under the table, bidding him look at how the flies kneaded the flapjacks with their specks of feet. But Fred was gone.

No one spoke until the plate was empty.

Mr. Mallory went out to the road with a rock in his hand. He hurled it up the road, in the direction the wagon had gone.

—

The day after, he stood in the barn door watching Enid milk the cows. As she lugged the buckets to the house he followed close behind, empty-handed. After breakfast, he ordered her to kill three hens, the tame black one she could hold in her arms and the old Barred Rocks. She stripped their feathers by the toolshed where he could keep an eye on her while he repaired a whippletree. He told Doreen to keep her in the house.

Enid spent the afternoon on the front porch, shelling peas.

Crickets rasped. Shush of wind in the spruce trees and the endless booming concussion of the unseen surf. Chicken blood crusty on her cheek, her thumb stained green.

Someone knows I am here. Someone had to of told that girl.

Enid had been driven to this house. She did not know how far they had come, for she had fallen asleep and it was pitch dark when she arrived and she had stumbled into a half-lit room where Fred, younger and smaller than she was, sat on a chair with his hands gripped in his lap.

Could I run away.

Whatever Mr. Mallory was plotting would be worse than anything she might encounter in woods, road or town.

Take a sack of bread and cheese. Might be wild berries.

Creep through the woods, just out of sight of the road.

She slept under a bearskin, knew the coarse black hair and the thick, curled claws.

Take a kitchen knife. One of them long ones.

—

The next morning, Enid was not at the breakfast table and the cow bawled in the pasture, unmilked.

Mr. Mallory shoved Doreen out the front door.

"I told you to keep an eye on her," he roared.

She fell to her knees.

"I was asleep, like you," Doreen screamed. She stumbled to her feet, slapped at her skirts, furious, brushing away dirt. Both of them stared up the road, where, in the opening, sunlight flashed in the spruce trees.

"Git on up that road and find her."

"I can't . . ."

"You git on up along there and find her."

"I—"

He snatched up the shovel and prodded her in the small of the back, forcing her to stumble over the sun-baked soil.

The cow stretched her neck, continued her gut-deep complaint. Mr. Mallory heaved the shovel as far as he could. It clanged, end over end.

SIXTEEN

Sisters

~

FLORA TRAILED HER FINGERTIPS across the woven tablecloth. The regularity of its criss-cross pattern calmed her. She sat with a cup of tea at the kitchen table of the Anglican parsonage. Pies with lattice crusts cooled on a cupboard shelf. The minister's wife was snapping green beans into a bowl.

"Reverend Snelcroft, in Halifax, wrote to the Overseer of the Poor in Pleasant Valley, Mr. Fairweather," Flora explained. "He said my sister was to be placed with Mr. Albert Mallory. The hostler at the inn knew a driver who would take me there. Mr. Perley Hayes. He had heard tell of the Mallorys. He drove me up there."

She gestured, vaguely.

"But the Mallorys said . . ." her voice faltered. "They didn't know any Enid Salford."

A practised listener, the minister's wife watched Flora keenly through steel-rimmed spectacles. She clucked with sympathy.

"Shame. What a disappointment for you." Her voice was apologetic. "But I'm sure my husband never heard anything from Reverend Snelcroft."

Flora opened her mouth to protest. Closed it. The minister's wife reached forward and patted Flora's wrist, distressed.

"I'm quite certain. My husband tells me everything. A minister's wife, you see, has to know."

Flora looked out the window, hiding her disappointment.

"I'm sorry, Flora. He would especially have told me if it was something to do with children."

Swallows, like a row of pearls, made the clothesline sag.

—

She spent the rest of the day asking. At the docks. In the dry goods store. At the train station. At the livery stable, the shoemaker's shop, the blacksmith's, the milliner's. People paused in their work, surprised. They looked at her with puzzlement, listened to her query, responded with sympathy. No one had heard of a young English girl named Enid Salford.

By the end of the day, she could no longer bear to tell the story.

At the inn, waiting for supper, Flora sought the breeze, choosing a table by an open window, but even so, beads of sweat prickled her scalp. She felt lost, bereft, as if a cherished picture had been torn from her hands and cast onto a fire.

A young woman pushed open the screen door. Dusty, scuffed boots, one set precisely in front of the other, warily stepping over the floorboards to the front desk. She spoke with the clerk, who took note of the washboard-wizened dress and missing buttons before nodding towards Flora. Flora witnessed the exchange, watched the woman slipping between the dining room tables, slumped like a folded napkin.

"You the one lookin' for an English girl?"

Flora nodded. The young woman's eyelids were swollen by blackfly bites.

"I cm'in town to see my brother. He tol' me someone named Flora from this hotel came to the docks askin' about an English girl."

She paused, eyeing Flora. Flora squeezed her cloth napkin, focused on each word, like extracting gold from sand.

"I know where that girl is. She's up to Black Creek. At the Mallorys'."

"I went up there. But Mr. Mallory told me . . ."

"He's a liar. Mr. Mallory. He's bad. He's real bad. My husband gots a distillery. Mallory buys from my husband. They drink. I heard him talking about that girl. He was some angry. Said he asked for a boy."

Flora was seized with trembling.

"You're sure."

"Yuh. Sure."

Flora took coins from her bag.

"Thanks," she whispered, pressing coins into the woman's hand. She felt the brush of fingers. The woman vanished, a ripple of motion, then stillness, like the disappearance of a fox.

—

Perley Hayes appeared at the door of his house.

"You been up there once, he told you she ain't there. *She ain't there.* You got no reason to go up there again."

Flora stood straight. She lifted her chin and stared down into the man's eyes.

"I think she's there. I was *told* she is there."

He drew the back of his hand over his nose, wiped his hand on his pants. He settled into himself, staring past Flora, over the harbour. "Askin' for trouble and I don't want to be no part of it."

"I'm scared for her."

"Just askin' for trouble."

"I'll pay twice what I paid yesterday."

He worried his hair with one hand.

"Could you be at the inn at 5:30 tomorrow morning?" She spoke calmly, as if he had already agreed.

His eyes touched hers. Reluctant.

"On your head if he gets riled up."

"On my head, then."

—

Just at sunrise, the hired man knocked over a hoe propped against the side of the parsonage barn. He picked it up and carried it inside.

Started, stepped back.

A body, under grain sacks. On the new hay. He clutched the hoe, tiptoed close. Female, neither child nor woman. Dirt-encrusted fingernails. A rash of fly bites and sores. Arms bloody with scratches. Flakes of skin on her lips, hair caught up in a knotted rag.

He jogged to the house and burst into the kitchen. The minister's wife was spooning tea into a pot. Oatmeal bubbled on the wood stove.

"Miz Wallace, there's a girl asleep in the barn."

She, too, started, tea leaves spilling from the spoon.

"Is she anyone you know?"

"Never seen her before."

The door from the back stairway cracked open. The minister appeared, crooked spectacles, half-awake. Seeing the hired man, he stepped down into the kitchen.

"Harold, Cullen tells me there's a girl in our barn."

"What do you mean, Cullen?" the minister asked, adjusting his spectacles.

"Sleeping. She's some filthy. Skin and bones. Arms all scratched, like she was picking raspberries."

"Oh, my heavens, Harold. The lost sister?"

"Most probably."

"Cullen, rush right over to the Pictou Inn and get them to wake up that girl. Flora is her name. *Flora*. Bring that Flora back here straight away."

Cullen hurried from the kitchen.

"Harold, I'm going out to the barn."

She pushed the oatmeal to the side of the stove. She took molasses cookies from a crock, wrapped them in a cloth, hurried out the door and down the path.

The girl was sitting up. She froze as Mrs. Wallace came into the barn, pulling the sacking up over her shoulders.

Mrs. Wallace knelt beside her.

"Molasses cookies. I baked them yesterday." She held one out to Enid. "I had a girl like you but she's all grown up and has two children. My husband is the minister, you know, and he's the nicest man. I have oatmeal making on the stove. Now you get onto your feet and we'll go up to the house and I'll make you some tea."

A hand slipped from beneath the sacking, accepted the cookie.

"Thank you," the girl whispered.

English?

"You know, dear, your sister is looking for you."

"My . . ."

"Your sister. Her name is Flora? Is that right? Are you Enid?"

The sacking slipped from her shoulders. Collarbones, like a chicken carcass. Hay clung to her dress, made of flour bags.

"I seen her," the girl said. Her voice was hoarse, as if it had not been used for a long time. "She ain't my sister."

Mrs. Wallace pulled Enid to her feet, put an arm around her, led her to the house. Reverend Wallace, watching in the window, was ready with the blanket that Mrs. Wallace wore over her lap on winter nights.

Enid sat in the rocking chair. Mrs. Wallace eased a cup of tea into her hands. They set a spoon and a bowl of oatmeal sprinkled with fresh blackberries on the table next to her. Mrs. Wallace fussed at the sink, postponing her own breakfast. Mr. Wallace took a cup of tea to his study.

Cullen opened the back door and stepped into the kitchen.

"She isn't there," he said, glancing at Enid, who had taken the bowl of oatmeal into her lap and was hungrily eating. "Flora. She and Perley are on their way to the Mallorys."

Enid set down the oatmeal and stood. The blanket fell from her shoulders. "You got to stop her."

"Why, Enid?"

"Fred . . . they'll think I told. He'll hurt her."

She was seized with a fit of trembling.

"I run from him. I run."

—

Perley Hayes stopped the horse just before the curve in the road, where it led out of the trees and into the clearing.

"I got to water the horse. There's a stream here. You kin walk. It's just around the corner and down."

Flora felt a beat of fear.

"You don't want him to see you."

"Horse needs water, is all."

He climbed down from the wagon, not meeting her eyes. She hesitated, wondering if her instinct was a product of desire or the adjunct of disappointment, a foolishness she would regret.

Flora left the thought unfinished, unheeded, and slipped down onto the road. The sun had risen—spruce needles caused the light to quiver.

"I shouldn't be long," she said. "And if I am, you going to come looking for me?"

He was unbuckling the harness, seemed not to hear.

—

The homestead lay below, an opening in the trees surrounded by a split-rail fence. She heard the broken crow of a young rooster; smelled the smoke that spiralled from the chimney. Dampness rose from the soil as she walked down the hill. Her heart quickened. He was only like Mr. Tuck, she reasoned. Coarse, rough. He was only like the men in the workhouse. Or the hired hands on the farm where she had lived with the Quigleys. Perhaps he had been abandoned as she had been herself. And there was a woman. She had seen her, peering over the man's shoulder; surely she would be a softening influence should Mr. Mallory be angry. The rooster crowed again. Close, now, she could make out the waking farm's details—a cow belly-deep in weeds, disconsolate with bursting udder; the rooster on the fence stretching his neck. She wondered if Enid might be in the barn, or a shed. She felt sudden misgiving. Perhaps there was nothing sinister about this. Perhaps they only wanted to keep her for the help she gave them. Or perhaps Enid herself was afraid to leave this place. Perhaps she did not want to return to the world where a sister could abandon her; where a child could be bundled onto a ship and shipped across an ocean. Perhaps she thought that whatever came next might be worse than this desolate, secluded farm.

Flora stepped around sun-glazed hollows in the path where hens made dust baths. She approached the house warily, mindful of the dog. It occurred to her that if a young woman should emerge and be presented to her as *not* being Enid, she would have no way of knowing whether or not this was the truth.

Fourteen years old, she thought. *Fourteen*.

The door of the house swung open. Mr. Mallory stood in the doorframe, unbuttoning his flies. She froze as he began to fumble with his underdrawers. He sighed, closed his eyes. A golden stream, steaming. She heard a hollow knocking sound, as if something within the house had fallen over.

He called back over his shoulder. "I ain't done with you."

He opened his eyes as he tucked himself back into his trousers, and his gaze felt on Flora. He reeled backwards, threw up an arm.

"What the bejesus you doing here?"

His words were slurred. His eyes widened, squinted.

"Fuckin' women."

Wee-min, Flora heard. *Fuckin' weemin*.

He came towards her, one long step caught up by a sideways lurch. He stopped, clasped his face in one hand as if the light were an anguish. He pointed back up the hill.

"By Jesus, you get off my place."

"Who is it? Who you talking to?" A woman's voice.

"Shut up."

Mrs. Mallory's face appeared in the window, distorted by the glass, cheeks smashed to purple, open bleeding wounds around her eyes. She gripped her mouth with bloody fingers.

Mr. Mallory took another reeling step. "Get off out of here."

Flora backed away.

"Mr. Mallory, I was told that Enid Salford was here. I need to see her."

Whiskey, sour breath. Shirt half-unbuttoned. Black hairs on his chest. A streak of blood on his cheek.

"Perley Hayes bring you? Cunt bastard. I'll see to . . ."

The dog came up from the barn, a silent energy, like wind. Flora screamed, flailed her arms, felt teeth on her forearm. She tore from the dog's grip, ran towards the house. The woman pulled the door wide. Flora tripped, fell over the threshold. The woman snatched a cloth from the stove bar, thrust it at Flora. Mr. Mallory followed Flora into the house, slammed the door behind him, rammed a bolt over the bar latch. Flora huddled on the floor, pressing the dishcloth to her wound. The dog hurled itself against the door.

"Shut the fuck up."

Silence. The click of the dog's nails.

Mr. Mallory sat at the table. He picked up a stoneware jug and tipped it to his mouth.

"All night," the woman hissed at Flora. Accusing. "This been goin' on all night."

She huddled against the wall, hands to bleeding mouth. Smashed crockery. A broken chair, its rush seat ripped loose. A bowl of stew on the floor, its contents congealing on the rug.

Flora's mind became a ray of light, searching. The door, locked. Could she pull the bolt back? The dog, waiting. Another door, leading into a hall.

Drinking all night.

"What to do with her," he muttered to himself. "What in the *hell* am I going to do with her. Fuckin' women." He roared at his wife. "You let the girl out of your sight. She's gone and told. They sent this... this..."

Pointing at Flora.

"No one sent me," she said.

"*No one sent me.*" He tipped the jug back until she could see the matted underside of his beard.

"Alright, then," he whispered. "Two women I got to dispose of. How to... though... uhh. Dispose..."

He sat forward, abruptly, elbows on knees, head in hands. He shook his head, muttering.

"...deal with Hayes... horse... whore bitch..."

The woman and Flora looked at one another. The woman's eyes went to the poker, hanging on the back of the stove. Flora's eyes. She signalled to the woman with the slightest lift of a forefinger. *Wait.*

"Mr. Mallory?"

"How the fuck you know my name? Where you from, anyway. Never seen you around..."

"I'm not from here. I don't know anything about you, except that..." She took a deep breath.

"*...that you have my sister.*"

Stillness, suddenly. Mr. and Mrs. Mallory, shocked into complicity.

"What sister?" he said.

"Enid Salford is my sister."

"You ain't one of them people who's in charge of them English kids?"

"No. I'm Enid Salford's sister, and I've been looking for her for a very long time. I was told she was here at your farm."

"Well, then, you got *her* to blame." He tipped forward until his feet were beneath his torso; rocked himself up and staggered over to his wife. Bracing himself with one hand against the wall, he kicked her with each word. "She-let-that-damn-girl..." Harder. "Out-of-her-sight. Her-ignorant-slut-fault."

Flora scrambled to her feet. She seized the back of his shirt.

"Stop that. You'll kill her."

He turned and gripped Flora by the shoulders. She tore from his grasp, knocked the jug from the table. It broke into three large pieces. She picked up a piece, backed away, holding it towards his face. He punched her in the stomach. Her skirt tripped her as she doubled over, turning to run, the bolt beneath her fingers, trying to shove it back, screamed as she felt a stab in her shoulder, the point raking down through the fabric of her sleeve. Bloody shard in his hand.

Men's voices, horses.

She screamed. Mrs. Mallory screamed.

"Help! Help us!"

Mr. Mallory thrust her aside. She knelt, clutching her shoulder. The door wrenched open, his boots on the dirt, a stagger, shouting, running, the shard in his hand like a spear.

"Off my property! You got no—"

Air on her face, the smell of summer.

Mrs. Mallory on her side, furled, like a caterpillar. Mr. Mallory, stumbling across the clearing, waving his arms as if the men were crows and could be frightened away. Two men flinging themselves willy-nilly from their horses, running towards him.

Perley Hayes, then.

Horse and wagon coming around the bend.

SEVENTEEN

Fresh Bread and Freedom

~

AS SOON AS THE doctor finished cleaning the dog bite and stitching the stab wound, Perley Hayes drove Flora to the parsonage.

Mrs. Wallace hurried out, tightening her apron.

"Thank heavens," she said. She stepped forward, cupped Flora's face, examining the bandage. "You are white as a ghost."

"I need to see her."

Flora followed Mrs. Wallace down the hallway. Her heart began a rapid beating. Her shoulder began to throb. She felt faint, ran one hand along the yellow-flowered wallpaper.

"I couldn't give her a bath," Mrs. Wallace whispered, finger to lips, just before they stepped into the kitchen. "She ate oatmeal, had some tea."

A girl perched on the edge of a spool-rung chair. The chair was pushed back from the table, as if she were about to jump up. She clutched her hands in her lap.

Purple shadows beneath her eyes. Knuckles, elbows, the bones of her arms. A wide mouth, drawn downwards. Matted hair.

"Enid?"

The girl's eyes held her, without recognition. Flora stared back. She was not certain, herself, whether this was her sister.

She pulled a chair from the table and sat beside the girl. Sunshine washed over a loaf of bread, a spray of crumbs.

"Are you Enid Salford?"

"I am."

"Did you come from England? Did you come from a workhouse in Tetbury?"

"I did."

Flora drew a shaky breath.

"Enid. I am *Flora*! I am Flora."

"My sister Flora?"

Hope in the girls' eyes, a flicker. Flora remembered the feeling as it had once been for herself—irrepressible, treacherous.

Flora laid her hand on the girl's clenched fist.

"Enid, I am your sister. I truly am. I came looking for you. I'm Flora."

The minister came from a front room, holding a pen. He sat at the end of the table, looked from girl to girl.

"I've been writing to her for years," Flora said. "I don't think anyone ever sent my letters. 'Cause I never got a reply."

"Why did you run away from the Mallorys, Enid?" he said. He spoke as if he had asked this question several times already. "We need to know if they have done something that needs to be brought to the attention of the police."

She would not tell them what she had seen, Flora realized. One could not speak of evil. She knew the isolation of horror, remembering how Matron's helpers had held a little girl, working a bar of soap into her mouth. Or how they fondled your private parts when they bathed you. You hid it away, even from yourself—worked it into the deepest soil of your mind.

Sunshine slanted through coloured panes, making a nimbus of the girl's matted, filthy hair. Flora noticed that it was the same light colour as her own. Tears welled in the girl's eyes, slid down her cheeks. She was staring at Flora as if seeing her for the first time. Hope, stronger. Eager.

"My sister? My Flora?"

The girl suddenly rested her cheekbone on her hand, as if she were too tired to hold her head up. She sprawled forward, head on folded arms.

They stared at the girl lying amidst jam and bread, in the clean kitchen with its white wainscot and checkered curtains.

Flora looked at Mrs. Wallace's stricken face, and spoke softly.

"She's only asleep."

—

The girl slept for hours at the parsonage before coming to Flora's room at the inn. Flour-sack dress clutched tightly around her gaunt frame, she huddled at the window's edge, peering down. It was late afternoon, and the bricks of the dry goods store across the street were flushed a warm red. A top hat, a parasol—people passed, below, on the sidewalk.

"He's down there, looking for me."

Flora joined her at the window.

"Do you see him?"

"No."

She could not rid herself of the stunned feeling that this fourteen-year-old girl, almost as tall as she was herself, was an imposter. Yet in the rich light she could see that the girl's face bore a similarity to her own.

"I'm going to run you a bath."

"Run me a bath?"

The girl spoke nervously, and Flora wondered if she was remembering the brutal scrubbing she had received at the workhouse.

"I'll let you bathe yourself," Flora said. She went into the bathroom and turned the spigots. The girl followed her, stood in the bathroom door. "Hot, see. Cold. I wish Ma could see this."

"Ma. Did we call our . . . our mother Ma?"

"We did. Ma and Papa."

"I don't remember a father."

Your little hand, Flora thought, running her own hand back and forth in the light-rippled water. The river stones, knocking against one another. The grave's raw dirt. No relatives, only the priest and some people from the farm where Papa worked. She rose and left the bathroom to this unknown girl who was neither the child Flora remembered, nor Enid as she had imagined her. She heard a small, dunking splash. Then silence.

"Is it all right? The temperature?"

The girl did not answer and Flora turned to see that she was bent forward in the tub, weeping, beating her forehead with the heels of her hands.

Flora wet a cloth made of knitted string, rubbed it with soap, passed it up and down the girl's back, squeezed it onto her shoulders. She dipped it again. Aroma of coconut. Eased the cloth along the knobby spine. Bug bites on the back of her neck, but no marks of whip or hand.

The girl clutched her legs, buried her face in her knees. Her body shook, she wept in spasms that Flora's cloth could not subdue.

"He were cruel to him, beat him with a big belt. I saw them in the...'n then he... the boy, he..."

Flora asked no questions. It would have to be coaxed out, Reverend Wallace had told her in the parsonage kitchen while the girl slept. If there were some wrongdoing on the part of Mr. Mallory, he'd told Flora, they would have grounds to keep Enid from his custody.

"Sit back so I can wash your face." She tugged gently at the girl's shoulder.

The girl sat up and tipped her head back, eyes closed as Flora passed the cloth over her face in slow, coaxing strokes, like a cat's tongue. The water was turning brown.

"I remember my first time in a tub," Flora murmured. "I remember the first time I saw water coming from a tap. It was at the place I live now. Lift up your foot."

She knelt, lifted the girl's foot and worked the cloth between each toe.

"Now the other one."

She made the girl lie back in the water with her fingers in her ears.

"Now, bend forward. I'm going to wash your hair." Flora circled the soap bar over the matted tangle, raised a froth with her fingertips. Scabs, on the girl's scalp. Knots, to be gently pulled apart.

"Smells nice," the girl murmured. She cupped water in her hands, lowered her face into it. Her shoulders relaxed.

"You wash the rest of yourself," Flora said, when she had rinsed the soap from the girl's hair. She waited in the bedroom until the girl appeared in the doorway wrapped in the towel. Flora snugged a blanket over the girl's shoulders and gently steered her to a chair. She pulled another chair close and sat, facing her. They braved each other's eyes.

A fly buzzed on a curl of sticky paper suspended from the ceiling. The strip circled, touched by a breeze. The breeze carried the four-beat clop of hooves and the plaint of gulls.

"You talk different," the girl said.

Her cheeks sheened, apple blossom pink; her hair lay in wet-dark slabs. Her eyes struggled past the surface of Flora's, seeking the sister of memory.

Flora leaned forward, placed a hand on the girl's knee.

"What do you remember about that Tetbury workhouse?"

"Me and my sister, we went outside everyday and we walked round and round. In a circle. There were walls we couldn't see over."

"What did you and your sister do for work?"

"Hemmed gloves."

"You *are* my Enid. Your poor little hands. I remember them. Tiny little red . . . They tore you away from me. You were screaming."

She grasped Enid's hands. Her voice shook, her eyes filled with tears.

"Oh, Enid, I shouldn't have gone. I shouldn't have. They told me I would *better* myself in Canada and they would send you to me. They told me you would come over the very next year."

She wept, openly. She could not speak until her sobs subsided.

"They lied to me."

Enid glanced down at their clasped hands and then up at Flora. A layer dropped from her face, like mist, clearing. "I remember that. I do. There were a box, a green box. You packed. I cried. You went in a carriage."

"Yes."

"Was it a lady, like, who said you would better yourself?"

"Yes, a lady."

They sat, holding hands a little longer, feeling the beat of each other's heart.

"Let's get you dressed."

Enid stood and the blanket dropped. Flora glanced, quickly looked away. Spasmodic shuddering, ribs, the mound of pubic hair a forlorn extravagance between bony thighs.

Leg by leg, lifted. Underpants. Arms, lifted. Tentative, flinching at Flora's touch. One of Flora's dresses, dropped over Enid's head. Flora fastened buttons and ribbons, while tears gathered in Enid's eyes and spilled over her cheeks. She said nothing, only sat as Flora began working at her hair, cutting out mats and snarls with her sewing scissors until, finally, it could be brushed, and became a thickness filled with light and air, the strands floating, crackling. Flora's fingers flew, separating, braiding, winding the braid to Enid's head, pinning it in place.

"You can blow your nose," Flora said, giving her a handkerchief.

Enid did, then wiped her eyes.

"No, wait, you . . ."

Flora handed her a fresh handkerchief.

Enid rose and looked down at the full skirt, touched the white collar at her neck, arms willow-slender in the cotton sleeves; and Flora saw that she was not the wild, fierce girl the flour-sack dress had made her appear to be.

"Let's go get our supper," Flora said.

"He's going to come for me. I should stay hid."

"You're safe. He wouldn't dare come right into the Pictou Inn."

She reached for Enid, but the girl drew back, her mouth tightening.

She wrapped her arms around her own waist and made herself small, looking down. Desolate, terrified.

"Come," Flora said, gently, taking her by the hand. "You'll be safe."

In the hallway, the soles of their shoes clicked like hooves on the varnished floor. The smell of chicken pie and biscuits rose from the dining room.

Be patient, Flora told herself. Touch was a thing from which one recoiled. At the workhouse, you learned to wait, to be invisible, to do only what you were told. Eyes that met your own did not do so out of love. Enid's fear was a thing that Josephine and Ellen might know how to treat.

There was the long train trip to come.

There was the little room to show her, the bed with the quilt. The veranda shaded by lilacs and vines. Raspberry crush, the kitchen, the hens and the cow. Fresh bread.

And freedom.

EIGHTEEN

Someone Else's Happiness

"'TWAS ONLY KINDNESS I was showing." Ellen flipped a butter knife over and over. Breathless, her mouth working. "Saying she hates my good custard."

Only silence came from the dining room; evidently the boarders had broken off their dinner conversation to listen to the fracas in the kitchen. Yelling. The dog's barking. The crash of broken crockery.

Maud was on her hands and knees, picking up the pieces of a shattered bowl. Strawberry custard dripped from the cupboard drawers. Josephine stood in the kitchen door watching the sisters going down the hall—Enid, a swirl of rage, apron torn off and fluttering onto the floor, Flora stooping to pick it up.

"I was only asking," Ellen said. "Did she remember her parents. Does anyone ask me if *I* remember my parents? I wouldn't say no to a question or two. Just to show, you know."

"What? Show what?" Maud sat back on her heels. Her face was pained, confused. She had been excited to welcome a "little sister" into the household.

"Who a person is. Alls I wanted to know. Who is this girl who talks only to Flora. Who looks up from her good food only to say *I don't want any more.* Never a thank you."

"She's like a stray dog," Maud said. "Just afraid, I guess."

Josephine resumed her seat at the table. She had no appetite for the rest of her custard.

Enid had arrived two weeks ago. Still she would not meet their eyes. She sat hunched at the table, pleating her skirt into fans and then smoothing it out. Creasing, smoothing, creasing. Her face did the same thing, anxious ridges forming on her forehead, clearing away when Flora whispered to her, then rising up again.

"It is because of what we expected," Josephine said, pushing her bowl away. "Maud, put down that rag and come sit."

Josephine noticed Maud and Ellen exchange a glance of surprise at her tone.

It had crept over her, gradually, her own understanding of why Enid did not smile, not at beauty—the bee-laden blue delphiniums, the trellis smothered with roses—nor at new dresses, her bed with its bright quilt, Ellen's desserts. Enid was filled with a story too dreadful to tell, with resentment for the story itself and rage for those who had created it. The child knew neither what was expected of her nor of how she fit into this household.

"Ellen, I believe you have done the right thing to show her that you are interested in her. Perhaps we need to . . ."

She cupped her cheek, gazing out the window. Lilac leaves drooped in the still air. Sailor, standing, alert, stirred his tail.

"Let her be. Ask her nothing. Be as kind as we can. Leave the disciplining, if there is need for it, to Flora. One day, she will begin to shed her fear and anger."

"Sounds like someone else I know," Ellen said. She picked a bit of hull from a strawberry. "They be sisters, alright."

After they washed up, Josephine found Flora sitting on the bottom tread of the stairs with her head in her arms. Josephine paused. Her heart had not yet resumed its normal pace after the scene in the kitchen. She lowered herself next to Flora, tucking up her bombazine skirt. Flora did not look up but held out a hand for Sailor, who trailed

Josephine without fail, the *click click* of his claws percussion to the rustle of her skirts. The dog licked Flora's hand, once.

"She won't listen to me." Flora's voice was muffled.

Josephine thought of her advice to Maud and Ellen. She was accustomed to a different way of speaking with Flora, as if Flora were her partner, someone she might go to with questions of her own. The air was tense, as if Enid's sulking wafted down the stairs; and she realized, suddenly, the extent to which the girl had shattered the household's hard-won peace.

"I could not do without you, Flora," she said. She drew a breath, not knowing what she intended to say next.

Flora raised her head, clearing her face with both hands. She stroked Sailor. Her hand trembled.

"Are you thinking that you should send me and Enid away?"

"No. No! Certainly not." Josephine realized that she had revealed conflicted feelings.

"I'm trying," Flora said. She did not blink, fighting back tears. "I'm trying to see her as the Enid I remember. But she's not."

"She's probably doing the same. Trying to see you as the sister she lost."

"We were both lied to. Stolen. Used like animals."

"How used?"

"Why do you think they name it the *work* house? We did nothing but work. Like we were being punished for something we never did, but we felt bad about ourselves anyway. Like it was our fault being poor, being orphaned. Like it happened because we were bad children. We made gloves. Every day. Hour after hour. You should have seen the bruises on Enid's hands."

Josephine sensed an outpouring long in the making.

"Then we were used again. Told we should come over here to have a better life. Oh, here, here with you, it *is* better. But . . ."

"Oh, Flora."

"I see clean faces, happy faces. People who enjoy life and think people are good. *You* think people are good, don't you? You think the world is made of people like you and . . ." She made an encompassing gesture. "People who live in these houses. Mr. and Mrs. Fairweather."

Flora's eyes were dark. Her voice raised. Sailor scrambled to his feet, panting.

"I have never, ever in my life felt like I belonged anywhere. I've never ever felt like I had the right to shop in a store, or walk down a street. I've been looked at like I were a . . . dangerous dog . . . rabid, wild. Or else a thing to be used. I came to Canada because I was told I would get a better life. I dreamed of it. All the way over in that ship, I cried, thinking of little Enid, left behind, and then I hoped, I *hoped*, I imagined a pretty house and kind people who would help me and send for my sister. I saw myself saving money. She told me that's what was going to happen. That lady who came to the workhouse. She lied. When I got here, I was made to work, worse than in the workhouse. To do things *I had never done before*. We got no training in England. We got no training in the workhouse. We was treated like cows. Fed, told to walk in circles for exercise. Got stood in washtubs and our privates felt up by nasty women. Got fed less than you would feed Sailor and sent to bed."

They watched through the screen door as Mr. Tuck walked across the grass and entered his workshop. Evening light saturated the red rose petals, their sun-baked sweetness filled the hall.

"Only thing we learned was to sew gloves," she whispered.

Josephine pulled Sailor close, put an arm around him, ran her fingers through his black fur.

Flora took a long breath, watching the sunlight casting the screen's pattern onto the floor in trembling trapezoids. She hunched forward, her arms still clasping her legs. There was no sound from upstairs and she wondered if Enid had stolen to the top of the stairway and was listening.

"Something happened to Enid," she said quietly. "Something to do with that horrible man in Nova Scotia. She told me she weren't . . . wasn't ruined. I asked, and she said no, she wasn't ever ruined but the *boy* were ruined. What boy, I said. What do you mean, he were ruined? How can a boy be ruined? And she won't tell me. And I think there was something else, more bad. 'Cause there was no boy there. And she won't say what become of him."

Josephine's hair was coming loose from its pins. Strands clung to her forehead, damp with perspiration. She picked crumbs from her sleeve. She felt reckless, the casting off of propriety. Carrie would be pleased. *Two woman sitting on the back stairs, sharing their truths.*

"I'm sorry, Flora. Sorry that I never took the time to ask you."

Flora buried her head again.

"We can't *hurry* Enid. We have to wait for her to know that she can trust us. Realize that her life has changed. As I have myself been waiting, ever since Simeon died. Waiting for things to change within myself. It's something that you can't rush. Like vegetables, you know, seeds..."

Josephine's voice was uncertain, treading on uncertain ground.

Flora straightened, suddenly. She locked eyes with Josephine, her own pleading, yet firm, forceful.

"I got to keep her here with me, Josephine. I got to. Please don't send us away."

Josephine felt a wave of sadness, not grief, but a simpler sorrow, the longing to put things right.

"Flora, not only do you have the *right* to be here, but your presence has been a necessity. Without you, I might still be huddled in my bed. You make me feel that I am cared for, not because I am a mother, or a ... captain's wife ..."

She reddened, treading too close to emotion. Flora was watching, intently. She was listening, Josephine realized, only for assurance.

"I will not send you and Enid away. Of course I won't." She drew a breath. "I said to Ellen that we must not ask Enid any more questions. No matter how well intentioned. We will wait for her to tell us her story. Can you ... Flora, can you try to teach her some things? Only *you* should speak to her about her table manners. Only *you* should teach her how to behave. Teach her politeness. Respect."

"Yes," Flora said. "I have been trying but I'll do more. Ada taught me some of that. I were . . . I was at that farm for five years. I got the odd smack. Didn't hurt me none."

"Any," corrected Josephine. "We'll ask Maud to teach her grammar."

—

Flora and Enid sat cross-legged on their beds, whispering in the darkness, all the summer nights. They told small stories, long ones. At first, in mid-July, the sky was light enough so they could make out each other's features as silence lengthened between the ending of one story and the beginning of the next. Then August came, with towering thunderheads and the smell of goldenrod. They wore flannel nightgowns and whispered until they realized darkness by loss, their faces without expression, only the hint of eyes and teeth.

What was it like the day after I left? Who took my bed? Who sat next to you at the dining table? Did those three girls keep picking on you? Did that woman still secretly help you, remember how she'd prick the leather with her awl?

They sat listening to the crickets while Enid sifted the contents of her memory. *They were mean to me. Yes, she helped. I dunno, can't remember.* The stories released and rose, random as bubbles. Enid told how she had been met by Mr. Mallory at the train station after she had watched the passing farmhouses, all the way from Halifax, and hoped that hers would be as pretty, with red and green trim, rose bushes and apple trees. She said nothing more about the boy other than he was named Freddie, had disappeared, and had something to do with the shovel leaning against the house on the first day that Flora arrived.

—

Flora was snipping carpeting into squares and oblongs, making more miniature rugs.

"You should get your sister to help," Mr. Tuck suggested. "I'll pay her." He spoke with an easy tone, as if he did not care whether she took up his suggestion.

"My sister is too busy in the house."

She told Enid not to have anything to do with Jasper Tuck. She asked Ellen to give Enid extra sewing in the evening.

—

Tired, Flora walked heavy-footed up the stairs and along the quiet hallway, passing the washroom that smelled of lavender and the crack of light around Ellen's door. In their room, Enid sat on her bed bent over a lesson book. She had begun to fill out, her cheeks firm. She read a sentence out loud, proud, then slapped the book shut and fell back on her pillow, arms behind her head. She watched as Flora undressed.

"What are we going to do, Flora? You and me going to live here the rest of our lives?"

Flora pulled her nightgown over her head and did up the laces under her chin.

"I have a plan," she said. "I think we'll have our own house someday, Enid. I'm saving money."

She went to the corner beside the dresser, lifted the floorboard, took out the sock and sat on Enid's bed.

"This is money that Mr. Tuck pays me. He's got a new plan, now. He's going to have me go to fancy homes and show off the miniatures and get more people to order them. He got me a beautiful dress to wear."

"Where is it? Can I see it?"

"It's . . . he keeps it in his workshop."

"Has Josephine seen it?"

"No. It's something I . . . I don't think . . . It's a secret, like, this money. It's because . . . I saw something."

Between them, suddenly. A less than perfect understanding.

"Enid, it's for our own good. I'll tell you someday, but if you don't know, no one can make you say. It's just something that I shouldn't have seen. For some reason Mr. Tuck doesn't want anyone to know how much he pays me. It's only money, I tell him, but . . ."

She examined the sock, absorbedly, not looking at Enid.

"He wants to have a factory, one day, where he makes the little houses, and he will hire me to work there. It's all I can think to do, Enid, to become independent. So we can have our own house."

"Don't Josephine know that he pays you?"

"Doesn't. *Doesn't* Josephine know."

"Doesn't Josephine . . ."

"Yes, but I pretend that it's just a little bit. Pocket change. I told her it's fun for me. Fun to work on the little houses."

Flora knelt and slid the sock back beneath the floorboard. She wished, suddenly, that Enid were younger, a little girl she could tuck into bed, a child who would do everything she asked her to do, who would believe anything she told her.

She climbed into bed and pulled up the blanket. She folded her hands on her chest. Enid, too, settled beneath her covers. They listened to the crickets.

"He were just a little boy," Enid murmured, sleepily. She yawned, rolled over and burrowed into her pillow. "One time there was a screaming in the night and I thought it was a woman. He come into my bed and we pulled the covers over our heads. He said it was a bobcat."

Flora waited, but heard only Enid's slow, deepening breathing.

"We pretended he was my little brother," Enid murmured.

"Did he do that often? Come under the covers?"

"Only that one time." Her voice grew faint with sleep. "I wasn't supposed to talk to him."

—

Josephine was wakened by a sharp cry. *A fox.* She lay, listening, but the sound did not come again. It was too early to get up. Even the dawn chorus had not yet started, only the first tentative chirps. She lay in the hard, narrow bed watching as the wallpaper, the dresses and petticoats hanging on hooks and the pine chest of drawers gained colour in the rising light. She pondered her life. It drained away, the status she had enjoyed—daughter of a factory owner, wife of a sea captain. Now she was becoming—who? what? The matron of a boarding house. Would she grow old in this house? Would she and Ellen become like an old married couple, growing closer and closer as their roles merged?

She heard the sound again. Human, not fox. An anguished, half-strangled shriek.

She threw off the covers, ran into the hall. The cries increased in volume, coming from Flora's room. She rushed in, found the sisters on Enid's bed, Flora holding Enid in her arms, rocking her.

"Shh, Enid, Enid, it's only a dream."

Josephine slid onto the bed, stroked Enid's head.

"Night terrors, they are so awful. You're awake now, Enid, aren't you? You're here with me and Flora."

"Fred," Enid choked. She drew a long, shuddering breath. "Freddie." She sat, covering her face with her hands, rocking forward and back. Wailed. "Can't stop it, can't stop it."

Flora took Enid's hands and drew them from her face. "Look at me, Enid. Look. You are in our bedroom. Josephine is here with us."

Enid's eyes were stricken.

"I see it over and over and over and over. The same—"

"Tell us," Flora said, softly. She stroked her sister's cheek. "It will make it stop if you tell us."

"We made a swing, in the barn. It was a rope, to haul things up into the loft. We swang on it. He were sleeping in the barn, they didn't want him in the house. I found kittens, I knew Mallory would send us to drown them so I got up early and I took one out to him."

Hands, gripping her mouth. She began to rock and moan.

"Tell me. Tell me."

"He hanged hisself. He hanged hisself on our swing. Oh, Flora. His feet were . . . I run in and told them."

"Oh. Oh, Enid."

"I seen him carry Fred off. Fred under one arm. Shovel in the other hand. Doreen and me, we watched from the door. He said he'd kill me and her if we ever told. It happened the day before you come, Flora."

"Oh, Enid."

"I should've gotten up earlier. Oh, Flora, if only I'd gotten up earlier."

—

Later that day, Josephine walked to Harland's store and told him the story.

"And this happened *the day before Flora arrived*. It accounts for the man's violence."

He sat at his desk, hands in fists on either side of the blotter. He watched her, barely blinking, his mouth drawn down at the corners. When she had finished, and fallen silent, he dropped his forehead in his hands.

Josephine heard the voices of his daughter and a customer. She saw the pages of a ledger, opened to today's date.

He drew a long breath and sat up.

"I will contact the Pictou constabulary," he said. "If I need to go to Nova Scotia, I will." His voice was grim and she imagined that this time he would brook no objections from Permelia.

His face hardened and he did not see her, even though he stared straight into her eyes.

—

The next morning, Josephine slid her legs over the side of the bed and stood, all in one motion. She stretched her arms over her head.

For the first time, she did not think immediately upon waking about Simeon's absence, but rather about Enid and the boy in Nova Scotia. The words themselves had been so difficult. They did not relate to one another. *Boy. Rope. Hanging.*

She tried to imagine what could make a child want to die. *We look forward. Like reading a book, we want to know what comes next.* Fred, she thought, knew the answer—what came next was only despair, and he could no longer face it. There was no one he could turn to for help, and never would be. Like a kitten drowned in a pillowcase, he knew he would vanish without anyone noticing his absence.

Josephine slid open a drawer and studied its contents.

No child should ever have such feelings.

The boy had not a single person to love him save Enid, whose friendship had been forbidden. His life was of value simply to service the man: milking, weeding, lugging, even—Josephine closed her eyes and drew a breath—fulfilling his sexual urges.

I am choosing my clothing, she thought, suddenly realizing that this was a step forward. She had not taken the wrinkled bombazine mourning dress from its hook—a habit, by now—but pondered a fresh shirtwaist, a green skirt.

Dressing, she considered the rehabilitation of Enid. The girl was accepting Maud's grammar lessons. *Repeat what she tells you,* Flora urged.

She pinned up her hair. Josephine herself had taught the girl to play checkers and Old Maid. She gave her a basket containing knitting needles, a skein of cotton yarn and a simple pattern for making a washing-up cloth. She took Enid's hands in her own and guided them over a purl stitch. She sat beside her and listened to her read. Enid's favourite primer was about a girl named Flora. "*Flora has been to pick flowers in the woods. See, she has some in her apron. Flora sat on a bank and made a wreath of flowers, and now she puts it on.*" She pronounced the words carefully, her accent still much more pronounced than her sister's. Her *th*'s like *f*'s.

Josephine went down the back stairs, smelling the first smoke of the morning fire.

Enid's healing would need planning, care. She could not have explained it to herself, the steps she would take: it was a compendium of details, known and absorbed since Simeon's death. Oddly, it leavened the weight of everything else she had undertaken: bookkeeping, the needs of pantry and laundry, the complaints of the boarders— these tasks felt less onerous, as if they were now part of something precious and rare.

After the day's chores were done, the women sat on the veranda. Josephine and Ellen took the rocking chairs, Sailor settled at Josephine's feet, while Flora, Enid and Maud perched on the steps. The floorboards retained the day's heat; the birds were quiet, purposeful, flying from bush to tree. August leaves made a dry shirring. The breeze smelled of wood smoke and roasting meat. In the garden beds, lilies had shut, sepals tucking away stigma and anther for the night, like locked houses.

They watched as two boys dashed into the road to retrieve wobbling hoops. A high-stepping bay horse trotted downhill, pulling a hooded chaise, passing a wagon creaking slowly upwards, loaded with barrels and boxes, returning to the countryside after a day in town. Harland's father, The Commodore, paused to bow as he made his twice-daily constitutional, his little terrier panting at his heels; and the MacVey sisters swept past in white dresses, carrying ivory-tipped walking sticks, waving with lace-gloved hands.

Ellen adjusted her spectacles and swept open the newspaper.

"Do ya's want to hear about what the women are doing, now?" The paper was running a brand-new column: *For and About Women*.

Enid hugged a yellow gingham dress around her knees. She brightened, expectant; she liked Ellen, and Ellen, sensing it, had had a change of heart.

Maud and Flora exchanged a smile. Yesterday, they had complained to Ellen of her fascination with murder.

"Yes."

"Seven Maine schoolmarms, tired of boarding house life, are planning to erect a cottage for their own use. They have saved a few hundred dollars each and their building enterprise will be undertaken on the co-operative plan."

Ellen lowered the paper and removed her spectacles.

"There's a thing, now. No men in the house. Just ladies, like us."

"They're likely suffragists," Maud said. "What do you think, Mother?"

Recently, George had announced to Maud that he would wait until she was twenty-one before discussing selling the house. He had reminded her, however, that the property on Queen Street, *so perfect for Mother*, might not still be available at that time, and that if *she should change her mind* they might take Mother on a drive to see it. Even in memory, she felt a wave of irritation. He had adopted his uncle's tone of voice, choice of words, mannerisms. She longed to report the conversation to Lucy, to lay plans for how they might thwart George.

"Are *you* tired of boarding house life?"

Josephine was startled by the question. "What? Am I . . . why, no, Maud. No, I have grown quite accustomed to it. It is a way to stay in this house where everything holds a memory of your father. It makes . . . it simply, you know . . . it *changes* our dream into a new dream that somehow includes the old one. No, I wouldn't want to."

She raised a hand, suddenly, as if she were attending a meeting.

"Oh! I forgot to tell you all. I had a note today from Aunt Azuba. She wrote to say that a date has been set for presenting the suffrage petition to the legislature. She says this is the most important suffrage petition ever to come before the government. She says that if this petition fails there is fear that the momentum will die and it will take years to get back to where . . ." She paused, considered, resolved something. ". . . to where we are now. So she asks if we would start a special committee just for our town. For the sole purpose of gathering signatures."

Ellen lowered the newspaper to her lap.

"Now, then," she sighed. "As if we had nothing else to do."

"Oh, but we should start a suffrage committee. Mother, we should." Maud fidgeted at the top of the steps, fanning her face with a hosta leaf, surreptitiously unbuttoning her collar and the top two buttons of her dress.

"I agree, Maudie," Josephine said. The dog sat up on his haunches. She worked her fingers into his white ruff. "I took the liberty of saying we would do it. That *I* would do it, at the very least."

Maud half turned to her mother. Her voice took on Carrie's pedantic tone. "I feel as if there would be no point to my life, Mother, if it fails. Why should I try for an education, if men still won't let me vote? As Carrie says—why should we marry if . . ." She waved her hand vaguely at her mother, the house. "As you have experienced, Mother." She turned to Flora. "You'll help, won't you, Flora? You and Enid? You spoke so well that one time. Remember the march, when they threw water on us? Wasn't that fun?"

"It's about the vote," Flora murmured to Enid. She laid her hand on Enid's to stop her from pleating and smoothing her skirt.

Mr. Sprague and Miss Harvey came around the corner of the house. They were "stepping out" together. Miss Harvey held a parasol against her shoulder. She twirled it, making its white ruffles float out like the petals of a daisy. They strode down the hill on the sidewalk.

"For example," Maud explained to Enid, darkly, lowering her voice. "Say they get married. Everything she has earned in the factory office, everything she owns, becomes his. Or might as well, even if the new law says otherwise. Cousin Carrie says they find loopholes to keep us in our place."

Flora straightened her back, watching the couple going down past the big houses and feeling indignation at Maud's words. She realized that she had herself imbibed these ideas at the women's meetings. Enid was new to such understanding; only wistfulness crossed the girl's face as she, too, watched the couple.

Ellen, finger pressed against the article where she had left off reading, narrowed her eyes behind her spectacles. She watched as Mr. Sprague, wearing a brown linen jacket, and Miss Harvey, in a white dress with green stripes, turned the corner past the house with hydrangea bushes. Mr. Sprague was evidently expounding on something, for he slowed his pace, describing something in the air with his hands.

"Them two. Skinny and bony. Pity the cook they hire."

No one knew Ellen's story. Flora and Maud whispered about her. *Maybe her husband murdered someone. Do we know if she was married?*

No, not for sure. She simmered, never quite coming to a boil; behind her compressed lips, they sensed secrets, resentments.

"I agree we should start a committee," Flora said. "We'll help, Enid, won't we?"

Enid nodded—*of course*—chin in hands, gazing out over the grass with its purple and white flowers too low for the lawnmower's whirring knives. Her hair, soft and heavy, coiled at her neck. Pink, at last, Flora saw, in her cheeks. Her compliance in Flora's offer to volunteer was all of a piece with washing dishes or learning to read or improving her grammar. Enid was increasingly agreeable, quieting within, watching Flora, picking up cues and copying them. Released, and relieved.

Ellen sighed, again, and picked up the paper. "That's that, then. Just when pickling is starting."

—

It rained, all the next day. Enid hunched over her sewing, silent, as she often was when she had had bad dreams. Flora tried to make her smile.

"Give her time," Josephine murmured, passing in the hallway, a stack of folded sheets in her arms. "You can't make someone's happiness."

That evening, Flora left Enid in the kitchen, darning the heel of a sock. Ellen was bottling pickles amidst steam smelling of vinegar and mustard seeds.

Outside, on the street, pinwheels of spray rimmed the wheels of passing carriages; raindrops rolled down the Solomon's seal leaves, plinking a puddle beneath the workshop window. Flora entered the barn.

Mr. Tuck was expecting her. An array of wood squares, matchsticks, glue and clamps covered her workspace. She was making miniature tables. First she put together the table aprons, then glued matchstick legs to them. She sanded the squares of wood and positioned them atop the apron and legs. Her fingers shook. Tired, she breathed out to steady herself, wondering why a man like Jasper Tuck would have chosen this work, requiring sparseness of movement as he transformed the immutable and massive materials of a mansion—timbers, spikes, bricks—into components as frail as tissue.

"Your sister working?"

"I told you. She's sewing. She's always sewing."

"Got a lot of sewing needs in that house."

"As a matter of fact, we do. Clothing for nine people. That's a lot of mending. A lot of darning."

He held a chisel in one hand, tapped it with a hammer, incising a line.

"I want you to go out on the next fine day. Go out in the dress and talk to a lady. Take the house for her to see. Before it gets too big and heavy."

"What lady?"

"The sisters told me about a friend of theirs." *Tap tap tap.* "Lives over on Summer Street." *Tap tap.* "Big white house."

When Flora had first seen the dress, touched its white wool, heard the rustle of its petticoat, she had been a different person, a girl without someone to care for. Enid's presence changed things in a way Flora did not know how to explain to Mr. Tuck. It was not the making of the houses that she minded. It was being Mr. Tuck's salesgirl, his representative. Now that she spoke, in effect, for both herself and Enid, and worked towards their eventual establishment as respected citizens of the town, she could not bear the thought of walking through the streets like a dressed-up doll, pulling the miniature house. Even if Mr. Tuck were to drive her, she could not see herself climbing down from the wagon and going up to a house wearing a dress that a man had bought for her, one that fit with frightening precision. She could not see herself speaking in a warm, false voice about the virtues of owning a house that looked *just like your own,* attempting, for her own pecuniary gain as well as Mr. Tuck's, to convince a woman—whom she might have encountered at a suffrage meeting—to buy something unnecessary, made by an indigent man with no family or friends, who had come out of nowhere after

Josephine was no longer the beloved wife of a sea captain but the grieving manager of a lodging house.

She trembled to the extent that she could not hold the little table, so picked up a piece of paper faced with pulverized glass, for smoothing. She recognized fear by a blood taste in her mouth and a darkening around the edges of her eyes. She could not say yes. She could not say no.

"Sometime next week, I was thinking." A curl of wood shaving clung to his collar. His eyes were as alert and unfathomable as a racoon's. "The next fine day."

"I will be picking beans on the next fine day. You know you can't pick them when their leaves are wet."

"*Can't* you. Missy smart-one, you are. Don't know what the missus would do without you."

That, too, was a worry. She was both beholden and indispensable.

He set down the hammer and chisel, running a finger along the incised line, drawn lips exposing his teeth. The *scritch-scratch* of Flora's glass paper was loud, as if expressing her feelings, and she laid it down. Their eyes touched.

"How much money have I given you?"

I earned it, she thought, indignant, but suddenly could not speak, could not stand up for herself, as when she bargained for firewood and hay or argued robustly for her pricing on eggs and butter or snapped at Mr. Sprague if he complained *You tuck them sheets so tight a man can't get into them.* Enid's presence had made her aware of her strength and determination; yet, also, more careful.

"How much?" he repeated.

"Five dollars and seventy-three cents."

He glanced down at the money drawer. "You and I have a secret. Don't we."

"Yes."

"You don't get much money from Josephine, do you? No. No, you don't. You going to pick them beans or sell a house?"

"Sell a house."

There was no need, she thought. He could have treated her like a partner. He could have asked her pleasantly.

"You and me going to make a business, aren't we? One day I plan to live in a house like this." He reached over and drew a finger along the roof of the little house, like stroking the ridge of a dog's skull. He grinned, his eyes hard. He made a vague gesture towards the lower streets lined with large, shingled buildings: the boot factory, a tannery, a woodworking plant, greenhouses, foundries. "*Tuck's Miniature House Factory* . . . one day you'll be my main girl."

She resumed sanding. The future that he sketched was so real that she pictured herself passing Mr. Tuck's mansion, set on the hillside with a view over the eastern hills, as she walked home to her own imaginary house, where Enid would be tending a flock of hens.

"How you doing with that glass paper?"

He hooked his chair back with one foot and came across the floor. She folded her hands in her lap and hunched her shoulders. It occurred to her that whenever she caught Enid in such a posture she always whispered *Enid! straighten your back, look up, stop fanning your skirt*—a kind of pleading, since Enid's pain was a thing she did not want to witness.

He stood behind her. She felt as if a draught blew over her head, stirring her hair, a vague brushing. Or as if a daddy-long-legs had wandered over her scalp. She did not dare move, although in the effort to remain still, her neck quivered.

—

Harland arrived at tea time. It was a hot, still afternoon. The sky was lurid; thunder crumpled, a sense of danger prowling the outskirts. The wisteria-shrouded veranda seemed a place of safety, threatened.

"Sometimes, yes, I do wonder," Josephine said. Her throat thickened at the question—*Did she wonder, worry or fret over how he had died.* She was snapping the stem ends from green beans. She had not worn a corset for months, now. She felt the soft swell of her freed belly, hidden beneath an apron; saw the bright green of the beans in her lap. An ash basket held the snapped-off stems; woven, honey-coloured strips held lines of shadow and light. "There's no one who can tell me how he died, only that the ship went aground and they saved the women."

"No doubt he was in the process of saving them," Harland said. He leaned forward, picked a stem end from the floor and dropped it into the basket in her lap.

Even if Permelia should die, she thought, flushing, and Harland were to ask for her hand in marriage, she could not imagine removing her clothes in front of him. She could not imagine his moustache pressed against her face or his fingers touching her breasts. She did not know how other women did this, marrying for a second time. She had given herself to Simeon; together, they had graduated from embarrassed fumblings into discovery of the body's magnificent gifts. Now she was on the cusp of allowing the past its due and proportion, a reduction, while gathering to herself this day's weather and the needs of the present; and as the past drifted away, day by day, the more frequently, it seemed, Harland visited. She became aware that it was she who had found direction and he who was lost.

She longed to ask him about Permelia—how did he *feel* about her— so instead spoke of her love for Simeon. Like plunging one's hands into the carcass of a hen, she thought. Grasping the heart.

"I loved Simeon so dearly. He was my best friend. The only person I felt truly knew me."

"You had a good marriage," he said, as if conceding something long unspoken. "I'm glad, Josephine, although I am grieved that it has come to an end."

She snapped the ends from several beans, listening to the muttering thunder. She would ask, then. Since the question lay, waiting.

"And you?"

"There are difficulties, as you have no doubt realized. Yes. Difficulties. I will admit to my part in her frustration. I am too engrossed in my . . . my interests. My other interests."

"Weather records," she said. She snapped the beans more quickly.

"Yes, weather, of course. And the store. And, now, Flora and Enid. Which Permelia simply cannot understand." He flushed, fingering the rim of the straw boater he held on his knees. His lips tightened over the words Josephine knew he would not speak, the words Permelia used to describe such girls as Flora and Enid, who had been brought over to Canada by the boatload. The *worst* elements. From the *poorest* class. *Infesting* our country.

"Flora worries, terribly," she said. "She wants to repair the damages done to Enid. She feels responsible."

Flash of lightning, a crackling boom. Josephine started and the beans spilled from her lap. She rose and tugged chair and basket deeper into the veranda. Harland continued speaking as he, too, moved his chair farther back. The first drops of rain drummed the porch roof.

"Which she is not, certainly," he said. "The Mallory case is going to court. I received a letter. Both man and woman are in prison. No doubt the poor woman is glad enough to be under a sound roof. They have written to say there is no need for Enid to testify. I came, today, in fact, to tell you this." He lowered his voice. "They found the boy's body. The wife has said that he was . . ." He avoided her eyes. "Abused."

She snapped a bean, thinking that her own future was no longer bleak. Thunder rumbled away down the valley, leaving the quickening patter of raindrops.

"I can keep Flora and Enid," she said. "I can keep them. Maud will leave soon. I really could not run this boarding house without Flora."

He took a long breath through his nose and closed his eyes. "If you would let me . . . help pay . . ."

She felt intimacy rush up, violent as the thunder. *You. Me.* A matter of allowing, after being asked. Yes, she thought, immediately, a reflex, pleased. And then, after a moment, heard the newly learned response: no, of course not.

Blood rushed to her face. She picked a stray stem end from her skirt.

"If I could just *see* it," Enid pleaded. They were washing dishes, after supper. The thunderstorm had blown over, but they could still hear a far-off, intermittent rumble. The new cat, a stray, crouched over a bowl of milk, shoulder blades like grasshopper's legs.

"It's just a house," Flora said. She swirled the dishcloth over the bottom of a cast-iron frying pan and handed the pan to Enid, who dried it and hung it on a hook behind the wood stove. For once, Ellen was not in the kitchen. Mr. Dougan had stopped by for a visit and she had taken him out back to inspect the raspberry canes he had planted last summer.

"Not the house. Course I would like to see that, too, Flora. And all them little bitty things."

"Those. *Those* things."

Enid sighed, annoyed.

"*Those* little bitty things, then."

She picked up a cut-glass sugar bowl, examined it closely, running the tips of her fingers between the pyramids. "Mr. Sprague knocked over the pitcher that matches this, didn't he?"

Flora watched her, hands working in the soapy water, feeling for the cupcake moulds. Enid's face, in its new fullness, was perhaps a version of the father Flora could barely remember. Round brown eyes. Hair darker than Flora's, strands of red and brown mingled with the blonde. Yet people said to them, *Oh, you must be sisters.* My sister. I have a *sister.* Flora felt the wonder of it, that she was not alone.

"He did," Flora confirmed. "He talks with his hands."

Enid's giggle came like rain after thunder, released. She put her hand over her mouth.

"Flora. I meant the dress."

"What are you talking about? Here." Flora dumped a handful of the cupcake moulds in the wire drainer.

"Your *dress.* That Mr. Tuck got for you. I want to see it."

Enid had been talking about the dress ever since Flora had told her about it. To still her curiosity, Flora described it in detail. The soft white wool, the blue velvet underdress.

"Enid. It's not *my* dress. It's his. It's like . . . it's like one of his tools. It's just a thing to make us more money."

"But I . . ."

Enid set down one of the cupcake moulds. She had dried it with extreme care, as Flora had instructed, so that no rust would form at the tin seams. Swallows nesting in the eaves, above the open kitchen window, made a sweet, contented chirping, like pegs being turned in tight holes.

"I would like to try it on," she whispered. "I never wore a dress like that. Think I would feel like a princess."

Flora's hands continued to work in the soapy water, gathering the forks, pinching and working her thumb along their tines. As evening gathered the light, the house darkened, drawn towards its nighttime self—captured gold in the nap of chairs and cushions, books beneath glass-shaded lamps—and she traced a thought so complex she could not express it, how she and Enid were at the beginning of their life together, sheltered beneath this stout and complex roof, caught in the mesh of Josephine's family; and yet, still, she felt the thing that she and Enid had never been without—danger, fear—so familiar as to be an essential part of them. The fear seemed to be growing, since she could not trust that this house would always be theirs. For it would not. One day, they would be cast to the winds like fledgling birds. She and Enid were still alone, and the danger, she realized, was that of the two worlds she had begun to inhabit—Josephine's and Mr. Tuck's—it was his with which she was most closely aligned and upon which their survival depended.

I can do it, though, she thought, lifting a handful of forks and dumping them in the drainer. She pictured her work for Mr. Tuck like a path which she must follow with extreme caution, navigating places which ordinarily she would avoid.

"No," she said. "He wouldn't let you try it on, Enid. I'm his saleswoman, that's all it is. It's just a costume. You keep your mind on reading, writing and arithmetic."

Flora untied her apron and hung it on the wooden rack. She turned from the rack and saw that her sister was staring bleakly out the window, dishcloth hanging in her hands, and wondered if Enid had been seized by the treachery of memory, if the coming of dark reminded her of nights in the Nova Scotia house.

NINETEEN

A Dark Ghost

~

SHE PULLED UP HER sleeve, studied her wrist. Scratched.

"There's a sale on in Hampton, tomorrow, at the hardware store," Flora told Josephine. "Mr. Tuck asked me if I could come with him to pick out some of the more feminine appurtenances for his little house—material for curtains and bedspreads. I could see about some things you need. Corner irons to repair the window screens. And that stove bolt for the grate. I could pick up some matches and stove polish."

"Of course," Josephine said. "Of course, Flora."

She gave her two dollars in case she found any bargains.

—

Flora told Enid that she was getting up very early the next morning.

"I have to go to a sale in Hampton. Don't get up with me."

—

Jasper Tuck stood close, both hands on her.

"You want them to think no one else will have a miniature like theirs," he said, twitching at the dress, adjusting the tabs across her chest.

They left at daybreak. Flora noticed spider webs strung from the grass, so heavy with dew that some strands had separated and now drifted, forlorn remnants. They drove to Summer Street and waited beneath an elm tree until the milk wagon had passed by, making deliveries, and maids had begun to open front doors.

The horse fretted, lifting his hooves, stamping them down.

—

A maid not much older than Flora opened the door. Sleep crusts in the corners of her eyes, rough-pored skin, teeth like crooked clothespins. She frowned at Flora, then glanced past her at the miniature house on the veranda.

"Yes?"

"May I speak to Mrs. Dunfield?" Flora said. "I'll wait here. I don't need to come inside."

A shadow quivered across two milk bottles. The girl came onto the veranda and picked up the bottles before vanishing back inside.

Mrs. Dunfield came to the door. A white dress of cotton lawn fell around her slender frame. Her eyes were quick, comprehensive. She studied Flora, then checked beyond to see who might be waiting in the street. She frowned upon noticing the miniature house.

"Good morning, ma'am." Flora had no idea what to say next. She felt thick, garish, perspiring in the petticoat and velvet underdress, this white wool gown, which, she suddenly realized, was inappropriate for this late August day whose heat sounded in the spreading throb of insects. She could not say *I am Josephine Galloway's servant*. She could not say *I am Mr. Jasper Tuck's assistant*. She could not say *I am a Home Child who was saved from the auction*. She could not say *I am running Mrs. Galloway's boarding house and taking care of my sister who we have just rescued from dire circumstances*.

"You are the girl who spoke at the tea meeting, aren't you? With Mrs. Galloway? You are the girl she rescued from the pauper auction. Flora, isn't it?"

Flora had not foreseen this.

"Yes, ma'am. Flora Salford."

"Will you step in? My, it's going to be a hot day." The woman's eyes, though, remained on the miniature house. "What is that?"

"It's a miniature house being made for the MacVey sisters."

"Why yes, indeed. Oh, my goodness. It is exactly the same as their house, isn't it?"

"I am helping make it," Flora said. "I made the windows and some of the . . ." She took a breath. "I was sent to see if you would like to buy one. He would make an exact copy of your house. There would be nothing else like it, not anywhere in the. . ."

She felt the pent words drain and die. Her neck quivered.

The woman came out onto the veranda and let the screen door fall shut behind her. She looked closely at Flora. Then she motioned to two white-wicker rocking chairs, shaded by a trellis of clematis.

"Come," she said. "Sit down." She set her hands together, palm to palm, and pressed them between her knees. "Tell me. Who is *he?*"

Flora leaned her head back to expose her sweating neck. The wicker was damp, cool. The green floorboards were freshly painted.

"Mr. Jasper Tuck. He makes miniature houses."

"I heard of someone . . . down near the coast? A man going from house to house . . ."

"No, it's not him," Flora said, quickly. Whoever *he* was. Surely Mrs. Dunfield had misheard. "Mr. Tuck is from up north."

"Where, *up north?*"

She recognized what she had felt, when, instead of throwing corn to the chickens, instead of making the kitchen fire with the good, dry kindling, instead of serving oatmeal to the boarders, she had removed her apron and her brown gingham dress in Mr. Tuck's workshop and submitted to putting on the dress he'd picked out for her.

Shame.

"I don't know the province. It's what he told Mrs. Galloway when he came to the boarding house."

"Who are his people?"

New Brunswick was like a vast house with interconnecting rooms, hallways, closets with familiar contents, parlours filled with friends and relatives. She had learned to say, *I'm a Salford. My people are English.*

"He's not from around here. He says he has no people."

"What's his name?"

The wrong questions, she thought. Not—How much does it cost? How long will it take to build? Will it look *just exactly* like my house? It had never occurred to her that she would *not* sell a miniature house to this woman of evident wealth.

"Mr. Jasper Tuck," she said. "His parents were killed in an accident."

"Were they." Mrs. Dunfield plucked at a thread in her cuff. A cat jumped up onto the veranda railing and wove its way on cloud-quiet paws.

She shook the thread from her hand and reached over to touch Flora's sleeve. "Whatever you're doing to help this man, I would advise you stop."

—

Flora went down the street and fetched Mr. Tuck.

Mrs. Dunfield stood like a dark ghost behind the screen door as Mr. Tuck and Flora carried the house down the pathway. They moved awkwardly, arms extended, as if carrying a body.

—

She had not considered that they would be returning in broad daylight. All the twenty-minute ride back, she slumped on the seat, sweltering, the armpits of her dress soaked. As the horse turned up the lane, she hoped that Josephine would be busy at her desk, that Enid and Ellen would be in the kitchen. The harness was outlined with a yellow froth of the horse's sweat; purple-black flies hovered as if suspended from strings. Mr. Tuck drew horse and wagon to a standstill behind the barn and Flora slid down and ran into the workshop. She began a frantic tugging—buttons, tipped to fit through holes. Hooks, behind her neck. Panic changed the place's shape, brought details into focus. Saddle rack marks, pale, on the walls. Cobwebs, and the expanse of workbench where the miniature house had been, and a small brass duck on a windowsill.

Jasper Tuck came through the door. He threw down a paper parcel—stove bolt, corner irons and matches he had purchased to validate Flora's supposed trip. He sat on the edge of a chair, hands on his knees.

"What did you say to her?"

"What you told me to say. That it would be the only house like it. That it would be just like her own house."

"What did *she* say?"

Flora could not tell him that every subsequent statement from Mrs. Dunfield's lips had been about him. *Who was he? Who were his people? Where did he come from?*

"She said it was beautiful. She said they couldn't afford to buy one but maybe someday. Someday, she said. She would like to have one."

"You're lying, aren't you."

"I don't lie." *But sometimes I have to.*

He was a sprung hinge, on his feet, grasping the tab of cloth across her breast, pulling her to him. She cried out, pushed against his chest.

"She wanted to know about me. Eh?"

"I said you came from up north."

"You could have tried harder." He grasped her shoulders and shook her.

"I don't know anything about you." Her head snapped forward, flung back. His thumbs dug into the hollows beside her collarbone, opposing fingers like steel.

She drove her head into his chest, twisted. She brought up her knee and he bent forward, released her. She felt desire between her teeth, the bite she had not taken. They stared at one another, panting. She heeled her hand into the violated hollow, rubbing the pain.

"Why wouldn't I want to sell one of the houses?" Thick, hot. "Of *course* I want to. It's *my living, too*. I can't help what happened. *It wasn't my fault.*"

The clicking of a lawnmower, snipping off the tops of the grasses. Their own breath.

Grief, in her throat, like all the disappointments she had ever suffered: a dormancy, awakened.

—

Enid sat at the kitchen table, reaching down to retrieve onions from a bushel basket at her side. A rack of Mason jars steamed, sterilizing, in a blue-speckled tub on the wood stove.

"This house has changed," Ellen said.

She was in one of her moods. Nothing was right. The dill seed was too soft. The cucumbers were the wrong variety. *Mmm*, Enid agreed, diffusing, as Flora had told her to do.

"Never would have seen a cracked windowpane when Captain Galloway was alive. Veranda floor was fresh-painted every spring. Once he brought a carton of ready-made pickles from one of them countries. Portugal, I think. No, Greece. Now, they were nice little cucumbers."

Enid said nothing. She was worried about Flora, who had gone to Hampton with Mr. Tuck and had not yet returned. There had been so few men in Enid's life. She did not remember her father. In the workhouse, men and boys were reduced to the sound of gravel-making in the hidden yard. Hammers on rocks, chinking. On the ship, she had seen sailors up close, sluicing the vomit-slimed floor of their cabin. Watch caps, whiskers—like horses, mute and powerful. Once she'd arrived in Canada, there were men on the Halifax streets, hunched on the seats of wagons, walking the aisle of the train. Never speaking to her. Never touching her. Only their eyes, watching. Then the boy. Mr. Mallory. Jasper Tuck.

"She'll be all right," Ellen said, interpreting Enid's silence. "I've heard her stand up for herself."

"But you don't trust Mr. Tuck."

"I only met two men I trusted. Mr. Dougan and Captain Galloway."

"What about Mr. Fairweather?"

Ellen's sleeves were rolled up. The flesh of her upper arm hung in a fan of fatless wrinkles. The white skin quivered as she chopped onions, fresh from the soil. She paused to wipe away onion-tears. "We'll see about Mr. Fairweather."

"He found me. He saved me."

"That he did. 'Tis not you I worry about with that one."

A cricket, close by on the side veranda, started up his strident sawing.

"Were you ever married, Ellen?"

Ellen continued chopping the onions. Her mouth tightened at the corners. She took a breath that lifted her chest beneath the water-spotted bib of her apron.

"Was. For a time. Your age, I was."

The knife pivoted onto its point beneath her hand. Fell through the onion. Its juices, released.

"I ran out of the house. A mass of bruises, I was. There was a dog on a rope and I let him loose. He scurried down the lane, scared as me. I remember it was pouring down rain and the fields were covered with blackbirds. They all flew up and me running through the mud. And I thought *free as birds. Free as birds.*"

She wiped her eyes on her sleeve.

Flora walked into the kitchen. Amid the tang of onions, she thought nothing of Ellen's tears. She went to the sink and turned the tap and filled a glass with cloudy water. She drank with her back to them.

"Flora?" Enid said. "Did you go to Hampton?"

On the stove, the Mason jars made a thin tinkle as the water came to a rolling boil. Flora rinsed the glass and set it into the dish drainer. She turned to them, her eyes dark, furious. She tossed a wrapped parcel onto the table. "The bolt. And other things."

Enid dropped her knife.

"Was it Mr. Tuck? Did he . . ."

Flora smiled, strained. "No, no. I'm just tired, Enid. It was a long, hot morning and in the end we . . . we didn't get very much."

"I'll go next time," Enid said. "Why couldn't I? I would like to see Hampton."

Flora shook her head, looked away.

Ellen crossed her arms, knife in hand, watching the sisters. Her eyes narrowed, as if this might help her understand all that had not been said.

—

A letter came from Lucy in the morning's mail. Josephine slipped it into her sleeve and did not mention it to anyone. She wished to read it in privacy, feeling a furtive, half-shamed hunger for its contents.

In her bedroom, she unbuttoned her cuffs and rolled them back. Today she had chosen to wear black, like the Queen. Clothed in grief.

She slit the envelope with an ivory letter opener Simeon had brought from India.

August 30, 1889

Dear Mother,

Thank you for your letter. I have had quite the week.

First, at work, I got in trouble again for organizing a group of women to go to the foreman and demand a separate toilet. We are sick of the conditions, you can't imagine and I won't describe, but he got very angry with us and docked me a week's pay for being the "ringleader" as he called me and so I have had to go to Cousin Carrie's for my suppers this week.

Then we had a march through the streets on Sunday afternoon. We held banners calling for the vote. Buckets of water were thrown at us, as well as degrading insults which I will not repeat.

Afterwards we went to a wealthy woman's house where there was a big parlour and we held a meeting. Her husband burst in with some of the other women's husbands. He roared at his wife and told us we would "never succeed" and that we "didn't appreciate the protection and guiding minds of husbands" and made us leave.

We went to another place where we could be safe and we were pretty upset, you can imagine. What we discussed was men's sense of superiority and how they are afraid of losing it. They say we have innate traits which are appropriate only for childrearing and home-making. These traits are "emotivity, caring, supportiveness, and intuition." We can't reason, they say, because of our emotionalism. They believe it would be "race suicide" if we were allowed out of our sphere because the stresses upon us would damage our reproductive systems. At the bottom of it all, we decided, men are terrified of losing the power they hold over us. And so we decided that they are in fact weaker than we are. This gave us a sense of pride. We refuse to absorb these false descriptions of who we are any longer.

Are you getting names on the petition? We hope to have over ten thousand signatures.

Are you getting signatures for Mr. Fairweather's almshouse petition?

How is your boarding house business doing? How are you, yourself, doing? Do you wish you did not have so much work?

I send you much love,
Lucy

The window was open, and she could smell the cidery tang of apples; overnight, the Yellow Transparent had dropped most of its fruit. All around the tree, deer tracks made black holes in the dewed grass.

Another autumn was upon them: bees burrowing in the borage, slow-winged; leaves gathered against the porch lattice, smelling of frost.

She sat back in her chair, one hand on the letter and the other on her heart.

How are you, yourself, doing?

Lucy's questions made her realize that the gains she had made within herself did not show as outward attributes. *Do you wish you did not have so much work?* Work, she thought, suddenly exasperated by the question, was a necessary thing—as Lucy should know from her studies into the rights of women. When she had been unable to rise from her bed, she had felt a sickness not of the body but of the soul. Since she had begun working, she felt no longer lost but necessary, her goal to improve the lives of all those who lived under her roof, even knowing that this circumscribed world was in jeopardy, since the house would never be hers, save for her dower right. Outrage, seeded by injustice, changed the way she walked, spoke and listened.

How can you own one-third of a house?

How can you not be the legal mother of children you have borne in pain and joy?

How can all you brought into the marriage become your husband's property?

Lucy, who had left in anger as if the family's misfortune were a thing Josephine herself had caused, had become an unwitting catalyst. She had no idea, Josephine thought, that the fury ringing from her daughter's letters had become newly comprehensible, both affirmation and recognition.

Holding the letter, she went to the window and watched orange leaves detaching, riding the air, a slow and erratic spin, *round, round, round*: touching down on the green grass.

Harland was walking up the street. He paused at her lane, looked up at her window. She waved, and he waved in return. He seemed to make a sudden decision, turned into the lane. She hurried downstairs and was at the front door to greet him.

"Come in, Harland. I was just going to have a cup of tea."

He had stirred his hair into disarray. The buttons of his vest were misaligned, the second one in the first hole. He set his linen hat on the sideboard next to Mr. Sprague's derby. Light fell onto a chinoiserie vase filled with peacock feathers.

They sat in the turret room. Flora brought a tea tray. Steam curled from the teapot. A white bowl held late-crop raspberries, full-lobed, seedy. Butter cookies circled a plate, each one buttoned with strawberry jam in a thumbed dent. Flora turned, weaving a subtle route between chairs and around the piano. With a quick glance over her shoulder, she closed the door without making a sound.

Josephine poured tea for Harland. She poured for herself. On the mantelpiece, the clock made a clicking hesitation as the minute hand shifted.

"Did you come about the petition, Harland?"

It was the only point of reference between them, since Enid had been found, and the court case completed, and Mr. Mallory sent to prison, and Doreen bundled off to the county poorhouse.

"I need . . ." His hands shook and the cup rattled in its saucer. He set it down, untasted. ". . . advice."

"Of course, Harland. I have asked the same of you, so many times." She thought of Lucy's letter. *We refuse to absorb these false descriptions*. If a woman had asked for her advice, she would not demur. She reached forward and touched the cuff of his shirt. "What is it, Harland?"

"Permelia and I have had the most terrible fight of our marriage. Words have been spoken that can never be forgotten. Words have been shouted that cannot be unsaid. It began after supper, last night. We raged on and off, and then it started up again after breakfast. She came to the store. She laid down her demands. She had them all *written out* on a piece of paper. She . . . she simply laid down the paper and walked out. I have not been home yet."

He pressed a hand to his face. In the cave of his palm, his breath was shaky, hoarse. He took down his hand and leaned his head against the back of the chair. A tear brimmed in one eye and rolled down into his moustache.

"What were her demands?"

"Most were to do with the business. She feels I am not running it well. She thinks I spend too much time on my weather station and my notes. She thinks I'm resting on my father's accomplishments and am not responding to the 'changing times.' She has been going over the books behind my back. She wants me to fire the people I now employ, except for my daughters, of course. She wants changes made to the store—how it looks, what I buy, who I hire. She wants things for herself, as well. A new stove, dresses for the girls, things I have been . . . putting off."

"Well. It could be worse. I would assume you can afford to do at least some of those things."

"Yes. That is not . . . really . . . I should not paint my wife in such a negative way. She is a good friend to the girls, a loving and attentive mother. She is an upstanding citizen, as you know from all her committee work and . . ."

He made a circle in the air with his fingers.

". . . and so on. In fact, Permelia has more business acumen than I do. Were we better suited in temperament, perhaps we could run the store together. But that is the crux of the issue. We could not run a business together. We cannot make a marriage together."

"Oh, Harland."

"Truly, Josephine. I do not know how I am going to return home tonight. I don't know how I can walk into the house and smile at the girls and sit down at the dinner table and talk about the day. I feel like . . ."

He held his gaze on the uppermost part of the tall windows.

"I would like to be heading west with—"

"A fur cap?" She smiled, joking. "A gun and a tent and a trapline and snowshoes?"

He dashed at the wetness on his cheek with the back of his hand. She wanted to do for him what she would have done for Simeon. Run a hand through his hair. Straighten his collar.

"Josephine. I have only one life. And you have only one life."

"And you have a good life, Harland. You will repair this."

"No. My marriage is a thing that never existed. There is nothing to repair."

"No love between you?"

"Love. So much talk of love. Love for Christ. Love for our fellow man. I search myself. I suppose I love my daughters, in a kind of way. Although sometimes I wonder if they love me. They take on their mother's attitudes. Sometimes I wonder if I . . . I think that what I feel for . . ."

"Love is . . . wanting to tell someone every beautiful thing you see. Sharing the love you feel for your children. Not . . . oh, not finishing a sentence because you know the other person could finish it for you. Love is . . . feeling your . . . your . . ."

Her voice thickened. Even as the tears came, she watched herself, as if another Josephine were acting a part; she forbade herself to cry, and still the tears came, changing her into a person of whom she had no control, who might say anything.

"My last gift to him . . . remember, Harland, it was Christmas when he was expected . . . still wrapped, still in his . . . bureau . . ."

Harland was on his knees beside her chair. He took her hand. He slid an arm over her shoulder and pulled her to him. She wept against the white linen jacket, smelling Permelia's Sunlight soap, feeling his lips pressed to her head and his breath on her scalp.

Just for a minute, she thought, just let me rest here for a minute, as if he is the husband I have lost. It occurred to her, then, that although she was not in love with Harland she did, indeed, love him dearly.

Her tears subsided. She was in her own parlour. A man was on his knees beside the tea table with his arms around her. She pulled away. He returned to his chair.

"We could marry, Josephine. I could divorce."

She pulled a handkerchief from her sleeve and wiped her eyes. She avoided his eyes and knew that in this avoidance he, too, returned to himself. He patted his vest and looked down.

The buttons. Awry.

"Have they been that way all day, Harland?" she said.

He looked up at her.

"You know, I care for you dearly," she murmured. "We can go on together, caring for one another dearly. You know this, Harland. It is another kind of love."

He bent his head and did not answer. She watched his fingers, working the buttons.

—

No one watched as Josephine pulled her nightgown over her head. No one noticed how the satin ribbons were worn or observed the stitches where she had repaired the cambric ruffle. No one murmured tender words.

She climbed into bed and lay back against the pillows. The kerosene lamp on her bedside table pulled from the darkness the wallpaper's entwined flowers. Out the window, she could see the lights of a neighbouring window, interrupted by the shiver of leaves.

She put her hand to her hair, the place his lips had pressed.

Divorce, disgrace. The failure of a marriage. Should she accept his offer, the failure would be her inheritance as much as his.

She closed her eyes and realized she could succumb to the longing to be loved. A kiss. His hands would slide to the small of her back. She would bend and fall back.

She saw how far she would fall, then, from the woman she was in the process of becoming.

PART IV

September 1889 – June 1890

TWENTY

Brass Duck

~

FLORA STOOD IN THE dust and scraps of the empty workshop. She felt a childlike rush of tears.

He was sweeping the floor, his mouth ugly.

"Did they . . . did they like it, Mr. Tuck?"

He stopped and crossed his arms, imitating her. "*Did they like it, Mr. Tuck?* What do *you* think?"

"I just would like to have seen . . ."

She would like to have seen the sisters exclaim over the perfect, tiny carpets. The curtains, with their barely visible stitches. The matchstick windows, the feather-light tables. She would have liked to have seen how they did not notice glue, brads, all the meticulous work of measuring, whittling and sanding, but saw only their results, like something from a fairy tale. *Oh, Rosamund, isn't it exquisite? Don't you love it?*

He was in a terrible temper. "Oh, they liked it good enough. They liked it."

"Well, maybe they will show it to other people and we will get more orders."

"Somebody snitched to them as to how I was taking advantage of you. Must have been what you told that one who didn't order. That Mrs. Dunfield."

"I never . . ."

"Told me they would 'withhold' a certain amount of what was owing unless I promised it would go straight to you. So I promised. But it ain't. Going to you. Because I put down good money for that dress and you won't wear it, so now you'll work for me until you earn back what I paid for it."

"You could take the amount they were going to withhold and put it towards the dress."

"You think that will be enough? Hey?"

Flora turned away and pressed her forehead to the window. It was the first day of September, the sky a brilliant blue, the clouds larger, closer.

He had laid hands on her once. She would give him no reason to do so again. The sock filled with coins, hidden beneath the floorboard, was becoming heavy. She did not know what else she could do to make money. Every effort she made in that regard—eggs, mittens, butter—went towards maintaining Josephine's household.

He slammed the broom into its corner, picked up a scrub brush and dipped it into a bucket of water and lye. He drew the bristles deep into the grain of the table, bore down.

"I'll wear the dress. It was just too hot, that's all. I'll try to order up another house. I can tell people to go to see Hilltop. I can ask the sisters if they would mind."

He avoided her eyes, muttered something to himself.

"What?" she said. She wanted to snatch the brush and throw it in his face. "I didn't hear."

"Never you mind," he said. "Just git."

—

The following day, at breakfast, Ellen noticed dark circles beneath Flora's eyes and a corresponding anxiety in Enid. Josephine, as well, seemed unaccountably agitated, as she had for several days.

Get them out of the house . . .

She sent the girls to the grocery store.

"I can't make my cookies until I get more oatmeal and molasses. Beds can wait."

Enid and Flora walked down the hill. Frost lay as if strewn from buckets—behind sheds, in ditches. A maid stood on a veranda, shaking a small carpet; dust rose in a cloud and then unravelled.

"He thought if I wore the dress I would be able to sell the houses."

"Why, Flora? Why do you have to wear the dress?"

To hide the guttersnipe. To make me a lady.

Flora sought patience, impatient not with Enid but with the situation she found herself in. Mr. Tuck, and his sulks. The miniature houses, only an idea, now, since the house they had made was gone.

"Anyway," Flora said. "I said I'd put the thing on and go around again."

Enid said nothing, and Flora, waiting for a response—commiseration, perhaps, or protest—could not read her expression.

—

After lunch, Enid went out to the garden. The shell bean vines had collapsed, their leaves crunchy. Red and white speckled beans pushed open the stiff pods. She pulled the plants up by the roots and piled them in the wheelbarrow. She pushed the wheelbarrow into the barn and gathered the beans into bunches, weaving lengths of string into the dry, wish-boned stems. Behind her, large doors stood open, framing the green fields, the red and golden hardwoods spiked with spruce trees.

She wore a brown gingham dress with full sleeves. An apron. She had stuffed her hair into a cap, tied at the back.

Jasper Tuck opened the door of the workshop.

His hair fell over his forehead, shading his eyes. He leaned against the wall, ankles crossed.

"You want some nails? For to hang them?"

"Oh." She looked up at the barn wall, where she had thought to find enough protuberances to hang the bunched beans.

He went back into the workshop and came back with a hammer and nails. He set a neat line of nails along the wall.

This morning Ellen had wondered aloud what Mr. Tuck was doing with himself, now that he had finished Hilltop.

Lots of things he could be doing. Mr. Dougan, now. Would have fixed that latticework. Would have glazed them storm windows.

I could ask him, Josephine had mused. *But I can't pay him, you see.*

It occurred to Enid that they were all, to some degree, afraid of Mr. Tuck, although aside from moodiness he gave them no reason to be.

Enid lifted the handles of the wheelbarrow. She saw the subtle, almost unconscious motion of his hand, bidding her to set them down.

"You like it here?"

"Do you mean here at Mrs. Galloway's or here in Canada?"

"You choose."

"Well. I'm not so sure about Canada. Strikes me as a hard place," she said. "But I like Mrs. Galloway's house."

"You like being with your sister."

"Oh, yes! Flora can do anything. Can't she?"

Except wear the dress with pleasure, in order to sell his houses . . .

A tight smile. "Yes, indeed she can."

She could surprise Flora. *She* could do it, and then tell her it had been done. *Flora, I sold a house, you can make money again.* And maybe, too, she could help with the cutting and sewing, and it would be as if they were back in the felting room but without the terror of Matron's inspection.

"Mr. Tuck, I would like . . ."

He pushed himself away from the wall with one foot. He stood across from her and put his hands on the sides of the wheelbarrow. He leaned forward and his eyes went to her hair.

"What would you like, Miss Enid Salford?"

"To see that there dress. The one you got . . . you know."

"Yes," he said. She thought he spoke to himself. *Yes.* She was not certain what she meant by it. He turned and walked back towards his workshop. Uncertain, she bent to lift the wheelbarrow. He heard the creak of the axle and stopped. "Hey? You coming with me?"

She followed him into the workshop. She smelled the bright, clean aroma of paint, turpentine, wood shavings. Immaculate windows sharpened the house across the lane, like a focused lens. Sun lay on the surface of the work table, so scoured that droplets of dried paint were as if intentional and the wood grain, ridged, held no dirt, only streaks of blue or white, the dent of a hammer. On the wall was a row of miniature tools, oiled, sharpened: chisels, hammers, knives. The brass handles of a chest of drawers were a grid of shining, golden shells, upside-down.

"You keep it so neat, Mr. Tuck."

"Waiting for the next job. Which . . ." He stared at her, and she thought he wanted her to speak but could not imagine what she should say. He turned, abruptly, and went to a chest shoved up against the wall. He squatted, lifted the lid. A rustling, like paper. He stood, the dress laid over his arms. He held it out to her.

"You want to put it on?"

She lifted a finger to stroke the blue velvet.

"I'll go out there in the yard and stand under that tree. See? Right there where everyone can see me. I'll set my back to the barn. I'll be looking out at the street. You crack open the door and give me a whistle when you're done."

He went out. Enid withdrew to the back of the workshop and removed her clothes, glancing over her shoulder. He remained by the tree, sturdily fixed, arms crossed. The dress smelled reassuringly of Flora; slightly too big, it was easy to slide into. Her arms, sleeking along the lining of the velvet sleeves. Her feet, stepping into the circled overskirt. Shoulders, shrugging into the jacket. Her fingers flew, tipping the buttons into their holes. She patted herself down and looked up to see a reflection, in a mirror. The mirror was as clean as the windows. She saw that the dress was loose over the breasts, yet the lacy frill at the neck's edge cupped her chin and she looked into her own wide eyes and felt a stirring of love for her beauty.

"Mr. Tuck." She cracked the door. "Mr. Tuck."

She glanced over at the house. *What if one of them were to come out.* She retreated to the back of the workshop.

He came back into the workshop and did not look at her until he had made certain that the door latch had settled properly. He turned. The expression she had thought would come over his face—delight, wonder—did not arrive and she realized it was Flora's reaction she'd expected.

"Bit too big," he said. He crossed the floor. He was shorter than Mr. Fairweather and lean as Mr. Mallory; his thin lips reminded her of the workhouse children who never had enough of anything. Fred, she thought, lifting her arms, since he was reaching for her waist . . . *would have looked like Jasper Tuck, had he grown up.*

He set his hands on her, lightly, and revolved her until she stood with her back to him. He gathered up the loose material; pulled it tight against her breasts.

"About an inch," he muttered. "Seams."

He turned her again.

"Still," he said. "You'll grow. You'll be growing fast with the likes of that Ellen's food."

"Do you want me to try to sell some houses? I will, if you want me to."

"You going to tell Flora?"

"I thought . . . maybe if I sell one. Then I could tell her."

"And why is that? Why wouldn't you tell her that you are selling houses for me?"

"She wouldn't . . ."

"Want you to have anything to do with the likes of me."

He looked sideways, out the window. His hand was still on her waist, as if she were made of china and he kept her steadied so she would not tip and fall. *The likes of me.*

"It's not *you*, Mr. Tuck. It's me. She's afeared for me. She won't let me go down into the town alone."

Still he stared through the immaculate glass. She sensed his unknown story, most likely similar to her own, and felt the sprouting of pity. She wondered if her own father might have wanted her for an assistant; might have inspected her, soberly, as Mr. Tuck had. She saw that Mr. Tuck might change his mind and then she would never again wear the dress. She felt a passionate attachment to the dress, as if her own loveliness were shaped by it. She wanted, for the first time in her life, to care for Flora.

"Mr. Tuck, your houses are like a dream come true. That's what I would tell people. *His houses are like a dream come true.*"

The sentence tilted her, the edge of a slide.

His smile flickered, vanished. He lifted his hand from her waist and circled his finger. She rotated, again, unconsciously lifting her arms into the air.

"Flora is the beautiful one," she said. She felt the need to explain this so he would not expect too much.

He stepped closer, held her shoulders.

"She might be the beautiful one. But you and me. You and me, Enid. We're a secret, the two of us. Aren't we?"

He raised a finger to stroke back a strand of hair that lay across her forehead but changed it into a warning shake.

Teasing, she thought. He left the workshop and again stood under the tree. Her own gingham dress was like a wilted leaf, softened by washing and the sunshine and snap of the clothesline. She tied the strings of her cap. There were more beans to pick, rows and rows, lying dead and dry in the soil.

—

Enid told Flora that she had met a girl who was working in one of the other big houses on Creek Road. Sometimes she and this girl, Colleen, would walk in the pastures up behind the houses.

Flora felt a pang of jealousy and chastised herself for it. Enid had never had a friend.

September drew to a close. After supper, darkness sifted down and the few feeble crickets fell silent. With dishes done and the house readied for morning, Flora and Enid went up to their bedroom to study.

"What are you reading, Flora?" Enid asked. She was practising her addition. *11 + 17. 23 + 10.*

"*Then all around was heard the crash of trees / Trembling awhile and rushing to the ground.* It's a book about how men and oxen cut down all the trees and turned the forests into farms."

Rustle of turning page. The scratching of Enid's pencil.

Flora dropped her forehead onto the heels of her hands and stared at the poem's illustration, an etching of mighty trees and men swinging axes; the largest of the trees was in the process of falling, and Flora felt sad for it, and for the young birch trees that bent beneath it. Mr. Tuck had not asked her to go out prospecting for new customers, and so there were no little houses to make. Josephine relied on her to keep the boarding house running; this was Flora's work, yet it yielded only room and board. She had only erratic slices of available time, which were all right for a job with Mr. Tuck; but she did not see how she could work in the tannery or the boot and shoe factory or the steam laundry. Mr. Tuck had not asked her to go around in the dress. His face was closed, forbidding. She figured he was hatching a new plan.

Flora wondered if she and Enid would ever leave this house, no matter how far they furthered their education.

She pictured the drawer filled with banknotes. Orange, grey and green.

—

Occasionally, Enid waited for Mr. Tuck on a side street. She wore the dress, concealed by a cloak. He picked her up with a horse and buggy from the livery stable.

Enid knocked on doors. If admitted, she unrolled large pencil drawings that Jasper Tuck had made of his creations. She explained about the similitude of the reproduction. *Who is the maker?* she was asked.

Mr. Tuck had told her not to point him out as he waited in the buggy. She was to say that Mr. Jasper Tuck had recently moved to town and that he constructed these houses in his own workshop. *Should you be interested,* Enid said, *we kin ask if those as owns one of his little houses can let you see it.* She stood straight and fearless, proud of herself in the beautiful dress. Women sent her away with cookies or a loaf of bread. They smiled, giving her pats on the shoulder and glancing at the man on the buggy as they followed Enid to their doorways. One asked if Mr. Jasper Tuck was her father.

After the third such visit, Mr. Tuck no longer spoke when she climbed back into the buggy. His eyes skipped to the closing door, the face in the window. His expression masked any emotion. He lifted the reins and clucked to the horse.

—

Josephine took down the Simpkin's Tooth Powder monthly calendar from its nail and turned it to October. There was more sky visible between the branches; the rooms of the house seemed larger in the unimpeded light.

"Do you remember the pirates?" she asked Carrie, who had stopped to visit. Carrie was on her way to the train station, heading back to St. John after visiting her parents in Whelan's Cove.

"I remember it more as a sensation," Carrie said. The turret room was chill, and both women wore merino shawls. "With pictures strewn around like pieces of a jigsaw puzzle." She spoke briskly. "My dear dead dog, Gig. I remember that. And how I helped my mother make my father's hair into little braids to bind the wound."

Josephine realized she should not have forced this from her husband's cousin, who had never asked her how she had felt upon visiting the scene of Simeon's death.

"I'm sorry, I should not have asked."

Flora came in with a plate of oatmeal cookies, fresh from the oven. Carrie's eyes followed her as she left the room.

"She seems sad," she said. "Is she still pursuing her studies?"

Josephine felt a pang of guilt, realizing her own preoccupation ever since the precarious moment with Mr. Fairweather. "Yes, I believe she studies in the evening with Enid."

"What will become of them? The sisters?" Carrie leaned forward to take a cookie from the plate. "They must have a life of their own, someday."

Her eyes were calm, as if the question were simple, but Josephine saw it encumbered with Carrie's understanding of what constituted a life—women as players in a political drama, their choices weighted with historical significance. Josephine wanted to protest that she had saved the girls from poverty and degradation. She wanted Carrie to acknowledge the gracious house with its linens and carpets, and how even if the girls were to some degree servants within it, it was their home. She wanted to proclaim the advantages of her own deep affection for them. Yet she was struck by a pang of shame.

She found she could not tell Carrie the degree to which she loved, as well as depended upon, Flora. Or how she and Maud and Flora and Ellen murmured to one another about Enid—delighted to see that she had stopped pleating her skirt on her knee, thrilled when they noticed she had begun to look people in the eye, improve her grammar, smile. She could not tell Carrie that on some mornings she woke to her loneliness and felt as lost, as vulnerable, as Flora and Enid.

"I don't know what will become of any of us. Them, me, Ellen. My own daughters. I can only go on, day by day. Keeping food on our table and a roof over our heads."

"Men's laws left you in a pickle, of course, and now you avoid working out your own situation by being pleased with the improvements you see in the girls."

"There is only one way that I can see of to *work out my situation*, Carrie. Simeon's will could not be found, and because of that, I have nothing. He would not have wished this upon me, but those are the facts and cannot be changed. I will live in this house the rest of my life, unless all three of my children decide to sell it. Which I heartily hope they will not. But if they did, and should I relinquish my dower right, the portion I would receive from the sale would pauperize me. I am doing the only thing possible, running a boarding establishment. It is an invaluable help having Flora and Enid here. I hope it is a help for them as much as it is for me."

Her face grew hot. Mr. Fairweather. *Divorce*. His desire to spend the rest of his life with her. The fearful sweetness of the moment, which she could not resist nurturing.

Carrie, misinterpreting the blush, leaned forward and touched Josephine's arm. "Oh, Josephine. You know, I believe I spent too many years of my childhood with only my mother. No playmates. My father was of necessity a stern man. I did not learn the niceties of conversation. I am too direct. I'm sorry."

"It's not . . ." Embarrassed, Josephine leaned to peer out the window. She had seen a movement on the lane, a flash of green, and thought it could not be Mr. Tuck's coat, as it was too bright.

—

Enid listened but heard no sound. She opened the door and slipped into the workshop.

In the corner where she had changed into the dress, just where she'd expected it to be, she found her white satin ribbon. Ellen had given it to her and she wore it like a necklace, treasured it. It lay between a wicker wastebasket and the wall. Farther back, in a corner, she saw an object—box, book, wallet, spectacle case—clearly lost, in want of rescue. She scrabbled into the darkness, lifted something cold, smooth, heavy. A paperweight? A toy?

A brass duck.

She squatted, cleaning it on her skirt.

It was so unlike Mr. Tuck that she knew immediately that it must have belonged to one of the children, Maud, perhaps, or George. Perhaps they'd forgotten it while visiting Mr. Dougan. *Oh, he kept the place spotless,* Ellen had recollected. *Loved to oil the harness, the bridles. Mr. Galloway had a nice riding horse. Mr. Dougan, he kept those stirrup irons shining like the best silver.*

Enid had once possessed a cloth doll with wooden head, arms and legs. She could not remember it, but Flora told her that Ma and Papa made it for her. It went missing in the workhouse, Flora said. *Some other little girl stole it. You cried for days.*

She held the duck in the palm of her hand until it was warm. She rubbed the round circle of its eye until she fancied it looked happy and recognized her.

Back in the house, as Enid climbed the stairs, she heard Flora laugh, probably at something Ellen had said. Farther off, the murmur of voices in the parlour. She went to her bedroom, dropped the ribbon on her bed. No one wanted the duck, she reasoned—she'd only brought it into the house where it belonged, although it was hers now. She tucked it under her pillow with only a bit of the beak showing. *So you can breathe.* Later, she would find a better hiding place for it.

She went back out to pull the last of the turnips.

—

At four-thirty, Ellen put a hand to the small of her back.

"Must go lie down," she said.

Flora stooped to slide a sheet of biscuits into the oven. "I can make the pie."

"You got to crumble the savoury fine and pick out the stems. Remember Mr. Sprague. *Needle in my throat,* he said."

Ellen went upstairs. Passing the door to Flora and Enid's room, she paused, noticing the ribbon on the bed. She saw something else, curious. She stepped into the room and lifted the pillow.

—

As Flora put the finishing touches on the supper table—cut-crystal saucer of pickles, silver-plated butter dish, knife inserted in its prong—the boarders were coming down the stairs. Returning to the kitchen, she noticed that light had drained from the sky, the barn roof a silhouette against the cooling blue.

"Where's Enid?"

Maud was sitting in the rocker, patting the cat. "Haven't seen her. I thought she was upstairs washing her hands. I'll call her."

She jumped up, went out.

The cat, offended, rubbed against Ellen's ankles. Ellen, revived from her brief rest, was spooning mashed potatoes into a bowl; she stamped a foot. "Go on with you."

Maud returned, shortly. "She's not upstairs."

"I think she's in the garden," Josephine said. She was stirring a custard.

"I'll go check. It's not like her to be late." Maud was in the hall, shoving her arms into a woollen sweater.

"But it's getting dark," Flora said. She felt her breath, shortening. "It's almost night."

She carried the chicken pie into the dining room. Ellen followed with the bowl of mashed potatoes. Miss Harvey, Mrs. Beaman and Mr. Sprague were pulling back their chairs, discussing a bicycle race that had taken place in St. John.

"Is Mr. Tuck coming down?" Ellen said. She stood with the bowl of steaming potatoes balanced on the flat of her hand. A pat of butter loosened, pooled.

"Didn't see him."

They listened.

Mrs. Beaman, sitting, loosened her waistband with complacent tugs. She unfolded her napkin, surveying the table as the women set down pie and potatoes and hurried back to the kitchen.

Flora put her hand on her chest, pressing down on her heart's heavy pound.

"Mr. Tuck is missing," she said to Josephine.

The back door opened. Maud stood, panting.

"She's not in the garden."

Laughter, the clatter of silverware.

Ellen put out her hand and brought it down slowly, as if pushing something away. "Flora," she said. "Did you see that brass duck on Enid's bed?"

"Mr. Tuck's brass duck? The one from the workshop? On Enid's bed?"

"What are you talking about?" Josephine said.

"The children, they never had a brass duck?" Ellen asked her.

"I don't remember any such thing."

"Dear God in Heaven." Ellen snatched up her glasses, went to the corner where articles about the axe murder trial were still pinned to the wall.

She ripped a yellowing paper from its tack. She sat at the table and ran her forefinger down a column until she found what she was looking for.

"This testimony was from a woman who used to visit the one that was murdered. She had gone to the house on the very day the woman was killed. *After* she was killed. *I saw that nothing was missing from the chest of drawers except a large box containing her savings and a small brass duck that had been of particular notice, as being the only decorative item amongst her possessions.*"

"There could be other brass—"

"*Taken*," Ellen said. "*Taken* by the axe murderer."

"The axe murderer was hanged, Ellen."

"Maybe," she said. "Or maybe they hanged the wrong man."

"Oh. Oh, no. No. No."

"*What*, Flora?"

"The drawer. He has a drawer stuffed full of money. Banknotes. Like a lifetime of savings. He threatened me if I ever spoke about it."

—

They ran into the falling night, trailing half-buttoned coats. Mr. Sprague and Mrs. Beaman clustered in the doorway. Miss Harvey was putting through a telephone call to the town constables.

Harland noticed them from his dining room window. Light behind him, as he opened the front door. Table napkin fluttering from his hand like a moth. Flora veered from Ellen, Josephine and Maud.

Up the path.

She called out. The words, panted.

"Enid and Mr. Tuck. Disappeared. We found. Something that makes us think he is the murderer."

"Murderer?"

"The axe murderer. Please, come, I'll . . ."

He dropped the napkin. Left the door wide open behind him. The others had continued, were turning onto Main Street. Flora and Mr. Fairweather broke into a run, passing houses where people sat to supper. They caught up at the town hall, where a constable stood on the steps, surprise in his round blue eyes. He had received Miss Harvey's telephone call.

They followed him into the office. He touched a match to the gaslights. Ellen stood at his desk, panting, holding out the article. He took it from her, sat. Read it.

"But they hanged that man," he said, slowly. He spoke to Mr. Fairweather. Streak of mustard on his shirt. One cuff, unbuttoned. He ignored the women as if they were a cluster of hens.

"Let me see it," Harland said.

He skimmed the article, eyebrows raised.

Ellen had not stepped back from the desk. She held herself as if in the process of falling to pieces: arms crossed, shoulders hunched, mouth pinched. Flora had never seen her outside of the kitchen.

"'Twas the brass duck." She nodded at the paper. "See how it says . . ."

Mr. Fairweather did not comprehend. Josephine drew a breath, preparing to explain. The constable looked back and forth, now, between Josephine and Mr. Fairweather, doubt creeping into his face, a hint of irritation. He ignored Ellen. He had been interrupted at his meal.

Flora pushed in front of Mr. Fairweather. Her heart—heavy, surging. She took the paper from the constable's fingers and slapped it down in front of him. He pushed back his chair, startled.

"*Look* at me," she said. "*You look at me and listen to me.* This is my sister has been took."

She enunciated each word like the distinct poke of a forefinger against the constable's chest.

"Took by Mr. Jasper Tuck. They're both missing. He lives at our boarding house. I work for him. He has a drawer filled with cash. I saw it. And a brass duck. Exactly what was stolen from that murdered woman. Cash, and a brass duck. *This brass duck.*" She worked the brass duck from her pocket, slammed it onto the desk. An unwashed teacup rattled in its saucer. "A murderer has my little sister. *He has my little sister.* We got to go after them. There's no time. *No time.*"

A second constable stepped into the room. Both men pored over the article with increased interest.

"You *seen* this cash?" the first constable asked Flora.

"Yes," Flora said. "An entire drawer filled with banknotes. In his workshop."

"Why didn't you—"

"Never mind," Mr. Fairweather snapped. His cheeks flushed. His clothing, like the constable's, was disarranged by his dash from the dinner table. "As she said. There's no time."

—

Reinforcements would arrive on the next train: four constables from St. John, three from Moncton.

The constables spread a map, traced the twisty roads.

"He will look for an abandoned barn. Or an abandoned house. Could be the old Carty place, up here on the Wallen's Ridge. Or there's another place down in Midvale . . ."

Mr. Fairweather murmured in Flora's ear.

"I've asked the others if they would like to return home. They said they would. I'll join the search." Harland knew of outlying and abandoned places in the vicinity from his time as Overseer. "Do you want to come with me?"

Clothes turned up . . . bruises on the insides of her thighs . . . scratches from a man's fingernails . . . marks of teeth . . . the whole forehead was broken in . . . blood . . . blood . . .

She turned and pressed her face into Mr. Fairweather's wool overcoat. He put his arms around her and pulled her close.

TWENTY-ONE

Like Beautiful Objects, Like Possessions

~

THEY TRAVELLED FAR INTO the countryside. As the sky changed from pink to dusky blue, darkness rose like water in the alder hollows, and orange maples turned black against the sky. The horse's hooves crunched the dirt in rapid concussion, the rhythm of fear. Soon Enid could see only the lantern swinging at the side of the buggy, an erratic sear illuminating goldenrod, dry ferns, and the flash of ironclad wheel. Squares of occasional windows flickered in the night—candlelight, a yearning. The moon rose, as on the night she had run away from Mr. Mallory. She slid forward as the road descended, entered a stretch of woods. An owl swooped, an intent darkness, undeterred by their passage. The road emerged into silvered fields—in their centre, like black pearls, a house and a barn.

She stumbled down from the carriage. He slung a carpet bag over his shoulder, took the lamp from the buggy and walked behind her, shoving her across a tangle of collapsed grass until a house loomed in the circle of light. He kicked open the back door. A hallway. A room with a wood stove, a bed, a table. She smelled something sharp and lively. A scrabble on the low ceiling.

"Racoons," he muttered. He set the lamp on the wood stove. He pushed her onto the bed. He set down the bag, then picked it up and stood with it in his arms. Finally he set it down on the floor beside the bed. He untied her hands, released her from the saliva-soaked rag. She clutched herself, shivering, trying to read his expression, but he was black angles, he was the scrape of chair legs, he was a chair held in one hand, swung close. He was swift sitting and kneecaps and the tap of a fingertip on her own thigh.

Broken window. The house held the silence of long emptiness.

"You don't know me, do you?"

She knew Mr. Mallory. You had to do what he wanted. You had to guess not only what he would want you to say, but with what quality of submission to say it. With what absence of judgment. Enid had watched Doreen and learned how to breathe, where to look, how to hold her shoulders, what to do with her hands. How to make herself into what he wanted. How to be like the air that he would take in, satisfactory and barely noticed.

"I got to decide if I am going to take you with me or leave you here."

He could leave her tied to the bed—feet tied, arms tied, gagged. The raccoons would creep down and attack her with their sharp-clawed, fingery paws.

"I got to know if you will be a help or a hindrance."

Absolute silence. No horse and carriage passed on the road.

"I will be a help."

"Will you, now? Because there was other women who said that to me. *I will be a help*. If they weren't, I did away with them."

To tremble. To still her trembling. To show fear. To be brave. Enid did not know. Moonlight on a piece of wallpaper. A flower. She fought against the image of Fred, turning on his rope.

"I took you because I want to have you."

"Yes. You can have me."

"Well, then. That's nice. You do what I say, you be my girl, you don't go running off to your sister, you come away with me, no one follows, we change our names. Understand?"

Why? She had done him no good. She had not sold a house. He had been angry with her. She did not understand.

"Yes."

They would have noticed her absence. They would be looking for her. Words were papery, fragile, like toy boats set onto a river. She could not say she was glad to go with him. She could not promise to obey him.

He was hunched like a raccoon, eyes in a mask, glints. He raised a finger and drew it across her throat. His finger traced her nose, the circle of her face, followed her hairline, came down over her cheek and her ear.

"Any man had you?"

"No."

"I'll be your first."

Could a heart hammer itself to death?

"Yes."

"Then you'll be my woman. You understand?"

She thought, now, that he wanted her not to understand.

"Mr. Tuck, I don't understand, but it's all right, I'll be your . . . your girl, anyway."

"And why is that? Why would you do that?"

Was he asking *Why would you want me?* or *Why would you hate me?* Did he want her to tell the truth? That she would do it only because she had no choice? She did not dare say it.

The tears came. She could not stop them. She kept herself from sobbing. Tears, mucus, the salty slime at the corners of her mouth. He slapped her face.

"Why would you do that?"

She had forgotten the question.

He pushed her down on the bed and unbuckled his belt. She panted, staring upwards, knees clenched. He would roll her over onto her stomach. She had seen Mr. Mallory climbing on top of Freddy, in the stall.

"I stole," she said, suddenly. She could show him how she could be a thief. She could make him believe in her usefulness.

I did away with them.

He tossed his belt onto the floor. "Stole what?"

"I found a . . . a brass duck in your workshop. I figured it to have been a toy. Of . . ." she could not sully their names. "Of one of the children. I never had a toy so I took it."

"When? When did you take it?"

"Today. I went to find my ribbon. I found the duck behind a basket . . . and I kept it."

"Give it to me."

"I . . . I don't have it. I hid it in my bedroom."

"Did you hide it well? So no one would see it?"

The beak.

"Yes," she lied. "I put it under a floorboard. No one will find it."

He dropped to his knees. He put his hands on her neck and pressed her against the damp cot. She could not turn her head from side to side. She could not breathe.

"When you're my girl," he hissed, whispering even though no one could hear, not the racoons or the owls or the rising moon. "*You will not take my things.*"

My neck. Breaking. Stars at the edge of rising water.

The hands, lifted.

To breathe. Shuddering. Her own hands, small and soft, on her own skin. Sweet skin.

"I'm sorry." Her voice was hoarse, strained.

He sat on the floor, against the wall. The moon, now, was shining directly into the room. A pile of droppings, in the middle of the floor. A cast-iron tea kettle on the stove. The belt.

The racoons, upstairs, made no sound. Wind, the sigh of grasses, leaves.

No crickets, no frogs.

This is how it had come to Freddy, when he had reached for the rope and settled it around his neck. You are walking straight ahead, not knowing you approach a threshold—and a door slams closed. You walk into it. You and the door meet.

Enid dropped her face onto her knees, held herself. The doll. She saw it, now. Wooden head with no face, wooden arms and legs. No name, no eyes or mouth; yet she had given it the life she should have had. A wedding. A daisy for a bonnet. Rhubarb leaf for a gown. Crooning, songs. *Hear that, dolly,* held to the sky when the night birds sang.

Dying.

"I had one . . . toy . . . just wanted . . . another. Didn't know it was . . . yours, Mr. Tu—"

"Ain't a toy. *No more than my houses are toys.*"

"No," she whispered, frantic, wiping her face. "No, no, I didn't mean to say toy."

He sat with his wrists on his knees, hands hanging. Fingernails, like onion skin. The tremulous rush of air going into his nostrils, the huff of its return. She heard an eerie yipping coming from field or forest; remembered the scream of the bobcat, *it's not a woman,* Freddie told her, but still she had dreaded the sound, *like a woman being murdered,* she told him, the sound she always feared they would hear coming from Doreen.

Why would Mr. Tuck want a brass duck. Duck, Tuck, luck.

A charm.

"I'm going to ask you one thing, Enid Salford." He made a pistol with his finger but aimed it at the carpet bag and then shifted it to the iron stove with glints of metal like slitted cat's eyes. "I am going to ask you one thing and I will know if you are lying. If I so much as *think* that you are lying, then I am going to put my hands around your neck. And I am going to strangle you."

Say yes. Say nothing. Say nothing.

"I want you to tell me where you put that duck."

The floorboard was where Flora hid the money. Flora had never told anyone but her about the money.

"I put it under my pillow."

"Any part of it showing?"

"The beak. The beak was showing."

He snatched her chin, wrenched her face towards him.

"That's true, isn't it."

She nodded into his hand. He released her. He bent forward, holding his forehead.

Flora, Flora, Flora.

Roaring in her ears, a throb behind her eyes, her chest aching with the pressure.

She would hear the *clock-clock* of hooves coming up the road. They would be looking for her. They would come.

He planted his hands on his knees and pushed himself up. He hitched his pants at the waistband, testing. He picked up the belt. He buckled her hands to the scrolled metal headboard, all the while whispering to himself. He picked up the carpet bag and slung it over his shoulder. He did not look back.

The drumming of hooves on dirt was like a scattering. Pepper on the night. Sprinkled.

Fewer.

Fewer.

She heard a soft thump upstairs, again the scrabble of claws. She struggled, wrenching her hands, feeling the skin on her wrists stretching. Her breasts. She could not cover them with her arms, bend forward, protect her face, belly. She could only kick. She could kick at the raccoons when they jumped up on her. She could scream.

Another thump, close overhead. A second racoon, following the first.

Scritch scritch. A rapid, wild raking. Would a scream frighten them away or signal her vulnerability? They would approach, hunchbacked, with their sidling, sneaky scuttle. Eyes, glinting.

Flora and Josephine and Ellen and Maud would by now have alerted Mr. Fairweather and everyone else they knew. *Enid has been stolen by Mr. Tuck.*

Ellen: *You keep clear of that one.*

Flora: *Stay away from him.*

She explored with her fingertips. Her thumb touched the bar of the buckle, her finger straightened the prong. Slipped, snagged, slipped, snagged.

She gave up.

Tears. She licked them from the corners of her mouth.

Try again. Maybe he didn't tighten it as much as he could have.

She pressed back against the headboard to loosen the belt. She bent the belt upwards with thumb, fingers, nudging the leather over the prong.

Nudging. Nudging.

She heard the thump of a racoon coming down the stairs.

"You get away," she shouted.

The prong slid down. She pushed it back up, bent the leather. Panting, now.

Over and over.

The prong suddenly, miraculously, slid from the leather. She worked the belt through the bar. It slithered to the floor.

She pulled up her legs and sat cross-legged on the bed, bent forward, forehead on knees, rubbing her wrists. Trembling. Let them come, those racoons, she thought, feeling vicious contempt.

I can attack. I can run.

When she escaped from the Mallorys, there was no house on Creek Road; no Josephine and Ellen and Maud; no white-painted bedstead and patchwork quilt and chest of drawers with leaf-shaped pulls. No sister.

No hope.

Only fear.

"Get up," she whispered, swinging her legs over the side of the bed.

"You are just hungry and thirsty, that's all, Enid. You're not even hurt. You get up, now. You walk home."

—

In Mr. Fairweather's carriage, Flora clutched her face, as if to blind herself would also hide the scenes in her mind—Mr. Tuck with an axe; Enid, cowering; she saw the spurt of blood, like when she chopped off a chicken's head but hideously magnified. She cried out, a wail into the heat of her hands. Mr. Fairweather patted her shoulder.

The moon was rising in the east. Fields spread away on either side; horse and carriage made the only movement, a beetle crawling across silk.

He tapped the horse with his whip. His voice jolted as the mare, startled, broke into a canter and then resumed a faster, swarming trot.

"It's not too much farther. There's a house and barn along here. The constables thought the house had been sold. Well, perhaps it has, but last time I passed by it was still empty. I used to visit an old man who was born and died on the farm. Lonely and a bit strange in the head."

The mare laboured up a long hill, then down, into the flickering shadows of a spruce hollow.

"Just along here, now," he said as they came out of the woods. "There. There it is."

A house and barn. No lights. He turned the horse. They went up a long lane, lurching over ruts.

"What if he's armed, Mr. Fairweather? What if he shoots at us?"

He patted his pocket. "I am armed, Flora."

The horse drew up in front of the desolate house. They climbed from the far side of the carriage; ran, bent low. The lantern swung from Harland's hand; he held the pistol in the other.

The door creaked on rusty hinges. Silence flowed from the house. The hallway smelled of lard, plaster, filthy fabric. The lantern's glancing light touched oilcloth worn through to floorboards; animal scat; a dented saucepan.

Mr. Fairweather held the lantern high, inched into the front room. Flora followed the lantern's path, eyes wide yet not wanting to see.

No blood. No Enid.

Could have strangled her . . .

They went into all the rooms of the house, downstairs, upstairs. Mr. Fairweather went into the cellar through a rotten hatchway. He came back up, coughing.

"Nothing down there. Now, Flora, I'm going to explore the sheds and the barn. I want you to go back to the carriage and stay down."

"But—"

"*Please.*"

She saw that it was for her sake that he wished not to state his reasons. Safety, sanity. She stepped out of the circle of lantern light. She went back to the carriage. Her skirt snagged and she tugged it, heard the rip of burrs. The mare shifted her front hooves. One, then the other. Her whinny was a ruffle, anxious.

Flora put her arms around the mare's neck, breathed the scent of horse flesh, comforting as cornbread, cinnamon. She set her foot on the metal step, climbed up and huddled on the carriage floor.

Enid, hanging from a beam in the barn.

Enid, strangled and tossed into a shed.

She refused the images, seeing, instead, her own story: Enid's little hand holding hers as they mounted the steps of the workhouse; Enid at the kitchen table in Nova Scotia—*Are you really my sister?*—a clean nightgown, peepers and the summer moon; the crackle of static beneath hairbrush. On it went, the river that should not stop, that must not, would not. She shivered against the boards, waiting for gunshot, a wail, shouting.

Footsteps. Mr. Fairweather climbed into the carriage and lifted the reins.

"There is no one. But they have been here. I saw a pile of fresh manure. He'd tried to hide it, kicked it apart. We'll see if we can tell which way they went."

The horse went back down the track. At the road, Harland and Flora climbed down. He swung the lantern.

"I can't tell," he said. "Can you?"

Hoof marks. Large, small, workhorse, pony, shod, unshod. Like ripples on a brook.

Harland stood, looking into the darkness, the lantern hanging at his side.

Enid was a hole in Flora's heart, a rent into which anything could fall.

—

Harland and Flora drove all night, until at sunrise they found themselves at a small train station. The station master had not seen a man and a young girl.

He promised to watch for them.

—

Enid crashed down into sleep, woke in wet grass. Bewildered, she sat, absorbing the unfamiliar darkness and silence until she came fully awake. *Mr. Tuck.* She scrambled to her feet, unsteady but already poised to run. The moon was obscured by hills, now, and she came into a hollow and entered the woods she remembered driving through with Mr. Tuck, when she had thought her life was coming to an end. She shouted as she strode, the cape swinging, the hood sheltering her from the forest. She thought of buckwheat pancakes and maple syrup.

"I am a girl, you wild animals! I am not good to eat!"

Her voice jolted.

"I am Flora's sister. I can read. I know my multiplication tables. I have crossed the Atlantic Ocean. I am Enid. I am Enid Salford who lives in Pleasant Valley, New Brunswick, Canada."

She remembered the eye of the little duck and how when she had cleaned it with her finger it had seemed to know her, and be glad to be hers.

TWENTY-TWO

Warning to Travellers

~

JOSEPHINE WOKE TO ELLEN'S cry.

"Oh! Mrs. Galloway! Mrs. Galloway!"

She ran down the hall in her nightgown, her heart a thick presence, racing. Dawn light touched the plaster walls; chill air wrapped her ankles, coming through the side door, standing half-open.

Enid lay on the kitchen floor, curled like a cashew. In the stove, a newly laid fire roared; Ellen knelt by the girl, her hands hovering, not knowing where to touch.

Josephine dropped to her knees. She felt along Enid's body, frantic. Firm shoulders, ribcage, the shuddering rise and fall of breath. Bits of grass and fern in her hair. Eyes squeezed shut, fists pressing cheeks.

"Where were you, Enid? Are you hurt? Can you talk?"

She lay on the floor and curled against Enid, gathering her, soothing as she had comforted her own children in their illnesses. Waking, in the night, she had dreaded to think how Enid's loss would cast both her and Flora into despair, how the walls of her own recovery would crumble. She realized that even as she held the girl in her arms, feeling her shuddering breaths, her joy was barbed, tinged, as if at this moment another Enid lay murdered.

Footsteps, hurrying downstairs. Maud, and the boarders.

"Oh, the poor thing."

"The Lord be praised."

Ellen, stiff, pushed herself to her feet, one hand on the table. She slid the stove dampers shut and shoved the kettle to the hottest lid.

"Can you sit up, Enid? Flora and Mr. Fairweather are looking for you." Josephine plucked a strand of hair from Enid's eye. "She needs to be soaking in a tub. Ellen, will you—"

Enid scrambled to her feet. Dazed, teeth chattering, she walked between Josephine and Maud. In the bathroom, she slid from their arms and collapsed on the rag rug. Miss Harvey appeared at the door, frightened face looking over a blanket clutched to her chest. She laid it over Enid, while Josephine shook Epsom salts into the water. Sunlight quivered through the window and turned the steam to gold.

All three women supported her as she stepped into the tub. She wept as Josephine squeezed hot water over the nape of her neck. "Oh, poor Flora. She don't know, she don't know I'm safe . . . she's thinks I'm ruined or killed . . ."

The women exchanged looks.

"I'm not," Enid sobbed. "I'm not ruined . . . but I think I was almost killed."

—

Flora climbed down from the carriage beside the portico, where limp nasturtiums hung from a trellis, bearing faint residues of red and yellow. Night frost had completely burned off the nearby roofs of Creek Road. Mr. Fairweather leaned across the seat, as if reluctant to relinquish their intimacy of endeavour.

"I will phone and let you know what I learn from the constables."

She let herself into the house. Maud came running out of the kitchen.

"She's found, Flora! She's here!"

"Here? *Enid?* Enid is . . ."

"I mean she's not *found*, she returned. She walked into the house. A farmer picked her up on the road. Mr. Tuck had her, he took her to an empty house . . ."

Their boots trampled up the uncarpeted back stairs. ". . . she said that when she told him she had taken the brass duck, he . . ."

Flora, on the threshold of the bedroom, saw Enid in the white bed with a blanket around her shoulders, a cup of tea cradled in her hands—blue scoops beneath her eyes and the unblinking gaze of shock.

Enid put down the cup, spread her arms. Flora flew to her side, embraced her. Both girls burst into tears, seized by the violence of grief that had not come.

—

WAS THE WRONG MAN HANGED? POSSIBLE AXE MURDERER
BOARDS AT MRS. SIMEON GALLOWAY'S HOME.

SISTER OF HOME CHILD TAKEN BY POSSIBLE MURDERER.

RUNAWAY MAN MADE MINIATURE HOUSES.

MINIATURE HOUSE IN POSSESSION OF MACVEY SISTERS.
WE HAD NO IDEA, MISS MACVEY SAYS.

—

Evidence mounted: Jasper Tuck's absence of connection to any person in the local area; and a rumour that two significant facts had been overlooked in the axe murder trial. Around the time of the murder, a man selling handcrafted toy fishing boats had been seen near the residence of the murdered woman, and a carpenter had gone missing from a house-building crew. The constables verified to the local paper that the murdered woman's money had never been found. Neither had a small brass duck, mentioned by a witness as having vanished from her dresser.

Train stations were watched; livery stables and hotels were placed on alert. Posters were disseminated warning people not to take in a stranger with a missing wolf tooth, black hair and a wiry stature.

For two days, reporters frequented Josephine's lane until she was driven to distraction and phoned Mr. Fairweather.

—

Warm rain brought down the last leaves, carpeting the lawn as if with a decaying quilt. The air smelled of wood smoke.

Harland stood beneath the portico.

"Mrs. Galloway has no new information. She asks that you respect her privacy and has asked me to tell you that she will answer no more questions."

Josephine and Ellen, watching from the hall, saw two men break away from the group and approach the barn. They made blinders of their hands, looking in the workshop window.

"He's a good speaker, he is," Ellen remarked, jutting her chin at Mr. Fairweather, whose voice rang out, as it had, Josephine reflected, on the day of the pauper auction. He'd been sorry for the job he'd had to do. He was not sorry, now. He relished his role as Josephine's protector.

A reporter raised a hand. "Why are you speaking for Mrs. Galloway?"

"I was the auctioneer on the day Flora Salford was sold at auction to Mrs. Galloway. The missing girl, Enid, is Flora's sister. Both girls now live here."

Another reporter called out.

"Wasn't her sister at the Mallory place, in Nova Scotia? The man of the house now in custody for the death of a young boy?"

"Yes. But that is of no relevance."

"Could this Mr. Jasper Tuck be any relation to those Mallorys?"

Harland remained calm. Firm.

"No."

The rain changed from a patter to a teeming downpour; the reporters tucked their pads into pockets and went away. Mr. Fairweather came into the kitchen. He sat in a rocking chair. The fire made a faint, sporadic crackling. Bread rose in the warming oven. Josephine was digging in the caddy with a teaspoon; Ellen was making applesauce.

"Where are Enid and Flora?"

"They are upstairs. We are trying to keep them from seeing the newspapers, but Flora has glimpsed some of the stories. Enid weeps until we think she will be sick."

"Flora reads to Enid," Ellen added. Her face bore conflicted pride. "Storybooks."

"Maud's old books. The kind those poor girls never had."

"Under this very roof, he was," Ellen said, stirring apples. Rain drummed the veranda roof. "He was under our roof, Mr. Fairweather. I lie in bed at night, my mind going round and round. We all could have been killed in our beds. Savaged, first—raped, and then murdered. I think about the poor man they hanged. Then I think of Enid off alone with the likes of . . ."

"Ellen, Ellen. Please." Harland sighed, putting his head back against the chair.

Josephine, pouring tea, was thinking about a rumour Maud had overheard when standing in a line at the grocery store. *Mr. Fairweather is seeing quite a lot of Mrs. Galloway.*

—

Flora sat beneath the window, reading aloud from a small book with gilt-edged pages. Enid, in bed, held her knees, the quilt around her shoulders.

"*. . . and her daughter secretly warned the travellers to be very careful not to eat or drink anything as the old woman's brews were apt to be dangerous. They went to bed and . . .*"

Enid drew a long breath and laid her cheek on her knees.

Flora closed the book on her finger and stared out the window. A leaf fell, twirling. They had heard Mr. Fairweather send away the reporters. They had heard him come into the house.

They listened to the drumming of rain. A blue jay cried.

"So sad," Enid said, her jaw working against her knee. "That bird. Like he's lost someone."

Flora watched the raindrops.

"What are you thinking about, Flora?" Enid murmured, still looking sideways, her gaze unfocused.

"How the rain is like nothing becoming something."

"No, really."

"How everyone is talking about us. How it seems like we can't get away from bad things. How it's like we were born nothing, and we will stay nothing."

Flora's hair pillowed at the nape of her neck, held off her white lace collar by a blue ribbon. Her eyes were resolute, sorrowful.

Enid whispered, "Flora, you are so beautiful. Just to look at you is to see goodness."

"It's only a danger," Flora said. "It makes men want us. Like possessions."

"I know," Enid said.

"Why do you think he took that duck, Enid? I think it's the strangest thing. Just a toy."

"I think . . ."

Enid could not speak of Mr. Tuck without tears. She had turned the duck over to the constables. The dress, too, had been confiscated.

"I think he wanted it same as why I wanted it. I don't feel sorry for him, Flora. I think he is a madman. But maybe . . . maybe once he was a boy like Fred. Maybe it was a part of not being poor. To have a thing, for no reason. Just a toy."

The sisters listened to the sound of the rain, a hushing. Flora opened the book and resumed reading, her voice gentle, even though the story uncoiled a tale of the worst and the best of human nature.

—

Nothing was heard of Mr. Tuck. No hotels reported seeing him. He was not spotted at any train station. No stories were brought in from the countryside of a man asking for food and shelter. No vagrant was sighted in any town. Constables could not locate him in Moncton, St. John or Fredericton.

The horse and carriage, however, were found and duly returned.

—

A week after Enid's ordeal, Flora and Enid decided they must face Mr. Tuck's workshop. Their shoes left black circles in the morning's silvered grass as they crossed the lawn to the barn. Stepping over the threshold, Enid began to tremble and Flora took her hand.

"It's all right, Enid. He's not coming back."

The tiny tools were gone. The dresser drawer hung open.

"I wish there were something of his," Enid said. "I want to smash it."

Flora looked at the chair where she had spent hours cutting out pieces of carpet, or sewing, or making the miniature windows.

"He's gone," Flora said, "But he's not. He's out in the world, waiting to find another woman to use. Or kill. He let another man hang for his crime."

They listened to the drip of melting frost; the croon of hens on the other side of the wall.

Enid stared around the workshop. "I thought I seen the worst with Mr. Mallory and Fred. I feel like I can't go out in the world. I feel like I got to just stay in my bed."

"We have each other. Fred didn't have anyone. Fred thought no one loved him."

"I loved him. The dog loved him."

"It wasn't your fault, Enid. Fred probably didn't know what love was."

She thought of how she herself knew more about love now, having suffered the cruel possibility of its loss. How it was a thing like light. You could not describe it to a person who had never seen it. And yet, indescribable, it was something you trusted when, lonely in the dead of night, you waited for morning.

"I *got* to ruin something that was his," Enid said. She was pacing around the room, touching the bench, opening a cupboard door. "Are we bad girls, Flora?"

Flora had wondered the same. She had determined to value herself by the degree of kindness so freely given by the Creek Road household.

"We are good, Enid. We have always been good. And now we live with good people. Josephine, Ellen, Maud . . ." She spread her fingers, tipped her palm towards the house.

"Yes," Enid said. "Yes, we are so lucky. Flora, let's just sit here for awhile."

Flora sat at her old place. Enid slid gingerly onto Mr. Tuck's chair.

Flora wondered if Ellen, too, thought of herself as a bad person. If not bad, then *less*. She pushed down her rage against Mr. Tuck because she did not know what she would do with it when it came.

"We will have to be on our guard for the rest of our lives, Enid," she murmured. "Not only for him but for the likes of him."

Flora watched her sister, who slumped, chin in hand. Brown and green plaid dress, the body burgeoning beneath it, womanly—yet in Enid's eyes, such sadness. As if she were still running, trying to leave something behind, knowing it would come again. A threat, in unknown form.

"I know, Enid," she said. "I know what we should do."

TWENTY-THREE

Reckonings

~

FLORA AND ENID SAT side by side on a small divan. Outside, men scaled ladders, installing storm windows. Enid's hand was poised as if to pleat her skirt, but then clenched against the impulse; Flora noticed how the shapes of their knees were visible, knobs beneath their flowered skirts, whereas the MacVey sisters were like well-feathered hens, bones and flesh hidden within flouncing carapaces of ruffles and ribbons and trailing necklaces.

"Grace. You are avoiding the issue. I think the girls are right."

"Oh, yes, yes. No, I quite agree. It's just . . . hard to come to the actual *truth* of it. That our lovely . . . little house . . ."

"It is no longer a *lovely little house*. We have been mentioned in the papers. I cannot bear to look at it anymore."

"Yes, oh, yes, Rosamund."

Grace bent forward, widening her eyes, hands clutched as if containing a small creature frantic for release. Behind her, light glinted on a domed glass cage filled with stuffed birds.

"Well, then. Let's do it now."

Rosamund picked up a cane leaning against her chair. She stood and went onto the veranda.

"Please come," she called to the men. Grace, Flora and Enid rose as the men climbed down and stomped into the hall. Rosamund spoke to them in a low voice, making lifting motions. They glanced at one another. Tanned, scarred hands dropped to their sides, and they followed Rosamund as they trooped through an archway rimmed with mahogany spindles. Grace and the young sisters followed.

In the grand parlour, October sunshine slanted onto Mr. Tuck's creation, set on a pedestal. The men walked around the miniature house, muttering to one another, their boots silent on the Oriental carpet. Flora felt sudden anguish for the cedar shingles, the size of a baby's fingernails, covering turrets, veranda roof and dormers; for the shiny red trim; for the flagpole with its cloth Red Ensign; for the shiny, raisin-sized brass doorknobs; for the windowpanes, which she herself had set into their frames.

In one hundred years, she thought, no one would remember that the house had been made by a murderer whose victim had borne the marks of teeth on her wrists and hands; whose blood had sprayed a pattern of stars on the surrounding walls. Yet to allow the house to stand on display in the sister's parlour was to turn one's back on the murdered woman herself: Mrs. Elsa Cavanaugh, from County Tyrone, fifty years of age. Whose savings Flora had seen. Whose cherished duck had ridden in a murderer's pocket, had nestled beneath Enid's pillow.

Grace put her hands over her mouth. "Oh. So sad."

"Yes. It is very sad." Rosamund put an arm around her sister's waist as the men lifted the house. "It is all very sad. But imagine if one day that monster came back and sneaked around and peered into the window and saw that we still had the house he had made."

"He would think that what he had done didn't matter. Or that we believed him innocent."

"That's just it."

They followed as the men carried the house through the door, down the hall and onto the veranda. Men, house and women paraded past the laundry yard where maids were hanging sheets; past the hen house and the donkey barn. They wove between the apple trees. At the paddock, Rosamund held the gate and the men angled the house through the opening. The donkeys lifted their heads and tipped their ears, grass trailing from black lips.

"Here," Rosamund called, striding ahead, beckoning. "It is always very damp here."

The men set down the house in a slight depression.

The miniature house was diminished by the wispy grasses, the shrivelled wasp-clung apples, the clumps of donkey manure.

"A facsimile is a thing that dies once the bloom has worn off," Rosamund said, tapping a turret with her cane. "We would tire of this. It does not change, like a real house. There is no heart to it. I prefer to see it as a wicked man's trick."

Flora noticed a cracked window, although she had seen how gently the men had lowered the house to the ground. She knelt and ran her finger over the veranda floorboards. She remembered the sketch, then the detailed drawing, and the gradual accumulation of wood, glue, glass, nails. Clouds sailed over the orchard, disintegrating at their edges like ancient fabric, and she thought how everything, in various ways, vanished and then began again. She wondered what she should do with the money Mr. Tuck had given her, still hidden beneath the floorboards. She thought of her dream, carefully nurtured: a job in Mr. Tuck's factory; the white house that she and Enid would own, with roses and a wooden fence.

The men returned, one with shovels over his shoulder, the other pushing a wheelbarrow filled with paper and shingles. They dug around the house, slicing away turf, leaving raw soil. They set down buckets of water. One man split shingles over his knee and the other made a skirt of crumpled newspaper around the veranda and the walls and the gables and towers. They criss-crossed broken shingles over the paper. Rosamund folded her arms and then flung them up, shooing away the donkeys, who strayed close, curious. The men leaned chunks of split birch wood against the sides of the house, careful not to break a single windowpane, nor nick the paint, nor snap a balustrade.

One drew a box of matches from his pocket. He glanced at Rosamund. The roof of the house came to the man's hip.

It is only a thing, Flora thought. *It will gather dust. The shingles will come loose on their brads; the curtains will stiffen. The paint will peel.*

Rosamund nodded.

The man struck the match, cupped the flame in his palm and touched it to the paper. The paper flared and blackened. The little flame vanished into the crumpled ball. Smoke came like silent black breath and then a ragged fringe of fire burst from beneath the miniature veranda; it licked up, catching the steps, the posts. The men circled the house, cracking matches, igniting paper beneath the kitchen window, beneath a turret, beneath the portico. The fire made a sharp, steady crackle. Heat radiated and the men tipped water onto the bared soil and onto the grasses at the soil's edge, and the women backed away, hands to their faces, coughing. Beyond, the real house was so massive in contrast as to appear to lean back against a tapestry of blue sky and leafless lindens. The fire grew to a muted lion's roar, momentarily enveloping the still intact house in rapacious light. The posts crumbled, first, tearing away the veranda. Spurts of flame shot from the turrets. The roof collapsed and then the fire began a louder snapping, as if it devoured dry spruce needles. Within minutes, the little house was a pile of sticks, melting glass, blackened fabric. A burning curtain detached and was borne away like a butterfly. The men shovelled the outer edges of debris into the fire's lessening heart. Flora poked a burning table back into the flames. She saw a carpet, blackening. She saw the tiny iron stove that Mr. Tuck had bought in Hampton. The men dashed water, causing hissing puffs of steam.

"So quickly!" Enid murmured. She held Flora's arm, limpeting herself, as she had ever since the abduction.

"Be glad it was not our real house," Rosamund remarked. Her voice was harsh. She turned away and slid the back of her hand up a donkey's furry face.

Flora was brushed by a sense of relief. She felt an urgent need to go home and clean the workshop with vinegar and hot water, to scrub its floor and shelves and windows, and then do the same to the room Mr. Tuck had slept in, putting clean sheets on the bed, airing the blanket that had touched his cheek.

"Her name was Elsa," she said. "The woman he murdered. Elsa Cavanaugh."

The smoky breeze stirred their skirts, their collars and ribbons. Shovelling soil onto the pyre, the men considered them in fleeting glances.

"Rest in peace, Elsa Cavanaugh," Rosamund whispered.

Burn in hell, Jasper Tuck, Flora thought.

Pulling Enid close.

—

Gas from the lighting fixture left a familiar, sour redolence in Harland's throat. At his desk, he was designing advertisements for the Christmas season. *Fairweather's Gentlemen's Clothing,* he wrote. *Quality Attire for the Modern Man. Have on offer . . .*

Permelia had criticized his advertisements. He scratched out *Have on offer* and substituted *We Sell as Low as Any.*

His employees were exclaiming over items, rustling paper, unpacking a shipment of goods. He read over the bills of lading. *Fancy Lisle Socks. Black Taffeta Silk Umbrellas. Peccary Hogskin Gloves.*

His mind was on Josephine, seeking an excuse to visit her. The hunt for Jasper Tuck was in the hands of the police. The courts were reconsidering the murder of Mrs. Elsa Cavanaugh. Enid was safe. Mr. Mallory had been brought to justice.

It occurred to him that a woman had multiple needs a man could solve. Someone to shovel her lane. Firewood. A broken door on her kitchen range.

He pulled out his pocket watch and saw that he would not be expected home for dinner for another half-hour.

Josephine untied her apron, leading him to the turret room.

"I'm going to my dinner," he said. "I just had a moment and thought I would stop in."

She folded the apron and set it on her lap. The cloth was soft and made a small, square package.

She reflected upon an opening remark. Three weeks had passed since the disappearance of Jasper Tuck. The news had faded in importance. No reporters came to the house. Enid was fragile, but recovering. Maud was in her final year at the Pleasant Valley Academy. His interest had always centred on Flora, as the link that attached him to Josephine. Flora was occupied with many things. Which one should she tell him about? Her arithmetic studies? Latin?

"Are you well, Harland?"

She had seen a jar of dyspepsia powder on his desk. She wondered about the ravages of his wife's sharp tongue, how it sculpted him, shaving away the parts Permelia found unacceptable.

He held his hat on his knees.

"Nothing to complain about, Josephine, thank you. I was wondering about your spare room. Now that Mr. Tuck . . . I thought you might need help finding a new tenant."

"Flora has taken care of that. She met someone at Humphreys and Teakles' who knew someone who knew . . . you know how it is. I made sure, though, that the person was well regarded around town. It is a Miss Caroline Macpherson."

"The Harold Macphersons?"

"Yes, those Macphersons."

"That's good, then."

His lips worked as if he wished to speak but had nothing to say. He ran a finger over the hat, not looking at her.

"I wanted you to know that I am always at your service. If you need a man for doing any little . . . or perhaps *large* . . . thing. Carpentry, or gardening, or the like. I can always help you find someone. Or, of course, do it myself, if I can."

Josephine listened to the words that he spoke; heard, as well, the ones that lay beneath.

"Thank you. I feel that between Flora, Ellen, Maud and myself, we are becoming a very capable team. But of course I shall ask you if . . ."

She broke off.

"We want to see one another, don't we, Harland?"

"I didn't—"

"I know you didn't. You have never been the least bit improper. But now that the problems you have helped me with are solved, there is no reason for you to come here. And . . . and you know . . . people have begun to talk."

Flesh thickened along his jaw, making a slight droop. Fine black hairs darkened his wrists. His shoulders were slumped; his clothing shielded him, like armour.

"Harland. My dear friend. I wonder if you are prepared to divorce Permelia."

He considered his fingers, spread out on his knees. The fingertips tightened. "I have looked into it, Josephine. And I have concluded, regretfully, that I cannot."

She realized that he would rather have postponed this question. Or left it unasked, unconsidered.

"It is as I expected." She stroked the folded apron, not meeting his eyes. "No, you needn't tell me. I can well imagine all the . . . oh, the disastrous consequences."

The boarders were letting themselves in the front door, hanging coats and hats on the rack. A draft travelled across the floor and touched her ankles.

She did not care if Mr. Sprague or Miss Harvey or Mrs. Beaman or the new boarder should see. She leaned forward and put her hand on Harland's. She lowered her voice.

"Harland, in these months since Simeon died, I have felt extreme affection for you. If things were otherwise, if . . . you, for example, were a widower . . . I might have considered . . ."

She could not say *there is a difference between affection and love.*

His eyes filled with tears. The boarders vanished into the dining room. He took her hand and lifted it to his cheek.

He pressed his lips to it.

He laid it back, gently.

"I suppose, then, that I should not visit."

"Not without Permelia," Josephine said.

He stood. She, too, rose to her feet, letting the apron cascade from its folds as she tied it around her waist. His polished shoes were silent on the carpet; he stepped across a slant of light like crossing a brook. He stopped with his hand on the doorknob. They could hear the clash of cutlery; Flora's voice, less English, now.

He opened the front door, paused as if to speak, looked at his shoes. He walked down the drive, and she remembered when he had remarked upon his father, The Commodore, who exercised—rain or shine—with his little dog, and how she had thought, then, of the loneliness of old age.

—

Ellen pushed a kettle of beans to the back of the stove, added a stick of wood to the firebox. She sat in her rocking chair and did not pick up her knitting. Maud did not open her history book. Josephine gathered a white shawl around her neck. Flora and Enid sat in chairs at the kitchen table, their pencils dropped onto pages of arithmetic.

"What he must have thought of us," Ellen said. "Serving him dinner. *Would you like milk with your tea, Mr. Tuck?*"

"I should have turned him from the door," Flora said. "I should have said, *We have no more rooms.*"

"But how could you have known, Flora? He was a perfectly decent-looking man. No, if there is fault it is mine. I should have asked around before taking a stranger into my home. *Our* home," Josephine added, glancing at Maud.

Flora wondered if George was still encouraging his sisters to sell the house, or if their determined resistance had made the idea fade away. Still, Josephine would never own the house; once the children achieved their majority, if they did not sell the house but allowed their mother to continue living in it, would she need to pay them rent? Would she be able to keep Ellen, Flora and Enid? Flora did not know, but imagined this as a worry that darkened Josephine's relationship with her children. Nor did Josephine entirely own the furniture, or anything else in the house. She *managed* the property. Her best recourse would be to remarry. Flora had noted that Mr. Fairweather had ceased visiting and that Josephine seemed quieter, and yet, oddly, at peace.

Maud pressed a hot facecloth to her pimply forehead. "It makes me feel sick. To think how he would have been laughing at us. Being polite to a murderer. Thinking that he was an ordinary person. When he was—when he *is*—a monster."

Josephine reached forward to pat Enid's shoulder. "Never fear, Enid. He will not come around here again. Somewhere, someday, he will be hunted down and caught and brought to justice."

"Maybe," Ellen said. "Or not . . ."

Flora caught revelation in her tone. "Why do you say that, Ellen?"

It had come upon them, tonight, after the dishes had been washed and dried and put away: the reckoning. A gash had closed, and yet would not be healed until the manner of its affliction was discussed.

"I should tell you," Ellen said. "I should tell you, and you'll not see me in the same way ever again."

Josephine glanced at her, surprised.

Ellen picked up a pair of stork scissors. Snipped threads from her apron with its beaky blades.

"Well, then. My father was a man something like Jasper Tuck. Fine looking, made the ladies take pity on him with stories of, oh, you know, being ill done by one thing or another. We had a cow and pigs and all . . . and I suppose he did the odd job, being a child I didn't know, just that he reeled home from the pub after dark and when me Ma heard his steps on the road she hid me and my little brother away out of sight. I never knew what it was she'd done wrong, that he had to come home to punish her. I thought that it must be me he wanted, for badness I'd done. I thought she took my part, the slaps across the face, the punches, the kicks when she was knocked down on the floor moaning with her poor arms covering her head. Me under the bed or peeping through the wardrobe door. So the one night, he tripped and struck his head and then he didn't move. I remember how quiet come over the house. How long she sat there, like a dog, panting. Then she put a mirror to his mouth, put her fingers to his neck. She tied his hands behind his back and she tied his ankles together and she took a pillow from the bed and she . . ."

Fingers pressed against her lips, Ellen took a long breath.

". . . sat on his head."

Flora covered Enid's hand with her own, sliding her fingers into the grooves between the knuckles.

". . . flopped around . . . Then he was dead. She untied his arms and legs. Put the pillow back on the bed. Not a one of us, not me nor her nor me brother, not a one of us ever said a word. We went to the funeral and not a person in the village as didn't pity us."

"Good for her," Maud breathed.

"I'm as good as a murderer, you see."

"He would have killed your mother one day," Flora said. "Oh, I heard stories in the workhouse. Your mother was as good as dead, Ellen, and she knew it. She had no choice."

Josephine, shocked, sat with hands clasping her face.

"Oh, Ellen. To have seen such a thing as a child." She drew a long breath, shaking her head. "Oh, Ellen. Terrible. And no one . . ."

She broke off, as if searching for stronger words.

"No one, believe me, Ellen, *no* one would blame you. Flora is right, she was only saving herself. And saving you. She did it for you and your brother. So you wouldn't be killed."

"Well. 'Tis many years ago now and not a night goes by I don't pray to the good Lord to watch over her in heaven." A tear glistened on Ellen's cheek and she removed her glasses and wiped her eyes on her sleeve. "Now. I've told it. How many years I've been keeping that inside me is a thing I wouldn't want to tell."

"Not Mr. Dougan?" Maud said, suddenly. "You never told Mr. Dougan?"

Ellen shook her head and began to laugh. "He always said I was like to be a murderer myself, the interest I took in crime."

They heard a shriek and a burst of laughter from the front parlour.

"He's done it again," Enid murmured. Mr. Sprague manoeuvred the Ouija board shamelessly.

Ellen dropped the stork scissors into her basket. She rose, shook tea leaves into the brown pot and filled it with boiling water.

"What are we going to do?" Josephine asked.

Maud lowered the cloth from her forehead and glanced at her mother.

Ellen, Enid and Flora exchanged glances.

"Me, my children, and you three," Josephine continued. She poured the tea. The kitchen rang with the tinkling percussion of cup and saucer. Outside, the last light had faded from the sky. "Maud and Lucy and I have discussed this. Of course, I have not had a chance to talk to George."

George seldom visited, citing busyness.

"Lucy and Maud have told me that they do not intend to sell the house when they reach maturity, even if George . . . well. That's as good as done, then, since all three must make the decision. I intend to stay on here, and will continue taking in boarders. Maud's grand-parents have recently informed me they will pay for her to attend the Ladies' College in Sackville next year. As for Lucy, we don't know her plans but I do not expect her to return to Pleasant Valley. It is my hope that you three—Ellen, Flora, Enid—that you three will stay here, and do as you think best. It is my dream that you, Flora, will assume a larger role in running this establishment and that beyond room and board I might someday offer a share of whatever income we can glean. And it is my hope, too, that you, Enid, will go to school. Perhaps even starting this year."

Flora set her teacup back in its saucer. She noticed dried pie dough on her sleeve, picked at it.

"I know you are not my daughter, Flora," Josephine said. "But you are no more a servant to me than is Ellen. As I understand it, and from what I have learned from Cousin Carrie, as we try to be *persons* we must become something new. I am not a wife. I am not a homeowner. I'm just . . . we're just . . . friends, I suppose. Pieces of the same puzzle."

Making a life.

Flora brushed her sleeve. She said nothing.

What, after all, she thought, had she imagined for herself other than two things—one, hazy as sunshine through mist, was a house of her own; the other, the one that had nurtured her through the long, lonely years with Ada and Henry, had been to find Enid, whom she had betrayed without meaning to—Enid, running up the road in her dream, always vanishing. Enid was solid, now, at her side, murmuring with an anxious tone—*Flora?*—as if it were she who must care for Flora and not the other way around.

Josephine's offer was the second choice of her life, she realized. The first choice had been based on Maria Rye's story, a bright concoction spun of things that a pauper child might desire. This new offer, however, was a real possibility, and such possibility, she saw, was also what a pauper child might desire, and now she knew its truth: the tall windows, the verandas and linden trees, the claw-footed tub with its iron spigots, the maple-leaf dresser handles, the oak telephone. Too, she herself was no longer a lost child, but had been saved, and had herself saved Enid, and might say that just as Josephine was no longer *only* a widow, she was no longer *only* an English orphan.

The dream of a white house with roses and a chicken pen shrivelled like a drawing crumpled and tossed onto a fire, and all that was left of it was a sock weighted with ill-gotten money which, she saw now, must be taken from beneath the floorboard and given to the police.

She skipped several stages of her answer to Josephine. Her eyes focused on the shapes she drew on the table with the tip of her finger, a large square with lines drawn across it.

"We could make Mr. Dougan's tack room into a cottage so we could take on more boarders. I *know* we could barter for work. We'd need a carpenter and a mason. You could put two bedrooms, like this, and this. If we . . . give me your pencil, Enid."

TWENTY-FOUR

A Different Outcome

~

ENID STOOD BENEATH THE trellis on the back stoop nervously clutching a book bag to her chest. It was fall, and the school year had already begun. Flora, standing in the doorway, remembered Enid at the parsonage table, her hair in hanks, flour-sack dress hanging from bony shoulders. Her mouth, a slash of misery. Now, shiny blonde hair was parted in the middle and caught back in a chignon, like Josephine's. Enid had starched and ironed a green plaid dress herself.

She looked neither at Flora nor at Maud, but out towards the street. Her lips trembled, her breath was rapid. Excitement, fear—each mitigated the other, making her uncertain.

Maud, one step lower, hitched her own books and held up a hand.

"Come," she urged. "I'll show you the way."

—

Flora found a mason and a carpenter who were willing to transform Mr. Dougan's tack room (as they called it, now, never Mr. Tuck's workshop) for a steady supply of bread, eggs, preserves, socks, and pickles.

Work began in November, just as the first snowflakes wavered into view.

Ellen and Flora made forays to the attic. They brought down chairs in need of scrubbing, paint or upholstery; found abandoned paintings, moth-eaten blankets, a frayed braided rug. After supper, in the early darkness, they stitched or scrubbed or painted. They carried the finished articles to the back shed and covered them with sheets—surveyed the growing pile, pleased.

"Now if only Mr. Dougan were here to see this."

Miss Harvey and Mr. Sprague announced their engagement, but stated their intention to wait a year before marriage.

Josephine was invited to join a newly formed reading club. Members took turns choosing a program of readings and invited other members to stand at the front of the room and read aloud their given selections. The club rotated from month to month, house to house. Dress was formal—black tie, gowns. Husband and wife were not allowed to sit next to one another, and seating rotated after each segment of the evening.

"Harland and Permelia Fairweather are members," Josephine told them, over supper.

"Are you going to join, Mother?"

"It means I will have to host, you know. We will have to serve wine and spirits and use my marriage tea set and polish the silver."

Her voice quivered, very slightly, and she picked a thread from her sleeve, not meeting anyone's eye.

—

December 4, 1889

Dear Mother,

And Maudie, Flora, Enid and Ellen, for I know Mother reads my letters aloud! I have been continuing my studies of Blackstone's Commentaries and I have conceived the desire to become a lawyer. How I will do this I do not know for my wages are barely enough to pay for food and you should see how thin I have become but never fear, I am filled with the energy of conviction! The petition has now been circulated over the entire province and Carrie and I continue to travel on Sundays to speak about it. We will bring a copy to you with the latest wording. It states: "Your petitioners therefore humbly pray your honourable body to enact a law providing that full parliamentary suffrage be conferred on the women of New Brunswick, upon the same terms and under the same conditions as that now accorded to men . . ." Isn't it fine!? I am SO EXCITED. There are a few men in the legislature who we are quite certain will support the petition. One of them recently stated that a law that debars one-half of society from the franchise is "unjust"; another man said it was his "fixed principle" that women should have equal rights with men in "every walk of life." Mother, I'm sure that when a few men have the courage to state such things, they are speaking for other men less bold. It is a sign of the times, I'm sure of it.

As for my work, it continues to be hot and difficult. I have been having dizzy spells from not eating enough. I fell the other day and have a bruise on my temple. I don't know how I could keep going at this if it were not for my dreams of how I might organize the other women. I am not doing this, yet. I don't know how I could do it without being fired. I am always a little set apart from myself, as if I'm hovering overhead and seeing this slave labour for what it is. Don't worry, Mother. I realize I will not last long here. I will either become too weak to work or will have to admit that I can't exist on such wages. Although other women do! Thus, so should I. I will try, since what I will do next I do not know.

Josephine's hand gripped her mouth. She drew a long breath, shaking her head.

Come home, my darling, she thought. You can always come home.

*I know that my life will change once we receive the franchise. I feel
that I will be the happiest I have ever been on that glorious day and
that I will be freed of the weight of injustice.*

*My hand tires, as does the wick of my lamp, so I will send you all
my love.*

*Your,
Lucy*

—

Editorials appeared in the papers citing police incompetence and the
rush to convict in the case of the man hanged for the crime of murder-
ing Mrs. Elsa Cavanaugh. In parlours, barbershops and railway carriages
all across Canada, Mr. Jasper Tuck was indicted.

Jasper Tuck vanished.

Flora told Enid a story to put her mind at rest. "This is what *I* think
happened, Enid. He was walking in the dark and he saw a carriage coming along the road. He bolted into the woods, to hide, and there he . . ."

They sat in their flannel nightgowns, hair in braids, feet in socks.
Flora lifted her hands, shaping the story, and shadows rose and fell on
the wallpaper.

". . . tumbled down a steep hillside that he couldn't see. He broke
his leg. He . . ."

". . . tried to crawl . . ."

". . . and then he lay back, played out, and just then . . ."

". . . a pack of wolves."

They listened to the spatter of icy snow on the window, the fluting
moan of wind.

"Most likely he was too far from a farmhouse and he starved to
death," Flora said. "His body is being covered with snow right now. In
the spring someone will find his skeleton with nothing but boots and
a belt."

Josephine warned George as soon as he arrived.

"The boarders have finished their own Christmas dinner. We're just resetting the table." Her voice was slightly breathless. She held his hat as he shrugged from his wool coat. "Today, we are using the dining room."

"Don't you alw—"

Lucy and Maud ran into the hall. They patted George on the back.

"Merry Christmas, George!"

They were flushed from the heat of the kitchen, floury with last-minute preparations.

Ellen rang the dinner bell.

I am used to this new family, Josephine thought as they assembled around the table, a haze of steam rising from serving bowls. She watched as George pulled out his chair, smiling stiffly, attempting to hide his discomfort at sitting down with women who once would have served him. Maud had made her usual place settings, names written on cardboard, decorated with water-coloured sprigs of holly. George was not sitting at the head of the table. Rather, Maud had placed Ellen where, all the years of George's childhood, his father had sat.

"I did it by age," Maud said. "See? Enid is at starvation corner."

Flora laughed. "What does that mean?" She had forgotten to remove her apron, worked at the knot.

"The last to be served."

"But you will still say the blessing, please, George," Josephine said.

After the blessing, Josephine filled the plates, which were passed all the way around the table, pausing at Ellen's end for the addition of gravy. Finished, she sat back, smiling. She broke a roll and spread it with butter.

"Mother," George said. He had been glancing around the room. "I noticed shingles missing on the veranda roof."

"Yes. I know."

"And one of the storm windows has a broken pane."

Maud waved her roll, swallowed. "A branch smashed into it, George. In that November storm, the big one."

He cut his turkey into small pieces. He held himself close, elbows, mouth, eyes. Josephine noticed the parting in his hair, a white line, as if drawn with a ruler.

"Oh, Ellen. I have missed your rolls! And your gravy," Lucy said.

"Flora makes the gravy now," Ellen said. She sent Lucy a tight smile, avoiding looking at George.

"But who do you have for these things?"

"For what things, George?" Josephine asked.

"House maintenance. There's no Mr. Dougan. You can't let the place . . . just . . ."

"Run down?" Maud said. She did not wait for Lucy to speak first, as she once would have. "You think we are letting the place run down, George?"

"It will, with no man on the property."

Josephine's and Maud's eyes touched.

"You . . ." Maud began. Her nostrils flared. "Have no idea . . ."

Josephine held up a hand, interrupted. "Did Cousin Carrie and her husband go down to the coast for Christmas, Lucy?"

"No, Mother. Aunt Azuba and Uncle Nathaniel went to St. John. Carrie has an important meeting between Christmas and New Year's. It's to do with the petition."

"What petition?" George asked.

"The suffrage petition, of course. Oh my goodness, George. You need to leave the office more often."

"The *office*, as you call it—"

Maud interrupted. "Did she convince him?" she asked Lucy, as if continuing a conversation.

"Mr. Turner? Yes, she did! That's what I was about to tell you. Yes, she did! He will speak up for us in the legislature. He has great influence."

Josephine saw that Flora and Enid would remain silent if she did not draw them out.

"Mr. Turner is a member of the legislative assembly for St. John," she explained.

"You don't honestly think it will pass in the legislature," George remarked, at the same instant.

Maud began, "You just interrupted Moth—"

"Why not?" Lucy demanded. Flushed.

His tone, Josephine thought. *Exactly like my father's.*

"It . . ." George spoke directly across the table, addressing Lucy. He had not looked at Ellen, who sat on his left. Or at Flora, on his right. "It would be like asking you to climb up a ladder and fix those shingles. Or take down that storm window. You wouldn't want to do it, once you saw what it really required. You wouldn't, for example, want to have to . . ." He, too, flushed. His voice rose. ". . . manage a floor of factory workers. Like I have to."

Lucy and Maud laid down their forks and looked at one another.

George smiled, slightly. He worked at a piece of crisp skin with knife and fork. "You see, it is just the way—"

"No," Lucy said. "It is not the way. Not any more, George. You forget that I *work* on a factory floor. I see *children* working on a factory floor. You may think you treat your workers well, and perhaps you do, but other men do not. Men make laws, for example, that render married women the property of men."

Maud drew a breath and opened her mouth. She leaned forward, hands in fists beside her plate.

"Girls," Josephine said. "It's Christmas. It's the first time we've all been together since . . ."

A different silence.

"And now we have Flora and Enid. And it's Enid's first Christmas with us."

"All right, Mother, I understand," Lucy said. Dangerously. "But one last thing and then we will talk of . . . of the weather." She pointed across the table at her brother. "You are wrong about us. I will prove it to you."

"And so will I," Maud added, under her breath.

"Enid was in the pageant," Josephine said. She reached over and patted Enid's hand. "Oh, I was so proud of you. Weren't you proud of her, Flora?"

"She was . . ." Flora paused, pondering her sister. "I only wish our ma and papa could have seen her."

Enid did not speak, but leaned forward, eager to see the expression on Ellen's face.

George was silent for the rest of the meal. Josephine noted that he took a sober appraisal of every person at the table. His sisters—animated, informed. Ellen—entirely changed in appearance as she smiled at Enid, the lines in her cheeks folding upwards, softening her expression. The English sisters—at ease with the family, as Josephine had taught them to be. Herself—at peace.

Afterwards, when they did not go into the parlour, since the boarders were playing Parcheesi, he seemed at a loss, as if he could not retreat with them into the kitchen. As if there would be no room for him there.

—

Ellen said she did not feel capable of taking around the petition.

"What if they ask me questions, like? I'll stay home with Enid."

Enid spent Sunday afternoons in Ellen's kitchen, earnestly filling out worksheets or doing sums or writing essays with the aid of a large dictionary, while Ellen's arthritic fingers pushed and lifted, knitting mittens and tasselled caps. For barter, for sale.

Josephine, Flora and Maud spent these afternoons visiting women in the towns and villages around Pleasant Valley, explaining the petition, offering it for signing. Excitement mounted, exponentially. They could feel it in church parlours, where they met members of the YWCA, missionary societies and women's auxiliaries; in temperance lodges, where they attended meetings of the Women's Christian Temperance Union; in women's homes, where they were guests of honour at literary societies, tea parties, or sewing circles. In the countryside, they spoke to determined women crowded into farmhouses.

Everywhere, women fanned out, covering the entire province—Carrie and her cohorts, from St. John; other suffragists, from Sackville, Moncton, Fredericton, Campbellton.

On a Sunday evening, coming home on the train, in the flush of an evening sunset, Flora sat on the edge of her seat feeling sharpened, as keen as the point of a pencil. She studied the names written in ink—*Gladys Templeton, Beryl Fanjoy, Alice Streetham, Rose Campbell, Marcia Jones, Beatrice Davies, Florence Camps.*

Her own name, at the top.

Flora Salford.

She wished that Maria Rye, or Matron, or the men who had bid for her at the pauper auction, or even Jasper Tuck might in some ghostly manner populate the other seats. Exiting the train, she would pause and stare into each of their faces. They would see within her own eyes all the other women who had signed the petition: an irrepressible multitude.

—

By April, Flora and Ellen had prepared everything needed to furnish the new rooms, and the rooms themselves were ready for occupancy. Josephine began to mention, quietly, and to the right people, that she was accepting two new boarders.

Flora acquired a Barred Rock rooster. He woke the entire household at the break of day and rode the hens with a mighty flapping of grey wings. She named him Prince Albert and waited eagerly for the first hen to claim ownership to her eggs. She took the cow to a neighbour's bull, and watched the mating, and walked her home again. She planted a forty-foot row of peas when the snow still lay on the fields.

—

Lucy's letter arrived on the day when all the women of the household, even Ellen, were in a frenzy of preparation. They made cold meals for the boarders and a picnic for themselves, packed satchels for the train ride to Fredericton. Tomorrow, the suffrage bill was to receive its second reading in the legislature and women from all over the province were going to witness the vote.

At supper, as they cut into Ellen's rhubarb pie, Josephine read the letter out loud for the second time.

June 23, 1890

Dear Mother,

I can hardly hold my pen for excitement. I have been accepted into the Wellesley Female Seminary in Massachusetts! Cousin Carrie encouraged me to apply and begs you, as do I, to accept her offer to pay for my education. It may be that after all I might become one of the first women lawyers. I will finish out the summer here at the factory if I don't get fired! I will begin at the seminary next September. Mother, I will change the laws. I will fight for the rights of women and children. And of course, by then, we will have the right to vote.

Josephine pressed the letter to her breast. Not for me, she thought. Change takes time. *But for them.*

Maud speared a piece of buttery crust with her fork. "The more I learn about how we are treated by men, it's as if my heart is actually swollen with anger. It can't be healthy. It's like wearing a corset." She forked the pie into her mouth, chewed, swallowed and turned to Ellen. "You and Enid haven't been hearing it, but everywhere we've travelled this spring, *everywhere*, women are talking about the laws, and how they work in favour of men, and about how women make no laws. And then we all talk about how most women are more affected by the ills of society than are men. And so, of course, would be in a better position to make . . . better laws." Maud threw her arms wide, narrowly missing Flora's head. "But I am *so excited* for tomorrow!

Mr. Turner has been talking all over the place, encouraging other men to his side. To *our* side. I can hardly believe it, but . . . no, I can, I *can* believe it. Who could have believed Lucy would go from working in a cotton factory to studying at a women's seminary in Massachusetts? Oh, Mother. Let me see it again."

"Remember how Lucy wrote that she was growing so thin she was becoming weak?" Josephine said, handing Maud the letter. "I was about to tell Carrie to go and rescue her."

"Well," Maud sighed, satisfied. She handed the letter to Ellen. "She has. In a way. Rescued her."

—

The number of women arriving at the legislature to witness the vote was so great that chairs were set onto the floor of the House of Assembly Room—behind the fixed seats and beneath the tall windows—and all the upper galleries were filled.

Josephine, the girls and Ellen sat in the topmost row of the side balcony; they leaned forward to watch the floor below.

"I just heard that the petition received over twelve thousand signatures from every corner of the province, from both women and men," Maud said to Flora, as the din of arrivals continued.

Women flooded in, found their way to seats, compressing their skirts, murmuring apologies. Ellen pulled a fan from her bag, endeavoured to make a cooling breeze of the stultifying heat. The tall windows had been opened; over their heads, holes in the ceiling sucked the air, but Flora felt sweat rolling down her cheeks. The balcony at the far end of the enormous room looked so steep that it seemed as if the women were pasted there like wallpaper. On the floor, some men sat tidily and others sprawled at their appointed desks. The clerk spread papers on a marble table, set before the Speaker's dais.

On the dais, the Speaker stood and the room quieted.

"O Lord, our heavenly father," he said, "high and mighty, King of kings, Lord of lords, the only Ruler of princes, who dost from thy throne behold all the dwellers upon earth: Most heartily we beseech thee with thy favour to behold our most gracious Sovereign lady, Queen Victoria . . ."

Flora's mind wandered as the business of government wended its confusing path: first, a message from the Gentleman Usher of the Black Rod, after which a group of men left the room, while those left behind spoke, stood, sat, strolled. The group returned. Men rose, then, seemingly at random, and asked leave of the Speaker to speak. Speeches ensued. Then counter-speeches. Flora could not see that any conclusions were reached or actual work accomplished. It seemed a deliberate obfuscation or postponement of the bill which so many women had travelled to hear, and restlessness unsettled the chamber. Women removed their hats and ran fingers through sweaty hair. A parasol slid to the floor with a loud bang. The members of the legislature murmured to one another behind the backs of their hands. They cast slighting, amused eyes at the women.

Josephine crossed her arms.

"So rude," she whispered to Flora. "Perhaps it is always like this but somehow I doubt it. I believe this was planned for our benefit."

". . . consolidate and amend the law . . ."

Flora had risen before dawn. She had milked the cow early, and set the milk to cool, and fed the chickens and brought in firewood. She yawned, her eyelids thickened.

". . . upon accepting the office . . ."

". . . dispatch of public business . . . rate of stumpage . . . non-navigable waters upon ungranted Crown land . . . suffrage bill which was referred to committee and will now resume consideration."

Flora ran sticky palms down her skirt. Maud's teeth closed on the back of a finger. Which man, Flora wondered? Which man would rise to speak for them?

Two members stood and reversed a previous decision they had made to oppose the bill, citing the extraordinary number of signatures to the petition.

Maud caught Flora's hand and squeezed it. Excited whispering rose from the floor until the Speaker stood and called for order.

The member from Kent County rose. Flora was predisposed to think well of him, following, as he did, the men who had supported the bill. He stood with one hand slipped through the lapel of his jacket; a short beard jutted from his chin.

"I am disappointed in the speeches I have just heard from the Honourable Members from York and St. John. I wish to remind this house of inalienable facts which we would do well *not to forget*. Despite the presence of the fair sex in our chamber today, I will speak frankly and without mincing matters, with all due apologies. I make the following points. *Number one.* If a woman is given a vote, then, like a man, she is logically bound to perform certain duties: behind all legislation there is physical force, so she must be prepared to serve in the military—"

A stir of laughter, quickly suppressed.

"—and perform constable duty."

More laughter.

"She must be prepared to perform road work, pay poll tax, serve on juries or to *hold public office*. If she is entitled to a full share in the making of laws, *then she is liable to do her share in enforcing them*."

He stared out over the room. Men crossed their legs, glanced at papers, stifled yawns, raised eyebrows at one another. Flora felt a flush of hatred, and by the women's silence, felt the brewing of rage.

"Number two. A woman and her husband are one, and therefore she is legally incorporated. His political voice is hers, and therefore there is no need for her to enter the hurly-burly of politics, for which her delicate constitution is ill able to withstand. Moreover, despite this petition, which I see has been padded by the votes of men, it is not clear to me that the *majority* of women desire or indeed are even interested in having the vote. I believe that even if they had the vote they *would not exercise it*."

Shouts of protest from the women.

"And number three. What are the particulars, I would like to know, that these women are upset about? Can they enumerate them? Are they tyrannized by this despotic legislature ruled by men? Do we not exercise judicious reason? If they are suffering, we do not hear any complaints. To conclude, I believe that many of those sitting in this chamber . . ."

"Some of us are women." A woman half rose from her balcony seat.

Another woman called out. "Enumerate? Let's start with not having the—"

He raised his voice. ". . . have forgotten that it is the very noble qualities that women bring to the home sphere which make her *not designed* for the political sphere. The woman's role is to be wife and mother, *that is the divine will!* Society shall rise or fall upon that exquisite skill that she brings to the raising of children and the nurturing of her husband. I conclude with a quote from Alfred, Lord Tennyson: *Man with the head and woman with the heart . . . all else confusion.* Thank you, Mr. Speaker."

Uproar.

Women stood from their seats, waving pamphlets, shouting, hurling abuse at the Honourable Member from Kent County.

The Speaker stood and waited for complete silence.

"The debate now being ended," he said. "We will put the bill to a vote. All in favour, please say *yea*."

A chorus of yeas.

"All opposed, *nay*."

The bill was defeated.

Flora was swept down the spiral staircase by a tide of grim-faced, silent women. At the bottom, they stepped into a crush of people in the vestibule. The Honourable Member from Kent appeared in a doorway.

"Coward!"

"What's that?" He flushed, sought the speaker.

The woman who had spoken strode forward, drew back her arm, and slapped his face. Another woman shouted "Ignorant coward!" She, too, slapped him. Other women shoved forward, shouting, punching. He crouched, holding his head. Members of the assembly rushed to surround him. They hurried him down the hallway towards the safety of the Legislative Library, a scuttling phalanx, while even though the front doors had been open to the air, women continued to mill in the vestibule, chanting—"Full suffrage for women! Full suffrage for women!"—hoarse from heat, fury and profound disappointment.

—

The station platform was crowded. Dresses, parasols, hats. Sweep of silk. Restless, rustling.

Lucy and Carrie stood with a group of St. John women, speaking in low voices. They summoned energy, Flora observed. Their eyes were dark with anger and determination. They were laying plans.

The train hissed and squealed to a stop. Josephine and Maud climbed up the steps and entered the carriage. Ellen, who seldom left the house, gripped both Flora's and Enid's hands before taking a breath and setting a foot onto the metal step.

No one spoke as the train left the station and gathered speed, a regular jolting that smoothed into a sleep-inducing sway as they passed eastward along the river.

Flora pressed her face to the window.

The first time she had taken a train in Canada, she had been coming from the Protestant Orphanage in St. John. Late spring, and the fruit trees had been veiled by pink blossoms, the fields lush with grass, unbruised by hooves or weather. The houses seemed whiter in memory, even though it was the same time of year. The barns, too, had seemed freshly painted, and the sky a darker blue. She'd watched a woman wearing an apron scatter corn to her chickens while tea towels tossed on a clothesline; and Flora had thought that she would step onto the Pleasant Valley train platform and be greeted by a kindly family.

She had travelled with hope. She had lived with hope, even when she guessed Ada had not mailed her letters, even when she'd mounted the steps of the train platform to be sold at auction. She had held Enid in her heart.

Hope, she thought, watching cows on a raft being poled out to the interval islands, was perhaps what allowed buds to burst from twigs, or brought grass from the soil, or gave chicks the energy to break their shells.

She reflected that she had only lost hope once, after Enid had vanished and Ellen had remembered the brass duck. But it had returned.

Enid slumped, rested her head on Flora's shoulder.

The vote failed, Flora thought. Her heart lifted.

But we didn't.

She drifted off to sleep, thinking of the boarding house, and of her cow, and of Enid's schoolwork, and of the next petition she would champion, making up its words to the rhythm of the clattering wheels.

Election Act . . . amended . . . have the right . . .

Some True Things, Notes and Historical Reference Material

NOTES:

I have used the spelling *St. John* for the city now known as Saint John, New Brunswick. The former is how the name was usually spelled during the time period of the novel.

Mount Allison University has had many different names between 1843 and the present, related to a male academy, female academy, commercial college and the university. I've endeavoured to use names appropriate to the years mentioned.

The regatta held in the novel is based on an account of the Jubilee Regatta held on June 20, 1887, in Saint John, in celebration of the Jubilee of her Majesty, Queen Victoria. I do not name it as such in the novel, however, since the events of the novel and the actual event do not coincide.

Some readers may be aware of a terrible murder that occurred at the time of this novel in the vicinity of Saint John, and for which a man was hanged. Mr. Tuck's story bears some resemblance, but is not intended to depict the true and tragic events. The articles read by Ellen in *The Sister's Tale* are adapted from the real accounts of this murder, known as the Little River Tragedy, as reported in *The Daily Telegraph*, Saint John, New Brunswick, 1878.

The town of Pleasant Valley is loosely based on the town of Sussex, New Brunswick, just as Whelan's Cove is based on present-day St. Martins. Tyne Cove and Black Creek are entirely fictional. All the characters of *The Sister's Tale*, except for George Francis Train and a handful of well-known political and historical figures, are products of my imagination.

The philanthropist Maria Rye (1829–1903) is real, although the part she plays in this novel is invented, including her letter to Mr. Fairweather.

George Francis Train (1829–1904) was a highly eccentric Bostonian who did, in fact, stun the town of Sussex in 1887, when he secured a position at the local paper. After denouncing the pauper auction, he was dismissed and sent packing. Every detail about him, as mentioned by narrator or characters, is true. Including the purple gloves.

The Commodore (the name is my invention) is based on an eccentric bachelor of the period, Dr. Goodfellow, a dentist who wore a paisley shawl around his shoulders when he went for walks "with the ends drooping to the ground," as described by Grace Aiton in *The Story of Sussex and Vicinity*.

Sussex had its first telephone exchange and operator in 1891. I took the liberty of changing the date to a few years earlier.

—

TRUE THINGS:

1889: The last pauper auction was held in Sussex, New Brunswick. The Kings County Almshouse and Poor Farm was established in the Parish of Norton, New Brunswick.

1895: An Act Respecting the Property of Married Women showed a dramatic transformation in New Brunswick women's legal rights, including "Married women may hold real and personal property" and have "full control of property, possessed at time of marriage or acquired after."

1917: I took the liberty of changing the date of the second reading to the women's enfranchisement bill. The actual mobbing of a member of the legislative assembly occurred in June 1917, when a private member's bill calling for women's enfranchisement went into second reading. After being roundly expected to pass, it was voted down.

1919: Women gained the right to vote in provincial elections in New Brunswick.

1920: The Dominion Elections Act was amended so that every "eligible" Canadian over the age of twenty-one, male *or female*, could vote in federal elections.

1929: Women became "persons." On October 18, 1929, the word "person" in Section 24 of the British North America Act was finally understood to mean men *and* women, in a ruling overturning the Supreme Court of Canada by Canada's then highest court, the Privy Council in England. Lord Sankey announced: "The exclusion of women from all public offices is a relic of days more barbarous than ours."

1934: A bill passed, allowing women to hold provincial office in New Brunswick.

1939: The Child Migration program was ended in England.

1967: The first female member, Brenda Robertson, was elected to the New Brunswick legislature.

2010: British prime minister Gordon Brown apologized to Home Children: "We are sorry that instead of caring for them, this country turned its back. And we're sorry that the voices of these children were not always heard, their cries for help not always heeded."

REFERENCE MATERIAL:

For those interested in learning more about Home Children and women's lives in the late 1800s, here are some of the books I am indebted to:

Re Home Children:
Sean Arthur Joyce, *Laying the Children's Ghosts to Rest: Canada's Home Children in the West* (Hagios Press, 2014); Joy Parr, *Labouring Children: British Immigrant Apprentices to Canada, 1869–1924* (McGill-Queen's University Press, 1980); Phyllis Harrison, ed., *The Home Children* (Watson and Dwyer, 1979); Kenneth Bagnell, *The Little Immigrants: The Orphans Who Came to Canada* (The Dundurn Group, 2001); Marjorie Kohli, *The Golden Bridge: Young Immigrants to Canada, 1833–1939* (Natural Heritage Books, 2003).

Re paupers and small town life:
Grace Aiton, *The Story of Sussex and Vicinity* (Kings County Historical Society, 1967, '71, '79); Elaine Ingalls Hogg, *Historic Sussex* (Nimbus Publishing, 2010); K. Wayne Vail, *Yesteryear Sussex*.

Re women and suffrage:
Gail G. Campbell, *I Wish to Keep a Record: Nineteenth-Century New Brunswick Women Diarists and Their World* (University of Toronto Press, 2017); Janet Guildford and Suzanne Morton, eds., *Separate Spheres: Women's Work in the 19th-Century Maritimes* (Acadiensis Press, 1994); Mary Hallett and Marilyn Davis, *Firing the Heather: The Life and Times of Nellie McClung* (Fifth House Publishers, 1993); Constance Backhouse, *Petticoats and Prejudice: Women and Law in Nineteenth-Century Canada* (Women's Press, 1991).

Online and archival materials:

I used too many archival and online sources to list, but here are some of the most valuable: Shannon M. Riske's dissertation (University of Maine) *"In Order to Establish Justice": The Nineteenth Century Woman Suffrage Movements of Maine and New Brunswick*; Elspeth Tulloch's *"We, the Undersigned": A Historical Overview of N B Women's Political and Legal Status 1784–1984*; and *The Report of the Royal Commission on the Relationship of Capital and Labor* [sic] *in Canada* (NB, 1889).

ACKNOWLEDGEMENTS

I would like to thank the following for help with an early (very different) draft of this novel: Steve Goudreau, David Lutz, David Macmillan, Don McAlpine, Amber McAlpine, and the staff of the New Brunswick Museum Archives.

The Sister's Tale was immeasurably helped by the following: David G. Bell, University of New Brunswick professor emeritus, for answering many questions about "intestacy and the widow"; Bev Harrison, former Speaker of the Legislative Assembly, for historical legislative protocol; David Mawhinney, Mount Allison archives, re women students in the late 1800s; the staff of the Sussex Regional Library for help with microfilm of *The Kings County Record*; Francesca Holyoke, University of New Brunswick archives, for advice and information re women's lives; Gregory Marquis, University of New Brunswick Saint John, re nineteenth-century policing and historical spelling; Peter Larocque, New Brunswick Museum, for answering endless odd questions; and most of all, Janice Cook at the Provincial Archives of New Brunswick, who listened, pondered, searched and supplied me with the key. Deepest thanks to all.

At Knopf Canada, thanks to the terrific team: my publishers, Anne Collins and Martha Kanya-Forstner, as well as publishing director Lynn Henry, managing editor Deirdre Molina, designer Talia Abramson (love the boots!) and publicist Sharon Gill.

Thanks to Tilman Lewis for a meticulous copy edit and Angelika Glover for careful proofreading.

Enormous thanks to my brilliant editor, Craig Pyette, who worked on this novel during the unprecedented stresses of the coronavirus pandemic. Heartfelt thanks for unwavering commitment to finding the deepest levels of *The Sister's Tale*, for helping me tell the story in the best possible way, and for laughter, challenges and friendship.

To my dearest agent, Jackie Kaiser, thanks once again for truthful advice through many drafts, steering me down that most turbulent river towards the next novel, steadfast with comfort, encouragement, determination and love.

Thanks to my family: Jake, Sara, Maeve, Bridget, Mark, Beverly, and most of all my beloved mother, Alison Davis, at ninety-seven vibrant and strong, publishing her memoir, giving workshops, bright-voiced on the telephone—so far away and yet so close to me.

To my husband, Peter. Always, everywhere, sharing, seeing, understanding—my eyes, my ears, my heart, my soul.

© Peter Powning

BETH POWNING'S previous books include the bestselling novels *The Hatbox Letters*, *The Sea Captain's Wife*, and most recently *A Measure of Light*, a *Globe and Mail* Best Book and winner of the inaugural New Brunswick Book Award for Fiction. Her works of memoir include *Home: Chronicle of a North Country Life*; *Shadow Child: An Apprenticeship in Love and Loss*; and *Edge Seasons: A Mid-life Year*. In 2010, Beth was awarded New Brunswick's Lieutenant-Governor's Award for High Achievement in English-Language Literary Arts. She lives on a farm near Sussex, New Brunswick, with her husband, the renowned sculptor Peter Powning. Learn more at www.powning.com/beth. Follow Beth on Facebook @bethpowningauthor, Instagram @bethpowning and Twitter @bethpowning.